PRAISE FOR JERUSHA AGEN

"Jerusha Agen once again delivers top-level suspense and thrilling action. *Covert Danger* kept me looking over my shoulder and flipping pages. Fast-paced suspense at its best."

DIANN MILLS, BESTSELLING AUTHOR OF
CONCRETE EVIDENCE

"Hang on! This action-packed story doesn't let up until the good guys win!"

NATALIE WALTERS, AWARD-WINNING
AUTHOR OF *LIGHTS OUT* AND THE
HARBORED SECRETS SERIES ON *COVERT
DANGER*

Hidden Danger kept me reading and on the edge of my seat from page one through the end. Jerusha Agen writes a gripping suspense filled with danger, romance, and K-9s complete with a strong faith thread.

SHAREE STOVER, BESTSELLING AUTHOR
OF *FRAMING THE MARSHALL*

"Fast-paced, explosive thriller. I couldn't turn the pages fast enough."

CARRIE STUART PARKS, AWARD-WINNING, BESTSELLING AUTHOR OF *RELATIVE SILENCE* ON *RISING DANGER*

"*Rising Danger* grabbed me from the first chapter and never let go. Don't miss this edge-of-your-seat story of suspense and romance."

PATRICIA BRADLEY, AWARD-WINNING AUTHOR OF THE *LOGAN POINT* AND *MEMPHIS COLD CASE SERIES*

WAYLAID

BOOKS BY JERUSHA AGEN

GUARDIANS UNLEASHED SERIES

Midnight Clear (prequel novella)

Rising Danger (prequel)

Hidden Danger

Covert Danger

Unseen Danger

Lethal Danger

Terminal Danger

WINDY CITY WESTONS SERIES

Waylaid

Wasted (Fall 2025)

Watched (2026)

SECURITY LEAGUE SERIES

Protected (prequel novella)

Rescued (Spring 2025)

SISTERS REDEEMED SERIES

If You Dance with Me

If You Light My Way

If You Rescue Me

WAYLAID

WINDY CITY WESTONS | BOOK ONE

JERUSHA AGEN

 SDG Words, LLC

Soli Deo Gloria

Are not two sparrows sold for a penny?
And not one of them will fall to the ground apart from your Father.
But even the hairs of your head are all numbered.
Fear not, therefore; you are of more value than many sparrows.

Matthew 10:29-31

CHAPTER
ONE

Chicago. August 28. 9:26 p.m.

A POP PIERCED THE NIGHT.

A gunshot? Spring Weston's stomach clenched as she ducked lower over the handlebars of her bicycle and peddled hard. A shooting wouldn't be a surprise in that neighborhood, but she'd rather avoid a run-in with a stray bullet.

She glanced into the hazy darkness on either side of her as she kept her pace steady, light raindrops mixing with sweat on her face.

Nothing moved in the glow from streetlamps.

A white van waited next to some business with barred windows. The building's sign was a yellow blur as she whizzed by, maintaining her racing speed.

She tapped the backlight on the timer attached to the handlebars. Great pace. Faster than she should be at mile ten. Adrenaline and nerves must be driving her legs.

Drugs. Doping. On *her* team.

The anxiety wadding in her stomach threatened to choke her. She puffed out a breath, willing her muscles to relax as she kept pedaling at the same clip.

She glided through a curve into the headwind. Rain pelted her face.

"Doping? Are you kidding me?" Cliff's denial echoed in her ears, louder than the wind that rushed past. *"I run a clean team. You know that."*

"But I saw Megan…popping pills." Spring had watched her coach, desperately hoping he would offer some explanation she could believe.

"How do you know they were drugs? She takes supplements all the time."

"Megan told me what the pills were."

Cliff laughed. "She told you? That'd be pretty dumb if she was doping, wouldn't it?"

Spring frowned at his jovial grin. "Megan didn't think I'd care. She thought it was expected. She said—" Spring moistened her lips. "She said the whole team is doing it."

"Well, there you go."

Spring raised her eyebrows.

"Obviously, she was just joking. She knows you don't take drugs." Cliff's grin angled sideways. "You know what a kidder Megan is. You gotta learn to lighten up and not take things so seriously."

She stared at him. Why couldn't he be more convincing? Offer some explanation or at least a denial that he was involved?

He had stepped closer to her, his grin softening into a smile that seemed to hide something. "Come on, Spring. Don't you trust me more than that?"

She had trusted him. But she knew what she had seen Megan take, what Megan had said. It wasn't a joke. At least not to Spring.

She shifted her shoulders, trying to relax as she surged through the neighborhood she was moving too fast to see.

The rain weakened, but her tense thoughts pelted her from the inside.

If only it wasn't true. If only she hadn't met Megan for a training run and seen her take those pills.

Spring pressed her lips together, trapping her breath longer than she should. She had no hard evidence to prove doping on the team. Only what Megan had told her. Would anyone believe her if she reported it? She could hardly believe it herself.

But she couldn't knowingly compete on a team that was doping. Every win would mean nothing. And the scandal could come out once she made it to an elite team. Everyone would think she had doped, too.

Lord, give me wisdom. Calm slid through her chest with the prayer, soothing the tension and allowing her to breathe more evenly.

She would have to report what she knew. Whether or not anyone believed her wasn't her responsibility.

Relief flowed to her fingers with the confidence that she'd made the right decision.

Readjusting her position over the handlebars, she focused on pushing her pace back up. A praise song from church started to play in her head, lending a driving beat to her pedaling rhythm.

She sailed into the curve under the overpass, the road wet enough to make her slow just slightly.

She sped into the straightaway.

A rumble behind her.

Ugh. Traffic. Unusual for the area at that time of night.

She drifted closer to the curb to let the driver pass, not slowing her pace.

The rumble grew louder. Why wasn't the car passing?

She glanced back.

A white blur slammed into her bicycle. Catapulted her.

She flew, airborne.

Her breath caught as time stood still.

A concrete abutment waited for her.

She was going to die.

August 29. 10:17 a.m.

"That fool coulda killed us."

Torin Cotter glanced at the damage to the woman's blue sedan. A large dent creased the corner of the front bumper. Six hundred dollars' worth of damage at the most.

But fire lit Mrs. Marston's dark eyes as she crossed her thick arms over her chest and glared at the driver Officer Price interviewed thirty feet away on the sidewalk.

"Good thing you and your granddaughter were wearing your seatbelts, ma'am."

She humphed and yanked her gaze to Torin's badge. "You a sergeant, right?"

"Yes, ma'am."

"You gonna do somethin' about that fool? Yank his license or somethin'?" Sweat glistened on the dark skin of her forehead as hot sunlight glinted off the severely short hair that contrasted with her round features.

Torin felt the watchful gaze of Mrs. Marston's granddaughter. Probably no more than five years old, the little girl stared up at him with big eyes. He gave her a small smile as he answered her grandmother in his calmest tone. "We'll do what the law dictates, ma'am. Now, if you can tell me one more time what happened."

"I'll tell you what happened." Her full lips pursed together. "That fool come out of nowhere and hit me and my baby!" She lurched toward the other driver, who met her fury with a derisive laugh.

Torin put out his hands, not touching her as he controlled the space with his body. "Mrs. Marston, you have to calm down. Your granddaughter's watching you."

The girl had actually turned away and was looking at the brown two-door that had collided with her grandmother's car, but the point still stood.

The woman puffed a breath that didn't sound calm enough to put Torin at ease.

"Tell you what, I'm going to go over there and speak with the other driver."

She opened her mouth to protest—

"In order to find out who deserves what, I have to talk to him. I'm going to have Officer Price get your side of things in more detail, okay?" He met her angry gaze with a slight smile. "I need your help here, ma'am."

"Oh, I'll help. So long as he gets what he deserves."

"Yes, ma'am." Torin turned and signaled with a flick of his fingers that Price should switch drivers with him. He didn't like the smirk the male driver had given the woman. And he didn't like the spiteful set of the man's jaw as he watched Price walk away.

Explained Price's sigh and look of relief as he passed Torin. "Cop hater, Sarge. Watch it."

The tall driver crossed muscular arms across his chest as he glared at Price's back. Torin never could understand how race-based cop haters targeted black officers like Price even more intensely than white officers.

Reining in the instinct to defend his fellow cop, Torin stopped in front of the man whose license had ID'd him as Claudius Jackson.

"What do you want?"

Torin kept his expression impassive. "To get out of here as much as you, I'd guess."

Surprise flickered behind the hostility in the man's eyes for an instant.

"You can speed this up by telling me what happened."

"I told the other cop."

"He's a patrol officer. I'm with accident investigations. You'll have to tell me before we can move on with this."

Jackson lowered his arms and glanced down at the smartphone he held in his large hand. Checking the time or messages? Odd moment to lose interest in the conversation.

A red flag popped up in Torin's mind.

"That crazy lady hit me."

"That's not what she says, or the witnesses."

Jackson glanced at the three bystanders who lingered with a growing crowd to watch the show from the sidewalk on the opposite side of the street. Then he checked his phone again.

He shifted his weight as he gripped the phone too tightly at his side and lifted his gaze.

Why the sudden tension in his body and around his mouth?

"They were probably texting and missed the whole thing." He smirked again, but something lurked in his eyes besides animosity. Nerves? Or was it anticipation?

The hair on the back of Torin's neck lifted away from his skin. The guy hadn't been edgy before. Not like this.

Five people had gathered behind the chain-link fence that enclosed the small park at Jackson's back. Ethnic minority hangout on one side of the street and affluent, white-owned, historic houses on the other. Could get ugly if Jackson decided to start something.

"The witnesses say you ran the stop sign and hit her car without slowing down at all."

"You tryin' to pin something on me? So you can beat me up?" He took a step toward Torin. "Put a bullet in me?" He grinned, far from friendly. "Got too many witnesses this time."

Torin wasn't even wearing his gun. But he wasn't about to announce that fact to this guy. "I think you know we aren't going to do that. If you can relax and work with us, we'll be able to let you go in a few minutes."

Jackson dropped the challenging stare to check his phone again, the corners of his mouth tensing. He looked up with a sneer. "You ain't got no right to keep me out in this heat. I got rights. I want to stand over there." He pointed to a patch of shade under a tree about twenty feet down the sidewalk.

A warning bell joined the red flag waving in the back of Torin's mind. "Once we're done here."

"If I get heatstroke, man, you're gonna pay. We got enough of your oppression."

Torin met Jackson's gaze for the second the fidgety guy could hold it. "Okay." He kept his focus on the big man. "Officer Price."

In his peripheral, Torin saw Price walk toward them. "Mr. Jackson is concerned he's going to overheat. Would you escort him to that shade over there and finish getting his story?"

Price nodded. "After you, Mr. Jackson."

Torin met Price's gaze briefly as he passed, following Jackson. Price moved his hand to rest on his hip, closer to his weapon.

Good. He wasn't about to be taken by surprise.

But the alarms in Torin's head grew louder, his gut tightening. He scanned the scene as Jackson peacefully walked to the tree.

The bystanders still watched from the other sidewalk, their number increased to seven people. Four women, one adult male, two children. Appeared harmless and calm.

Sunlight beat down on the charcoal street, illuminating every inch of the accident scene. Seemed an unlikely scenario for someone to try an ambush.

Maybe ambush wasn't what Jackson had in mind. Maybe he simply had drugs in his car.

Warranted a closer look.

Torin headed toward Jackson's two-door where it stood at an angle to the sedan on the street.

Something moved on the other side of the car.

Torin tensed.

A fuzzy cloud of black hair appeared at the edge of the trunk, then the small head of Mrs. Marston's granddaughter came into view.

Torin smiled, taking in a breath to combat the kick of

adrenaline. "Hey, there. Can you do me a favor and wait with your grandmother over on the sidewalk?"

She watched him with solemn eyes as he walked to the car.

He glanced through the windows.

The interior was clean. Almost squeaky clean. Like it was new.

But the registration said the car was seventeen years old, and it had the rusted frame to prove it.

His muscles tensed as he peered at the dark interior.

He sensed something at his side.

The girl. She tugged on his pant leg.

"You need to go to your grandma, okay? Right now." Alarm forced a sharper tone than he wanted, but it worked to make the girl turn and head away.

Then he saw it.

A backpack on the floor by the back seat.

"Hold it, Jackson!" Price's shout cut through the heat.

Torin jerked to see Jackson running. Away.

Oh, no.

Torin sprinted from the car, grabbing the girl in his arms. "Bomb!"

He clutched the girl to his chest as he ran, sheltering her with his body.

The world exploded behind him.

CHAPTER
TWO

October 6. 8:23 a.m.

SPRING'S MOUTH dried to sandpaper as she stared at the smartphone on the table positioned across her propped-up hospital bed.

The phone vibrated again, rattling against the fake wood-grain surface.

It stopped.

Spring closed her eyes. They stung from staring so long without blinking. She opened them again, her gaze automatically returning to the phone. She squeezed her lips together, then let them go.

Her hand moved to the phone as if it had a mind of its own.

She should ignore the message. She didn't have to see.

But her fingers lifted the device, and she checked the screen.

Her breath jammed in her throat.

The text logo signaled a new message. She tapped it.

You have a visitor. Don't tell him anything.

The words jumped off the screen to crawl under her skin. She swallowed. How did the texter know before she did that she had a visitor? She wasn't expecting anyone. Especially a *him*. Maybe her dad? She checked the clock on the wall across from her bed. No, he'd be at work that time of the morning. And his visits were growing fewer.

Her wandering thoughts only worked for a couple of seconds to take her mind off the fear that tightened the few muscles she could still feel. If she only knew who the texts were from, they might not be so frightening. And what didn't the texter want her to tell?

A burning pain surged through her leg. She reached to rub the worst spot.

But she couldn't feel the touch of her own fingers. Couldn't stop the burn. She gritted her teeth.

The phantom pains were becoming more frequent. Another thing to tell her physiatrist.

All the good it would do. Her brain wasn't any more used to her *limited mobility* than her heart was. *Limited mobility, lower limb dysfunction, thoracic injury*. The lengths the people at the Chicago Rehab Center went to just to avoid speaking the truth would be funny if she could still laugh.

Kind of like her dad and most of her four siblings who visited occasionally. No one wanted to say the P-word. Except Victoria, of course. A physical therapist had to talk about it.

Speaking the truth couldn't make it hurt more anyway. Spring would prefer an honest reaction to her paralysis instead of her dad's behavior when he visited—forcing a smile now and then between looking at her like she'd failed him more than ever before.

She clenched her jaw tighter as the burning sensation increased. She pushed her head back into the pillow, teeth jammed together as she searched for something to take her mind off the torturous phantom.

The colored picture hanging on the wall next to the window.

The pain slid to the background as her heart warmed. She could see the focus and effort Jerome had invested in the crayon drawing of what looked like the sun shining on a flower. Remarkable that the four-year-old could even sit still long enough to complete such a drawing.

A tiny ember of happiness, an emotion she'd just about forgotten, glowed inside as she pictured his compact body bouncing around the playroom at Sunshine Day Care with unquenchable energy.

Who was driving Jerome home now? What if his mom hadn't found any—

"Spring?"

Her raw nerves jolted at the masculine voice in her room. She turned her head to see familiar brown hair with hints of gray at the temples and a tanned face with weathered lines. Her coach. Former coach now.

The pain in her leg started to creep back, almost as if her wounded spirit caused it. "Cliff?"

He grinned. "You sound surprised to see me."

"No." She blinked at him, taking in his shorts that showed off cyclist's muscles and the windbreaker that couldn't hide the round torso he'd gained since his racing days. "Just..." She trailed off and leaned her head back against the pillow, hoping he'd let it go with fatigue as an excuse. She was surprised. No one from the team had even called her, let alone come to visit.

"Did you get the flowers?"

She nodded, though she didn't remember. Her room at the acute care hospital had looked like a greenhouse with all the bouquets and potted plants. By the time the flowers had died, the well-wishers seemed happy to forget about her. That she was still in a bed. That she'd never get well, as their cards had wished.

"So, how are you doing?"

Spring looked at him. Cliff never had been known for tactfulness.

He winced. "Sorry. Dumb question." He stepped closer to

the bed and put out his hand, resting it on the sheet a few inches away from her arm. "I'm so sorry this happened to you. The whole team is."

His pity clotted her throat like an oversized cotton ball.

"Rotten luck." He tried to smile again, but it didn't lift the lines curving downward on his brow. "It's been rough without you. You were our best rider. But I guess you know that."

Spring resisted the urge to hack out the cotton, instead clearing her throat enough to steer him in a different direction. "Who took my spot?" She rubbed the tip of her finger on the smooth sheet where it covered her useless leg.

"Lana."

Made sense. Her times had been nearly as good as Spring's in training.

Spring should be happy for her. Of all the women on the team, she was closest to Lana. They were friends. Training partners, thanks to being within driving distance of each other. Spring shouldn't feel like a ton of bricks were just added to the weight of her fate. Her uselessness. Her pain.

"We picked up a new young rider named Kendra Flickson. She's no Spring Weston, but she has some potential."

"Good." Spring amazed herself with how pleasant she managed to sound, despite the load crushing her chest.

"You're not all right." Cliff's voice softened to a pitch she'd never heard him use before. "Are you?"

She brought her gaze up to his face. Then wished she hadn't.

His eyes were filled with the pity that made her want to vomit. He'd pushed her, screamed at her, teased her, cheered her. Never looked at her like she was about to die. Or as if she had already.

"Why are you here, Cliff?"

He looked away, pink tinging his tan neck. "I felt badly about..." He took a breath and looked at her. "About our last conversation. Right before..." He gestured to her legs.

The memory slowly started to return, like something out of a mirage long forgotten. A different time. A different life.

They'd had an argument.

The doping.

So that's why he'd come.

Heat dried the numbness in her chest as irritation crackled to life. First visitor from the team, and he was only there because he was worried about his hide? Probably wanted to find out if she'd reported her suspicions.

"I wanted to apologize."

Her gaze shot to his. Apologize?

"I should've taken what you said more seriously." His lips angled in a half-smile. "I looked into it and found out you were right about Megan. She was doping, but she had just started. She's suspended from the team for at least a year."

Wow. That would nearly kill a competitor like Megan. They may not have been best friends, but Spring had hoped she could crack Megan's protective shell someday and help her face the personal demons she tried so hard to hide. "I didn't want to get anyone in trouble."

"Hey, somebody's got to keep the rest of us honest." Cliff grinned. "I just wanted you to know that I did listen to you and that she was the only one on the team who was doing it."

The memory of Megan's laugh jangled in Spring's ears. Her careless smile as she'd told Spring everyone on the team was doping. Probably what anyone would say to excuse what they were doing. Wasn't it?

A surge of pain seized Spring's otherwise invisible leg. She gritted her teeth.

"You okay?"

She managed to nod.

"Maybe I should go. I've worn you out."

She forced out a breath. "No, you didn't." He didn't have to think she was an invalid as well as paralyzed.

But the tension of discomfort framed his awkward attempt at a smile.

"I don't need to keep you, though." She tried for a friendly tone as she gave him the out he so obviously wanted.

"Yeah, I should probably go."

Of course he should. No reason to hang around the paralyzed ex-cyclist. "Bye, Cliff."

"Right." He started away from the bed, then paused and looked back. "Spring—"

She braced herself. Anything but some profuse statement about how sorry he was for her.

"Thanks for telling me about Megan."

Surprise softened her coiled muscles.

"You know I run a clean team. Wouldn't want anything to ruin our record. Or sully your wins."

She nodded, watching him leave as something niggled at the back of her mind in response to his parting words. There was something odd about them. That comment about her wins. Almost as if it was some sort of veiled threat.

But he'd barely looked at her when he'd said it, and his tone had stayed the same.

Her gaze went to her phone. Those anonymous text messages were messing with her mind.

The phone vibrated.

She jumped inwardly. Did someone know she was watching it just then?

She picked up the cell, her throat drying as she checked the screen. New text message.

Nice job. Keep quiet and you'll be fine.

She slammed the phone onto the mattress next to her leg, as if that would banish the fear creeping through her. The texter couldn't possibly know what she'd said or hadn't said. Uncertainty teetered her conviction, and she glanced up at the corners of the room. No cameras.

She was being ridiculous. Paranoid.

The texter was a liar anyway. She wouldn't be fine. She'd never be fine or truly alive ever again.

Cliff could've spared himself the visit. She had too many

problems of her own to be worried about a team that had forgotten her as soon as she couldn't pedal.

Biggest problem of the moment: figuring out why she should try to survive till tomorrow.

———————

9:05 a.m.

Torin drummed his fingers on the clean surface of his desk. The only sound in the office.

An edginess he couldn't explain filtered through his nerves. Maybe the explosion was finally catching up with him. But that wasn't the memory that had returned to hijack his dreams during the last week.

The calendar, the approaching date, held the explanation.

But he wouldn't go there.

Torin opened another case file on his computer, forcing himself to focus on the details of the woman and child killed in a collision with a semi. A mother and daughter. A wife.

Torin's ribs pinched inward as his fingers tightened on the electronic mouse.

Keep it together.

He slammed his palm flat against the desk. He would not lose it. Not at the station.

This traffic case was different anyway. He could help these people if he focused.

Dodging the memory's icy fingers, he pushed himself to peruse the file to see why their case had so far gone unsolved by Officer Raymond during Torin's absence. Torin could at least get justice for this woman. For her family.

His gaze caught on the semi driver's testimony. Didn't match with the distance and speed at point of impact.

Torin scribbled a note on the pad of paper next to his keyboard.

"Hail, the hero." Powell leaned in the doorway of Torin's office with a sideways grin.

Torin directed his gaze back to the screen as his jaw clenched. *Easy.* The rookie officer's funnyman persona usually slid right off his back.

"A hero behind a desk? Shouldn't you be out on the street, saving somebody?"

"Knock off the hero bit, Powell."

The grin faltered under the glare Torin didn't manage to quell. "Sure, Sarge. Didn't mean to take away from what you did. It was awesome."

"It was nothing."

"Saving a little girl's life?"

"I did what every cop would do. I'm not a hero." And if the rookie had been around three years ago, he'd know that.

"Okay, Sarge. The lieutenant wants to see you."

The uneasiness returned. "Right." Torin closed the files and logged out of the computer as Powell disappeared into the hallway.

The lieutenant likely wanted to talk about one of two topics. Neither was good.

Torin walked out into the hallway, then through the room of desks and cubicles.

Sergeant Myers glanced over his cubicle wall. "Great work, Cotter."

A series of similar remarks followed from the officers Torin passed.

"Welcome back."

"The hero returns."

"Nice save."

Torin acknowledged the calls and smiles with a tight nod. There should be a ban on cops watching media coverage. They'd clearly bought into all the hype and news stories that were trying to make Torin out to be some superman. Was he the only one who remembered the truth?

He reached the glass door of the windowed office where

Lieutenant Airaldi's black-haired head hovered over papers on his desk.

The lieutenant looked up as Torin entered.

"You wanted to see me?"

He nodded. "Have a seat."

Torin sat in the chair opposite Airaldi's desk and tried to appear more relaxed than he felt.

Airaldi looked at Torin under bushy black eyebrows. "Five weeks."

And four days.

"How's it feel to be back?"

"Good, sir."

"Any pain still?"

Only inside. Torin kept the thought to himself and cleared his throat. "No."

"Good." The lieutenant leaned back in his chair, tenting his fingers in front of him as he watched Torin. Never a good sign.

"You did a wonderful thing, Cotter. In general, of course, and for the department, as well."

Torin tensed. A *but* was obviously coming.

Airaldi let silence fill the office, making the muffled sounds of activity outside the door seem deafening.

"Was there anything else, sir?"

"You don't like the attention, do you?"

Torin met Airaldi's astute gaze. "No, sir. I was just doing my job."

"True. But doing it well." He leaned forward, sliding a sheet of paper on his desk an inch to the side. "Except for one thing that bothers me."

Here it came.

"The documentation from the incident says you weren't wearing your weapon. And you didn't deny that in your own statement."

Torin resisted the urge to clear his throat. He'd been expecting this during all five weeks of injury leave. If only he'd been able to come up with an explanation he could admit to his lieutenant. "Yes, sir."

"So you weren't wearing your weapon though you were on duty?"

"No, sir." Torin met his gaze, fighting the urge to glance away and fabricate a clever excuse.

Airaldi tapped a thick index finger on the desk. "You've been with CPD for how many years now?"

"Ten years, sir."

"And you're a sergeant." Airaldi stared at Torin with the intensity of his grandmother after his one and only attempt at graffiti. "You know you're required to be armed when on duty in the field, correct?"

"Yes, sir."

Airaldi's eyebrows lifted, nearly blending with his dark hairline. He sighed when Torin said nothing else. "You know I could write you up for this, Sergeant."

Torin nodded.

"I *should* write you up." Airaldi shoved the loose papers into a file on his desk. "But..." He paused, gave Torin another assessing glance. "Instead, it looks like you're going to receive an award."

The bottom dropped out of Torin's stomach. Make that three unpleasant topics the lieutenant could pick from. He hadn't believed the rumors were true.

"You don't look too happy about that either." Irritation crept into Airaldi's voice.

Better tread carefully. "It would be an honor, sir." Torin moistened his lips. "But what I did—it was nothing. Certainly doesn't deserve an award. I was just doing my job."

Airaldi held his gaze for a moment, then a small smile softened his angular features. "I like a humble sergeant, Cotter. I'll keep you posted on the award." He grabbed another file from the stack on the corner of the desk. "I won't keep you from your work any longer. I'm sure you have a lot to catch up on."

Torin stood and headed for the door, his sausage and egg breakfast curdling in his stomach.

"Oh, Cotter."

Torin paused with his hand on the doorknob, looked back to see Airaldi peer at him from under shaggy eyebrows.

"The next time you decide to do nothing, make sure you're wearing your weapon." Airaldi's dark eyes hid all but a glint of expression, which could be either humor or anger.

Not taking a chance either way, Torin left the lieutenant quickly and made his way back to his own office, focusing on the cases waiting for him to investigate. To bring closure. Justice. Peace.

He swung through his office doorway and stopped.

A man sat in Torin's steno chair, wheeled several feet away from the desk. He stood, but not hurriedly, as Torin assessed him.

Sixties, 5'11" with medium build, brown hair and glasses, tailored navy suit, expensive shoes. A visitor badge swung from his lapel, but he didn't have an escort. Heavy connections or law enforcement background.

"Dr. Henry Weston." He extended his hand for a confident shake.

A doctor with lofty connections, apparently. Torin returned the firm grip. "Sergeant Cotter."

"Gary Stinson tells me you're in charge of the accident investigations unit."

Superintendent of Police? Connections in high places all right. And not afraid to use them first thing out of the gate. "How can I help you?"

"My daughter was in an accident over five weeks ago, and we have yet to see any progress with the investigation. I'd like you to do something about that."

"I see." Torin kept his expression clear of the irritation that raked over him with the doctor's commanding tone. The man was clearly used to getting what he wanted. "What is your daughter's name?"

"Spring Weston."

"Well, Doctor Weston, I just returned from leave, but I'll look into her case and see what the status is."

"The status," Weston folded his arms across his gray dress shirt, "is nil. As I said, no progress has been made. There's an Officer Jannick in charge of the case, and I don't believe he's qualified to handle it. Someone hit my daughter and left the scene. I know that's a felony."

"I assure you Officer Jannick is more than qualified for his job, Doctor." And this guy was making Torin less and less interested in looking into the case.

Weston lowered his arms and stepped toward Torin, holding his gaze. "My daughter was paralyzed in that accident, Sergeant."

Torin hid a wince.

"She's a paraplegic now. She was a professional cyclist."

Compassion warred with Torin's anger at the gall of the man. "I'm sorry to hear that. However, we investigate every case equally, with the utmost effort and thoroughness."

Weston's features softened slightly, whether intentionally or not, Torin couldn't tell. "I would like justice for my daughter, Sergeant Cotter. Surely you can understand that."

Torin's chest tightened, his throat thickening. "I can't promise the results you're hoping for, but I will look into the case personally."

Weston watched Torin with intense hazel eyes. He nodded, extending his hand. "I appreciate it."

Torin accepted the handshake with the unpleasant feeling that he'd made some sort of deal that put him on the losing end.

"I'll be in touch, Sergeant." Weston's remark as he left the room almost sounded like a threat.

Having met the overbearing doctor, Torin had no doubt Jannick would be all too happy to hand over the Weston case. But after one dose of the father, Torin wasn't certain he wanted anything to do with the daughter. Probably a privileged, spoiled woman used to getting her way as much as her dad.

But still someone who deserved justice if a crime had been committed. If it was a hit-and-run, she and her family would have a chance at closure when the perpetrator was caught and punished. If only finding closure for someone else could bring Torin a taste of the same.

CHAPTER
THREE

October 7. 8:38 a.m.

SHE COULDN'T TAKE it anymore. The walls closed in around her. She couldn't move. She could never move again.

Panic surged up Spring's throat, catching on the scent of chemical-laden air. This is what her life would be like for the rest of her days.

She leaned her head away from the pillow that cushioned her propped-up position in the bed. Didn't dare tip farther or she'd pitch forward completely. If only she could reach the window, she could lean out and end this misery.

Guilt tightened her stomach. Had she seriously sunk to that? Having suicidal thoughts? Maybe it didn't matter now that God had abandoned her.

Victoria would remind her that wasn't true.

At the moment, nothing seemed truer. How could—

A rumble severed her thoughts.

The phone. Vibrating.

Another anonymous text. The panic clutched at her throat. Why couldn't the texter leave her alone? Wasn't she suffering enough?

A cop is coming. If you tell him anything, you will pay.

A shiver tingled through her neck and arms. The texter knew what the police were doing? How?

"Miss Weston?"

She startled and jerked her head toward the doorway. Her gaze landed on a handsome man who was definitely not the officer that had interviewed her before. This thirty-something man sported a surfer's tan, while his chiseled jawline and sandy brown hair framed a collection of nearly perfect features. Perfect, except for a slight dent in the bridge of his nose, as if it may have been broken at some point.

"Are you Spring Weston?"

The question snapped Spring out of her embarrassingly close examination of the stranger. Had he asked her that more than once? "Yes."

"Sergeant Torin Cotter, Chicago PD's Major Accident Investigations Unit. I'll be taking over the investigation of your case." He met her gaze with bright green eyes that sent a jolt from her stomach to her chest.

Oh, boy. Heat rushed to her cheeks. The other investigator had visited her a couple times, too, but he had been comfortably older and overweight. She hadn't given a second thought to how she looked or that he was seeing her in this condition.

But something about the way the sergeant's tan sport coat emphasized his broad shoulders and trim physique made her hand involuntarily move to her straggly hair as the other one pulled her sheet a little higher over her nightshirt.

"You let a cute guy see you like that?" Treese's voice echoed in Spring's head. Her little sister would be all over Spring for appearing so unattractive in public. But she had never cared about getting prettified. Why care now when she only had half her body to work with? As if a man like Sergeant Cotter would even give her a second look if he wasn't being paid for it. No man would now.

"Looks like you have some young fans." The sergeant studied the colored pictures on the wall. "Relatives?"

"Children at my job."

He switched his gaze to her. "Your file says you're a pro cyclist."

That was her. Pro cyclist—the reason she hadn't made a priority of starting a family when she'd had the chance. There was supposed to be plenty of time to fall in love and get married after she made it big in cycling. After she'd proven herself. Succeeded. She was only twenty-eight. She was supposed to have a long time yet. She swallowed as her gaze dropped to her useless legs under the sheet.

"Not true?"

"Cycling doesn't pay the bills at the moment." At the moment. As if that would ever change now.

"Sorry to hear that."

A business-like apology without much sincerity. But at least he wasn't looking at her with the pity most people couldn't hide when they saw her.

"I'd like to get the facts of your collision, if you don't mind."

"I already told the other investigator everything I remember."

"I'm sure you have." He took out a miniature tablet from the pocket of his sport coat and found a pen in the chest pocket of his sky blue button-down shirt. "But I'd like to review to see if there's anything we missed the other times. I want to find the person who did this to you, Miss Weston." Those green eyes locked on her face, causing a funny flutter of her pulse.

Maybe he was more sincere than she thought, but he was still just being a cop.

"The incident occurred at approximately nine thirty p.m. on the twenty-eighth of August. Is that correct?"

She nodded.

"Can you tell me exactly what you remember happening?"

If you tell him anything, you will pay.

The text flared in her mind. Her breathing shallowed. But she had to tell him something. "I was riding on the street in the dark. It was raining a little. Not a lot really. And all of a sudden I was flying through the air. I don't remember anything after that." She gripped her hands together so he wouldn't see her fingers trembling.

"I'm sorry if it upsets you to relive it." His gaze moved from her hands to her face.

He'd seen. At least he supplied a harmless excuse for her nerves.

"As you were probably told, there were no cameras in the area of the collision." He watched her as if looking for something. "No witnesses that we've been able to find and no leads through the physical evidence. So your testimony is the bulk of what we have to go on. Have you been able to recall if there was a person or another vehicle you may have forgotten initially?"

She shook her head.

"Perhaps you can tell me something about the vehicle that hit you. Could you hear it as it approached?"

If you tell him anything, you will pay.

"I...don't remember." She looked at Jerome's picture on the wall, fighting to keep her breathing normal.

"Did you see any part of it? Maybe a glimpse of the color or size?"

"I didn't see anything and I don't know anything." She turned her head to face him, but couldn't meet his gaze. Her pulse pounded in her ears. She couldn't admit she'd seen white and heard the rumble of an engine behind her. Not with the threatening texts she'd been getting ever since she was coherent enough to talk in the ICU.

Keep quiet. Or we'll have to kill you. The first text message she had received was the one the texter repeated most often. Always telling her to keep quiet.

She didn't even really know what she was supposed to

keep quiet about. She could only remember that white blur and the engine's rumble. The pain. Waking up to find out her life was over.

"And you don't remember seeing anyone else in the vicinity." The statement held obvious doubt. Did he know she wasn't telling the whole truth?

She made herself meet his watchful gaze. "No." At least that part was true. "I told you, it was raining."

He just looked at her, his brown eyebrows lowered slightly.

She glanced away with a sigh. "There's no point in investigating this at all. That other officer hit a dead end." She fiddled with the top hem of the sterile white sheet before she looked up again. "I thought it was a closed case by now."

"No, ma'am." His gaze grew intense. "Not on my watch. I'll find a lead to follow."

She looked into his eyes, and her heart skipped a beat. Did he really care?

"But I'm going to need your help." He took a couple steps closer to the bed.

Her pulse took off at a sprint. Why hadn't she at least brushed her hair that morning?

"Had you ever cycled through that neighborhood before?"

"Um." She licked her lips, trying not to let her gaze linger too long on his tanned features or the short locks of light brown hair that brushed his forehead. "Yes."

"The same route? Same street?"

"A few times."

He looked up from making a note on his tablet. "Did you always do so at the same time, on the same days?"

"No."

"Okay." He made another note, then pinned her with those bright green eyes. "You probably heard the sound of the vehicle as it approached, but you may not have recognized the noise for what it was at the time. I need you to think back."

With those serious eyes locked on her and her pulse trying

to outpace the Tour de France riders, she wasn't sure she could think, period, let alone about that night.

"Did you hear any noise at all just before you were hit?"

She could tell him about the engine noise she'd heard, couldn't she? It shouldn't make any difference. There was nothing remarkable about it. "I might have heard something. But it wasn't anything significant."

He nodded. "Anything at all will help."

"It was just a—"

Her phone vibrated.

She shut her mouth, her breath braking as she stared at the phone on the little table in front of her. The texter couldn't know she'd said something. He couldn't.

"Do you want me to hand it to you?"

She jerked her head up. Then caught the full meaning of his offer. "There's nothing wrong with my arms." She knew she snapped out the words, but she didn't care. The zing of nerves, embarrassment, and anger overcame the attraction she'd let sweep her away.

Sergeant Cotter obviously didn't see her as anything but a crippled victim in a case file. She was stupid to expect anything else…from anyone.

Torin would have smacked his own forehead if it wouldn't appear unprofessional. What was he thinking, asking her a question like that? He sounded like he thought she couldn't do anything.

He was honestly surprised he hadn't made a stupid mistake earlier, given how tongue-tied he'd been ever since she had turned her face his way. The woman's ID photo didn't do her justice. He was completely unprepared for the nearly-black hair framing her face with soft waves that begged to be touched as they flowed down to brush the tops of her small shoulders. And her smooth, pale skin that worked like a canvas for her full, deeply distracting lips. She wore no makeup, and she clearly didn't have to.

He'd taken a full five seconds to remember the next thing he was supposed to say. After that, he'd delivered the rest of his questions on autopilot, trying to pay attention to her answers instead of the way her big brown eyes pulled him in. The way her delicate hand, marred by a brownish bruise, pushed back the thick clump of hair from the left side of her face when she got tense.

Which she seemed to be the whole time he was there. He didn't usually have that effect on women, but then no woman had affected him like this either. Not for a long time.

He swallowed past his dry throat. He knew better than to go there. Pretending to write something important on his notepad, he used the movement to glance at his wristwatch. Seven and a half hours before quitting time. Before another day would be done. Another day that he didn't let anyone down. Didn't hurt another person.

But then, he'd be closer to tomorrow. He wasn't ready to face that.

He yanked his mind away from the memories that threatened to surface and focused on the woman who had become even quieter than before.

Her already light complexion was stark white.

The phone in her hand must be the culprit. She stared at it like it was a cockroach she couldn't put down.

"Ma'am? Are you all right?"

She started, slapped the phone face down on the table that crossed her lap. "I'm fine."

Definitely a lie, exposed by the trembling of her fingers as she drew her hand away from the device.

Torin's cop instincts pushed the hair up on the back of his neck. She was obviously being close-lipped about the collision. Not telling everything she likely remembered. But he'd chalked her silence up to depression over what she'd lost. He could see not caring about the hit-and-run driver when finding the perp wouldn't bring back her mobility. Maybe.

"I'd like you to leave now." She stared at the wall in front of her as the color slowly returned to her pallid cheeks. "I'm tired."

He threw his first theory for her silence out a mental window. Appeared she had some reason beyond dashed hopes for why she didn't want him investigating her case. And the reason could be on her phone right now.

"Are you sure there isn't something else you'd like to tell me?" If she was in trouble, he didn't want to leave her alone to deal with it.

"Can I help you?" A woman spoke from behind Torin.

He turned to see two ladies, late twenties, enter the room.

The slim, auburn-haired one assessed him as she approached. "I'm Spring's sister, Victoria, also one of her physical therapists. And you are?" The woman stopped next to Spring's bed as the other therapist, he gathered, walked around to the opposite side of the bed and started unfolding a wheelchair.

He met the sister's gaze and felt like he was looking into her father's. "Sergeant Cotter. Chicago PD."

"Oh." The protective glint in her hazel eyes softened, a change he couldn't imagine ever occurring with Dr. Weston. "Are you investigating the accident?"

"Collision. Yes, ma'am."

Her eyes widened slightly. "You're with the Accident Investigations Unit."

"Of course he is, Victoria." Irritation flattened Spring's tone. "That's why he's here."

A slight smile curved Victoria's lips. "No, I mean I recognize you. You're the officer on the news, aren't you?"

Torin cringed inwardly.

"Oh, that's right!" The shorter, dark-haired woman straightened from opening the wheelchair, a smile on her face as she stared. "You saved that little girl from the car bomb."

In his peripheral, he spotted Spring's gaze swing his way. He resisted the urge to run his fingers under his suddenly tight collar.

Victoria's smile grew to a beaming show of teeth. "I didn't recognize you at first."

Thanks to the youthful ID photo the media had used. If the department would allow him to grow a beard, he'd be even harder to recognize.

"I saw the news coverage when…" her smile wobbled as she cast a glance at her sister, "when Spring was in ICU."

Torin glanced at Spring, but she shifted her gaze to the wall.

"Did you ever catch the bomber?"

"Yes, ma'am."

"Good." Victoria's lips pressed into a serious line. "Do you know why he did it?"

"The bomb was meant for police officers on the scene. Beyond that, I can't say."

She frowned and slowly shook her head. "I don't understand why some people want to attack the police. I'm personally quite fond of law and order."

The shorter therapist laughed. "Right?"

"Victoria." The one word from Spring carried both annoyance and chastisement. Perhaps a difference in opinion there?

Victoria glanced at her sister, but aimed her statement at Torin. "Did someone put you on Spring's case instead of Officer Jannick?"

"I'll be handling the investigation from here on."

"Wonderful." She turned to look at Spring, whose red rose-tinted lips formed a frown. "Did you answer all his questions?"

Torin didn't miss the condescension.

Spring glanced at him before bouncing her gaze back to Victoria. "Of course."

"They can't help you if you don't let them."

Pink color tinted Spring's face, from anger, judging by the flash in her eyes.

"Hate to interrupt, ladies, but we have to get moving." The other therapist smiled at Torin across the bed. "I'm afraid we're going to have to ask you to leave. Spring has a PT session."

"I sent Victoria a text." Spring's voice was stronger, her frustration obvious as she glared at the two therapists. "I'm not feeling up to it today."

"You don't feel up to it because you haven't been doing the exercises to build your strength." Victoria's tone matched her sister's. "You'll never feel up to anything if you don't work at it."

"Don't patronize me, Victoria."

"Don't waste my time. You're doing a PT session today whether you like it or not. Some of us want you to get better."

Not condescending. Just pushy. Judging from the subtext, Spring might need such a sister right now.

"I'm sorry," Victoria turned to Torin with a kind smile, "but Angie's right. You'll have to finish asking your questions later."

"Of course." He slipped his notepad into his pocket. "I do have a few more." Or more like fifty. "I'll come back in an hour or two. Ladies." He dipped his head toward the women and turned to leave.

"Oh, Sergeant?" Victoria's voice stopped him.

He looked back.

She smiled. "Thank you for working on this. It would mean so much to us if you could find out who did this to Spring."

His gaze found Spring behind her sister just in time to catch the pink flush in her cheeks before she looked away.

He headed out of the room to the hallway where visitors and rehab center employees traveled in both directions. Didn't feel right to leave Spring after what he'd seen. The fear had been gone from her eyes when he walked out, but not from his memory.

Careful. He mentally battled the protective instincts that told him to stay nearby, to go back in and question her until she revealed what had scared her. It was a battle he had to win.

He was retired from the protection business. Permanently.

CHAPTER
FOUR

October 7. 9:00 a.m.

SPRING GRUNTED as she lost her balance and her chest tipped too far forward. "I told you." She could barely breathe. Her heart knocked against her ribs. But not only because of her awkward position.

How had the texter known?

Victoria pulled Spring back up by her shoulders. "You can do it if you just engage your muscles more. Your abs and lower back have to do more work now. It won't feel like the way you used to sit up. You have to learn the new way."

"Maybe I don't want to learn the new way." Irritation was a welcome distraction from the knot in her belly. At least the only other people in the gym at the moment were on the far side of the large, equipment-packed room. These exercises were humiliating enough with only Victoria and Angie watching.

"Why don't we try something else for now?" Angie glanced at her cohort before directing a smile at Spring.

Victoria sighed. "Fine. Long-sitting?"

"Sounds good." Angie nodded. "Okay, Spring. We'll do

some of the work as we lower you to the floor, but I want you to do as much as you can, okay?"

Spring pressed her lips together and jerked a nod. Poor Angie probably had no idea she'd be caught in the middle of sister squabbles when she had agreed to let Victoria assist with Spring's therapy. The idea had even sounded okay to Spring at first.

"Put your right hand here on the front of the armrest."

Spring followed Angie's direction, trying to ignore the churning in her stomach. The text that had come when the sergeant questioned her clawed its way to the front of her mind.

You talk too much. Now I'll have to teach you to be quiet.

"Let's see..." Angie's upbeat tone nudged at the tension winding through Spring's body. "Eventually, we'll want you to put your left hand down here on the caster." The PT tapped the small front wheel with the toe of her shoe. "But since you don't have the trunk control to lean that far yet, I'm just going to have you push off the armrests with both hands while Victoria and I help you to the mat."

Spring tried to fake attentiveness while her mind roiled with questions. How did the texter know she'd been going to tell Sergeant Cotter about the sound of the engine? A shudder waved through her body just as the two women placed their hands on either side of her under her upper arms.

"Are you cold?" Angie leaned in to meet Spring's gaze.

Spring shook her head, forcing a swallow down her dry throat before trying to speak. "I'm fine." Except for the fear clenching her chest. What did the texter mean about teaching her to be quiet? Maybe she should figure out an excuse to go back to her room for her phone. Could be more messages.

"Okay. One, two, three, lift." Angie called out the signal, and Spring pretended to push off the chair, letting the PTs do the lifting.

They lowered her to the thickly padded mat on the floor, leaving her useless legs stretched out in front of her.

"You call that pushing?" Victoria raised her eyebrows as she looked down at Spring with a challenging stare.

Probably trying to goad Spring into fighting to preserve her pride. But even if she hadn't just received a secret threat, her sister's trick wouldn't work. Spring wasn't the same person she'd been before the crash. When would Victoria get that?

"Now try to balance as best you can with your upper body." Angie slowly let go. "But if you feel yourself tipping, go ahead and brace yourself with your hands behind you on the mat."

Spring felt Victoria's stare and looked up. "What?"

She planted her hands on her hips. "You didn't tell him anything, did you?"

Sergeant Cotter. Wondered when they would get back to him. The anxiety running through Spring's veins heated, channeling into frustration. "I answered all his questions."

"Sure you did. Without telling him anything that could help, right?"

Spring glared at the colorful stability balls parked across the room.

"I don't understand why you won't cooperate with the police. They're trying to find the person who did this to you."

Spring tilted her head up to aim the glare at Victoria, bracing a hand behind herself. "And I suppose that will make me walk again?"

Victoria pinched her lips together, clearly trying to hold back whatever she wanted to say.

"At least the guy is cute."

Spring glanced at Angie to catch her wink. Heat rushed to Spring's cheeks.

"She noticed." Angie dimpled as she grinned.

"I think we all did." Victoria laughed.

"Then why didn't you ask him out?" Spring directed the comeback at her sister.

She frowned. They both knew Victoria would never do something so wild and impulsive. "It would have been pointless." Victoria crouched and began repositioning Spring's legs in front of her body. "I wouldn't have stood a chance with the way he was looking at you." She met Spring's gaze. "Or trying not to." Her lips curved into a satisfied smile.

"That is no lie, girlfriend." Angie giggled as she knelt at Spring's other side.

Spring stared at Victoria, her cheeks burning. "That isn't funny."

"I didn't mean it to be." Victoria didn't blink.

"You know I don't have a chance with men anymore. And especially not one as…"

"Handsome as Sergeant Cotter?"

Spring glared at her sister's smile. "Stop it, Victoria. My paralysis is not a joke."

Victoria's mouth straightened as her eyes filled with concern. "You're selling yourself short. You can still get married, have children. Live a normal life."

"I know you get paid to say stuff like that, but it won't work on me." Spring let her frustration sharpen her tone. "Why don't you just stick with the exercises and save the pep talks for someone who buys it?"

"Maybe I would if you would actually *do* the exercises. You're not even trying to get better." Victoria's voice pitched higher. "Don't you want to regain your mobility?"

"Will I ride again? Will I race?"

Victoria didn't say anything. She didn't have to.

Angie quietly started to guide Spring through another exercise, giving her instructions for transferring from the floor to her chair in a subdued tone.

Victoria got to her feet and took her position at Spring's other side.

"Good, Spring." Angie smiled when Spring gave a half-hearted attempt to help as the PTs hefted her into the chair again.

"There's a lot more to life than cycling."

Spring stifled an eye roll at her sister's statement while

Angie made sure she was sitting correctly in the chair. Round two.

"What about the kids who sent you all those drawings with that get-well card? They love you, and you love them."

Spring stiffened. "You know working at the daycare is just to help me get by until I get a better paid spot on a team. Cycling is my career."

"Your obsession, you mean." Victoria stepped in front of Spring so she could send a challenging stare.

"I don't say that about your passion for PT."

"That's different. I love what I do."

"And I don't?" Frustration ballooned in Spring's chest.

"Loving something and living for it are two different things."

Spring narrowed her eyes. Victoria would never understand.

"I know you two have some things to work out," Angie straightened and looked at Victoria, "but I don't think this discussion is helping with the therapy."

"This has everything to do with Spring's therapy." Victoria crossed her arms over her pale green twinset. "She's way behind and we all know it." She turned her do-what-I-say-or-else gaze on Spring. "There's no reason you can't sit on your own yet or do your own transfers. You're young and strong. You can't do it because you aren't trying. Because you've given up. Merely because you can't be a cyclist—"

"Or maybe because I can't walk and never will!" Blood rushed hot in Spring's ears as she shouted the truth. "Maybe because now I'll never get married, never have kids, and officially be the biggest failure this family has ever had!"

Victoria blinked, finally silenced. At least for a second.

"Never mind." Spring gripped the hand rims on the wheels of her chair and started to push. She grunted. Took more oomph to get moving than she thought.

"Spring, where are you going?" Angie still managed to sound pleasant despite what she'd had to witness.

"Left my phone in my room." Spring didn't look back as she pushed harder, slowly making her way to the door.

"Let her go." Victoria's instruction to Angie reached Spring's ears as she rolled out of the gym and into the hallway.

Anger fueled her strength as she pushed herself through the passing people, the skin of her hands already starting to burn under the unfamiliar pressure of the rims.

Victoria probably thought she'd won, getting Spring to push her own wheelchair. Victoria always got what she wanted, one way or another.

Why had Spring agreed to let her sister assist with her PT? So what if the two therapists had gone to school together? Angie was the real rehab PT anyway. Victoria just had to be in control and in charge like usual. She'd always loved being the oldest Weston sibling way too much.

Well, they were adults now. Victoria wasn't in charge anymore.

Sweat dripped down Spring's face as she continued to push the chair, not even to the end of the first hallway yet. Her shoulders started to hurt. It was Victoria's fault Spring was even trying to wheel herself such a ridiculous distance.

She would talk to her physiatrist tomorrow about revoking Victoria's permission to assist. Her sister should go back to her life and let Spring do what she wanted with whatever was left of her own.

Spring slowed to a snail's pace, her shoulders screaming. She was a cyclist, not a weight-lifter. Her strength had always been in her legs. Legs that were weak as jelly now. Even worse, really. At least jelly was strong enough to hold fruit afloat.

Fire surged in her triceps and shoulders as she panted from the exertion she wasn't used to, all for an inch of movement at a time. Victoria had been trying to get Spring to push her own wheelchair for weeks, but it was hard without the ab and back muscles strengthened enough to use her upper body.

Also Spring's fault, Victoria would say. Spring was supposed to be doing her exercises.

But what was the point? She couldn't live like this. She just couldn't.

If that last text meant what she feared, she might not have to.

———

Torin watched Spring fade to a stop in the hallway. Standing across the hall from her, he glanced at the people who passed between them. Some aide would probably stop to help. Or maybe she didn't want any.

But something in her gaze, the sadness that cloaked her features, pulled him to her. He couldn't just leave her sitting there alone. And he was waiting to talk to her anyway.

He pocketed the phone he'd been using to answer emails and crossed the hallway, choosing his words carefully so he didn't insult her this time. "Miss Weston?" Not brilliant, but should be safe.

She turned her head quickly toward him, allowing him to spot the deep hopelessness in her eyes before she masked it.

He'd seen that look before. In the mirror.

"Were you waiting for me?"

"Yes."

"Oh." She looked ahead. "I was going back to my room for my phone. I forgot it."

He reached toward one of the handles at the back of her chair. "May I?"

She nodded.

He couldn't tell if he'd offended her again or not, but he lost track of that concern as soon as he started to push her chair. An entrancing scent wafted up from her dark waves of hair, carrying all other thoughts from his mind. The aroma of berries. Soft. Sweet.

"Look out."

Spring's warning call brought him to his senses just in time to swerve around a man in a suit who was too busy texting to watch where he was walking. Torin hadn't been too alert himself.

"Sorry." He turned the wheelchair around the corner and forced his mind not to dwell on the distracting fragrance of her hair. Searching madly for something else to think about, he mentally latched onto the phone. Why did she want it so badly? Something to do with the message that had scared her earlier?

"We got interrupted when we were talking about something you heard just before the collision. Can you describe it?"

She didn't answer.

He should have waited to ask when he could see her face.

Why was she so hesitant to answer what should be a harmless question? Harmless for her, at any rate. Not so much for the driver who hit her, if her answer led to a clue.

"This is my room." She pointed to the open doorway that he knew led to her room. But it gave her something to say instead of answering him.

He carefully turned the chair through the opening left by the propped-open door and wheeled her toward the bed. Her phone still lay on the table, which had been swung out to the side of the bed.

As soon as they neared the table, Spring reached to grab the phone. She pitched forward, the phone clattering to the floor.

Torin's pulse lurched, and he stepped around the chair. "Ma'am?" He reached for her shoulders but wasn't sure if he should move her. She would sit up if she was okay, wouldn't she?

"I lost my balance." Her voice was muffled against her knees. "Can you lift me up?"

He quickly grabbed her shoulders, then thought to soften his grip as he pushed her back up. He let his hands linger on her small shoulders, not sure he should let go.

"I got it now." Her cheeks flushed an attractive pink as she avoided his gaze.

"Sorry." He dropped his hands and straightened.

"I'm supposed to be able to lean forward on my own. Sit up and lean to push the wheelchair better. I haven't been doing my exercises. Which doesn't make my sister very happy."

So she was a nervous talker. Maybe if he kept her nervous, she'd volunteer more information about the hit-and-run. But the idea of making her stay uncomfortable around him didn't sit well.

He spotted the smartphone where it had fallen and bent to pick it up. His gaze caught the beginning of a text message in a notification on the screen.

You talk too much. Now—

"I'll take that." She held out her hand.

He quickly gave her the phone, though all his instincts told him to hang on to it and read the rest of the message. But he wasn't out of line for accidentally seeing what he had when it was in plain view. Holding the phone longer and intentionally reading her messages would be a very different situation. He didn't need that kind of trouble.

Spring's gaze locked on the phone's screen. She tensed and her gaze flitted up to Torin, her dark eyes filled with alarm. Then she ducked her head as she turned off the screen and hid the device between her leg and the arm of the wheelchair.

As if he wouldn't think that was suspicious behavior.

Silence hung thick in the room as his mind raced, concern growing with every second. The text was rude. Harsh. Threatening.

She talked too much about what? The hit-and-run? Or maybe something else she was mixed up in.

Officer Jannick's documentation on the initial investigation and reconstruction of Spring's case hadn't mentioned evidence of criminal intent. But if the text message and her frightened reaction were connected to the crash, he needed to take a hard look at the evidence himself from a different angle.

The five words Torin had seen of the text sent a surge of anger through him. Hard to believe anyone would threaten a woman as lovely as Spring Weston. Though it shouldn't surprise him. He'd seen much worse.

Torin moved so he stood more squarely in front of her. He kept his tone level and soft as he began a new line of questioning. "Do you know of anyone who might have a grudge against you?"

"No."

Skin color didn't change. No quickness of breath or wandering gaze. "Have you ever felt in danger with anyone?"

"No."

"Ever been threatened by anyone?"

Her gaze darted away, and she moistened her lips before she answered. "No."

A lie. Or at least not the complete truth. She was covering for someone, even though that someone was likely putting her in danger. Maybe even put her there, in a rehab bed, unable to use her legs. Someone had a tight hold on this woman. Torin wanted to shake it loose.

He probably shouldn't admit he'd seen the message. Could get him on the wrong foot with her. But his gut told him she was in far worse trouble than the confession would bring him. He'd take the risk. "I saw that text."

Her eyes widened.

"I didn't intend to, but I did, and it sounded threatening."

Her skin paled as her gaze flitted away again.

"Do you want to tell me about it?"

She angled her head to face him. "You have no business reading my texts, even if the phone did fall. My messages are private." Her eyes sparked, bringing life into her otherwise morose gaze.

Torin squelched a smile at the unexpected spitfire. The woman had spunk.

Her chin lifted. "I didn't realize I was a criminal under investigation. Shouldn't you be looking for whoever did this to me?"

He sobered. Gave her a nod. "I'm sorry if I offended you. Just trying to explore all the possibilities. I'll leave you to your privacy and stop back when I have more information."

She opened her mouth like she was going to say something, then closed it.

He turned and headed for the door. She was right. What was he thinking? That he could protect her from whoever was bothering her? Even if she was in danger, he'd be the last person to be able to keep her safe. That had been proven.

Torin stepped into the wide, sterile white hallway and set a fast pace to the middle of the tenth floor where the crowd of elevators were clustered. He needed to stay focused on his job —solving this case, getting the file off his desk and her controlling father out of his life. Then on to the next collision and the next, keeping his head down and never looking back.

CHAPTER
FIVE

October 7. 5:10 p.m.

SPRING FIDDLED with the food on the dinner tray that sat on her lap, the sight of the Brussel sprouts nauseating her tense stomach. Never liked that vegetable even on a good day. Which this day was decidedly not.

Even the cupcake from her cycling team, *the* cycling team, tasted like cardboard. Maybe because of the card they'd sent with it. *Enjoy your freedom to indulge!*

The style of humor was a hallmark of the team, especially Lana. They hadn't meant to be cruel. But the reminder that she was no longer in training and never would be still stung.

She set the fork on the plate and moved the tray to the bed, careful not to lean too far forward in her chair. She might as well be in bed instead of sitting right next to it in the wheelchair. As if that were a great step for independence, toward getting her life back.

Something scraped in the hall.

She jerked toward the sound.

Her door was closed, as usual.

Now I have to teach you to be quiet.

The threat wouldn't leave her thoughts for more than a few minutes now that she was alone. The fear clutching her belly wouldn't let go either.

If someone wanted to hurt her…she was a sitting duck.

Frustration rose in her throat, mixed with regret. She shouldn't have snapped at Sergeant Cotter, nearly biting his head off. He probably did think she was a criminal he should investigate now.

But the thought that he could have realized the text was about the accident set her teeth on edge. If there would be dangerous consequences to talking about the crash, then she didn't want to think what would happen if she told the police about the threats themselves. Or if the sergeant found out on his own.

She needed to keep her phone with her at all times from now on. She couldn't risk Victoria or the hospital staff seeing the text messages either.

But how would she handle Sergeant Cotter? The look he had given her after he saw the text could have made a polar bear shiver. She felt sorry for any criminals he questioned. They probably crumbled and told him everything he wanted to know after two seconds under the hard anger in his green eyes.

She wasn't a criminal, though, and she shouldn't have to feel like one. She couldn't blame the sergeant. He seemed able to tell she was holding something back from him. He couldn't know it was nothing—just a blurred memory of the worst night of her life that wouldn't help him find the person who hit her anyway. And he couldn't know she was being threatened into silence about the little she could say.

If only she could figure out why. Why did someone care so much about her silence that they'd threaten to kill her if she said anything about the crash? The only possible explanation she could think of was that the texts could be from the driver, the person who'd stolen her life. Maybe the driver thought Spring could identify him. Or her. But Spring hadn't had a chance to see anything clearly before she was struck. The driver should know that.

Whatever the reason, she couldn't keep living like this much longer—receiving threats every day. Especially when they told her to lie to a certain handsome police officer who only seemed to want to help.

"Not on my watch." His jaw had tightened as he made the confident statement, but his eyes had held a sincerity and authenticity that few people had when they looked at her now. Most were too busy trying to hide what they really felt—pity, revulsion, discomfort, disappointment...

"I see you didn't like your dinner." The male voice made Spring start.

Dad.

Her breath returned at the sight of his familiar figure. What was he doing there at that time of day?

He stopped halfway into the room, wearing his office garb of dress shirt and slacks with a navy blue tie under a long white lab coat. The fluorescent lighting bounced off his auburn hair flecked with silver and his glasses, obscuring her view of his eyes.

Was he going to stay at that distance? She bit back the urge to tell him paralysis wasn't contagious, but there would be no point. He'd never been one for closeness anyway...at least not with her.

"They're supposed to have quality diet here. Exactly what you need to get well."

Get well. As if she had the flu or measles. Stifling an eye roll, she managed a civil tone. "The food won't make me walk again."

"Never underestimate the importance of diet in medical recovery." He took a few steps closer, aiming toward the end of the bed rather than her. Probably looking for a patient chart or something.

She felt a moment's satisfaction that she wasn't his

patient. Maybe there was one small thing to be thankful for. "What are you doing here?"

He slid his hands into his pockets and looked at her with Victoria's hazel eyes. "Visiting my daughter, of course."

"It's not even six yet. Aren't you working?"

"No more surgeries today." He pulled back the cuff of his coat to check his watch. "I have to look in on some patients on my way back to the office."

She raised her eyebrows, remembering the mere handful of family dinners he'd been present for, even after her mom was gone. Always claimed work got in the way. "So you came here."

"I wanted to see how you're coming along."

So that was it. She knew there had to be a reason for his surprise visit. "Victoria told you, didn't she?"

"Told me what?" If he hadn't become a neurosurgeon, he probably could've made his fortune from poker with his unreadable face.

"That she doesn't think I'm making enough progress."

"Are you?"

Spring looked at the gray sky out the window, crossing her arms over her T-shirt. "Am I what?" Two could play that game.

"Making progress."

She shrugged, hating the feeling of guilt that thickened her throat. "There's not much progress I can make."

"Nothing could be farther from the truth." The firm tone signaled an oncoming lecture. "If you work hard, you can get your life back. I spoke with your cycling coach—"

"You what?" Incredulity shot out the question.

"Yes, I called him."

"When?"

"A few days ago."

Was that why Cliff had stopped by? Because he realized she hadn't told her dad about her suspicions? Or because of something her dad had said.

"Though I don't see why that matters."

Irritation fired her cheeks. "Why would you call him?"

"To see about holding your spot on the team. Or at least opening it up to you again next year."

She could not be hearing this. "I don't know if you've noticed, Dad," she choked back anger, "but I'm *paralyzed*." She waved her hands at the wheelchair that supported her lifeless legs.

He folded his arms across his chest, undaunted as usual. "It's an incomplete spinal cord injury. You could recover much of your mobility. You already regained bladder function and lower trunk control."

She shook her head. "*My* doctors say that with the extent and severity of my injury it's very unlikely I'll recover any significant mobility, if any at all." She tried to remember the medical terminology as best she could. Maybe talking her dad's language would get through to him.

"They don't know the difference the Weston blood makes."

Great. The *You're-a-Weston* speech. "It can't work miracles."

He frowned. "Did I teach you to wait for miracles?"

She dropped her gaze as if she were the guilty kid he was making her out to be.

"They don't happen, and you don't need them."

She felt him lean in a few inches.

"If I didn't know better, I'd say you sound like you're giving up."

More like accepting reality.

"Westons," he paused on his favorite word, "do not give up."

She swallowed, avoiding his disapproving gaze.

"Westons are not afraid of hard work either. You can't get anywhere in life without skill and hard work. You have a skill for cycling. I said you could pursue it. Now you have to work to get back to it and work to excel."

The familiar points of his lecture pelted her like darts tearing the holes of an overused board. "I've told you this I don't know how many times, but it never seems to sink in. If you disciplined yourself and worked harder, you would be able to succeed like your brothers and sisters."

He stepped toward her, his presence making her feel like she was being boiled in a pressure cooker, though he stopped six feet away. "If your mother were here, she would be so disappointed to see how easily you're giving up again."

The dart hit the bullseye with piercing pain. Spring blinked hard. She would not let him see the tears fall.

He stalked toward the door, then stopped. Turned back. "I won't allow you to continue this way, Spring. You're a Weston. I expect you to work harder. Beginning with your first PT session tomorrow morning."

The highly acclaimed neurosurgeon marched purposefully from her room as if he'd delivered another infallible diagnosis or completed a brilliant surgery without breaking a sweat. Only this was her life he was talking about.

She had a paralysis he couldn't fix, and she had always been like a malignant growth on the Westons' record that he couldn't surgically remove.

She pressed her lips together, trying to stop the trembling of her chin. Her father still had the power to reduce her to a puddle of emotion, to her childhood desperation of wanting daddy's approval, simply by walking into the room.

He was wrong about her mom. Spring repeated that reminder over and over in her mind as the tears escaped and tumbled down her cheeks.

Her mother hadn't been a Weston by birth. Italian heritage had given her a dark beauty and laid-back approach to life that counter-balanced the intensity of Spring's dad. If she were there now, she'd take Spring's hand and tell her exactly what she needed to hear. She would somehow make everything right as only she had been able to do.

But even her mom wouldn't have been able to give Spring the use of her legs again. Nothing would do that. And all the blame her dad threw at her wouldn't enable Spring to change that fact. She was going to have to disappoint him. Again. She wasn't sure how many more times she could take doing that.

CHAPTER
SIX

October 7. 6:11 p.m.

VICTORIA CRANED to look over her shoulder at the pedestrians on the sidewalk through windows blurred with broken raindrops. The cloudy sky brought darkness early. But made Treese even later, apparently.

Victoria turned back and checked her slim watch.

"Relax, Vicki." Robert's dark brown eyes twinkled as a grin cracked through his beard. "She'll just be happy she tied you up in knots."

"I'm not tied up in knots." Victoria straightened the hem of her cardigan and clasped her hands together in her lap. She let out a breath in an attempt to calm the tension that was making her short-tempered. "And I certainly hope that's not why Patricia is late."

"Oh-oh." Robert set his smartphone on the small table next to his leather chair. "*Patricia.* Somebody's in trouble."

"You're going to be if you don't stop." Victoria glanced away before letting the tug at the corner of her mouth turn into a real smile that would reward her incorrigible brother. Though Robert was four years younger than Victoria, the

51

middle sibling in the group of three that were each one year apart, Victoria got along so much better with him than Spring, who was only three years younger than her. Why was that?

He often made Victoria laugh and rarely needed her correction or guidance. Only Hank also brought her more joy than challenges and irritation. Perhaps because he was the baby of the family.

Or maybe sisters were always bound to rub each other the wrong way more than brothers.

Victoria pursed her lips, holding back a sigh. Conversations crashed around them in the large alcove that still wasn't spacious enough. Too many people for her taste clustered in leather chairs and lounged on benches that lined two of the walls.

A clutch of three boisterous men sat uncomfortably close to the three leather seats Robert had angled toward each other to give an insufficient sense of privacy, or at least proximity.

The music from the main floor situated a few feet above the alcove thrummed louder, sharpening the throb of Victoria's oncoming headache. "We could have met at my house."

"And make Treese forty minutes late instead?"

Not to mention causing Robert to miss his favorite pizza in Chicago.

Victoria held back the comment, glancing at her watch again. Treese could be late to any location, even one only ten minutes from their father's house where she lived.

The raucous laughter of the men to Victoria's right abruptly ceased.

A current seemed to charge the air, as if a crackling energy had entered their midst.

Patricia had arrived.

She paused at the top of the steps, supposedly to look for her family, then waved with a gleaming smile. If gaining attention from onlookers was her goal, she'd succeeded.

The men of the alcove drooled as she sashayed to her

siblings in a black sheath and four-inch heels more suited to a night club than dinner with family.

"Hey, Robby." She bent to land a sweeping kiss on Robert's cheek before she angled the open chair closer to him and tossed Victoria a grin with too much sauce. "Am I late?"

Victoria caught the amusement playing on Robert's lips and held back the lecture her sister clearly needed. "Not enough to mention."

"Oh." A dimple peeked as Treese flicked her straightened, long brown hair behind her shoulder and sat down, crossing her toned legs.

Victoria hid a smile behind a sip from her water glass and arched an eyebrow at Robert. Treese had been trying to get her goat since the age of eleven. Victoria wasn't about to be any more easily manipulated fifteen years later. At least now, Treese's games were all in fun. For Treese, at any rate.

"Am I the only one who feels weird about this?" Treese leaned forward, the hem of her dress inching higher with the movement.

"About what? Overdressing for a sports bar?" Victoria couldn't resist. The outfit was outrageously inappropriate and flirtatious, at best.

"Pizzeria and brewpub." Mirth filled Robert's defense of his favorite restaurant.

"There, you see?" Treese tilted her hand toward Robert as if that won the argument. "I'm not overdressed at all. And Robby's wearing a tie anyway." She waved her hand at his work attire of navy blue slacks, tie, and pale blue dress shirt. "Now if you two will get serious for a minute…"

Robert chuckled as Victoria raised her eyebrows. She couldn't restrain the light laugh that escaped at the incongruity of such a statement coming from her baby sister's lips.

"What?"

"Nothing." Robert's lips twitched. "We'll try."

Treese pinned him with an exaggerated glare. "What I was trying to say was that this feels weird. To be here without

Spring." Her small hands tightened on the arms of the chair. "It seems wrong."

Robert shifted a somber gaze to Victoria.

"It's not wrong when she is the reason we're here." Victoria pursed her lips. "I'm at my wit's end with her. Her mobility is not improving and her attitude is deteriorating. We have to do something."

"Agreed." Robert tented his fingers in front of his chin, elbows propped on the chair arms.

"What can we do?" Treese uncrossed her legs and crossed the other one over the top. "I've meant to visit her more, but my schedule has been crazy."

Robert shook his head. "I'm not sure that would help. Visits seem to make her more irritable and depressed. Though I'm pretty sure that's her defense mechanism. She has a need for privacy and independence, a chance to grieve alone, but she also needs to know she's loved and supported." He caught Treese's stare. "What?"

"Please. This is our sister. You don't have to psychoanalyze her."

He grinned. "Are you kidding me? Psychoanalyzing you girls is what got me through school."

Treese wrinkled her nose. "Just don't try it with me, *Doctor*, if you know what's good for you."

"What can you do to me in that dress?"

Treese leaned forward and whacked his forearm.

"Children, please." Victoria stifled the urge to roll her eyes and become as immature as her siblings.

Treese pointed a finger at her big brother. "I can take you anytime."

"Wait till I change into my shorts. I'll meet you outside."

"One New Haven Style white pizza." A brave server inserted the pizza between the grinning adversaries, setting it on the petite table next to Robert and leaving them each with a small plate.

Victoria arched an eyebrow at her brother. "Are we going to taste any of that?"

"*You* can. I'll consider giving the princess some if she apologizes."

Treese answered his wink by sticking out her tongue.

This was the moment in which Spring would have said something clever and funny. Some pithy observation, at once witty and effective at restoring focus. Something completely Spring.

Victoria could only sit quietly and watch or scold and ruin their fun. Or, in this case, feel the pang of Spring's absence.

She softly cleared her throat. "Mind if I pray?"

Robert slowed his jaw mid-chew and lowered his slice to the stack of pieces on his plate.

"If it makes you feel better." Treese set her plate with the single slice she likely would not eat on her lap and crossed her arms as if that would keep Victoria's religion at bay.

A deeper pain burned in Victoria's chest as she closed her eyes and bowed her head. With her quick, oral prayer for wisdom to know how to help Spring, she added a silent prayer of her own for her siblings' salvation.

"You are going to eat something, right?" The ribbing recommenced immediately after Victoria's "Amen."

Treese smirked at Robert. "I prefer my protein without the processed wheat stacked with fattening dairy and slathered in oil, thank you very much."

"Olive oil has healthy fats." He wagged his finger at her before taking a huge bite of pizza.

Victoria should have brought her proverbial referee's hat. "Speaking of health, shall we return to the reason we're here?"

"Pizza?" Robert held up a hand before Victoria could properly deliver her frown. "I know. Poor taste." He glanced at Treese. "Pun not intended."

He set his plate on the table and wiped his hands on a napkin from the stack the server had left with the pizza. "The truth is, it's hard to objectively assess and treat someone when she's your own sister."

The concern that weighed on Victoria's mind reflected in Robert's eyes, lessening her burden just slightly.

"Hank called me yesterday."

They turned to look at Treese, her forehead crossed with rare lines. "He's worried. Just from the way she sounded on the phone when he last talked to her. He's angry, too." Her small jaw clenched. "It's wrong that whoever paralyzed our sister is walking around free out there somewhere."

"He's angry, or you are?" Robert watched her with a steady gaze.

Treese shrugged, the toned muscles in her shoulders and upper arms tensing. "Aren't you mad?"

"I want justice. The driver left the scene. Likely drove in an unsafe manner for the conditions. He or she could be prosecuted for that." He spoke slowly, as if choosing his words carefully. "I want what's best for Spring."

"She's afraid."

Robert and Treese swung their heads to look at Victoria.

"I can see it in her eyes. On her face." She stared at the stack of uneaten pizza on Robert's plate. "I hear it in the anger she aims at me."

"What is she afraid of?"

"I'm not sure." Victoria met Treese's brown-eyed gaze.

"Something other than facing life bound to a wheelchair?" Robert's question was logical.

"I think so." Victoria rubbed her upper arms through the sleeves of her cardigan. "I'm not certain. At first, I thought she was only scared of the paralysis. It would make sense. I think the change in her life is certainly why she's depressed. But lately, there's more actual fear in her demeanor. It's...different somehow."

She met her siblings' searching gazes. "Today, for example, she was trembling during her PT session. Her skin was so pale." Victoria shook her head. "I haven't seen her that scared since…" She picked up her glass of water. "For a long time."

"What if she's afraid of the jerk who hit her?" Protectiveness and worry warred across Treese's delicate features.

"Could be." Robert looked at Victoria. "Do you think she's still hiding something about the crash?"

"I do. It's not so much what she will or won't say, but the way she behaves when anyone asks about it. You saw it, didn't you?"

He nodded. "She shows some of the classic signs of deception. Of keeping a secret."

"We've got to get him." Treese's chin crumpled with the pressure her clenched muscles were putting on it. "What if she saw who hit her and now he's threatening her to keep quiet? People will do insane stuff to keep anyone from knowing they were stupid enough to hit somebody and run away. They'll pay blackmailers, kill people even."

Victoria cocked an eyebrow. "Have you been watching crime show marathons again?"

"I'm serious. Nobody can mess with our sister like this, ruin her life and then scare her every day without paying for it."

"Whoa there, Tiger." A small smile angled Robert's mouth. "Didn't know you cared."

The lack of a snappy comeback spoke more strongly than Treese's weak smile. She cared. They all did.

"You're right, though."

Victoria caught the darkening of Robert's eyes.

"Nobody's going to mess with our sister like that. I think it's time we got a little more involved in the investigation of the accident."

"Collision."

Robert's black eyebrows lifted at Victoria's correction.

"A distinction the new handler of Spring's case makes, apparently."

"New handler?"

"I suppose that may not be the correct terminology. A Sergeant Cotter is taking over Spring's case."

"Sergeant. That's a higher ranking officer than she had before, isn't it?"

"Yes."

"So is that a good thing?" Treese tilted her head.

"I think so. I met the sergeant today."

"And you like him." A smile curved Robert's mouth.

"I do." Victoria nodded.

"Wait, *you* like him?" Treese scooted forward in her chair. "How cute is this sergeant?"

Heat warmed Victoria's cheeks. "Honestly, Patricia. Robert didn't mean that kind of 'like.' Is that all you ever think about?"

"Ha! Classic symptoms of a crush. You're trying to get me off your back by turning tables on me."

"No, I'm trying to get you to act your age."

Treese gave Victoria a galling smile as she crossed her thin arms. "You're making my case."

There was only one way to end Patricia's fantasies before she had a fabricated ring on Victoria's finger. "If you must know, yes, the sergeant is attractive, and no, I am not interested, which is convenient because he only has eyes for our sister."

Treese's mouth dropped open. "Spring?"

"Do we have another sister?"

Robert chuckled at Treese's stunned expression. "Take a sip of water, Tiger. It'll help."

Victoria focused on her brother. "He seems competent and determined to solve Spring's case."

Robert grabbed his phone. "Cotter you said?" He typed something, likely the sergeant's name into his phone.

"Yes. He's the hero officer who's been in the news lately."

Robert glanced up at Victoria. "The one who saved the child from the bomb?"

She nodded.

"Wow." Treese's gaze bobbed between them. "So what did Spring think of him? Does she like him?"

Victoria cocked an eyebrow. "This isn't a soap opera."

"I don't know. It's pretty shocking, if you ask me."

"What's shocking about it?"

Treese met Robert's question with widened eyes. "That he likes her."

"The guy's got good taste."

"But she's paralyzed."

"Treese." Victoria's sharp scold attracted a few glances from the nearby groups. She lowered her voice. "Unlike some people, Sergeant Cotter didn't even seem to notice. And he certainly didn't let it diminish his opinion of our sister."

"That's not what..." Treese looked down at her knees, the frown that tugged her lips reminding Victoria of the ten-year-old who'd broken their mother's ceramic ballerina.

"I'll do some more research on the sergeant and make sure he's the best for Spring." Robert tactfully veered the conversation back onto the right road. "Either way, we'll give him as much help as we can."

"How?" No surprise, Treese rediscovered her voice quickly.

"I can take some time off." Robert glanced at Victoria. "You're with Spring every day, and we'll start showing up more often, too. We'll find out what we can from her and then spend the rest of our time digging through what she won't tell us."

"I'll do what I can." Treese shifted a clump of her hair to drape over her shoulder. "But it will have to be between clients."

He nodded at Treese, then moved his focus to Victoria. "And you're balancing two jobs right now, I know. We'll get together as much as we can, but we can text and call in between. First, we need a place to start."

"The cycling coach."

Treese and Robert blinked at Victoria.

"Just a suspicion. He never visited Spring until today."

"The day she got scared."

Victoria met Robert's gaze. "More scared, at least. I'm not sure it's connected, but she didn't seem happy to have seen him."

Treese wrinkled her nose. "But what would her cycling coach have to do with the crash?"

"I've been thinking about that. It's possible Spring recognized the driver who hit her. Perhaps her coach knows the person, as well. Or, he could even be the driver himself. Either way, Spring may not want to be the cause of him or her incurring consequences for an accident."

"Even if he's threatening her?" Treese's eyes widened.

Robert nodded. "That does sound unfortunately like Spring."

Treese glared at Victoria. "Don't tell me it's all that 'turn the other cheek' nonsense."

Victoria did her best to do exactly that and held her tongue, waiting the moment it would take for Robert to diffuse the situation.

"We'll start with the coach then." Robert's calm tone doused the crackling air between the sisters. "I'll call Hank and see if he has any ideas or wants to help."

"While he's in school?" Their father wouldn't thank them if they upset Hank's academic performance.

"Well, I'll at least keep him in the loop."

Treese let out a sigh. "Do you think we can do this, guys?"

"We're Westons." Robert grinned. "We can do anything we set our minds to."

Treese groaned as Victoria laughed. Her first laugh in a long, long time.

CHAPTER
SEVEN

October 7. 7:20 p.m.

THE BICYCLE WAS UTTERLY MANGLED.

Torin zoomed in on the digital photo that filled his desktop computer screen.

Blood smeared the twisted steel frame. Spring's blood.

Blood and worse were common sights in Torin's workday. Usually didn't make his chest tighten uncomfortably. He blew out a breath to release the unexplained tension.

From the state of Spring's bicycle after the crash and the other evidence he'd been reviewing in detail over the last hour, she was lucky to be alive.

The bullet car had struck Spring and her bicycle at an angle, which had probably saved her life. But the following force threw her and the bike into the bridge abutment, causing her paralysis and the destruction of the cycling equipment. According to the recon evidence, the bicycle had flown ahead of her and somewhat buffered the impact of Spring's collision with the concrete abutment.

The striking vehicle was estimated to have a closing speed of forty-six mph, well above the posted speed limit of thirty-five on that street. But speeders were nothing unusual. What was more unusual was the lack of evidence for the driver's attempt to avoid impact.

No skid marks to indicate braking. No impact evidence on any of the surrounding objects, tire marks leading off the road, or any other indication of a hard steer maneuver.

At least none Jannick had uncovered. Jannick was a solid investigator and Torin had confidence in his abilities. But Torin also preferred to see things for himself.

Jannick's assessment of the recon investigation concluded there was likely no criminal intent, though the driver committed the crime of hit-and-run by leaving the scene. The trajectory of Spring and her cycle indicated the vehicle struck her cycle with the front corner of the bumper, eliminating the chance that the driver could have been unaware of hitting her.

Yet, the rain and darkness of that spot under the bridge at nine thirty p.m., and the fact that impact occurred three hundred and eleven feet after a curve suggested accidental collision. A sad number of drivers in unintentional collisions did flee the scene, thanks to the limbic system inducing panic that led to irrational decisions.

But more often hit-and-run drivers had been in trouble before.

You talk too much…

Torin drummed his fingers on the desk as he mentally replayed the small snippet of the text message he'd seen on Spring's phone. Did she realize the collision might not have been accidental? He should interview her again. Maybe he could get her to admit more this time, confide in him about the text message and the fear it had lit in her doe-brown eyes.

He hoped the warm feeling that spread under his ribs as he pictured those eyes didn't have anything to do with his desire to interview her again. He knew not to get emotionally involved with victims of the collisions he investigated. And he would never become attached to any woman again. Period.

"Cotter."

Torin jerked out of his thoughts to see Lieutenant Airaldi standing in the doorway to his office. Torin stood. "Lieutenant." A visit from Airaldi wasn't unheard of, but neither was it common. Torin had the uneasy feeling he knew what this visit was about.

The lieutenant's sharp eyes assessed Torin and the files on his desk. "Staying late, aren't you?"

Torin glanced at his watch. "Yes, sir. Later than I realized."

"How are you holding up?"

Just as he feared. The lieutenant wasn't talking about his injury, but at least he was being mercifully vague. "I'm fine."

"You could have waited until next week to come back."

Until after tomorrow. "No need. I'm all right."

The lieutenant's eyes narrowed slightly as he met Torin's gaze. "I can give you the day off tomorrow. You should take it."

He shouldn't have taken the past five weeks off. His injuries had been horribly timed. Having no work to keep him busy as the anniversary of that horrible day approached only made him edgy and depressed, the attack of memories stronger.

He didn't need another day with nothing to do but sit and think about her, how in all this time life without her hadn't gotten better or easier. How it never would.

"Three years isn't long enough to heal from these things. I know that."

These things. As if they happened every day. But that wasn't how the lieutenant meant it. Torin glanced away. "Thank you for the card."

"The least I could do."

Torin shifted slightly, touching the tips of his fingers to the desk.

"Are you happy with MAIU?"

Torin swallowed past the lump. He wasn't happy doing anything anymore. But he made himself meet the lieutenant's gaze. "It's satisfying work."

"Most people aren't so fond of it." Airaldi's piercing gaze searched Torin's. "I still don't understand why you requested this transfer after what you went through. Most investigators want to transfer *out* of MAIU."

Torin nodded. He'd been warned many times while he pushed for the transfer from patrol. Veterans from MAIU and those who'd gotten out told him stories of the tragedies they had to witness, called away at a moment's notice on holidays and during family dinners to document horrific deaths that never should have happened.

But holidays only meant something when you had people to celebrate with. Family dinners were nonexistent without a family. And Torin would rather confront the tragedies on the roadways than the one that played over and over again in his mind. The one that gave him terrifying, living nightmares at target practice, even three years later.

"Well, I'm glad to have a man like you leading the unit."

"Thank you, sir."

Lieutenant Airaldi's chin scrunched as he dipped his head to Torin and started to turn away. He paused. "Oh, by the way, you heard about the budget cuts and restructuring we're going through?"

Torin's gut clenched. The lieutenant had that tone he'd learned to dread. "Yes."

"Well, more of the MAIU boys are going to have to put in patrol hours."

Patrol duty? His tight stomach plummeted.

"You might have to handle some patrol, too, depending on how the roster fills out."

"But—" The protest escaped before Torin could think of anything besides the panic speeding his pulse. He couldn't. It was inconceivable.

Airaldi looked at him.

"I can't."

The lieutenant's dark bushy eyebrows rose.

"I mean," Torin glanced around, as if he'd find the

excuse he so desperately needed lying on his desk, "I have so much work backed up." He gestured to the small stack of paper next to the computer. "And I always have a ton of work, of course." The excuse struck his own ears as lame.

"I know you're pulling a lot as head of the unit, but my hands are tied." Airaldi's voice was firm. No arguments to be accepted. "I'll try to keep you off patrol if I can so you can maximize your time here. Or it will be minimal duty, especially till I'm sure you're fully recovered from your injuries. Shouldn't be a problem."

Minimal duty. Just one shift would be too much. Anything could happen. A robbery.

He'd have to use a gun.

"Cotter?"

Torin fought to rein in his screeching heart rate and focus on Airaldi's lined face.

"Is there a problem?"

The question was a test. One Torin couldn't fail and keep his job, keep his secret. He mustered what little courage he seemed to have left and answered in a level tone. "No, sir."

"Good. Back to work, then." Airaldi turned on his heel and disappeared from the doorway.

Torin sank into his chair, but the off-white walls of his office seemed to close in around him. His breathing came in shortening gasps.

He could feel it coming this time. He had to get away.

If anyone saw him when it happened...

He pushed up from his chair and marched into the narrow hallway, headed for the garage. He tried to focus on something other than the vision of the shelves of snacks at the gas station. The smell of fuel on his hands.

The flash from the gun barrel.

Then he was sitting in the driver's seat of his unmarked car. No memory of reaching it and getting in. But plenty of other memories that would never let him free.

October 8. 12:15 a.m.

Spring gasped as another surge of pain ripped through her belly. She pressed her hand to her stomach. Didn't feel tender on the outside, but inside something was cutting it to pieces.

Biting her lip against the pain, she tried to think clearly. Had the physiatrist said anything about stomach cramps as a side effect of her injuries? Maybe the medications.

Yes, that had to be it. One of the medications must be causing this. Though she wasn't taking much anymore. Not that she remembered.

It was amazingly hard to remember or know anything at the moment. She'd never felt such agony. Made the phantom leg pains seem like pin pricks by comparison.

Another surge burned through her gut.

A moan escaped her lips as she clutched her abdomen, tried to roll over. Her dead lower body wouldn't let her.

Should she call someone? The hallway outside her door was quiet. At least she thought it was. Couldn't hear much beyond her own groaning and the pain that radiated every-where, seemed to be ringing in her ears.

There was a call button...somewhere by her bed. Wasn't there? She hadn't paid attention when they'd told her.

If she could just get on her side, the change in position might offer some relief. She should have learned the rolling over method Victoria had tried to teach her.

The cell phone buzzed on the table next to Spring's bed.

She turned her head, pulse quickening. Not now. She couldn't deal with a threat when she was being killed from the inside.

But maybe she could use her phone to call Victoria. She felt for the cell, sliding her hand around on the table without touching the device.

Why did that nurse insist on having Spring lay flat in the

bed where she couldn't see the top of the table? She wouldn't sleep anyway. She rarely did anymore.

Taking a deep breath, she tried to focus on using her ab muscles, but a slice through her belly made her gasp. She crushed her lip between her teeth to keep from screaming.

Was she supposed to use her shoulders instead anyway? She reached again, this time managing to rotate her shoulders and torso enough that she made contact with the phone. Gripping it in her fingers, she rotated back, the brightness of the screen in the dark room making her squint.

A text message greeted her.

This is your first lesson. Don't make me have to give you another one.

Horror reverberated through her body, the pain receding to give way to shock. The texter did this to her? How?

Another stab seemed to slash her stomach in half.

She dropped the phone, then fumbled for it on the sheet.

Her fingers trembled as she clutched the phone again, managing to type the question screaming in her mind. *What did you do to me?*

She tried to breathe as she waited for the answer she wasn't sure she wanted.

The phone vibrated against her sweaty palm.

It's not fatal. This time.

Fear swept through her with another gust of pain. She bit down on her lip. Typed. *Why are you doing this?*

The minute of silence dragged by like an hour as the agony pulsated through her stomach.

I told you to keep quiet.

Pain must inspire either courage or foolishness, because she asked another question without thinking. *About what?*

That night.

What about that night? Who hit her? She didn't even know the answer to that. Why wouldn't this person leave her alone?

Another tearing spasm made her bite back a wail.

The phone vibrated.

Don't call for help. They'll just tell you to stay away from cupcakes.

Cupcakes. Her heart paused. The texter knew what she'd eaten for dinner. Cold seeped into her blood stream, reaching every part of her body.

He was watching her. All the time?

She glanced around the darkened room, searching for a camera.

Pain slammed into the wall of her stomach. She squeezed her eyes shut, trying to breathe.

How could he have done this to her? Had he substituted something for her regular medicine? Or had he poisoned her food somehow?

Another text shook the cell.

Remember, silence. Or next time will be worse.

The texter could get to her even here in the rehab center. And his threats weren't empty.

Spring stifled a whimper as she clutched her aching stomach.

He'd made his point. She wasn't safe anywhere. Unless she didn't say a word. Not even to the handsome sergeant who'd given her a spark of hope.

A spasm hit her, and she twisted her head into the pillow.

Her Bible sat on the chair three feet from the bed. Out of reach. Just like its meaning and the comfort it used to give her.

Didn't God see her? Didn't He care about her pain?

No, He wanted this to happen or He wouldn't have let that driver hit her. Her greatest Comforter had turned into the cause of her agony.

She yanked her gaze to the ceiling, willing the next wave of pain to wash her life away.

CHAPTER
EIGHT

October 8. 6:40 a.m.

THE CRISP WIND brushed Torin's ears, like whispers of coming cold, approaching death.

The gravestone looked the same. No moss or discoloration clogged the ornate swirls and carved flowers Ivy's mother had insisted on.

Beloved wife and daughter. Gone before her time.

The etched words were engraved on his mind. *Gone before her time.*

He curled his cold fingers into his palms as he stared down at the symbol of his guilt. He should say how sorry he was. Beg her forgiveness. But the words lodged in his swollen throat.

He'd already tried that anyway. It didn't help. Nothing could.

The ring of his phone floated on the wind, as if it were miles away instead of in his pocket. He pulled it out, his stomach rolling over. Expecting the call never prepared him for it.

He tapped the answer option on the screen and pressed the phone to his ear.

Silence.

Then the words he dreaded.

"Why didn't you save her?" Miranda's voice cracked, but the bitterness still clung to her tone.

The question twisted the knife permanently planted in his gut. To say he had tried meant nothing.

"She should be here. I shouldn't have to—" She choked on a sob. She was different this year. Less wrath, more pain.

He could handle the anger. It was no worse than the fury he had for himself. Her pain, he couldn't take. He already couldn't bear his own.

"You haven't even found the man who shot her. Why haven't you found him?"

"We're trying." Derrick was trying. Torin had all he could do to function on the job, to avoid thinking about that day. But attempting to forget heaped betrayal on top of his failure.

"You've forgotten her, haven't you?"

He sucked in a breath. Hoped she didn't hear it. How did she always know his weakest point? The guilt crushed his ribs. He struggled to find his voice. "I could never forget." It was true. Hard as he tried, the memories of that day wouldn't leave him in peace. But he would never try to forget Ivy.

"I don't think you even loved her."

Heat surged up his neck. Didn't love her? He would have died for her. If he'd had the chance. He barely bit back the response he wanted to fling at Miranda. He had forfeited his right to defend himself.

She had reason to doubt his love. He'd let Ivy die.

"I want him caught. That's the least you can do for me."

"There's not enough evidence."

"You were *there*." Her hiss singed his ear through the phone. "Isn't that enough evidence?" The anger took hold of her voice, carrying her hatred across the miles to claw at him there at her daughter's grave.

Her bullet hit harder than the car bomb. Right where she'd aimed. But he had no grounds for a defense.

"I said you weren't good enough for her. You proved that when you killed her."

The words dug the knife in deeper. His due punishment.

"I want justice. Do you hear me?" Her voice grew louder. "I want justice."

A gust of wind swirled leaves around Ivy's gravestone. Leaves of gold and red, moving upward as if someone was calling them to defy gravity, to laugh at the realities no one could change.

"So do I."

"If you loved her at all, you'll get it for her."

"I'll try."

"Like you tried to protect her?"

His throat closed as the cold numbed his fingers. "I'm sorry."

Silence.

"You say that every year."

The background noise stopped. He looked at the screen.

Call ended.

His gaze latched on to the block letters etched in the stone in front of him.

Ivy Jefferson Cotter.

"Torin!" Her scream gusted toward him on the wind. He turned his back and fled, the dark memories nipping at his heels.

9:19 a.m.

"You've made good progress."

Spring looked up at Dr. Edward Berghuis as he rotated her to lie on her back on the bed again. Clearly, he was the surgeon and not the physical therapist or he wouldn't be saying that.

"The spine has stabilized very well. The swelling has gone down." He peeled off his examination gloves. He glanced at Victoria, who hovered on the opposite side of the bed. "I hear, however, that there may be some trouble progressing in physical therapy?"

Spring threw Victoria a glare.

The PT ignored it as she held the button that slowly raised Spring to a sitting position.

"Actually, your father called me yesterday."

She returned her gaze to the doctor as he stepped away to drop his gloves into the garbage slot below the counter by the far wall. "He called you?"

Dr. Berghuis smiled and turned back, his white coat swinging across his gray-striped dress shirt and patterned silver tie. "I'm afraid we surgeons aren't known for being good patients or good parents of patients. However, I did respect your confidentiality and referred him to you for specific questions about your health and progress."

"Thank you." At least one person around there treated her like an adult.

"I just hope your father doesn't decide to take his revenge on me when I need neurosurgery someday." Dr. Berghuis winked.

Victoria chuckled. "I wouldn't worry too much about it. Dad would probably do a terrific job even if he was trying not to."

"And I'd be very lucky to have your father doing the procedure. He's earned his reputation."

"So have you." Victoria smiled. "I'm so thankful Dad knew to ask for you to be Spring's surgeon."

"It was my pleasure."

Spring glanced back and forth between the two of them as Victoria took over yet another conversation. Spring was not the little child her sister seemed to believe she would be forever.

A beep sounded, and the doctor checked his pager. "I'm afraid I have to go." He looked at Spring. "But it appears my work here is done anyway. As long as you're not planning to go cycling and hit something anytime soon."

Moisture suddenly blurred Spring eyes, the remark unexpectedly stinging. She shouldn't be so sensitive. He only meant to be funny.

She forced a smile and shook her head, not trusting her voice.

"Good." He lifted his hand in a wave to Victoria as he swung around and left the room, holding the door open for Angie to enter.

The other PT smiled at Victoria. "Oh, good, you're here already." She transferred her gaze to Spring. "Ready to get dressed and get some work done?"

Spring frowned. Why was everyone so chipper today? They clearly hadn't spent the night in complete agony as she had. At least the stomach pain was gone today.

Not fatal. Just horrifying.

Without bothering to wait for a response from Spring, Victoria started to help Angie exchange Spring's gown for a pair of gray cotton lounge pants and loose-fitting red T-shirt. Needing other people to change her clothing was right next to bathroom help for the most humiliating results of her paralysis.

Maybe it would be better if the attack on her stomach had been fatal.

Spring tried to take her mind off the embarrassment by reaching to touch the pants when Victoria wasn't looking. They were the soft kind Spring used to love to wear around home after a long day of training. What she wouldn't give to feel that sweet comfort on her legs right now. She never would again.

Grief and anger twisted into a wad that clogged her throat

as the two women rolled Spring onto her side to finish getting the pants on. She was like a doll for them to play dress-up with. Just as lifeless and empty.

"Uh-oh."

Spring angled her head toward Angie.

The PT paused, staring at something. "Victoria."

Victoria leaned in to examine whatever had caught Angie's attention.

"What?" Bad enough they were dressing her like a Barbie doll. They didn't have to criticize her unclothed body, too.

Victoria's hazel eyes darkened as she met Spring's gaze. "You have a pressure sore." She pursed her lips while Angie started to bandage the area. "Honestly, Spring." Victoria looked at her as if she had just announced she'd flunked out of medical school.

Spring lowered her head back to the pillow, her cheek rubbing the hot cotton as she waited for the rest of Victoria's lecture.

"You know how to do bed rollovers. You're supposed to do them. And you're supposed to push yourself up to relieve the pressure when you're in the chair or the bed. You know that."

Spring shrugged one shoulder, not about to admit she couldn't remember how to roll over in bed because she hadn't paid attention when they'd shown her.

Victoria let out an exasperated grunt only Spring seemed to earn from her proper sister. "I can't believe you aren't taking this sore seriously. It could become infected."

Spring tilted her chin to meet Victoria's gaze, keeping any reaction off her face.

"You could *die* from it."

As if that mattered. Spring just looked at her sister.

"Oh, Spring." The frustration in Victoria's eyes melted to sadness as her delicate eyebrows pushed together.

A knock on the closed door stopped Spring from having to deal with the guilt forming a lump in her throat. Maybe she should've tried to mask her feelings. She didn't realize Victoria would take it so hard.

Angie stepped away to go to the door while Victoria finished pulling the pants on and rolled Spring onto her back. At least Victoria didn't lecture her anymore as she walked around the bed to position the wheelchair for Spring's transfer.

"You have a visitor." Angie smiled as she returned.

"Who?"

Instead of answering, Angie helped Victoria slide the transfer board under Spring, and then directed Spring to help with the transfer using shoulder strength she didn't have.

They settled her into the chair on top of an extra thick cushion Victoria had added, and Angie cast her fellow PT a secretive smile before she went to open the door. What were they up to?

Sergeant Cotter strode into the room, launching Spring's heart into a cartwheel she had no idea it could execute.

"Good morning." His lips curved into a smile, crinkling the skin at the corners of his eyes. That smile would probably disappear when she wouldn't be able to tell him anything more.

"I hope I didn't come at a bad time."

She'd forgotten how nice his voice was. Low-pitched with a slight roughness that complimented his rugged appeal. And his smile kept doing strange things to her insides. "No, not bad." She shook her head, her gaze unable to leave his face.

The blue sport coat he wore over a white button-down shirt lined with light blue stripes gave his eyes an entrancing sea green tint.

"Do you have more questions for Spring?" Victoria's voice snapped Spring back to reality.

The reality of an unknown texter watching her every move, poised to torture or kill her if she said one wrong word. From Barbie doll to puppet. How much worse could her life get?

She could have to explain the threatening text message to

Sergeant Cotter, for starters. She stifled a grimace, hoping that wasn't the reason he had come.

"First, I'd like to apologize." He watched her with his patient, confident gaze.

She lifted her eyebrows. Didn't he mean he needed to get an apology?

"For unintentionally…" He threw a glance at Victoria and Angie. "For when I picked up your phone."

She moistened her lips. He didn't have to be so nice. She already liked him too much. "I'm the one who should apologize. I overreacted."

"You had good reason to be upset." He reached into his sport coat pocket and pulled out the same small notepad he'd used the day before. But he looked at her instead of the pad as he continued. "I'd like you to know about a new wrinkle, a possibility that might shed some light on your case."

"You've found something?" Victoria's question reminded Spring her sister was there, standing just to her right.

How clichéd was that? Spring had actually forgotten anyone else was in the room.

The sergeant moved his gaze from Victoria to Spring. "Would you rather we discuss your case privately?"

Spring glanced at Victoria. She'd love to say yes, but her sister would not take that well. Victoria already knew all there was to know about the case anyway. "It's fine."

"I reviewed the evidence in detail yesterday, and I think you need to be aware there's a strong possibility that the person who hit you with the vehicle did so intentionally."

Victoria sucked in a breath.

Purposefully? Spring's stomach churned. She'd hoped she had misread his meaning when he questioned her yesterday. How could anyone intentionally paralyze someone? Why would they? She wanted to throw her questions at the sergeant. But she had to be careful. She could say something the texter didn't like without realizing it.

She took a breath and fought to keep her voice and expression calm. "What makes you say that?"

He watched her closely, his eyes slightly narrowed as if he suspected her again. "There's no evidence that the driver of the vehicle applied the brakes or made any attempt to swerve. The natural reaction would be to apply hard pressure on the brakes, even if at the last minute. The investigator at the scene didn't find any of the skid marks we would expect to see in that scenario."

"Couldn't the driver not have seen Spring?" Victoria stared at him. "It was raining, correct?"

He nodded. "That was Officer Jannick's interpretation of the evidence—that the driver didn't see her because of poor conspicuity in the unlit area on a wet night."

Spring cleared her throat. Victoria was not going to take over this conversation. "Conspicuity? Is that like visibility?"

"Almost. Conspicuity refers to something standing out against the background, usually movement, but even movement can be hard to see in the dark and rain."

"But you don't think that's what happened?"

"Officer Jannick's interpretation was the more likely one given the evidence and what we had to go on. But now I'm not sure."

Because of the text.

"Miss Weston," his direct gaze kept hers riveted to his face though she wanted to look away, "I don't know what the text I saw was about, but I need to ask you if it could have anything to do with the collision."

"What text?"

Spring ignored Victoria's question as a mental battle waged in her head. If only she were free to tell the sergeant everything she knew, about the crash and the text messages. But the texter seemed to know everything, even every word she said. She couldn't take the chance. She yanked her gaze from his. "No. No it doesn't."

"What text?" Victoria leaned toward Spring with an insistent tone.

Spring fought the urge to moisten her lips. Or hop her gaze along the walls. She looked steadily at her sister's delicate, slightly freckled nose instead. "It was just a text message he saw on my phone. From Treese." She glanced at Sergeant Cotter, surprised how quickly the perfect lie came to mind. "That's our little sister, Patricia." Shifting her gaze quickly to Victoria, Spring finished selling her fib. "She asked me not to tell anyone about Hank's party plans, but then she heard I told a friend at church."

Victoria arched one eyebrow. "That's ironic considering she's the one who couldn't keep a secret if her life depended on it."

"I can see how the message probably looked, Sergeant." Spring made herself meet his too-intelligent gaze, trying to ignore the surge of conscience. She hadn't lied since she was nine years old and told her dad she'd gotten an "A" in science. Hopefully Sergeant Cotter would believe her more than her dad had.

"And Hank is?"

"Our brother." A proud smile stretched Victoria's mouth. "We're celebrating his acceptance into Johns Hopkins' M.D. program. He's going to be a neurosurgeon."

She didn't have to sound like a mother who couldn't stop bragging about her children's accomplishments. The sergeant might not be as easily impressed by advanced medical degrees as were the Westons and their social circles.

"He was accepted in October?" A refreshing skepticism laced his voice.

"He applied for the Early Decision Program. It won't be official until November, but he'll definitely get in." Victoria spoke with the hallmark Weston confidence that drove the premature party plans.

"I see." The sergeant watched Spring instead of Victoria, his expression betraying nothing of the usual reaction her family was used to receiving. None of that *your-family's-so-accomplished* nonsense.

She liked Sergeant Cotter better all the time. Even if he was looking at her like she'd just confessed to being a fugitive from the law.

———

Spring Weston was lying. And Torin still couldn't figure out why.

She avoided his gaze with those brown eyes that were softer and more mesmerizing than he'd remembered. But he couldn't let them distract him from the fact that she was hiding something.

Was she protecting someone? Her fingers had twitched as if with nerves on the armrests of her wheelchair when Victoria had spoken about their brother. And her cheeks had flushed.

Could the brother be connected to whatever she wasn't telling Torin? Or perhaps it was a connection to her family in a different way? Might be worth exploring. "Are your siblings in the area?"

"All except Hank." Victoria answered though Torin had looked only at Spring.

"That's nice." Torin observed Spring as he pretended to jot a note. No change in color that time. Maybe the siblings weren't the problem. "I think I noticed in the documentation that your father was the first to be notified after the collision." He was certain he had, but a little faked uncertainty put people at ease. "Does he live in Chicago?"

"Naperville."

There. Spring's cheeks turned a lovely shade of mild pink. But the reason behind that response was likely not so lovely. Could she be hiding something about the collision for, or because of, her father? His visit to get Torin investigating her case could have been a ruse to throw him off the scent. Or perhaps the threatening text came because of something different related to her dad?

Torin didn't buy for one second that the text had been from her sister about a party. Spring's frightened reaction at the time and unease now when she tried to lie about it were far too obvious.

He'd have to pursue the possibility of her father's involvement, but not through questioning. With both daughters in the room, he was unlikely to get either to betray anything helpful about their dad if something iffy was going on. He'd switch lines of questioning and see what else he could dig up.

"Are you close to the other members of your cycling team?"

Spring's eyebrows dipped in more genuine surprise this time. "Most of them live elsewhere. Out of state."

"I mean relationally. Are you friendly with each other? Competitive?"

Her lips curved downward. "I hope you aren't suggesting they had anything to do with the crash. Or that I have anything against them. We're *teammates*." She emphasized the word and her sales pitch a little too much. But there was enough sincerity in the gaze she kept on his face that he suspected her fellow cyclers weren't to blame for her unexplained secrecy.

How could he get her to talk? To believe he could be trusted?

"We really must go now." Victoria's lips pursed. "Spring has a PT session."

So Victoria was protective, too. Probably a good thing. Despite Spring's story otherwise, that text told him she needed protection. And he certainly wasn't the one who could give it. "Sure. Thank you for your time."

Spring didn't meet his gaze.

He turned to go.

A vibration sounded.

He swung back.

Spring's phone trembled on the table over the bed. Her gaze jumped to it.

"Treese again?" Victoria looked at her sister with an unsuspicious gaze.

"Probably. It can wait."

Watching the color drain from Spring's face as she fought for a nonchalant glance his way, Torin's gut told him to stay. To find out what was going on. To make sure she was safe.

But she didn't want his help. And she'd be better off without it.

He walked out.

CHAPTER NINE

October 8. 11:10 a.m.

"She's lying, Robert."

"Okay." His calm tone carried through the smartphone Victoria held to her ear. "We suspected that, though."

She leaned back against the counter in the empty staff breakroom at the rehab center. "I don't mean solely about the collision." She let out a held breath. "I should explain. Sergeant Cotter came to question her more today, and he asked her about a text message."

"A text?"

"I was confused, too. He behaved as if he didn't want to have the conversation in front of me."

"Sounds strange."

"It was. But Spring told him to continue with me there, which I thought was a good sign that she didn't have anything to hide." Victoria pursed her lips together as her mind tried for the twelfth time to make sense of the scene she'd witnessed.

"But?"

"I don't know what the text message said, but it must have

been on Spring's phone, and the sergeant asked if it had anything to do with the collision."

"What did she say?"

"She said that the text was from Treese. About Hank's acceptance party."

"Oh. That's suspicious?"

"Treese and I decided to postpone the plans for now so we could focus on helping Spring. She wouldn't be texting Spring about it."

"You double-checked?"

"I did." She moistened her lips. "Robert, Treese said she hasn't texted Spring for at least a week, and she's never messaged her about the party."

Silence hung on the line.

"What do you think?"

His voice pitched deeper when he finally answered. "I think she's in worse trouble than we thought."

A shiver traversed Victoria's spine.

"Spring isn't a liar. Not by rule."

"You're right. She's never lied to me before."

"Try not to take it personally. Knowing Spring like I do, she would have to be highly motivated to purposefully deceive anyone."

Victoria slipped a loose strand of hair behind her ear and moved her hand back to check the bun held with pins. "Especially as a Christian. She knows lying is wrong."

"Perhaps." Skepticism skewed his tone. "But it's not healthy either."

"My point is that she wouldn't lie unless she believed she had to. That something..." Victoria's breathing grew shallow as her mind reached a realization before her words, "...bad would happen if she told the truth."

"I'm afraid so."

A whir punched through the silence.

Victoria startled.

The refrigerator cooling. That was all.

She breathed again.

"Victoria." His use of her full name was enough to signal the gravity of what he was about to say.

"I know. I need to see her text messages." She closed her eyes. How could she spy on her own sister? "She keeps the phone with her all the time. I don't know that I can do it."

"Treese is coming with me tonight to surprise her with dinner. I'll fill her in and see if we can get a look. If not, we'll try to get some more information out of her whatever way we can."

"I could simply ask Spring about it. I could tell her I know she lied."

"You could. But that would likely make her feel forced to lie again. Could make things worse."

So she had to spy. Victoria's stomach rebelled. It felt wrong.

"We're doing this for her, Vicki." Robert read her feelings even in the silence over a phone. "She's scared and miserable. She would do the same for any of us in a heartbeat."

Victoria pursed her lips and nodded. "Yes, she would."

There was one more thing Spring would do for them, as well. Pray.

That, Victoria could do with full confidence that she was giving Spring the best help she was able to give.

Please, Father, if Spring is in danger, protect her. Protect us all.

CHAPTER
TEN

October 8. 12:20 p.m.

"DID SHE CALL?"

Torin stared at the Chicago-style hot dog on the table in front of him, piled with all the traditional toppings. He peeled off the dill pickle, his stomach sinking like a rock that couldn't possibly absorb any food, let alone the works. "Like clockwork."

"You should change your number."

That jumped his gaze to Derrick's brown eyes. "She has a right to chew me out." His voice was husky with emotion, but he didn't try to clear it. He didn't have to pretend with Derrick.

"Every year? Right when she knows you're visiting Ivy's grave? I don't think so."

But Derrick didn't say Miranda was wrong. He didn't say what happened wasn't Torin's fault. Maybe he knew if he did, Torin would never meet him again for this annual lunch.

No, Derrick simply knew the truth, every detail of that day. Couldn't pretend Torin hadn't failed in the face of such evidence.

"Anything…" Torin let the question drift as the son of the hot dog stand owner emerged from the curtained kitchen, tying on a clean white apron. He went to the counter without looking at them.

"Anything new?"

Derrick chewed a big bite of hot dog, mustard and pickle relish dripping down his dark chin. He grabbed a hunk of napkins from the basket on the table and swiped the yellow green streak away.

The hair on the back of Torin's neck stood on end.

Derrick was a slow thinker sometimes, but not that slow. And he wasn't meeting Torin's gaze.

"What'd you find?"

Derrick set the remaining quarter of his hot dog in the basket and swabbed his fingers.

"Derrick."

"You should've tested for detective when I did. Then you wouldn't need to get your info through me."

Clearly a stall tactic. Derrick might not know why Torin didn't want to be a detective, but he knew Torin wouldn't have been allowed to work his wife's homicide.

He dropped the napkins and finally looked Torin in the eye. "Frankly, I'm not sure what I should tell you. You're not exactly on the path to healing yet, partner."

Torin spread his fingers out on the green painted table between them, tension radiating up his arms. "What did you find?"

Derrick's jaw worked as he assessed Torin, as if trying to decide how much to say. Or whether to speak at all. "We didn't find anything."

Disappointment caved inward, collapsing on the hope Torin didn't know he still had the ability to feel.

"Yet."

Torin had never felt so much like harming a fellow policeman in his life, much less his former partner.

"Okay." Derrick held up a calming hand. "Promise me you won't run off half-cocked with this. You'll handle it my way."

Torin nodded.

"I mean it."

Torin glared.

"Good enough." Derrick pushed his hot dog aside—unthinkable for the skinny guy with the bottomless stomach. "We got a call yesterday." He crossed his forearms in front of him on the table and lowered his voice, checking his peripheral. "Anonymous male. Said he has info on the robbery."

"The shooter?"

Derrick scanned the restaurant again. "He just mentioned the robbery," his gaze returned to Torin, "and the shooting."

Torin's mouth tasted like paper. His pulse pounded. "Think it's legit?"

"I don't know."

"But you're going to…"

"Of course. We're checking it out. He said he'd call back today to set up a meeting."

Torin flexed his hands, clenched his fingers into fists that he shoved under the table. "I want to be there when you talk to him."

A muscle twitched in Derrick's jaw, just like it always did when he was battling between regulations and emotions. "Can't."

"Can't or won't?" Torin knew his anger was misdirected, but he couldn't rein it in. "You don't trust me, do you?"

"You know you aren't supposed to be involved in this investigation. Our unit will handle it." Derrick leaned forward. "*I'll* handle it." His eyes filled with the kind of emotion Torin didn't want to see. "I've always had your back."

Torin blinked back the moisture that threatened to pool. "I know, man."

"Then trust me."

Torin swiped at his moist nose, glancing away, then again

at the one man he trusted more than himself. "You'll let me know as soon as you follow up."

"Of course."

A possible lead. After all this time. Justice for Ivy.

If he could just get the shooter, maybe he could finally find some peace.

The possibility tangled his gut into knots.

"You gonna eat that?" A grin pushed up the corners of Derrick's mouth.

Torin saw in his ex-partner's eyes what he was trying to do. The challenge glimmered. Better than pity and tears. "You bet." Torin grabbed his hot dog, stacked the pickle back on top, and shoved the whole thing down, one impressive bite at a time.

CHAPTER
ELEVEN

October 8. 5:16 p.m.

"H̲o̲w̲'s̲ ̲m̲y̲ ̲f̲a̲v̲o̲r̲i̲t̲e̲ ̲s̲i̲s̲?̲"

Spring couldn't help the smile that spread across her face at the sound of her brother's usual greeting.

"Hey." Treese elbowed Robert as she snuck past him, carrying a small plastic food container. The one-year distance in their ages seemed belied by their dramatic size difference as Treese shoved Robert's muscular six-foot frame with her five-foot-three, zero-fat body. "You just said I was your favorite."

"That was before I spent thirty minutes in a car with you." Robert's sideways grin landed on Spring, where she sat propped up in bed.

She rolled her eyes, the knot in her stomach starting to unwind. She would have thought she couldn't stand more family after Victoria had finally left for the day. But the antics of her younger siblings were at least a distraction from thinking about the last text she'd received or the phantom pains she would probably have later that night. "You know he says that to all of us."

Treese's long ponytail swung as she hopped up to perch on

the edge of the bed, looking ultra-fit and cute in her zippered fitness jacket and leggings. "I don't believe it. Everyone knows I'm his real favorite."

"You're everyone's favorite, baby Threesie."

Treese threw Robert a glare for the hated childhood nickname. But it took Spring right back to a happier time—the happiest of her life. When little Robby couldn't pronounce *Treese*, the nickname Spring and Victoria had created from their mom's Italian pronunciation of *Patricia*. When mom was still—

A soft *pop* drew Spring's attention to Treese as she lifted the lid off her plastic container. It appeared to contain raw spinach leaves, dried berries, and some unidentifiable seeds.

Spring wrinkled her nose. "That's not supposed to be for me, is it?"

"Should be."

"But thankfully, your favorite brother took charge of bringing you dinner." He set the brown paper bag he carried on the bed and pushed up the sleeve of his navy blue sweatshirt to dig inside. "Ta-da!" He held up two little white boxes.

"Chinese!" She stared in disbelief at the tell-tale containers. "Wow, you *are* my favorite brother now."

"What do you mean 'now'?" He grinned as he opened the boxes and set them next to her leg, handing her a plastic fork.

"He shouldn't be. That stuff is terrible for you."

Which was exactly why the sight and smell of her favorite cuisine was nearly enough to bring her to tears. No one had let her eat anything but regimented health foods since the crash.

Spring grabbed the closest box and peered inside, inhaling the mouthwatering aroma of pork slathered with her favorite Chinese restaurant's greasy stir-fry sauce. "Mmm."

"Rice is in the other box." Robert pulled the wheelchair closer to the bed and dropped into it like it was a comfy recliner. He rested a tanned ankle across the knee left bare beneath his khaki shorts.

"Your dietician would have a fit if she could see what you're about to eat." Treese arched her eyebrows in a weak imitation of Victoria's classic look of disapproval.

"One time won't be a disaster." A smile played on Robert's lips. "It's mixed vegetables and pork. Vitamins, fiber, and protein. Very healthy." He held up a finger at Treese. "And I'm the doctor here, so don't argue."

She snorted. "Personal trainers know more about diet than a psychiatrist."

"Psychiatrists know more about everything." He grinned and drew his fingers and thumb down his closely cut beard, drawing Spring's gaze to the feature she still wasn't used to seeing on her brother's face.

She had to agree with Treese. Their brother was good-looking anyway, but his beard, formed with the jet-black hair he'd inherited from their mother, defined his jawline and gave him added maturity that made him more attractive. A beard seemed to do that for some men.

Then again, some were devastatingly handsome without one. The image of Sergeant Cotter's face came to her mind. If he had a beard, it would probably be a sandy brown, maybe with some red—

"What?"

Heat rushed to her cheeks as if Robert had seen her thoughts along with her stare. She cleared her throat. "I thought you were going to shave your beard. And what are you doing here anyway? I thought you see a lot of your clients at night." Better not be taking even more time off for her. He'd already missed work to visit her when she was in the acute care hospital, nearly every day according to Victoria. Spring's own memory of those days was too painful and blurred to remember.

"Business is slow at the moment. And I haven't taken a real vacation in three years." He snatched the rice container to add some to his own little box of food. "I think I deserve a little R & R."

"You mean time to clean your house to within an inch of its life, I bet." Treese smirked. "At least you aren't at home to get rid of all my 'junk.'" She made rabbit ears with her fingers around the fork in one hand.

Robert laughed. "I'd be happy to come and get the place looking presentable again."

"Don't you dare. I want to keep my stuff, thank you very much." Treese shoved a wad of spinach into her mouth.

How could she eat that bland food? Spring took a mouthful of her actually flavorful dinner and savored the succulent, salty taste on her tongue.

"I heard there's a very cute new investigator on your case now."

Spring coughed, a piece of pork tumbling down her throat. "Wow, *that* cute?"

She glared at her sister's grin. "I don't know when Victoria developed such an imagination."

"Comes with working two jobs." Robert pushed a shrimp into his mouth with chopsticks and talked around it. "You get so tired you start hallucinating."

"I thought she was still taking time off from home health." That's what Victoria had told Spring she was doing when she muscled in on the rehab PT sessions.

"She used up her vacation time weeks ago. She's scheduling her hours around your therapy."

A guilty lump ballooned in Spring's throat. Just when she was trying to enjoy the Chinese. Wasn't her fault Victoria insisted on helping with the physical therapy.

"Don't look so glum. Vicki said that's the benefit of working as a home health PT. Flexible schedule."

One more imposition Spring had to feel badly about. One more way she'd become a burden to others.

"Done trying to change the subject?" Treese set her plastic container on the bed and crossed her arms, jacket sleeves stretching over tightly toned arms. "When is this knockout sergeant coming again?"

"How should I know?" Spring wished she had a cold glass of water to counteract the flush traveling up her neck. Treese would notice for sure.

"Because we *have* to do something about this." She indicated Spring's face and upper body with an upward sweep of her hand.

Here it came.

"Your hair looks like it hasn't been brushed in a week, and some makeup is really needed."

"I don't think she's intentionally mean." Robert's dark eyes danced. "She was just born that way."

"It wouldn't hurt for Spring to take care of herself." Treese put her hand on Spring's forearm. "Trust me—that sergeant will be hooked when I get done with you."

Spring yanked her arm away. "I don't want him to be hooked. And I don't need to look like some model from the waist up."

Treese blinked.

Robert watched quietly.

Spring set down the box of food, her stomach recoiling. She took a breath. Her siblings had made the effort to come and see her. She didn't need to make them sorry they had. "So, are you really using your vacation time to clean?" She forced a cheerful tone as she lobbed the question at Robert.

"That and other things." He nodded. "Cleaning is highly therapeutic."

"Not for those of us with hairbands we don't want thrown out." Treese nodded, but it didn't reach the gaze that still held hurt. "I wish you'd tell him not to come to the house to clean, too." She picked up her salad again.

"I wouldn't throw them out if you didn't leave them all over the place."

"At least the house will be clean when you come home." Treese's brown eyes aimed at Spring over a forkful of spinach.

Home. Her dad's house hadn't been her home for six

years. She couldn't live with him again. Not like this. She put her hand on her thigh, feeling nothing in her leg.

"I'm hoping to build a ramp before I have to go back to work."

"A ramp?" No way would their dad want that at his house, even if Robert built it.

"Dad isn't going to let you do that." Treese echoed Spring's thoughts.

Robert shrugged and brought his gaze to Spring. "He's just convinced this is temporary."

So he hadn't wanted a ramp. She knew it. He wouldn't want a ramp or widened doorways. A handicap-accessible bathroom. He wouldn't want her. Not like this.

She didn't either.

"Don't worry, Spring." Treese smiled. "It'll be fun living at home. After all," she dramatically pressed her hand to her chest, "I'm there."

"Don't scare her, Threesie." Robert rested the chopsticks in the open box held in his hand. "At least Hank will be at Johns Hopkins, so you'll only have Treese to deal with."

"See? Just us girls. It'll be tons of fun." Treese shot Spring a beaming smile before fishing with her fork for the rest of the dried cranberries.

As if moving back home at twenty-eight years of age, paralyzed, would be one big happy party. But it was unusually sweet of Treese to try to make it sound that way, so Spring bit back the negativity.

"Returning back to this sergeant," Robert shot a look at Treese, "and, no, I don't mean crushing on him." He brought his smile to Spring. "I want to know if you think he'll make more progress on your case."

She looked down at the sheet wrapped across her middle and shrugged.

"Well, does he seem experienced? More than the officer you had investigating before?"

"He said he's the head of the unit."

"That's good."

"I guess."

"You don't think so?"

She made herself look up, catching sight of Robert's raised eyebrows. "I don't see why everyone's so hung up on finding out who…" She glanced at the kids' drawings on the wall, fighting the urge to bite her lip. The texter could be listening. Or somehow know what she was saying. She had to steer clear of the topic all together. But discouraging them from trying to find the driver would make the texter happy, wouldn't it?

"You don't want to know who put you here?" Anger and shock mixed in Treese's voice.

"It won't give me my life back." Might end it, if whoever was behind the texts made good on the threats.

"It could help to know whoever did this was behind bars." Treese's eyes glinted. "It's about time you got some justice. Maybe we can h—"

"Stay out of it, Treese." Spring looked down and pulled the sheet up higher to avoid seeing more hurt in her sister's eyes. "It won't make a difference." Except putting her in more danger.

"Okay."

Great. Spring knew that tone without looking.

Treese was getting ready for a fight. "Then why don't you tell me why you told the sergeant—"

"Before I forget…"

Spring turned her head to see Robert pull his hand away from Treese's knee. Nice of him to make her stop the interrogation. He pointed his chopsticks toward Jerome's drawing, "Jerome wants me to tell you 'hi' and to ask when you're coming back to day care."

Her chest squeezed. "You talked to Jerome?"

He nodded.

Treese gave her brother a look that Spring might've been able to read if she wasn't so tired. "He's been picking Jerome up from day care and driving him home."

Tears pricked Spring's eyes. She blinked them back, managing to whisper thanks. Jerome's mother would be so relieved. She couldn't get off of work early enough to pick up Jerome and she didn't know anyone else she could trust with her little boy.

"No big thing."

Not to Robert. He was always helping others, always making a difference. No wonder everyone loved him so much. Including their dad.

"He's a great kid."

Spring nodded, not trusting her voice.

"He wants to come and see you. He asked if I would bring him."

Her stomach lurched. "No. He can't."

Robert frowned. "He misses you. All the kids do. Brittany says she'd like to plan a visit with all of them."

"No." Panic closed Spring's throat. "They don't want to see me like this."

"How do you know?"

She knew. And she knew her heart would break if their little faces contorted with fear or repulsion at the sight of her now. Her days of caring for kids, or anyone else, were over.

"Have other people not wanted to visit you?"

She stared at Robert. That was a peculiar question. "What do you mean?"

"We just thought it was weird the cycling team hasn't been here." Treese picked at pieces in what looked to be an emptied container.

We? Great. The whole family was apparently discussing her behind her back. What else were they thinking?

"I didn't realize Victoria was tracking my visitors," Spring failed to keep the irritation out of her voice, "but my coach... former coach visited just the other day."

Treese glanced up. "What did he want?"

Why would she want to know that? Did she know something about the doping? Spring's breath caught. Did their dad know?

Her gaze darted to Robert.

He grinned as if nothing was going on. "I would assume he just wanted to see how Spring was doing, Treese." Robert sent their younger sister a look that held an unusual chastising edge.

Oh, no. They did know something. Would they think Spring had been doping, too? The thought of her dad finding out swirled the food in her belly. Maybe Chinese hadn't been such a good idea.

Her phone buzzed, making her pulse jump. Another text? She picked it up from the sheet at her side. Trying to keep any reaction off her face, she checked the message.

Nice family. Tell them nothing. You know I can hurt you.

Icy fear slid through her veins.

He knew her family was there. He could probably hear every word she was saying. Somehow.

"Spring?" Robert's concerned voice reached for her. "Are you okay?"

"No, I'm not okay." She snapped out the words. "I'm paralyzed." Trapped in a chair for life, trapped by these threats.

She looked up in time to catch the flash of pain in Robert's eyes. Remorse came too late for her to undo the damage. And apparently the texter would be happier if they left. "I'm sorry, guys. I'm just not in a very social mood tonight."

"Tired?"

"Yeah." She grabbed at the excuse Treese offered.

"We'll stop in on the weekend, okay?" She patted Spring's arm before sealing her container and slipping off the bed.

Spring glanced at Robert as he stood. "Thanks for the Chinese."

"Let me know when you want some more. Or anything else I can do for you."

She was one of Robert's charity cases now. A service project.

No, that wasn't fair. She'd never thought of what he did as patronizing when he helped others. And he never meant it that way. He was just there to serve, as he liked to say. It was in his blood. Their mother had been the same way.

"See you later." Spring laid her head back on the pillow, pretending she was going to rest, though the angle was too awkward for it. A nurse would come later and help her get in the right position to sleep. Or try to sleep.

She looked at the phone that someone was using to control her. To terrify her. No matter how much she hated it, she couldn't break free.

The texter had proven he'd follow through, at the very least putting her in more pain than she thought she could survive.

She set the phone down and closed her eyes, her heart racing too much to allow her to sleep. She'd been careful not to say anything about the accident. But if she'd messed up...

What horrors might await her tonight?

CHAPTER
TWELVE

October 8. 6:09 p.m.

HE WAS MISSING SOMETHING. Had to be.

Torin stood on the far side of the road where he'd parked his car and surveyed the collision scene, the breeze that touched his cheekbones armed with the nip of fall.

Too late to do the at-scene work of Spring's crash himself, but at least going to the site would help him see what he was missing in the recon report. Hopefully, a visual reconstruction of the collision in person instead of from his desk at the station would reveal something new. He wasn't content with Jannick's take on the collision anymore.

There had to be some evidence to go on. Some lead he was missing. He'd told Spring he would find one.

The memory of the look on her face when he'd made that promise was enough to make his swallowing difficult. Her eyes had grown larger, her lips parting for a moment, and he'd had to remind himself why he was going to ignore her beauty.

At least remembering Spring diverted his thoughts from the anonymous caller Derrick had told him about. He had to trust Derrick to do his job, far more objectively than Torin would be able to do with that particular cold case.

And Torin needed to do his job. As objectively as he knew how, even if the victim was having a strange effect on his mental state.

Torin removed his sunglasses as a car passed in front of him, traveling at least ten mph faster than the limit. The fading light of the setting sun wasn't ideal for a reconstruction of the nighttime crash, but much safer to avoid getting hit himself.

The reconstruction report matched up perfectly with what Torin was seeing. The curve ended a safe distance before the highway overpass, but he noted the lack of streetlamps or lighting of any kind beneath the overpass.

He waited for more cars to drive by, then crossed to the bridge abutments. Obvious which one Spring had hit. Scratches and silver paint transfer marked the concrete, blood drops still spattered among them.

The road was flat and covered by the overpass, making it less likely that rain would have rendered the striking vehicle unable to stop. He looked up at the underbelly of the highway above, the sound of whizzing vehicles indicating that rush-hour traffic was actually moving at the moment.

He verified that no lamps illuminated the underside of the overpass in the location where Spring was hit, then went to check the other bridge abutment. No paint transfers or damage there.

He was grasping at straws. Jannick and the rest of the investigative team would've found additional evidence if there had been any.

From his standpoint under the bridge, Torin scanned the houses back across the street since there were none on the side where he stood. Four of the small homes had windows that faced the road, within visual range of the collision site. Nine thirty p.m. and the amount of noise the collision must have made—one would think someone would have looked out. Seen something. But he wasn't surprised Jannick had gotten "no's" from the few people who'd been cooperative enough to listen to his questions.

Torin had been to that neighborhood more times than he would have wanted during his days on patrol. Repeated domestic violence calls at two locations about a block from there. A few gang-related calls. And a narcotics possession bust...on that very street. Sure, the little gray house with the chipped siding.

No wonder the area seemed so familiar. He'd probably have recognized the house earlier if he hadn't been so intent on examining the crash site.

Crossing the street again, Torin headed for the gray home, searching through his mental files for the name of the woman. Kasey. Mary Kasey. If she remembered who Torin was, she just might tell him something she wouldn't have shared with Jannick.

Hope buoyed his steps as he followed the cracked sidewalk to the Kasey house and turned to take the two cement steps that led to the door in one stride.

Muted sounds of a TV reached his ears.

He knocked on the frame of the screen door.

No answer.

The hollowed-out doorbell was clearly not in working order, so he knocked again.

The solid door behind the screen opened a crack. "What do you want?"

Mrs. Kasey's voice. As stubborn and strong as he remembered. "Mrs. Kasey? It's Sergeant Torin Cotter with Chicago PD."

"The police?" The door didn't open any wider.

"Yes, ma'am. We've met before. I'm the officer who arrested your grandson four years ago." The last thing he'd mention in most circumstances, but he was banking on the surprising reaction she'd given him the night he'd busted her grandson on possession charges.

"Oh, Officer Torin!" She flung the door open and pushed out the screened one, greeting him with a gap-toothed smile. "Come in, child. Come in." She waved him inside to the small living room that butted up against the door. "Bless my eyes, it's good to see you."

A grin stretched across Torin's face. The woman was something else. Only person he knew who'd greet a cop with such enthusiasm. Especially in that neighborhood. "How's Kenny doing?"

"Oh, you know, he doing so good now. Gonna graduate from night school come spring. And it's all thanks to you bustin' him that night."

"I wouldn't say that, ma'am. You brought him around."

"I sure needed your help to do it." She laughed. "I could not get through to that child till you put the fear of God into him."

Torin chuckled. "I'm glad it worked out."

"Come in and set a while. I'll get you some coffee."

"Afraid I can't stay, Mrs. Kasey. I'm on duty right now."

"You are?" She surveyed his plain clothes.

"Yes, ma'am. I'm a sergeant with the Major Accident Investigations Unit now. I'm actually investigating a crash that happened right outside your house here."

"You don't say." Deep lines creased the brow that had aged since he'd last seen her.

"The evening of August twenty-eighth at approximately nine thirty p.m. Do you remember hearing or seeing anything unusual that night?"

"My, that was a long time ago."

"A different officer would have spoken to you that evening. Asked you a similar question."

"Oh. Now you mention it, I do remember the police crawling all over out there. Lights and sirens like there was a fire." She shook her head. "Could barely get to sleep with all that commotion."

His pulse picked up speed. She remembered. And she was

talking so far. "That's the evening. Before the officers showed up, did you see anything?" He tried not to let his eagerness show.

"Mm-hmm. I believe I did. I remember 'cause I was watching the TV in there," she gestured toward the small television in the far corner of the room that displayed some dancing show, "and I heard something strange. Kind of like something smashing, I think." She nodded, her dark eyes drifting as she thought. "I knew it wasn't on my show so I got up and went over to the window in there to see." She stopped as if that was the end of the story.

She wasn't going to clam up, was she? "And what did you see?"

"I'm not sure. It was dark and raining that night, I remember."

"Yes, ma'am." He forced himself to remain calm, nonchalant. "But anything you can remember at all, even if it seems insignificant, would be helpful. I'd appreciate your help very much." Might as well play the personal card, too. If he could get a lead on the driver who paralyzed Spring...

"Well, I did see a white van drive away."

A white van? Jannick had found traces of white paint transferred onto Spring's bike. The trail for the paint's origin had quickly reached a dead end. "Did you see the driver?"

"No." She slowly shook her head.

"License plate? Or any labeling or marks on the van?"

She narrowed her eyes slightly, still looking thoughtful. "No, I couldn't see that. There could have been, though. It was dark, and the van moved real fast."

Torin battled a frown. Not the big lead he had hoped for. But it was still something. More than he'd had before. And he knew better than most how much they could find from one seemingly insignificant piece of information.

He smiled at Mrs. Kasey and extended his hand. "Thank you, ma'am. It was great to see you again, and you've been very helpful."

She held his hand between her rough, slightly wrinkled ones. "Glad to do anything for you, child. You just let me know if I can ever do anything else." She patted his hand. "You gave me back my grandbaby."

"Just doing my job, ma'am."

"Well, you just keep doing it, then."

"I will." He stepped away, opening the screen door. "Oh, one more thing." He paused, looking back. "Had you ever seen the van before?"

"Hard to know for sure. But I'd say so."

"You would." His pulse quickened. "In this area?"

She glanced away for the first time. Not comfortable answering that question for some reason. Even for him. "Don't much like to get involved."

He took a step inside again. "It's extremely important."

"Well, I'd say somewhere in the neighborhood, but I'm gettin' old. These eyes and my old memory ain't what they used to be." Her smile was as warm and real as before, making him wonder if he had imagined the change when he'd asked about the van.

But he knew he hadn't. As he repeated his goodbyes and made his way back to the car in the dim light, his mind raced.

A witness who saw a white van at the scene and ID'd it as one she'd seen before. Not wanting to admit where or say anything more suggested the van's driver might be involved in something illegal. No surprise in that area. It didn't have to be tied to Mary Kasey for her to keep quiet about it. Snitches were not dealt with kindly.

Satisfaction welled in Torin's chest as he unlocked his car and slid behind the wheel. He had a solid lead. Not bad for a day's work.

As Torin pushed the key into the ignition, a warning tingle slid up his neck. He glanced through the windows at the quiet sidewalk, the two cars passing by on the road.

The windows of the other houses were covered with curtains or darkness.

Why did he feel like he was being watched?

Verifying his doors were locked, he slipped on the sunglasses he didn't need so he could better survey his surroundings without being obvious. Still couldn't see anyone or anything unusual.

These days, being a cop was like walking around with *Shoot me* tattooed on his forehead. At least his unmarked car helped him avoid some of the hate.

Before giving anyone a chance for a direct shot, Torin started the engine, removing his sunglasses as he pulled onto the street. As the edgy feeling faded, he focused on the pleasant task he could now make his top priority in the morning. Uncovering a lead meant he had a reason to see Spring again.

CHAPTER
THIRTEEN

October 8. 10:16 p.m.

"THERE'S no reason to get so upset." Victoria placed a calming hand on Max's velvety head as she looked across the coffee table at Treese. "You're making Max nervous."

"You're the only person I know whose dog is more stressed than she is."

Victoria raised an eyebrow. "You must have some very stressed friends."

"No, you just have a weird dog."

"Hey." Robert lowered the leg he had crossed over the other and glared at Treese from the other end of the sofa.

"Sorry." Treese blew out a frustrated sigh as she popped up and paced to the fireplace where small flames fought for life amid remnants of wood.

Max started at the sudden movement.

"You're fine." Victoria moved her hand to stroke the big Leonberger's furry chest as he watched Treese's energetic strides with his large flop-ears perked alongside his head.

Treese stopped, arms crossed over her zip top. "I just don't see why he cut me off."

As if talking to Victoria about Robert while he was in the room would win her argument.

"I was about to ask Spring point-blank why she lied to you about the text message. She would've had to admit to whatever's going on."

"No." Robert leaned back into the sofa cushions, arms folded but exuding the placid wisdom that must work beautifully to put his patients at ease. "You would have forced her to lie to you, too. We talked about this earlier."

"I know." Treese's glare died as quickly as her bout of temper. "But that was before I saw how she guards that phone like it's a Saint Laurent handbag." She plopped onto the sofa next to Robert, swiveling her head to look at him. "And did you see the way she went all white when she read that text?"

Robert nodded, his dark eyes flickering in the dim lighting of Victoria's living room.

Treese's frown deepened. "Makes me sick."

"Me, too." Victoria met Treese's startled gaze. They finally agreed on something.

"We have to get to her phone."

Victoria sighed and stroked Max's head as he lowered his ears. "You mean I have to."

"You do have the best shot at it." Robert rested his ankle on the opposite knee. "But we can also follow up on the other lead."

Treese glanced at him. "We have another lead?"

"The cycling coach."

"Oh, right."

"Did Spring say anything more about him?" Victoria lifted her hand from Max's head as he slid to the floor, finally relaxing enough to rest.

Treese shrugged. "Just that he visited."

"That's not all she said." Robert touched his bearded chin with his thumb and index finger.

"It isn't?" Treese looked at him.

"She turned pale then, long before the text message."

"She did?" Treese's eyebrows pulled together.

"Yes." Robert nodded. "Her breathing grew shallow as soon as you asked what her cycling coach had wanted."

"I guess I was too busy wondering why you were giving me your 'shut-up' look to notice." She elbowed him in the ribs, apparently not as incensed as before.

Robert put his arm on the sofa behind her small shoulders and quirked an eyebrow at her. "You were being a little obvious."

"So I wasn't imagining her reaction to the coach." Victoria leaned forward in the armchair.

Robert met her gaze. "No, I don't think so. What do you know about the cycling coach?"

"Not much. Only that Dad is one of the team's biggest sponsors. He seems to have control over the coach. I don't believe Dad would have let him remain if he wasn't qualified."

"Probably right." Robert lowered his foot back to the floor. "I'll do some digging on his background and the cyclists. See if there's any criminal history we should know about."

"Criminal history? With Dad's money?" Treese raised her eyebrows as she leaned slightly away from Robert.

"Dad isn't infallible."

She snickered. "Try telling him that."

Robert grinned. "No, thanks." His attention went to the clock above the fireplace. "Whoa, sorry, Vicki. How early do you have to start work tomorrow?"

She smiled. "Early."

He cringed and got to his feet.

Treese stood with him. "I have to start early, too. It's no big deal. Totally worth it if we can help Spring."

And if a person had Treese's unending store of energy. Victoria rose from the chair to see them out.

"So you'll snatch her phone?"

Victoria winced at Treese's word choice. "I'll attempt to see the text messages. If I can."

She followed Robert and Treese to the door, pausing with

them in the entryway while Robert opened the door for Treese.

As their sister stepped into the dark night, Robert turned back to Victoria.

His eyes held a gravitas she rarely saw in his gaze. "If we can't turn up anything with the cycling team, you'll have to do more than *try* to get her phone." He gave Victoria's hand a light squeeze. "I have a bad feeling about this."

A chill traveled up her arm under her sweater. She nodded. "I'll look at her phone."

"Be careful."

He turned away, catching up with Treese who stood at enough of a distance she wouldn't have overheard.

Victoria watched as they reached Robert's car.

He looked back.

She waved, but her arm felt cold. Heavy.

She shut the door, automatically murmuring comfort to Max, who stood at a distance, staring at the door with his pensive eyes. *Lord, please give us courage and wisdom. Enable us to help Spring, no matter what that help requires.*

CHAPTER
FOURTEEN

October 9. 9:15 a.m.

"I TOLD YOU, I don't want to do PT this morning. I'm not feeling well." Spring's protests seemed to fall on deaf ears as Angie and Victoria adjusted her sitting position in the wheelchair. "Is anyone listening to me?" Her voice rose to a pitch even she recognized as childish. This is what she'd been reduced to. Throwing temper tantrums like a toddler before someone would acknowledge her wishes.

"Yes, I'm listening." Victoria stepped in front of the chair, hands going to her hips. "But I'm not going to watch you sink any farther into this depression. You need to wake up and take your life back."

"Like it's that simple."

"You're the one making it complicated."

"No, you are. I can't use my legs, Victoria."

"Ladies," Angie glanced between the sisters. "Please, let's start the morning with a little more patience and less anger, okay?"

"I'm sorry, Angie." Victoria took her hands off her hips. "You're right."

"I need my phone." Spring stuck out her hand toward the device where it lay on the unmade bed.

"Why do you *need* it?"

She met Victoria's challenging stare. "I'm not sixteen anymore, Victoria. You can't take my phone away from me."

"Here you go." Angie handed Spring the phone, giving Victoria a glance that was a mixture of surprise and sympathy. "Spring, how about you decide what you'd like to do for PT today? What would you like to work on?"

Spring blinked. That was a new approach. Angie was something akin to an angel the way she could put up with the squabbling sisters. "I'm sorry, Angie. But I honestly don't see the point."

The PT squatted down in front of the wheelchair. "I understand your frustration, Spring, but we only want to make things as good as we can for you." She rested her hand gently on Spring's wrist. "We can't give you the use of your legs again, but we can help you use everything else that God has given you."

That God had given her. He gave her this paralysis. This chair for the rest of her life. This living prison.

"Listen to her, Spring." Victoria stepped closer. "You can change things if you work harder. You can get better and learn to—"

"To what? Get my life back?" Frustration squeezed Spring's throat until she thought she might choke. "My life is over, Victoria. When will you get that?"

A solid rap outside the room made her start.

The door opened a crack, and the handsome face of Sergeant Cotter appeared, instantly crumbling her anger. "May I come in?"

"Of course, Sergeant." Victoria slipped into a ready smile as if they hadn't just nearly come to blows.

Spring couldn't hang on to as much of her irritation as she'd like to with Sergeant Cotter walking toward her, those riveting green eyes fixed on her face.

"I have some news."

She didn't know why her heart fluttered and she felt the need to smooth her hands over her black cotton pants. Could be the way the green stripes of his shirt intensified his eyes even more.

"We have a witness."

Spring gaped. "A witness?" Her pulse jumped. Was the texter listening? What would he do if he heard?

"It looks that way. She saw what was likely the vehicle that hit you. A white van. Does that sound familiar?"

The white blur, just before she'd been hit. But she couldn't say a word. She shook her head.

He watched her with that thinking look again. He was getting suspicious.

At least she couldn't squirm in her chair like her instincts wanted her to.

"Why is it that you rode through that particular neighborhood?" He was questioning her again.

"I..." She glanced away, only to see Victoria watching her just as intently as the sergeant. "I told you, I often went there." She took a breath. She didn't have to be so nervous. She was telling the truth. "The neighborhood doesn't have much traffic, so it's nice for training rides."

"The white van may have been a regular in that neighborhood. Had you seen a white van during any of your training rides before?"

"Um..." A white van stood next to that store the night of the accident. Her heart pounded, loud enough he could probably hear it.

The phone vibrated in her hand. A warning.

Her blood turned cold.

She pressed the phone against her leg. "No. Not that I can remember." It was true. She didn't remember seeing it there before that night. But as the sergeant's gaze rested on her hand clutching the phone, guilt crawled through her.

"We really should continue with her PT session." Angie gave him a smile.

Bless her. Probably trying to come to Spring's rescue once again.

"I'm sorry, ma'am, but this can't wait." His eyes held that edge of anger she'd seen before.

"You go ahead to your other patients, Angie." Victoria took charge as always. "We'll skip the morning session today."

"Okay. See you both later."

Victoria met her friend's gentle smile with a nod. "Thanks, Angie."

The sergeant watched Angie leave, then swung his intense, interrogation gaze to Spring. "How would you characterize your relationship with the members of your cycling team?"

The change in subject caught her off guard. She tried to breathe evenly as she scrambled to figure out why he'd ask that question. Could she answer it without getting into trouble? The texter couldn't be connected to the team, could he? Or what if the texter was a she?

"Fine, I guess."

"Fine?"

"Friendly. We get along."

He took out his mini notepad and pen from his pocket. "Any problems with your coach?"

Why would he ask that? Her heartbeat double-timed. She couldn't talk about the doping. Not with Victoria listening to every word. And telling a cop would be like reporting the doping to the authorities. She didn't have any evidence, and she'd probably end up with everyone thinking she'd taken drugs, too.

But she couldn't give him an answer without lying either. Evasion was her best option. "What makes you ask that?"

He lowered his notepad. "After reviewing the evidence further, I'm almost certain you were intentionally struck." He paused, probably to let it sink in. Which it did.

It had been easier to dismiss his theory the first time. Now he seemed so sure. But how could anyone purposefully do such a thing to someone? To her?

The texter. Maybe he, or she, wasn't trying to keep her quiet after *accidentally* hitting her. The texter, if he was the driver, could have hit her on purpose.

Her arms turned almost as numb as her legs.

"We need to find out who had a motive for killing you."

"Killing her?" Victoria moved to stand next to Spring, putting a hand on her shoulder.

The sergeant glanced at Victoria. "Yes, ma'am. The collision easily could have killed your sister. There's no evidence that the driver tried to avoid maximum impact."

"Spring?" Victoria angled to face Spring, her usually rose-tinged cheeks flat and colorless. "Why would someone want to kill you?"

As if it was Spring's fault. Of course she'd think that. "How should I know? I don't purposefully go around trying to make people hate me." She glared at the wall, crossing her arms over her chest as she clamped down on the phone in her hand.

"Miss Weston," the sergeant looked at Victoria. Even he was talking over Spring like she wasn't there now.

She didn't really deserve anything else. He had to know she wasn't being truthful.

"Perhaps I should talk to your sister alone."

Victoria pursed her lips together. She glanced at Spring, then back to the sergeant. "Certainly." Her tone was tightly controlled as she turned and gracefully walked from the room. Victoria never stomped, no matter how mad she got.

Spring's moment of relief that her sister had gone died when she felt the sergeant's gaze. She hadn't done anything wrong. She shouldn't feel so guilty. She squared her jaw and lifted her head, her gaze colliding with green eyes that were much softer than she'd expected.

The set of his mouth was as gentle as his expression as he watched her. "I know this is probably a shock to you. Most victims of a crime don't realize someone they know wants to hurt them until it's too late."

"Someone they know?" She tried not to look away.

"That's usually the case in a situation like this. A random stranger won't often intentionally run someone down."

"But that happens sometimes." She dropped her focus to the floor.

"May I?"

She glanced to see him gesture to the empty bed.

"Sure."

He sat on the edge of the mattress, putting him closer to her eye level, though not quite. "In my job, you learn to read people. To see who's in trouble and who's causing it." His intense gaze collided with hers. "You're in trouble, Miss Weston."

Her heart hiccupped.

He leaned forward slightly. "I want to help you."

"Why?" The dumb question came out before she thought. He was a cop. It was his job. And that's exactly what he'd say.

"Because you shouldn't have to live in fear."

Her next breath vanished. He knew she was scared. Did that mean he didn't suspect her of something? Did he know why she was scared?

The phone vibrated against her sweaty palm, jumpstarting her pulse. She fought the urge to look at it while her heart pounded.

"Don't you want to check that?"

She jerked to see his gaze on her phone.

He knew. Of course, he'd seen that text. Probably hadn't believed her explanation. Her lie.

She hid the breath she forced into her lungs. "It can wait."

"I don't have much patience for cat and mouse, Miss Weston, so let me be blunt. Is someone threatening you?"

She felt the blood drain from her face and turned her head away with the foolish hope he wouldn't see. Why did he have to ask such direct questions? She didn't want to lie.

"I know whoever it is has probably told you that something bad will happen if you cooperate with the police. But I can make sure that won't happen. I can protect you."

The phone vibrated again.

She closed her eyes, the device heavy in her hand. The memory of the pain two nights ago pierced through her.

The texter had promised worse. She didn't want to find out what that was.

"It's not your job to protect me, Sergeant." She met his gaze in time to see his green eyes cool. "I can't help you with the case. I've told you all I can."

He'd thought he had her. Torin dropped behind the steering wheel and slammed the door shut.

For a second, Spring had considered telling him the truth. He could see it in her eyes. She didn't want to lie.

Someone had a strong hold on her.

He should've stretched it out. Been patient and soft for longer. But depending on the type of threats she was receiving, there might not be time for the slow approach. He made the judgment call that she wouldn't lie to him a second time. He'd been right, in a sense. She'd managed to skirt by technically lying and still give him nothing.

Almost nothing. He did have her reaction to his question about the cycling team. Tense and evasive. Maybe the answer to the mysteries lay with her coach or teammates.

And a white van.

Torin shoved his car into gear and left the parking lot of the rehab center.

His phone rang, and he answered hands-free through the Bluetooth connection.

"Torin, you better come in."

His gut tightened at Derrick's grim tone. "The source?"

"Just come to my office. I'll fill you in."

"Be there in twenty."

Torin made the drive in seventeen minutes instead and hurried into the station at a jog. He slowed as he reached the office space Derrick shared with four other detectives. Two of those were at their desks and barely glanced at Torin as he made his way to his former partner.

He kept his breathing slow, normal, despite the racing of his heart.

Derrick looked up as Torin neared. He gestured to the empty chair at the corner of his desk.

Torin grabbed it, though sitting was the last thing he felt like doing. "What's up?" Amazing how nonchalant he managed to sound.

"You tell me." Derrick folded his arms across his chest, white shirt sleeves pushed up above flexing forearm muscles. His interrogation pose.

"What?" Torin didn't have to force any confusion into his question.

"You're telling me you didn't expect this?"

Torin hiked his shoulders, sure he must look as genuinely flabbergasted as he felt. "Expect what?"

"You're playing a dangerous game here, buddy." Derrick leaned forward and propped his elbows on the edge of his desk. "I could have you charged with interfering in my investigation, even if it is your wife's. Unless there's something else going on you want to tell me about."

"Whoa." Torin stood, though it'd be smarter to stay put. "Derrick, what is going on? If you think I've done something wrong, then you'd better tell me what it is so I can defend myself." He put his hands on the desk and leaned in. "But if you're trying to hide something from me about the shooting, you know I won't stop until I find the truth."

Derrick's dark eyes betrayed no emotion as he met Torin's glare. Until they softened a fraction. He leaned back again. "Sit down."

Torin lowered himself to the chair, resting his hands on his legs out of Derrick's view to hide their adrenaline-charged shaking. "Maybe now you can tell me why the suspect treatment."

"The anonymous source with alleged information on the shooting. We contacted him to set up a meet." Derrick tossed a pen a few inches against the side of his keyboard. "He said he'll only talk to you."

Torin's gaze jolted to Derrick's.

"You can see why I was suspicious."

"You thought I got to him?"

"Or something." Derrick still watched him with mistrust. "You have to admit, you'd wonder if you were in my place."

"Not if you were in my place."

Derrick watched him, then the corner of his mouth quirked up. "Point taken." He tapped a finger on his desk. "Do you know him?"

"I'm not sure. Who is he?"

Derrick sighed. "Wiley Boone."

Boone. The name was familiar.

Get down!

The blur of a man's face, dropping behind the counter.

"Torin." Derrick's voice startled Torin out of the memory.

"The gas station manager."

"Right." More memories clustered to attack his mind. He tried to fight, hold them off. Not here. Not in front of Derrick. He forced his mind on the present. "He was interviewed at the time." By Torin, Derrick, and the detectives. More than once.

"He says you saved his granddaughter's life. Wants to do you a favor."

"You don't believe him?"

"It checks out. The little girl you saved from the explosive is his granddaughter." The glint of suspicion was still in Derrick's gaze.

"But?"

"Have you talked to him?"

"Not since the investigation of the shooting."

"Did you know he was the girl's grandfather?"

"No."

"Did you contact him about the shooting?"

Torin stared at his friend.

"I have to ask, Torin."

"And I answered. No." Torin sighed. "Come on, man, you know me better than that."

"I used to."

Thick silence clouded the space between them.

Torin slid the chair back and stood.

"Hold it." Derrick flipped over a scrap of paper. "We're to meet with him tonight at ten."

"We?"

"I convinced him I'd better be there." A peculiar angle pulled Derrick's mouth.

Torin met his gaze. "Good."

Derrick handed Torin the piece of paper where the address was scrawled. "We're meeting at his apartment."

Torin stifled the relieved breath that would've given him away. No way could he have handled going to the gas station. "I'll meet you there."

"Outside the building. Promise me you won't go in before I get there."

"Sure." Torin turned to leave.

"Hey, partner."

He looked back.

"A good cop always suspects everyone. You know that."

An apology or a warning?

Torin nodded. "That's how I know you're going to find the shooter. You're the right cop for the job."

Relief relaxed the tension at the corners of Derrick's eyes. An apology, it seemed.

"See you at ten."

CHAPTER
FIFTEEN

October 9. 12:25 p.m.

SOMEONE WANTED HER DEAD.

A repulsive taste hit the back of Spring's throat, warning she might hurl, despite not touching the unappetizing lunch on the tray across her lap.

The thought she might vomit swirled more panic through her stomach. Someone would have to clean it up.

She stared out the window at the slate sky. She had to get a grip on her emotions.

It shouldn't matter. Whether the crash was an accident or not, she was paralyzed. Nothing would change that.

But it did matter. Accidents happened to everyone. She didn't really have anyone to blame if the driver couldn't see her that night or lost control of the vehicle. But who would do such a thing on purpose?

Why would someone hate her that much?

Was it the texter? She shivered at the memory of the texts she'd read after Sergeant Cotter had left.

I told you not to talk to the cop. You were warned.

I won't go so easy on you this time.

Her cell phone dinged. Probably vibrated, too, but Spring wouldn't know with it pressed between her useless leg and the wheelchair.

Could the texter read her thoughts now, too? Know she was thinking about his last threat? The thought was unhinged but that didn't keep dread from rippling through her upper body as she picked up the phone.

A visitor. Say nothing. I'm watching.

Could the texter see her as well as hear? Cold fear slipped through the limbs she could feel. She glanced at the ceiling, the four corners of her room. She'd looked before. Still no cameras. They'd probably be hidden somewhere.

A new thought drove her heartbeat faster. If the texter was the driver who wanted her dead, then would he kill her now? Tonight?

"Hey, girl."

Spring started. She craned her neck to see Lana Curtis's curly bob of black hair and bright eyes push in from behind the door.

"Lana." Warmth from the sight of a familiar, friendly face, calmed the palpitations in Spring's chest. "Hi. Come in."

Spring gripped the rims on the wheels of her chair and tried to turn. Didn't budge an inch. How was she supposed to do it again? Move one wheel forward and the other back? Or both back?

She stifled a grunt as Lana stopped on the other side of the bed.

Spring closed her eyes. Would the embarrassments never end? "Would you mind turning me around?"

"Oh, sure."

Spring's cheeks felt hot enough to cook a pancake as Lana easily spun the chair to face the room.

She stepped around the chair and went to the pictures and cards Victoria had put up on the wall.

Taller than Spring before she had to permanently sit, Lana seemed to tower as she crossed the room, her athletic build and conditioning obvious in her outfit of a short skort and tank under a fitted denim jacket.

Spring swallowed the envy that tasted no better than her lunch. That used to be her.

Lana pointed at the kids' pictures. "Cute." She turned to face Spring, resting one hand on her hip as a smile hovered around her mouth. "You look…"

Heat crawled into Spring's cheeks again. "It's okay. You don't have to say anything."

"No, I was just trying to think of something new to say. But I guess 'great' works. You look great." Lana smiled and stepped a little closer, but her eyes held a distance they hadn't before.

Spring bit back the defensive words she wanted to throw at her former teammate. *Nice of her to finally drop by. Didn't think she'd ever come.* Spring bit back the words and chose something more polite. "You, too." She cleared her throat. "Have you been training?" Dumb question. Of course Lana had been training. Her life hadn't ended.

"Oh, yeah. Megan and I just had a great ride. Not far from here, so I thought I'd stop in."

"Megan?" The image of her taking those pills jumped to Spring's mind. Of Megan laughing it off like a joke.

"Sure. You've been a hard training partner to replace." Lana grinned. "And you trained with Megan a bunch of times."

As if the only thing that would bother Spring about this was the thought of Lana training with someone else. "Cliff said she'd been suspended."

Lana shrugged, not missing a beat. "She still needs to train for when she comes back."

Frustration tweaked at Spring's resolve to be polite. Forget the pretense. This was probably the last time she'd see Lana anyway. "Did you know?"

Her grin slid off. "Know what?"

"About the doping?"

She held Spring's gaze. Not so much as a blink. Too little

of a reaction to be real. "I don't know what you're talking about."

"Oh, come on, Lana." The tray on her lap teetered as she swung her hand up. "We were friends. Don't treat me like an enemy."

She stalked close, stopping in front of Spring and leaning over, her dark eyes flashing. "You made yourself the enemy."

The hiss sparked Spring's heartbeat, but she kept herself from flinching.

Lana bent even closer, placing her hands on the arms of Spring's chair, boxing her in. "You were going to turn us in. All of us."

"You were taking drugs, too?" The words nearly caught in her dry throat.

Lana laughed as she pushed away from the chair, rocking it back with the force. She spun to Spring again, crossing her arms over her jacket. "You were always so sickeningly naïve. So righteous with your Bible and your preaching." She pushed her lips into a smug slash as she raked her gaze over Spring. "Look where it got you."

Spring stared down at the cold food on the tray. Couldn't argue with her own thoughts.

"You shouldn't have turned on your team, Spring. You should've known it wouldn't end well."

A tremor skidded out to Spring's fingertips. She looked up at Lana. What did that mean?

"Most victims of a crime don't realize someone they know wants to hurt them until it's too late."

Torin's words reverberated in her memory with the echoes of Cliff's parting statement the day he'd visited.

"Wouldn't want anything to ruin our record. Or sully your wins."

Had Cliff meant that as a threat? Maybe to her reputation, but he wouldn't actually hurt her any more than Lana would. Or would they? Torin asked her about motives. She thought no one had any, but...

"I heard you took my spot on the team."

"So?" Lana kept her defensive posture. "You won't be needing it."

Spring hid a wince. Since when had Lana become so vicious? Since Spring had threatened to turn in the team, apparently. But was she mean enough to want to kill? For her cycling career?

"You know I'm not here for a social call, so I might as well get to the point." Lana took a few steps toward her.

Spring stiffened, gripping the arms of her chair.

"You're out of the game now, so there's no reason to spoil it for others."

"You mean report the doping."

A sinister grin Spring didn't know Lana had contorted her features. "You're not getting me to admit anything." She started to turn away, then angled back. "Except for this—you squeal, and you'll regret it." She pointed a finger. "I promise you that. You don't have any proof, so keep your mouth shut."

She spun on squeaking sneakers and marched to the door, pausing with her fingers on the handle. She glanced back. "Take care of yourself, Spring."

The hard edge of her tone left no doubt in Spring's mind that, this time, the farewell was definitely a threat.

5:05 p.m.

Who do we have here?

Positioned in his car an inconspicuous distance down the street, Torin watched a man and woman leave the duplex where Cliffton Benecke lived.

The man was tall, black hair and beard, dressed in shorts and a sweatshirt. The brunette he seemed friendly with was petite and wore a more carefully coordinated outfit with the leggings and accessories young women seemed to favor.

Torin jotted down a note about their appearance. Watched

as they got into an expensive make of SUV parked on the street and drove off.

He checked the time before opening the car door. His stomach knotted as he stepped into the cool air. Five hours until the meeting with the source. Until he might finally have the information they needed to find the shooter.

The scent of rain lingered in mist as he headed for the house across the wet street, working to refocus his thoughts. Couldn't waltz into the interview for Spring's case thinking about his own problems. She deserved justice, too. He had promised to get it for her.

Her former coach Cliffton Benecke seemed like the best place to start, given her response every time Torin brought up the cycling team. But Torin would have to walk a fine line in this interview. He didn't have any evidence tying Benecke to the collision.

The coach opened the door before Torin reached the top stair. "Sergeant Cotter, right?"

Torin nodded and Benecke stepped back to let him inside a carpeted room dominated by a giant flat-screen TV attached to one wall. Appeared no one else was in the place, which looked like a typical bachelor pad, though slightly cleaner. "I hope this isn't a bad time after all."

Benecke lifted his eyebrows as if confused.

"I saw you had visitors as I arrived."

"Oh." Benecke let out a breathy laugh. "Just some friends. Stopped by unexpectedly." He stepped past Torin. "Hate it when people do that, don't you? I appreciate you called first."

And showed up early to observe, but Benecke didn't need to know that. He was already nervous enough.

The cycling coach walked toward a doorway to what looked like the kitchen, judging from the flooring change to vinyl. "Get you anything to drink? Soda? I'd offer you beer..." He grinned.

"Nothing, thanks."

"Okay." His hands went toward his jeans pockets, but

couldn't settle there. "Well, have a seat." He gestured to the long sofa while he perched on an end table by a chair.

Was the guy on edge because of Torin or the supposed friends who'd just left?

Torin took the end of the sofa and watched Benecke struggle to adopt a casual posture with one ankle propped on his knee. "No need to be nervous. This isn't an interrogation."

He let out another light laugh. "Sorry, but I don't have cop —police in my house every day."

"I'm just interviewing Spring's acquaintances to help with the investigation."

"Oh, sure." Benecke nodded with a smile as he dropped his leg. "Anything I can do to help." His mouth abruptly reversed to a frown. "Such a terrible thing that happened to her." He shook his head. "I couldn't believe it when I heard. I went to see her only…let's see…two days ago, I think it was. Can't get it out of my mind. So sad."

"Yes." Not as sad as the way the guy puffed himself up when spilling that he'd visited Spring. As if that earned him some merit badge.

Stay objective, Cotter. Benecke irked him, but that didn't mean he was Spring's attacker. Time to find out if he was. "Was Spring well-liked on your cycling team?"

"Oh, yeah." He lifted his knee, hooked his hands around it to hold it in midair. "She was one of the most popular girls on the team. Everyone loved her."

"What did you think of her?"

The knee lowered. A quick glance away, then back to Torin. "She was terrific. Great to work with. On time, reliable. Terrific athlete. Friendly. Respectful."

"Sounds ideal."

"Yeah, she really was."

"Did she ever have disagreements with anyone on the team?"

His brow wrinkled as if he were thinking for a moment.

"Not that I'm aware of. But, of course, the girls don't tell me everything. I'm just their coach." He donned his grin.

"Okay. How about with you. Did she ever have an argument or disagreement with you?"

"No, never." He moved his head side to side.

"Never?" Torin raised his eyebrows. "I've been on some teams myself, and I have to say I didn't always agree with my coach."

Benecke chuckled. "Well, she might not have always agreed with me, but she didn't share that. Like I said, she was always respectful. She sometimes would suggest something different or express an opinion, of course, but my coaching style is pretty relaxed." His gaze drifted to the curtained picture window. "We never argued about anything."

"Glad to hear it." Torin leaned forward, looked directly at the coach as he brought his attention back. "I'm going to ask you one more question, and I need you to give it careful thought before answering."

Benecke nodded and leaned forward, too, his mouth in a straight line. "Sure."

"Who would want to hurt Spring?"

He jolted, gaze dropping for a split second.

"Are you all right?"

Benecke stood. "Yes. Yes, of course. The question just took me by surprise." He turned away to the TV, then back. "No one would want to hurt her. Not that I know of anyway." He shoved his hands into his pockets. Hiked his shoulders. "Why would you even ask something like that?"

Torin kept his seat, unmoving except for his gaze that tracked the suspect. "Our investigation has revealed the likelihood that the collision wasn't an accident."

Benecke froze. "It wasn't?"

"No."

Benecke returned to sit, this time in the armchair next to the end table. "I don't understand. You mean someone..."

"Purposefully struck her with a vehicle."

He looked down. Shook his head, features contorting in what could be genuine shock or a solid acting job to save his hide. "That's awful."

Torin gave him a few moments to absorb the news. Or formulate a calculated response.

"I...I didn't know that. Before..." He lifted his head, his face a study in sadness, but not personal enough to reach his eyes. "I didn't know that before. Who would want to paralyze Spring?"

"The intention was probably to kill her."

Benecke's mouth gaped. "You're kidding. Spring?" A half-chuckle added believability to his incredulous expression. "Who in the world would want to kill Spring?"

"That's what I was hoping you could tell me."

The coach watched Torin's unchanging expression. "You're serious."

"Unfortunately, yes. The person who tried to kill her was likely someone she knew. So, I'm starting with you." An innocuous statement unless a person had something to hide.

And Benecke reacted like someone with a secret.

He sat straighter in the chair. "Now wait a second, I just told you how much I liked Spring. I wouldn't ever want to kill her."

Torin gave him a half-smile. "I only meant I need to interview her friends to get an indication of whether or not she has any enemies."

"Oh." The coach's posture relaxed slightly.

"But if you'd like to take care of any suspicion down the road, you could go ahead and tell me where you were the evening of August twenty-eighth at nine thirty." Torin took out his notepad from his pocket, giving Benecke a second to question his meaning. "Might save me some time if I were to have to come back to you." Torin looked up with an expression he'd practiced, one devoid of accusation or insinuation. Guilty parties tended to supply enough of both.

"I'm not sure why you'd need to know that." Benecke stared at the notepad like it was a press microphone.

"Just routine investigation."

"I'm being investigated?"

"Of course not." Torin pushed the notepad into his pocket and got to his feet. "I didn't mean to make you uncomfortable. You said you'd like to help, and it sure makes my life easier to have all the 'i's' dotted as I go. That's all."

"Sure, sorry." Benecke chuckled as he stood and rubbed his hand along the back of his head. "Didn't mean to get touchy. I'm just a private guy. But if it'll help, I was with Lana that night."

"Lana?"

"Lana Curtis, one of the girls on the cycling team. We had dinner." He grinned. "Do me a favor and don't tell the other girls when you talk to them?"

"Thanks for your time, Mr. Benecke."

He took the hand Torin offered. "Cliff, please. Anytime. Spring was like my own sister. I'll do anything if it'll help her out. Poor kid."

As Torin looked into those eyes covered with plastic emotion, he had no doubt Cliffton Benecke never helped anyone but himself. But shallowness and lying couldn't make a case to convince a jury of attempted murder. If he was Spring's attacker, Torin was going to need more to go on. Lana Curtis, alleged alibi, might be able to supply just that.

CHAPTER
SIXTEEN

October 9. 6:07 p.m.

"I never did like Lana Curtis."

Victoria hung her coat on the back of the chair and sat at the small round table across from her siblings, raising an eyebrow at Treese's remark.

Robert caught Victoria's look and grinned. "There is a reason for that statement—beyond Treese's usual prejudice, I mean."

Treese humphed and took a sip from the mug that probably held a skinny latte.

"Did you order anything?"

Victoria nodded to her brother. "Though I don't have much time. I have to see a patient at seven in Yorkville." At least they'd agreed to meet at the coffee shop infused restaurant and dessert bar this time. Much more to her liking than the brewpub. Talking would be easier without rowdy people and pounding music.

"Okay, we'll bring you up to speed quickly." The glint in Robert's eyes prompted Victoria to delay her own announcement.

"You discovered something?"

"Something big."

He glanced at Treese in response to her remark. "Not that big."

Victoria closed her eyes briefly. "Will you simply start at the beginning and tell me what you found?"

Another grin pulled up the corners of Robert's mouth. "Sure. We visited Spring's coach to see what he had to say."

"He said a lot." Treese smirked. "Just nothing very helpful or true, probably."

"I take it he didn't make a good impression?"

"Not for lack of trying." Robert shot a sidelong glance at Treese.

Victoria turned her gaze on her baby sister. "He flirted with you?"

"A lot of hits, no score."

"Wonderful."

"But beyond knowing the guy's normal, we didn't get that much from him." Robert wrapped his fingers around the mug in front of him. "I think Treese is right, though. He didn't seem to be telling the truth when we asked him if he got along with Spring."

"But he wasn't scary at all. I could keep him under control with my pinky." Treese waggled the mentioned digit. "Don't see why Spring would be afraid of him."

"She wouldn't have to be afraid of taking him on in a fight. Though he's not that out of shape." Robert smiled as he took a drink from his steaming mug.

"Are you saying he'd have to be for me to—"

"Can we stay on task?" Victoria shifted her stern gaze from Treese to Robert. "What makes you think he wasn't telling the truth about his relationship with Spring?"

Robert lowered his mug. "The telltale signs of deception were all there. Fortunately, he's not a great liar."

"But what is he lying about? Spring never mentioned any

problems with the coach or her team before the acci—" She stopped herself. "Collision."

"Right, that's what we wondered, so—"

"We went to Lana Curtis's apartment." Treese leaned in, hands clasping her mug. "Did you know she got Spring's spot on the team? Some friend."

"Before or after the collision?"

"After." Robert's eyebrows hovered, indicating he also caught the significance of that.

Treese glanced between the two of them. "I agree it's obnoxious, but I don't see how Lana wanting Spring's spot would give her a hold over Spring now. How could she have known someone would crash into Spring?"

Robert watched Victoria. "It wasn't an accident, was it?"

"Wait, what?" Treese sucked in a sharp breath. "You mean Lana did it to get Spring's spot on the team?"

An employee chose that moment to drop off Victoria's drink in a to-go cup.

"Thank you." Victoria waited until the girl was out of ear shot before answering Treese. "Let's not jump to accusations. We don't know who did it yet."

"But someone did it purposefully?" Robert's keen gaze seemed to see all of the truth.

"Sergeant Cotter came to the rehab center today and said definitively that he believes the collision was intentional."

"Is there new evidence?"

Victoria shook her head slightly. "My understanding is he's basing that conclusion on his own review of the same evidence."

"So someone paralyzed Spring on purpose?" Treese's small brow furrowed.

"Far worse." Victoria ran her tongue over her lips. "The sergeant believes the intention was to kill her."

"Kill her?" Treese's tone heated. "Kill our sister?"

Robert laid a calming hand on Treese's. "Keep your voice down."

She turned flashing eyes on him. "Aren't you upset?"

"Yes. But getting all riled up won't help us solve anything."

"You already knew this, didn't you?" She pulled her hand away.

"I had suspicions."

"You could've told me."

"I said suspicions, not certainty or evidence."

"Well, I for one am not going to let someone try to rub out our sister." Treese crossed her arms over her skin-tight red dress.

"Neither are we." Robert glanced at Victoria. "What did Spring say when the sergeant told her?"

"Not much. She seemed as shocked as I was. Perhaps more."

"So she probably didn't know someone wanted to kill her."

Victoria pursed her lips. "I don't believe she did."

"But then why was she already scared?"

"She received another text while Sergeant Cotter was there. She didn't look at it, but it obviously frightened her. I haven't seen her that pale since she told Dad she wasn't going to college."

"Didn't you check her phone?" Treese's intense stare showed she hadn't calmed down.

"No. I didn't have an opportunity."

Treese blew out an exasperated breath and looked at Robert. "Maybe I should do it." Typical Treese, always thinking she knew best and could do everything better.

He shook his head. "No, Victoria should."

"But she's being all careful about it." A familiar whine crept into Treese's tone. "We'll never get to the phone this way."

"We'll get to it with subtlety and sensitivity." He transferred his steady gaze to Victoria. "Can you do it?"

A sinking feeling weighed down her heart, but she nodded. "I think so."

Robert leaned across the table. "We learned something else

when we talked to another cyclist from the team. Megan Leone."

"Megan? I don't remember her."

"We asked Lana if Spring was friends with anyone else on the team," Treese rotated her mug in her hands as she talked, "and Lana said she trained with Megan since she's the only other team member in Chicago."

"Right." Robert pushed his drink to the side and folded his arms on the table. "I didn't find anything alarming in Megan's background when I researched the team, but there are some things about her that make me a little suspicious."

"Why would you say that?" Treese's eyebrows dipped. "She's the only one who genuinely felt bad about what happened to Spring." Treese turned her gaze to Victoria. "She admitted she overheard Lana and Cliff arguing the night before Spring's crash. They mentioned Spring."

Victoria looked at Robert. "Do you believe her?"

"Possibly. She seemed to believe what she said."

Treese let out a frustrated sigh. "Then why are you doubting it? Especially after what Victoria just told us?"

"Because of her symptoms."

"Symptoms?"

He nodded. "I'm almost certain she's on drugs."

CHAPTER
SEVENTEEN

October 9. 8:20 p.m.

I WON'T GO SO *easy on you this time.*

The text messages from earlier in the day played over and over in Spring's mind as the tension that started in her belly reverberated out to every inch of her body that she could still feel.

Should she tell someone? Ask for help?

She moistened her dry lips. Twisted the top hem of the sheet that covered her, wadding it in her hands.

Who could help her there?

And the texter would find out. Somehow.

She cast her gaze around the room, lit only by the moon glowing through blinds over the window and a nightlight plugged in under the kids' pictures. If only she could figure out how he knew everything that happened in this room. Maybe she could figure out a way to pass someone a message. Maybe Victoria.

But she wasn't there tonight.

Spring would have to face whatever the texter had in store on her own. Helplessly stuck in her bed.

Maybe she'd already avoided the worst by refusing to eat her dinner. Hadn't wanted to take the risk of ingesting another painful poison, if it had been given to her in the food last time. She couldn't be sure. But the texter had sent her that message about the cupcake.

Her breath caught.

The cupcake. From the cycling team.

Could they have poisoned her? Lana? Or Cliff. Were they behind the texts?

They couldn't be.

But she'd never seen such anger in Lana's face before today either. Hatred.

Could she be sending the texts? Or Cliff and Lana? Everyone knew they had a thing going.

She mentally reviewed their visits, when she'd received the texts, and what they'd said. Right before both had visited, she'd gotten texts that warned her about them coming, telling her to keep quiet. They wouldn't send such warnings themselves. And another text had come the instant Cliff had left. That wouldn't make sense.

Spring pressed her fingers to her temples. None of it made any sense.

A shuffle outside the door.

She jerked to look.

Light broke through the seams around the door as someone pushed it open.

She froze.

A dark silhouette stood in the light from the hallway.

"What did you say to him?"

Dad? Relief collided with a different kind of alarm. "Wh—" The word came out as a broken croak. She cleared her throat. "What?" Forget *Hi* or *How are you*, apparently.

He found the light switch and flicked it on. "To your brother. What did you say to him?"

Squinting at the brightness of the overhead lights, Spring

could barely see the blurry figure march toward her bed. "You mean when he brought the Chinese?"

"What?" Her father placed his hands on his hips under a gray sport coat. "Not Robert. Henry. He called me today."

"Oh."

His eyebrows lifted behind his glasses. "That's all you have to say?"

She stuck out her hands. If he wasn't so angry, the confusion might be funny. "What do you want me to say? I have no idea what you're talking about."

He pursed his lips, considering her with a mistrustful gaze she remembered too well. "Have you spoken to him recently?"

"What do you call recent?" She knew that was the wrong response before his eyes narrowed. Too evasive. "I just mean he calls me like once a week."

"Very well. Since you persist in pretending you have no idea what I'm talking about, I'll tell you."

Frustration ballooned under her ribs—a relief if it pushed out the fear. "Please do."

"Henry says he's not going to attend Johns Hopkins."

"He's not?"

Her father paced away from the bed, then turned toward her. "He says he no longer wants to become a neurosurgeon."

Uh-oh.

He walked with measured steps back to the bed, stopping close enough that Spring had to lift her chin to see his face. "Do you know what he wants to do instead?"

A foreboding tension crawled into her chest.

"He wants to become a physiatrist."

Because of her. She turned her head away, closing her eyes. She should've seen it coming. Hank was always so compassionate. He'd want to help other people like his sister, to heal paralyzed bodies when he couldn't heal hers. But he didn't have to change his whole career path because of what happened to her.

All that did was give her father another reason to hate her.

His dream of having his favorite child follow exactly in his footsteps had been about to become a reality. Until now.

She could feel his resentment reach for her across the space between them.

"Your mother always said Henry would be the one to follow after me. He had the makings of a brilliant surgeon from the time he was a small child."

She stared at the sheet where it cocooned her useless legs.

"He was destined for this. Thank God she isn't alive to witness what you've done. You would've broken her heart as well as mine."

Spring smashed her lips together, trying to hold back tears. "It's not my fault." Her mom would know that. "I didn't want to be paralyzed."

"Oh, yes, it is your fault." He waved a hand over her limp body. "None of this would have happened if you'd gone into medicine instead of pursuing this ridiculous sport."

Shock drove her gaze to his face. Was that really what he thought?

"Look where your rebellion has gotten you."

"Rebellion?"

"Yes, rebellion. You always went against everything I advised. I just hope you're satisfied now that you're destroying your brother's future, as well." His eyes were hard as he braced his fists on her bed. "I'm done trying to help you. If you want to keep running your life into the ground, I won't stop you. But don't think I'll let you destroy your brother without a fight." He turned on his heel.

"Dad, wait."

He kept moving.

"I didn't—"

He shut the door behind him, leaving her alone with her aching heart.

She'd made him mad plenty of times before. Disappointed and frustrated him. But he'd never looked at her like that. Like he'd given up. Like he didn't care anymore. Like she'd actually hurt him.

Her chest squeezed as if he were gripping it in his angry fist. She'd really done it this time. No mother, and now her father couldn't stand the sight of her.

She could call Hank, tell him to change his mind and become a neurosurgeon.

No, she'd seen the expression in her dad's eyes. He wouldn't forgive her, even if she could get Hank to switch back.

She'd always been wrong. Never good enough even when she'd had two good legs and a promising cycling career. At least then, she had the hope of someday making him proud.

But the way her dad had looked at her before he left, she might as well be dead.

9:55 p.m.

Three years and one day. Torin finally stood on the brink of the moment he'd been waiting for. Hoping for.

The ID they needed. Evidence to go on.

He shoved his hands into his pants pockets as he looked up at the brown brick apartment building, his car parked behind him. The brisk air made his blood rush faster. Or maybe it was just nerves.

The streetlamp backlit the billowing cloud of his breath. Cold enough for a coat. But he couldn't feel it.

What would Wiley Boone tell them? Had he known the shooter all these years? Kept it hidden until now because...

Torin blew out a long breath, the air puffing in front of his face. He needed to stay calm. Keep his mind off that day. Couldn't risk the memories assaulting him now.

Had to think about something else. Spring's case. He wouldn't have much reason to visit her tomorrow, thanks to his interview with Lana Curtis not being as helpful as he'd hoped. The cyclist had only allowed him a few minutes of her time, citing a training run. But a few minutes were all he'd needed to suspect she, like Benecke, wasn't telling the truth. Now if he could only figure out what the truth was, he'd be in business.

Both cycling characters were nervy about being questioned by the police. Both were supposedly best buds with Spring. And both were shocked to hear the collision was no accident. Or at least they pretended to be.

Trouble was, his background checks on them had turned up clean records. Nothing to point him in the right direction, other than Lana moving up to Spring's position on the team after the crash. From what he'd gathered, cycling at their level was far from lucrative, so it didn't seem likely Lana would kill for that reason alone.

He'd have to interview the rest of the cyclists on the team. Maybe talking to more of them would get him closer to the secret they were hiding, and to learning if it was the attempted murder of Spring.

The door of the apartment building opened, and two men sauntered out in black jackets, watching him with uneasy defiance as they walked toward him.

Maybe wasn't the best idea to stand on the sidewalk outside his car, even if it was unmarked and he wasn't in uniform. People in that neighborhood seemed to be able to smell cop regardless of wardrobe.

Headlights bathed Torin in plenty of protection as Derrick's unmarked black car appeared behind his.

Derrick got out, making no attempt to hide the holstered weapon at his hip beneath the hem of his sport coat. He glanced at the two men as they quickly shuffled past, then nodded to Torin. "How long you been here?"

Torin glanced at his watch. "Seven minutes."

"Been inside?"

Still suspicious. Torin probably would be if he were in Derrick's position, too. "Glued to this spot the whole time."

Derrick's grin flashed white against his skin. "Let's see what the man has to say, partner."

They headed toward the front entry of the aged apartment building. One of those that should've been torn down about ten years ago but instead housed more people than should be allowed. The smell of mold and decay assaulted his nostrils as he and Derrick went inside the unlocked building.

The sounds of squabbling kids, booming music, and TVs accompanied their trek up the stairs to the third floor and down the narrow hallway to Boone's apartment.

Derrick knocked.

No answer.

He glanced at Torin. Knocked again. "Mr. Boone?"

Silence.

He tried the knob.

It turned under his hand.

He nodded to Torin. Shifted to the side of the doorframe and drew his weapon.

Torin backed against the wall to the left of the door.

Derrick scanned Torin. Raised his eyebrows.

Looking for a gun.

Torin pushed back the sides of his sport coat to show he was unarmed.

Derrick's mouth tensed as he shook his head, then pointed at the door.

Torin nodded, then slowly pushed it open.

"Police!" Derrick swung into the room, weapon raised as he scanned.

Torin quickly followed.

A man lay on the floor, sprawled on a tattered brown rug. Wiley Boone.

"Derrick."

"I see him." Derrick pressed forward to an open, darkened doorway, gun still lifted.

Torin carefully approached Boone, scanning the open living room, dining room, and kitchen. The man appeared to be alone, unless Derrick found someone in the other room.

He scanned the unmoving body. That face.

"Get down!"

Boone's features twisted in panic as he ducked behind the counter.

She screamed.

Torin shook his head. Not now. Could not lose it now. Derrick needed him.

Torin forced himself to breathe and yanked his gaze away from Boone's face. The man could still be alive. Torin had to do his job.

Like moving against a fierce current in waist-high water, Torin mentally pushed through the memories that threatened to crush him.

He didn't remember getting on his knees by Boone, but he was already there. He reached for the man's neck, not looking at his face as he checked for a pulse.

None. Skin was cold.

He looked more closely at Boone's body, trying desperately for a clinical perspective as the memories flowed to the background. No sign of violence or trauma on the man that he could see.

A cell phone lay on the floor about three feet from Boone, next to the corner of the chipped wooden coffee table. Thrown? Or knocked off the table?

"Apartment is clear." Derrick reemerged from the doorway, holstering his weapon. His gaze went to Boone. "Dead?"

"Yeah. He's cold."

Derrick pulled his phone from his pocket to call in the technicians.

Torin stood and walked around the open area of the apartment while Derrick spoke on the phone.

The apartment was fairly neat. Only a few dirty dishes stacked in the sink, candles placed in decorative positions on the counter and on the bookcase that held knickknacks instead of books.

A younger woman, probably in her twenties, stared out at Torin from a paper-framed photograph on a shelf. Boone's daughter?

"When did you say you got here?"

Torin turned to see Derrick watching him over the body. He held back the defensive response he'd like to make. Kept his voice calm. "Nine fifty." If Derrick was honestly suspicious of him, Torin wouldn't help his case by trying to plead his innocence.

He walked back to the body, standing on the opposite side as Derrick. "What do you think?"

Derrick placed his fists against his hips and looked down at Boone. "No visible trauma. Could be a heart attack. He's sixty-seven. Not in great shape." Derrick's dark gaze lifted to Torin's, telegraphing the truth they both knew.

"But the timing."

"Never did believe in coincidences."

"Makes two of us."

Derrick landed his hands on his hips. "We'll treat it as a possible homicide until we learn differently."

Torin nodded.

"I'm going to ask you something, and I want the truth." Derrick stared at Torin, a muscle twitching in his jaw. "Did you come inside before I got here?"

"No."

"Did you talk to Boone after I told you he set up this meeting?"

"No."

"Did you have anything to do with his death?"

Torin held Derrick's gaze. "No, I did not."

"Do I have your word?"

"Do you need it?"

Derrick watched him. Shook his head, shoulders relaxing. "No. I know I can trust you."

"I thought you did."

"Hey, man," Derrick's tense mouth loosened into an attempt at a smile, "you know it's nothing personal. I don't believe you're capable of murder. But..."

"Desperate people do desperate things."

"Right." Derrick glanced at the open doorway. "I just hope we can figure out what he was going to tell us."

"Yeah." Not half as much as Torin. He stepped away to examine the rest of the apartment again.

"You're still not wearing your weapon on duty, are you?"

Torin's gut clenched. He turned to see Derrick's eyes flicker.

"I don't need it in MAIU."

"You're a cop out on the street. You need it."

Torin didn't respond.

"It's regulation."

"I know. I can't..." Torin turned away, moving toward the doorway of the bedroom. "It's safer this way."

No answer as he looked inside the room that held one double bed, made with a faded blanket as the bedspread.

He braced himself. Derrick could ask about the flashbacks. He'd been there twice when Torin trembled uncontrollably during target practice and had to leave early before the fear took over completely. Torin had made an excuse and tried to hide the shaking, but Derrick was a skilled detective. Smart enough to put the pieces together.

"There are some things I won't cover for you, partner."

Torin rotated. Met Derrick's gaze across the room. "I'm not asking you to."

"Maybe you should—"

The sound of footsteps in the hallway cut short whatever Derrick was going to say. Wouldn't have mattered what he said. It wouldn't bring back the only man who had apparently known something about the shooting. If only he could have told them what he knew before...

As the technicians went to work collecting evidence, Torin

ducked out. Little reason to stay when the only spark of hope on the horizon had just been killed, too.

October 9. 11:45 p.m.

A surge of pain shot through Spring's leg, the dead limb stretched across the bed. She pushed her head back into the pillow and gritted her teeth against the phantom pain that was far more tangible than the phantoms that assaulted her mind.

Every time that she'd disappointed her father paraded through her memory. His anger, insults, accusations. Her mother's soft eyes as she'd stand between them or come to Spring's room afterward to try to explain that Spring's father loved her. He only wanted her to succeed.

Stretches of the truth that Spring would never blame her mother for. She was trying to heal a child's breaking heart.

Maybe it would have been better if she hadn't tried. If she'd let Spring's heart break completely all those years ago. Before she got to this point of utter desperation and failure. To such hopelessness. A future imprisoned by a wheelchair, dependency, suffering.

A life where all she could do was helplessly sit there and wait for the attack of some unknown person who hated her enough to kill her.

The latest text had come five minutes ago. *I deal decisively with people who talk to cops. Time to teach you to be quiet. Just pray I don't silence you permanently.*

Pray. Something she hadn't done since before the crash. Unless she counted the hopeless prayer she'd screamed at the hospital ceiling when she was told she'd never walk again.

Her gaze fell on the Bible Victoria had purposely placed next to Spring's right shin on the bed. Probably wanted Spring to sit up in order to reach it. Victoria clearly didn't know how much things had changed.

She probably assumed Spring still read the Bible every

night, having the quiet time of study and prayer that used to calm her before going to bed.

But that night had happened. The night that changed everything.

She couldn't face the One who had allowed this to happen to her. It hadn't mattered that she'd been praying and running praise songs through her head as she'd cycled to the beat. If this is where that got her, she was more scared of praying than anything else.

She shouldn't feel that way, but she couldn't help it.

Burning seared through her right leg. At least she thought it was the right. Didn't really matter since her brain was making it up anyway.

Nothing mattered. She was sick of the pain, sick of this room, this bed, this immovable body. Sick to death of living like this. And sick of being manipulated by the very person who might have done this to her.

The hopelessness of those first hours of consciousness washed over her. She couldn't keep going like this.

The expression on her father's face before he'd left her room crossed her vision.

She didn't want to keep going. Not anymore.

She lifted the cell phone clutched in her hand. She typed a response. *Go ahead and kill me. I'd rather be dead.*

She set the phone beside her thigh as her pulse raced faster. What would the texter do now? She still couldn't imagine anyone wanting to kill her. What had she done to deserve that?

A phantom pain tore through her leg—the leg she couldn't even feel anymore. She gritted her teeth. Didn't matter what the texter would do. The prospect of a future with only half a body scared her more. The prospect of having to live with her dad, seeing his disappointment every day because of her failures. Seeing his relationship with Hank destroyed because she'd caused Hank to disappoint him. Poor kid had never done that before. He didn't know what he was doing.

The leg pain faded as a knot cinched in her gut—the same feeling she'd had as a ten-year-old when she had to show her dad the grade on her science report card. And her mom had again been the buffer between them. At least she didn't have to do that anymore. And she didn't have to see Spring like this. But then again, Spring wouldn't be chained to a hospital bed if her mom were still alive. She wouldn't have been cycling at all. She would have been doing what she'd—

The phone vibrated in Spring's hand.

She lifted it. Another text. A response? She opened it.

The knot jumped to her throat, cutting off her air as she read the words.

Your sister looked cute today. For a physical therapist.

Victoria?

Don't make me hurt her instead.

Spring's pulse pounded in her ears. The texter was watching Victoria, too? Her family?

She typed a response with trembling fingers. *Why are you doing this?*

She waited, barely remembering to breathe.

The phone shook in her hand. *You know why. You didn't see anything that night. Your sister's well-being depends on it. Don't test me.*

Spring swallowed. Made herself take in air. Had she already jeopardized Victoria's safety by what she'd told Sergeant Cotter? She hadn't even seen who hit her that night. She should tell the texter that.

She sent a message. *I didn't see who hit me. If it was you, you don't have to worry. I don't know who you are.*

The answer came fast. *Good. Then you won't mind keeping quiet about nothing. Especially when your sister's life is on the line. Trust me, I mean what I say.*

He didn't believe her. Was it Cliff, and he knew she might put two and two together about the doping? In a way, it would make sense. Could explain the threats even though she hadn't seen anything before the crash. But then why would he have texted her with a threat to keep quiet even when he had visited her? It couldn't be him.

If she could only figure out who the texter was, then maybe there would be a way to tell someone. To protect Victoria.

Maybe she could come up with a way to give a hint to Sergeant Cotter the next time he questioned her, letting him know Victoria was in danger. But he might not want to help her after she'd lied about being threatened. He'd had such an angry glint in his eyes when he'd asked her, like he thought she was a criminal who was hiding something from him.

Not that it bothered her. She didn't know the man at all. His opinion meant nothing to her.

She turned her head so that her cheek rested on the pillow, but the angle was too uncomfortable with the rest of her torso remaining straight. She could try rolling over, but why bother? The rest of her life, which she apparently still had to live, was going to be like this. Uncomfortable at best. She'd have to get used to it.

She tilted her chin down to see the clock on the wall opposite her bed. Nearly midnight. She stared at the minute hand as it slowly moved, hoping it would either put her to sleep or numb her mind enough so she couldn't feel the pain or the fear that clenched her stomach.

Instead, the memory of a certain handsome face filled her vision, those green eyes with the crinkles at the corners looking at her in a way that made her heart do a crazy flip.

She didn't care if it was crazy. At least it meant part of her could still feel something.

Besides, he was the nicest thing she'd had to think about since her world smashed into a concrete abutment.

CHAPTER
EIGHTEEN

October 10. 9:11 a.m.

TORIN WALKED to Derrick's desk at the station as the detective finished taking a swig from a bottled water.

He set the bottle down and watched Torin silently sit in the chair opposite the desk. Black stubble lined Derrick's jaw and, unless Torin missed his guess, he still wore yesterday's white shirt under the other of the two sport coats he kept in his locker. Apparently hadn't gone home.

Torin's chest tightened. He'd do the same for Derrick if he could.

"Preliminary autopsy says heart attack, but we'll have to wait on the samples they sent away to find out if it was drug-induced."

"Do you think it was?"

"I'm betting our killer didn't want Boone to talk to us." At least Derrick didn't imply the killer might be Torin this time.

"Any leads?" Probably wouldn't be. But Torin had to ask. Just like he'd felt compelled to check in as soon as he figured Derrick would be back in the office.

"None of the neighbors saw or heard anything. Or won't talk." Derrick glanced at Torin. "You know the drill."

Figured.

"But," Derrick opened a file on his desk and spun it around so Torin could see the contents, "we're tracking down the girlfriend."

The picture he'd seen on the bookshelf at the apartment. "Girlfriend?"

Derrick grinned. "Just a little younger."

"What about Mrs. Marston? She's the grandma of the girl that's his granddaughter, too?"

"Judging from her language when I contacted her, she doesn't like her ex-boyfriend very much. They were never married, and she says she hasn't seen him in ten years."

"So you think the girlfriend might know something?" Torin tried to keep the skepticism out of his voice. He'd been down this dead-end road so many times after the shooting.

"Even if it's only why she wasn't there all night, it should be interesting."

"Right." Torin couldn't join in his friend's chuckle.

Derrick frowned. "I won't give up, partner."

The phone on his desk rang between them.

Derrick lifted the receiver. "Detective Haynes." A pause. "Yes, he's here. I'll tell him." He looked at Torin as he hung up. "You've got visitors."

"Visitors?"

"In the lobby. They supposedly have information about a Spring Weston."

One of the cyclists? He was planning to interview more of the team that morning. But maybe Cliff or Lana had decided to tell him the secret they were hiding on their own. He wished. More likely it was finger-pointing time. Torin got to his feet.

"So what does this Spring Weston look like?"

Torin stopped, caught the peculiar grin on Derrick's face. "What?"

"Those storm clouds you wore on your face all night just cleared to bright sunshine, partner."

Torin stared at Derrick, trying to keep his jaw from slacking. "You need sleep, man." He left the office and headed for the lobby where unauthorized visitors remained until they had an escort.

His ex-partner had gone crazy. If Torin's expression had changed when he thought of Spring's case, it was only because of the prospect he could bring some peace and justice into the life of a woman who'd been dealt a nasty hand. He got that invested in all his traffic cases, especially the intentional hit and runs.

He would never consider caring about another woman. Derrick should know that.

Torin slowed to a more normal pace as he reached the door that opened onto the lobby. He glanced at the people waiting. No Cliff or Lana.

That couple. The tall, dark guy and the petite woman he'd seen leaving Cliff's place rose from the bench when they saw him.

He headed over and extended his hand. "Sergeant Cotter."

The man accepted the hand shake. Firm grip. Confident gaze. "I'm Robert Weston. This is my sister, Patricia."

Torin nodded as he shook the surprisingly strong hand of the sparkly-eyed woman. "Spring's siblings."

"That's right." Robert's serious eyes reminded Torin of Spring's, though his were a bit darker, almost black. "We've discovered some information that we think you should hear."

Great. Biased relatives trying to do police work never turned out well.

"It could help with your investigation."

The urgency in their gazes was impossible to miss. He knew what that felt like. "Then I guess I better hear it."

Smiles illuminated their faces. Would Spring's smile look like that if he ever got to see it? Inwardly shaking off the thought, he invited them to his office where he brought an extra chair he found in the hallway so there were enough seats for everyone.

He swiveled his chair away from the desk and sat down, facing the two amateur detectives.

"Victoria told us you believe the collision wasn't an accident."

Torin crossed his arms over his chest, assessing the brother who seemed to study him in return. "The evidence suggests it was intentional." The evidence, and the threats he felt certain Spring was getting.

"We think you're right." The sister's brown eyes that appeared to be flecked with green filled with an eagerness that matched her forward lean.

Torin held back a chuckle at the unasked for opinion. "What makes you say that?"

"Spring's afraid of something." She crossed her denim-clad legs. "We don't know what, but we think someone's scaring her. Like maybe the person who tried to kill her."

Torin lowered his arms. So they knew it, too. "Has she mentioned any threats? Perhaps text messages?"

Robert's dark gaze locked on Torin. "You noticed."

"Hard to miss."

"You mean you saw how she gets scared when she gets a text message?"

He looked at Patricia as he answered her question. "Yes, ma'am."

"And she never lets the phone out of her hand."

"I'm afraid I can't help unless she wants me to. She won't admit to receiving threats of any kind."

"You asked her directly?" Robert raised a thick eyebrow.

"Yes."

Patricia took in an excited breath. "We have a plan to—"

"To help with the investigation as much as we can." Robert clearly didn't want his sister to finish her sentence. What had she been about to disclose? "The two of us spoke with some of Spring's cycling teammates and her coach."

So Torin had seen. "What did you find out?" He glanced between the siblings, taking in Patricia's sour frown aimed at her brother.

Robert appeared undaunted. "Cliff, the coach, and Spring's teammate Lana both seemed to be hiding something."

Good observation.

"But Megan, another training partner of Spring's, was more helpful."

"She's really broken up about what happened." Patricia apparently wasn't silenced for the duration. "Actually cared."

"I also believe she may be taking narcotics."

Torin's eyebrows went up before he could stop them. How'd the guy know that?

"Perhaps I should have said, Sergeant, I'm a psychiatrist by profession."

Another sibling in the medical field?

"I've seen many drug addicts in all phases of addiction. My guess is that Megan has been taking amphetamines of some kind."

"Doping."

"That was my thought. She may have moved on from milder forms to something like meth now."

"Right, so we were thinking," Patricia uncrossed her legs and leaned forward, "what if others on the team were doping? Maybe all of them, and Spring found out. She could have threatened to turn them in."

"Do you think Spring would have been involved in doping?"

The siblings stared at him, Patricia's mouth falling slack.

"If most or all of the team were doping, it seems likely that Spring would, too." Though Torin hated to think it. "Unfortunately, athletes tend to follow each other or a coach's lead."

"You don't know Spring very well yet, do you?" A smile curved Patricia's lips.

Robert's features relaxed, too. "Spring is just about the

most moral person you could ever meet. Well, maybe next to Victoria."

The siblings exchanged grins.

"She would never, ever cheat. Or abuse her body like that." Patricia shook her head. "She'd be devastated if she'd found out the others were doping."

Warmth bubbled in Torin's chest, but he did his best to ignore the reason for it. "All right. But would she report it and give up her place on the team?"

"Absolutely." Robert's voice was firm. "Unless someone stopped her."

"That's a serious accusation."

He held up a hand. "No accusation. Just a possibility."

"But you found no actual evidence of doping, correct?"

The two glanced at each other before Robert answered. "Correct."

"Look, I appreciate what you both are trying to do. I understand your desire to find the person who did this to your sister. It's admirable."

"But you don't want us interfering in a police investigation, right?" Patricia watched him with a smile hovering around her mouth. "Robert said you'd say that."

"For good reason. We don't want you getting hurt if there's danger involved, and you could end up scaring someone off or unintentionally warning them so they can more easily get away with their crime."

"You're right, Sergeant." Robert got to his feet, glancing at his sister as if to suggest she should follow him. "We'll try to be more careful and let you do your job."

Torin stood and shook Robert's offered hand.

"Thank you for your time. I hope you'll look into the situation with Megan. I think she'll have a lot to say with the right encouragement."

Why did Torin feel like Robert had just sent him a secret message? And he noticed the psychiatrist hadn't actually agreed to stop investigating.

Patricia grinned as she rose and also shook Torin's hand again, seeming to let her grip linger. "I can see why my sisters like you so much." She winked.

Torin could have been knocked over with the touch of a handcuff. But thankfully Robert whisked his sister away and left Torin to recover in private.

Apparently Derrick wasn't the only one getting the wrong idea about Torin and Spring. Unless Patricia had been referring to Victoria. But she did say *sisters*. That meant Spring, too.

Had she said something to Patricia about him?

Never mind.

Torin sat at his desk to do some research on Megan, trying to keep his mind on the investigation instead of the way his pulse tripped over itself every time he remembered Patricia's parting words.

CHAPTER
NINETEEN

October 10. 10:15 a.m.

"THIS IS RIDICULOUS." Spring dropped her grip on the bar above her chair and caught her breath. "I can't even lift myself an inch."

"Yes, you can." Angie's dauntless smile beamed as the PT leaned in. "I know you can do this. You need to know it, too. You're stopping yourself before you've even started."

"Then why start at all?" When would they quit bringing her into the gym as if she was going to be able to do a workout or magically get all her strength back? She glanced at the other patients and PTs who did exercises nearby. Hopefully, they hadn't seen her pitiful attempt to lift herself up.

"I'd like to go back to my room." Or have this all somehow be over. Why, when she finally stopped caring if the texter killed her, did he stop threatening to do it? Spring had no options now. She was gagged more than ever by his threats to harm Victoria. The danger of the end she'd finally welcomed was aimed at someone else.

Because of her. She'd messed up again. This time even worse than disappointing her father. She'd put Victoria in harm's way. What could she do if the sergeant came back to talk to her today? What if she said the wrong thing without realizing it and Victoria—

"Stay with me, Spring." Angie's voice cut through her thoughts as the PT moved in front of the chair. "We need to figure out something to motivate you." She glanced around. "Where'd Victoria disappear to?"

Spring's heart hiccupped. Victoria was gone? "She was here just a few minutes ago." How could Spring not have noticed when she disappeared? Had the texter—

"There she is." Angie aimed a smile over Spring's head. "Looks like she must have gotten a phone call."

A call? Victoria would never take a call during a PT session, even one with her sister as the patient. Spring twisted to look, but couldn't manage to see Victoria until Angie turned the chair away from the chin-up bar.

Sure enough, she carried a phone as she walked toward them. Wait a second. Was that…?

Spring felt next to her legs for her phone. She'd had it with her on the chair.

Now it was in Victoria's hand.

She should be furious, but instead her breath swelled in her chest as her heart pounded.

Victoria stopped in front of Spring's chair. "Angie, would you leave us alone for a few minutes?" Her cool tone matched the frigidity in her hazel eyes.

Angie blinked at Victoria. "Sure."

"Thank you." Victoria didn't give her friend the usual smile as Angie left them alone.

"You took my phone." The accusation slipped out of Spring's mouth before she thought, launching into offense as she'd always done when Victoria had caught her doing something wrong when they were young.

Victoria's chin clenched as she went to the back of Spring's chair and pushed.

"I don't want to go anywhere but back to my room."

Victoria pushed her rapidly toward the other end of the gym instead, passing the other people without a word. She halted the chair in a corner, then stepped in front of Spring. "How dare you."

Spring blinked at the razor-sharp tone she hadn't heard Victoria use in years.

"How dare you keep this from me? How dare you *lie* to me?"

"You're the one stealing my phone." The defense was as weak as her mutter.

Victoria awoke the screen on the phone and tapped it with her finger.

Spring held her breath.

"Your sister looked cute today. For a physical therapist. Don't make me hurt her instead." Victoria held up the phone like it was a bag of illegal drugs she'd found. "Were you going to tell me the truth about these texts?"

She lowered the phone and looked at the screen again. "Because apparently these others aren't worth telling me about. The ones like, 'Keep quiet. Or we'll have to kill you.' Oh, and these are great—'This is your first lesson. Don't make me have to give you another one. It's not fatal.'" Victoria aimed flashing eyes at Spring as she finished reciting the message. "This time."

Spring worked up a glare. She couldn't say anything more or Victoria could still be hurt. "What do you want me to say?"

"The truth, Spring. For once."

She looked away, grinding her teeth until her jaw hurt.

"Oh, Spring."

She tensed. The sudden softness and hurt in Victoria's tone slid under her defenses as her sister crouched in front of her.

"Who is this who's threatening you? What did he do to you? The first lesson he talked about..."

Spring slowly turned her head to see grief in Victoria's gaze.

"Didn't you know you could've told me? I could—"

"Protect me?" Spring shook her head. "No. You'd just be in more danger than you are now."

"Why? Why am I in danger?" Victoria placed her hand on Spring's arm on the chair. "Why are you?"

"I can't…" Spring glanced away. "I can't tell you."

"Is it Cliff?"

Spring's breathing pinched.

"Was the team doping? You found out, and he—"

"It's not Cliff."

"How can you be sure?"

"Because the texts tell me to be quiet even when he's the only one I'm talking to!" She glanced around, hoping her volume hadn't called attention to them. A PT glanced their way, but went back to working.

"Did they come *while* you were talking to him?"

Spring swallowed. "No."

"Then it could be Cliff. A clever criminal would do something like that to make sure you never suspected him."

"How would you know?"

Victoria didn't even blink at Spring's snappish tone. "It's simply common sense."

Great. Victoria was going to take control of another part of Spring's life and probably get killed in the process.

Over Spring's dead body. "You know what else is common sense? A PT taking a patient back to her room when she wants to go."

"Stop it, Spring. This is serious. You need help to get out of this mess."

"That I've created, right? You sound just like Dad."

"That's not what—"

"I've had it." Spring let her voice grow louder purposefully this time. "Give me my phone and take me back to my room now or, I kid you not, I will scream." If more humiliation was what it took to keep Victoria safe in spite of herself, Spring would do it.

"Hey, ladies." Angie's calm tone washed over their tension like a wave dousing a fire. "I can take you back to your room, Spring." Her professional smile faltered as she glanced at Victoria on her way to the wheelchair.

Victoria placed the phone on Spring's lap, her cheeks flushed red.

Spring avoided her sister's gaze and tried to breathe normally as the friendlier PT silently wheeled her to her room.

Spring gripped the phone in a shaking hand. She stared at the blackened screen that temporarily hid the threats to her family—the only thing she had left that she cared about. She wouldn't tell anyone even the smallest detail anymore. She couldn't risk it.

She may not be able to live up to the Weston name or make her family proud, but she could do this one thing. She could do her best to protect them and hope they didn't end up hating her for the burden she would be the rest of her life.

CHAPTER
TWENTY

October 10. 11:01 a.m.

"YOU WANTED TO TALK TO ME?" Megan Leone's voice shook on the other end of the phone.

Torin paused to choose his words carefully, glad he sat in his office where she wouldn't hear background noises that might spook her. "Yes, I do. Thank you for calling back so soon."

She sniffed. Had she been crying? "I'll do anything I can. I feel so terrible about..." Emotion clogged her voice. "I can't sleep, I..." She drifted into silence.

"I understand. Would you rather talk about this in person?"

"No." Panic squeezed the word.

"Okay. No problem. Whatever makes you comfortable."

A heavy sigh blew across the line. "Can you just ask me what you want to know? I've gotta go."

He was losing her. He'd have to pick up the pace, but still keep his tone calm and unhurried. "Sure. I wondered what you can tell me about Spring Weston. Were you good friends with her?"

"Yeah." A muffled sound. "I always liked Spring a lot. She was...different than the other girls."

"How so?"

"She wasn't in it for herself. She cared about other people, you know?" She sniffed. "Don't see that often in cycling."

"Do you think some on the team might have resented her for being different?"

"I...I don't think so. I mean, she was nice." Megan's tone hardened slightly. Defensiveness? "Why should anyone not like her for that?"

"So no one would hold a grudge against her?"

A long silence.

Torin waited.

"Um...I didn't say that exactly."

Now they were getting somewhere. "Okay, let me ask you this. What would you say if I told you that Spring's collision wasn't an accident?"

No sharp intake of breath, no startled sound.

"Her brother and sister told me something like that when they talked to me yesterday."

Torin grimaced. Exactly what he didn't like about citizens doing their own investigating. They'd spoiled the reaction. But they meant well. And he'd do the same thing in their shoes.

He took another approach. "They told me they had a conversation with you. Spring's sister said that she thought you really cared about what happened to Spring. That you were the only cyclist on the team who did."

No reaction.

"Do you think that's true?"

"I care." Her voice tightened. "I care a lot. It shouldn't have happened."

"What shouldn't have happened, Miss Leone?"

"She shouldn't be...paralyzed."

"If you truly care about Spring, then the kindest thing you

can do for her right now is to answer my next question honestly."

Another sniff. "Okay."

"Do you know who would've wanted to kill Spring?"

Only Megan's light breathing drifted across the line.

Torin almost held his own breath as he waited.

"Maybe." The whispered word seeped into his ear, flooding his insides with anticipation.

This could be it. If he didn't blow it. "Will you tell me who you think would hurt her?"

"Cliff. Or Lana. I'm not sure."

Surprise, surprise. Torin leaned his elbows on the edge of his desk. "What makes you think they would hurt her?"

"I heard them talking…" Her voice trembled again. "He was really mad."

"Who was Cliff mad at?"

"Spring." She sniffed, followed by a swiping sound. She could be crying.

He'd better get through this fast before she became too emotional and shut down. "Why was he mad at her? Did he say?"

"The doping."

"What about doping?"

"Spring saw me taking pills." A sob wrenched her voice.

"Megan, it's okay."

"No, it's not! She's paralyzed because of me."

"You're doing the right thing now. You just need to hang on and get through the rest of this story to help Spring. Can you do that?"

Her sobbing and sniffing calmed.

"I just need you to tell me, was the whole team taking dope?"

She drew in a shaky breath. "Most of us."

"And Spring learned that from you?"

"Uh-huh."

"What day was that?"

A pause.

"August twenty-seventh."

The day before the collision. "And what day did you hear Cliff talking to Lana about Spring?"

"August twenty-eighth." Megan's grave tone and precise memory indicated the significance of those dates wasn't lost on her.

"One more question, and then I'll let you go. Did you hear Cliff or Lana say that they were going to hurt or kill Spring?"

"Cliff said they'd have to keep her quiet. No matter what it took."

CHAPTER
TWENTY-ONE

October 10. 1:22 p.m.

"ARE you sure you don't want to sit down?" Robert's dark eyebrows pulled together as he peered at Victoria. "There's a bench by the window."

She gave him an exasperated glance. "I don't need to sit down, Robert. We need to do something about this situation. I'm deeply concerned about her."

"I agree. I just don't remember when I've seen you look so pale."

She crossed her arms over her open coat and stared blankly toward Treese where she worked with a client at the far end of the small fitness center. "Those texts. They were so hateful, so threatening."

Robert's gaze darkened. At least he cared, too. "Did the caller ID say who sent them?"

Victoria dipped her chin. "No. Unkown number. I wish I knew who would send her such dire threats."

"I have a pretty good idea."

"Cliffton Benecke. You spoke with Sergeant Cotter about him?"

"Not him specifically. More about Megan." He cast a glance toward Treese.

She held up five fingers to signal the minutes remaining. Never mind that she was the one who'd told them to meet at her personal training center at 1:15.

Victoria let out a sigh. "Apparently she uses the same sense of time with her clients as she does for everything else."

"Welcome to Treese's world." Humor glinted in Robert's eyes.

"What did the sergeant say about your theory?"

"I think he was going to look into it, though he also didn't seem too excited about us sleuthing on our own." Robert rested his hands on the waistband of his khaki shorts. "Can't blame him. I feel the same way about amateur psychiatrists."

"And PTs."

A hint of a smile shaped his lips. "At any rate, we'll try to stay out of his way. But if Spring is getting death threats, I'm not going to sit back and wait for a stranger to find the person behind them."

"What about Lana Curtis?"

"Sure, it could be her instead. Or along with Cliff. Could really be anyone on the team."

Victoria nodded. "Do you intend to meet with Megan again?"

"I'm guessing a chat with the police will rattle her into spilling what she knows. I hope the sergeant keeps us in the loop if she talks to him."

"If who talks to who?" Treese bounced to Robert's side, her client packing up his duffel bag near the weightlifting apparatus.

"Whom." Victoria cocked an eyebrow at her tardy sister. "And you would know if you had bothered to be on time. At your own fitness center."

Treese lifted her hands with a shrug and a smile. "My place, my rules."

"Some of us have schedules to keep." Victoria checked her watch. "I have to leave in a few minutes to see a patient."

"Okay, but what did I miss?"

"We were right." Robert somehow spoke to Treese without a hint of irritation. "Spring is getting threats in text messages."

Treese sucked in a breath and turned her gaze on Victoria. "You got her phone?"

"See ya, Treese!" The client Victoria had forgotten was still there waved as he pushed open the front door.

"Bye, Lincoln! See you next week!"

Victoria closed her eyes against Treese's shout and waited until the door closed behind the client. "I looked at her text messages, if that's what you mean. I didn't keep the phone."

"And she was getting threats?"

"Yes. Someone threatening to hurt her, to teach her a lesson if she didn't keep quiet."

"There's more you aren't telling us, isn't there?" Robert watched her with his astute gaze.

Victoria took a breath. "The most recent texts I saw threatened someone else." She pursed her lips together.

"Who?"

She bit back the urge to correct her sister's grammar again. "Me."

"You're kidding." Robert's brow furrowed.

"I believe that's why Spring still wouldn't admit anything concrete when I confronted her."

"You confronted her?" Treese's mouth widened. "I thought we weren't supposed to do that."

Ignoring her sister, Victoria continued. "She did, however, acknowledge by inference that she was receiving threats. She spoke of her theory that she thought they couldn't have been sent by her coach because of the timing."

Robert nodded. "So she thought of him, too."

"Shouldn't we call the police or something?" Treese swung her gaze between them.

"Victoria already did that."

She nodded. "I called Sergeant Cotter, but he had already suspected she was receiving threats."

"Yeah, he told us she denied it, which is just crazy."

"Don't judge, Treese." Robert's eyes darkened with rare admonishment. "We don't know Spring's reasons."

"But the sergeant's going to help her now, right?"

Victoria shook her head. "He can't. Unless she reports the threats, he can't do anything about them. He said even my testimony about the threat to myself would be difficult grounds on which to obtain a warrant."

Treese blew out a frustrated breath. "Fine, but we have to do something. Our sister's in danger."

"We are going to do something." Robert's bearded jawline tightened. "The police might not be able to help her when she doesn't want it, but we can. We'll set up a rotation so one of us is with her all the time."

"I don't think anyone would try something during the daytime hours." Victoria slid her hand into the pocket of her coat and fingered her car keys. "There are so many people at the center. Staff and unexpected visitors stop by at unpredictable moments."

"Okay, then we make sure we're there at night."

"Right." Treese glanced at Robert. "And we should also tell Sergeant Cotter what we're doing."

Victoria pulled the slipping strap of her purse higher onto her shoulder. "Why would we do that?"

"If he likes Spring as much as you said, he'll want to know we're doing our best to protect her."

"Really won you over, didn't he?" Robert grinned down at Treese, then swung his gaze to include Victoria. "You should've seen her flirting with him."

"I was not flirting!" Treese's overdone expression of shock didn't hide the pink color that touched her cheeks.

"Do you even know how to talk to a guy without flirting?"

"Sure. I talk to you like this." She lifted a fist and plunged it into Robert's upper arm.

"Children." Victoria's snap called them to attention as effectively as when they were in her care. "We need a plan."

Robert sobered. "Right. I'll stay with Spring tonight."

"Good." Victoria pressed her lips together. "She might talk to you. I'm quite certain she still hasn't shared everything she knows, with us or Sergeant Cotter. But she won't open up to me."

"I'll see what I can do."

"I can visit Sergeant Cotter tomorrow to see if he got Megan to talk." Treese's mouth twitched with a barely restrained smile.

Victoria arched an eyebrow. "I'll talk to him when he comes to the rehab center."

Treese's chin tilted with familiar defiance. "How do you know he'll come?"

"He's visited every day since he's been on the case."

"Hmm. I guess he does care about a certain patient there."

Victoria turned away from the twinkle in Treese's eyes to look at Robert. "Do you want me to discuss your overnight stay with the center?"

"I'll manage it. I can pull out my doctor creds if I need to."

"Very well." Victoria adjusted her purse strap again. "I'll talk to you both later." She turned to go, but a touch on her arm stopped her.

She turned to see her own concern reflected in Robert's eyes. "Don't worry. We won't let anything happen to her or you."

She pressed her lips together to prevent the discouraging remark that wanted to escape. This time, helping may be out of Robert's reach.

But she knew the One who could protect them all. She whispered prayers to Him all the way to her next patient.

CHAPTER
TWENTY-TWO

October 10. 2:57 p.m.

A RAP on his office door made Torin look up.

Derrick leaned in. "Gotta go, partner." The glint in his eye told Torin he was onto something.

Torin squelched the quiver in his chest. *Don't start hoping.* "What's up?"

"Found the girlfriend." Derrick grinned. "She'll talk now."

Torin glanced at his computer screen, oddly reluctant to log out of the evidence file for Spring's case. The last hours of poring over it had rendered none of the evidence he'd hope to find that would prove or even indicate Cliff was behind the crash. There had to be something he was overlooking. He couldn't give up.

"Hey, did you hear what I said?" A frown replaced Derrick's smile. "I thought you wanted to be there for this."

"I do." Torin shoved out his desk chair, then leaned over the keyboard to log out of the software program. "Just processing."

"Sure. It's a lot to take in. A possible lead after so long."

Torin felt Derrick's eyes on him while he grabbed his sport

coat from the back of the chair. He fell in step next to the suspicious detective, not trying to explain. He didn't understand his reaction himself. What was wrong with him? He finally had what he'd been hoping for these three years—the possibility of information that might finally lead to the shooter. And he was letting himself get distracted by a woman he barely knew.

Not by her, really, but by her case. Probably because he was on the brink of solving it. He knew who'd hit her now. He just had to find the evidence that would prove it.

Dare he hope for the same with the shooting?

The chances of an actual lead seemed almost nonexistent a half hour later as he and Derrick stood in the dimly lit back room of a nail salon, interviewing Boone's girlfriend. Or trying.

Clavia Cameron seemed as interested in being helpful as breaking one of her red, two-inch fingernails.

Derrick's placid expression hadn't faltered yet. "Do you remember Wiley saying anything about the shooting?"

She shrugged one shoulder, sliding it farther out of the drop-shouldered dress she wore. "Nah." She bounced one of her crossed legs as she sat on the stool. "No, wait, I think he did one time. Can't remember what he said. Just he'd survived 'cause he so brave or whatever. He always talkin' about how big and tough he was."

Torin watched her from his standing position near the door that stayed open to the noisy salon. Was she really this ambivalent about the boyfriend and the secret that might've gotten him killed? Maybe it was an act she put on for cops.

"Did he tell you he had set up a meeting with us last night?" Derrick leaned against the counter behind him, apparently trying for a casual approach.

"Uh-huh."

"He tell you what it was about?"

"Just he was gonna have cops over." She looked at her nails, then glanced up at Derrick. "I thought he was crazy."

Her gaze drifted to Torin. "Said he owed one of you. It's you, right?"

Derrick glanced Torin's way, then back to Miss Cameron. "Why would you guess that, ma'am?"

"Seen him on TV. The cop that saved Wiley's grandbaby." She looked down at her nails. "That was nice."

She swung her head up with a sigh. "I guess I can tell you about his box."

Derrick pushed off the counter. "Box?"

"Wiley kept some junk in a shoebox. Made me swear not to look at it unless something happened to him. I was like, 'Whatever, Wiley.'" She rolled her eyes and swept her hand in front of her face. "He liked to be a real drama queen sometimes."

Torin's heart rate sped up. Odd thing to say unless he'd had reason to think something would happen to him.

Derrick kept his gaze on the subject. "And did you look at it after last night?"

"For real? I looked at it like a year ago when he told me about it. Just a bunch of weird junk." She slid off the stool, smoothing her dress and pushing her straightened black hair over her shoulder as she turned to the counter a couple feet away from where Derrick had leaned. "I brought it with me when you called this morning." She reached behind the counter and lifted what looked like a wooden ammo box. "Wasn't sure I should give it to the cops, but…"

She swiveled and took a step toward Torin, stretching out the box in her hand. "Wiley wanted to give you something. Maybe this was it."

He walked over and took the box, holding back the urge to immediately flip open the lid. Instead, he met her dark eyes. "Thank you."

She looked at him for a moment, then spun away—a real trick in a dress that tight. "You cops can keep it. I need to get to work."

"Thank you for your time." The flash of anticipation in

Derrick's gaze was impossible to miss as he passed Torin on his way to the doorway. "Let's go, partner."

The walk to Derrick's unmarked car felt like an eternity, the box growing heavier with every step.

His mouth was dry, and his hands dampened the box with sweat by the time they sat inside the vehicle, Torin in the passenger seat and Derrick behind the wheel. He pushed the box onto Derrick's lap. "You open it."

He lifted his eyebrows. "You sure?"

Torin nodded, staring out the windshield at the pedestrians jaywalking across the street. He couldn't risk losing control. Anything could be in that box. Pictures, names, something that would send him into a spiral he couldn't contain.

"Hand me the gloves."

Of course. Torin opened the glove compartment where Derrick always kept his latex gloves. He grabbed an extra pair for himself and struggled to pull them onto his moist hands. Gave him something to focus on.

"Here goes." Derrick slowly raised the lid off the box.

Torin gripped the armrest of the door.

"Looks like several notes, scribbled on scraps of paper."

Torin heard rustling paper but didn't look. His breath rose in his chest. Memories pressured his mind like water against a dam. Had to hold them back. He gritted his teeth.

"The one on top says, 'one thousand dollars,' then 'ask for more?' Here." Derrick extended the small square of paper, forcing Torin to look.

He grabbed the note before Derrick wondered what was wrong with him. Just a bit of paper shouldn't send him over the edge. He looked at the words scrawled in faded pencil, likely by Boone's hand. *$1,000. Ask for more?*

"A payoff?"

Derrick handed Torin another paper without answering.

Not from neighborhood. Tattoo 2 swords, blue shield.

Torin's pulse rapid-fired. A description of the shooter?

Boone had denied seeing or knowing anything at the time. Could he have been paid to keep quiet? Paid by whom?

"There's one more thing." Derrick looked at Torin. "A picture with a note on the back."

A surge of fear blasted through his chest. What if he couldn't handle seeing it? But he had to know. He took the four by six-inch photo, backside up, from Derrick's outstretched hand.

Two words were written in the same handwriting as the other notes. *He's back.*

Torin's breath halted as he turned the photo over.

A white van.

8:55 p.m.

Spring stared at the phone by her side, her fingers resting on the darkened screen. Why hadn't she received any more texts?

She should be relieved, but the silence scared her almost more than another threat. Did the texter know Victoria had seen the messages? Would he harm her now? Maybe that was why he wasn't texting Spring.

A gasp sprang from her mouth. She covered her lips with her hand. What had she done?

Her gaze searched through the darkness to find the Bible that Victoria had once again left next to Spring's leg on the bed.

Would God keep her sister safer than He had Spring?

Her fingers reached for the Bible by her calf before she thought she'd decided to do so. She stretched her arm as far as it would go, but was well short. Pushing with her other arm against the pillow that propped her up, she strained to reach the Bible.

She let go with a whoosh of breath. No use.

Another cruel joke, God?

The sound of slow footsteps in the hallway reached her ears.

She tensed. Silly. Probably just one of the nurses.

The steps stopped at her door. Didn't they?

She forgot to breathe as the door swung open.

A dark silhouette. The light behind prevented her from seeing any features.

Looked like a man wearing a long coat.

Her heart pounded against her ribs. "Dad?"

The man just stood there, an arm bent as if he had a hand in the pocket of his coat.

Her breathing stopped.

Voices carried from the hallway. Women, probably nurses talking.

The figure spun away and disappeared, leaving the door open.

Quicker footsteps approached.

Another shadowed outline swung into the room. "Hey, Spring Spring."

Her breath returned in a wave of relief. Only one person called her that. "Robert." She didn't know whether to laugh or cry. "What are you doing here?"

He flicked on the light switch by the door.

She squinted.

"Sorry. Too bright?"

She waved away his concern. "I'm fine." Except for her erratic pulse. Her eyes opened farther so she could see Robert walk in carrying...a pillow?

"Slumber party." He held up the red throw pillow that looked like a handstitched design with *World's Greatest Shrink* emblazoned in yellow across the front. He tossed the pillow onto the foot of her bed as she gaped at him.

"Just a second." He jogged from the room before she could find her voice.

The silence let her fear rush back. Was the dark figure still out there? Had he only left because Robert showed up? If her brother hadn't come, what would…?

Her breaths came in shallow spurts as fear squeezed her throat. Had that been the texter?

Robert appeared again, lugging a small green armchair in front of his body. "Not exactly the luxury recliner I was hoping for, but it'll have to do."

She blinked at him. "Do for what?"

"Our slumber party." A grin cracked his beard.

"You're going to sleep here?"

He set down the chair and flopped into it. "Unless we stay up all night talking." His dark eyes twinkled.

"But…" She struggled to find the words around her surprise. "You can't do that."

"Sure, I can."

She shook her head. "They wouldn't allow it."

He shrugged. "I'm a doctor. I'll write you a prescription." He glanced around the room. "So, got any video games?"

A smile tugged at her lips in spite of herself. "You're incorrigible."

"Ooh, big word." His grin broadened. "You sound like Victoria."

"Great." The sarcastic response dropped out before she thought. What if Victoria was in danger, and she was sitting there criticizing her? Spring glanced away, folding her arms over the blanket that crossed her waist. "Have you heard from her?"

"Victoria? Sure."

She turned her head to look at him. "I mean this evening."

His dark brows knitted together. "I talked to her on the phone twenty minutes ago. Why?"

"Did she seem okay?"

Robert leaned forward, propping his elbows on his knees and bringing his hands up under his chin. "What's wrong, Spring?"

She looked at the children's pictures on the wall. "Nothing."

Silence filled the space between them.

His voice was quieter, calm and steady when he spoke again. "You've always been able to talk to me. Remember?"

She brought her gaze to his face, to the understanding in his eyes and the hint of a compassionate smile.

"I'm told I'm a good listener."

The urge to tell him seemed to force words up her throat. She couldn't keep carrying this burden on her own. But she had to if she wanted to keep Victoria safe.

Though what if the texter knew Victoria had read his messages and was already going to hurt her?

She had to tell someone. And Robert was the most trustworthy and discreet person she could ask for.

She slid her tongue over her lips. "I've been getting... messages." She glanced at him for a reaction.

He just watched her with the same unflappable patience in his eyes, his hands lowered to hang relaxed between his knees. He looked as if he'd give her all night if it took her that long to speak.

She took a breath. "Texts. They're threats. Like..." she rubbed her thumb along the semi-soft blanket where it stretched over her thigh, "threatening to hurt me if I talk." She looked at him again.

His eyebrows lifted, his mouth in a concerned line. "If you talk about what?"

"I don't know." She blew out a shaky sigh. "I mean, I think I do, but none of it really makes sense. The texter doesn't want me to say anything about the crash, and he gets really mad when I do."

"What do you mean by 'he gets mad'?" Robert's even tone soothed the raw edges of her nerves. "Has he hurt you?"

She pinched the blanket between her fingers, staring at the fold. "Sort of."

Robert's hand covered hers.

She looked up to see him sit down on the edge of the bed next to her legs, resting his hand gently over hers.

He met her gaze without judgment, but his dark eyes smoldered. "I'm sorry, Spring."

Tears shot to her eyes, blurring her vision. She bit her lip, trying to hold them back. She dropped her gaze.

"Can you identify him?"

"Oh, no. He didn't hurt me like that." Embarrassment flushed her cheeks. "Not in person. I think he put something in my food to give me…cramps." Saying it sounded so pathetic.

"I'm glad you told me. You don't have to go through this anymore. We're going to protect you."

She looked up. "We?"

"Victoria, Treese, me."

Spring slid her hand out from under his. "You talked to Victoria. Did she tell you about the texts?"

"Yes."

"You could've told me."

He didn't look away. "I wanted you to tell me."

"Okay. Fine. So I admitted it. Now what?" Her pulse drummed a beat of anger and nerves. "We still don't know who the texter is or what he'll do. He probably heard me tell you now, and he'll kill me. Is that what you wanted?" That was unfair and she knew it, but so was having her family manipulate her and plot things behind her back.

"The texter hears what you say?"

She folded her arms over her chest again. "I told you he gets mad when I don't obey his instructions." Her gaze collided with the concern in Robert's eyes.

He was there for her, because he cared.

She softened her tone. "He seems to be able to hear what I tell people because he'll text as soon as I say something he doesn't like."

Robert let out a low whistle as he looked around the room.

"I've already looked for obvious cameras or microphones. But if there are any, they must be small."

He nodded and stood, his head turning as he examined the space.

She looked down at the silent phone next to her limp body. Why hadn't it buzzed? She tapped the screen. No new text messages.

She should have gotten one after telling Robert about the threats. "He knows about Victoria."

Robert paused in the middle of the room where he was surveying and looked at her.

"When I wouldn't do what he wanted anymore, he said he'd hurt her. But I suppose you know that, too."

"She mentioned it."

"Do you think he's following her now?" The sickening possibility stuck in her throat. "That he'll hurt her?" She ran her finger across the smooth screen of her phone. "She talked to me about the texts in the gym, but maybe he knows what I say there, too. If he knows she saw the messages, I'm afraid he'll..." Rising panic choked the words.

"Hang on, Spring Spring." Robert walked back to the bed. "Breathe for me, okay? Big, deep breaths."

She managed only a small gulp of air, then more with Robert's coaching until she could breathe deeply and evenly, the tension easing from her body.

"I won't let anything happen to Victoria or you." He sat on her bed again, holding her hand between his. "Has the texter sent you any more messages threatening her?"

"No. I haven't gotten any at all."

He watched her. "And that's unusual?"

"Very. I get several every day. More if I have visitors. But I didn't get any when you came." She lowered her voice to nearly a whisper. "Or when I told you..."

He nodded.

"What do you think it means?"

"I'm not sure."

"Do you think he's going after Victoria instead?"

"I can call her again to make sure she's okay, but it's possible the texter was bluffing. And you just called his bluff." A smile curved Robert's mouth.

Hope fluttered in her stomach. Was that possible? Could it be she had imprisoned herself by believing the texter was more dangerous than he was?

"Have you considered who the texter might be?"

She met his gaze. "Victoria thinks it's Cliff."

He didn't look surprised.

"Is that what you think?"

"Why don't you tell me what you think is true?"

She glanced away with a sigh. "I thought about it being Cliff. Or Lana. She really dislikes me now." Maybe even hated her. But Spring still couldn't believe Lana would want to kill her any more than Cliff would. She moistened her lips and brought her gaze back to her brother's. "I just can't believe it's them. Cliff wouldn't do something like that."

She lifted her shoulders. "Victoria said he'd text me threats about his own visit here if he was a clever criminal. But he's not clever like that. He might be behind…" She looked away as her cheeks flushed. Would Robert think she was involved?

"Doping on the team?"

Her gaze jumped to his face.

He gently squeezed her hand. "I know you weren't part of that. You were going to report them, weren't you?"

Her mouth felt like sandpaper. "Yes. But I know what you're thinking." She shook her head. "Cliff wouldn't kill me because of that."

"Okay." Robert's calm tone slipped like a cooling balm over her agitated nerves. "Would Lana?"

The hatred in Lana's eyes as she'd leaned over Spring's chair flashed in her memory. "I don't think so."

Robert's dark gaze reflected understanding, but she didn't miss the presence of doubt behind that compassionate front. He didn't believe her.

She couldn't blame him when she wasn't even sure she believed herself. What if she was wrong and Cliff or Lana really hated her enough to kill her? No, she just couldn't think that. They had been her friends.

"Whoever the texter is, I think it would be wise to tell the police about the threats."

The memory of the pain that twisted her insides that night sent a pulse of fear through her veins. She couldn't go through that again. Or the worse he'd threatened to do. "The texter especially didn't want me to tell the police anything."

"Hey." Robert moved her hand between his, prompting her to look at him again. "Don't give in to the fear. The person who's sending those messages can only have power over you if you give it to him."

She moistened her dry lips and nodded. Sounded good, but was Robert right? What if the texter was capable of everything he threatened?

"Sergeant Cotter seems smart and trustworthy. I'm sure he'd know how to handle this situation without putting you or Victoria at risk."

Sergeant Cotter. The memory of those intense green eyes sparked a different kind of flitting in her belly.

"Good thing Treese isn't here."

She heard the grin in his voice before she saw it.

"You're blushing."

"I am not." An actual smile lifted her mouth.

He released her hand as he stood, chuckling. "No comment." He looked down at her. "So you'll talk to Sergeant Cotter about the text messages tomorrow?"

What would the texter—

No. She wouldn't give him that power over her anymore. She wouldn't be a prisoner in this rehab center. She'd seek out the help the texter tried to keep her from getting. The protection.

She nodded.

"Good. I'm going to check this room for bugs, though I

admit that is definitely not my area of expertise." He tossed her another grin. "While I do that, I want you to tell me everything you remember about the night of the accident and anything else you haven't told me about the texter. Will you do that?"

She took a deep breath. "Yes." The flicker of hope burned hotter, warming her from within. Seemed too much to believe, but maybe, just maybe, she wouldn't have to be afraid anymore. Maybe she could be free.

CHAPTER
TWENTY-THREE

October 11. 7:25 a.m.

HE COULDN'T BELIEVE he was about to do this. Torin stood a few feet behind Derrick as the detective pulled up the digital case file of the shooting on his computer. Sitting in his desk chair facing the screen, Derrick had his back to Torin. Perfectly positioned to miss any signs of the panic sucking the air from Torin's lungs.

That's what it was. Panic. The tough cop was scared to death. Just to look at a case file.

He shouldn't risk seeing it. He might lose control, and the flashes of memory would take over as they'd done before. Derrick would notice, and Torin wouldn't be able to hide his secret any longer. Derrick would probably feel he had to tell the lieutenant.

But Torin had to know. If there was a possibility of finding the shooter, he had to try. He couldn't let Ivy down again. That was the only reason he'd agreed to go over the evidence with Derrick.

"There's nothing about a white van in the witness statements." Derrick shook his head as he stared at the screen

Torin was trying not to see. "No one claims to have seen a getaway vehicle at all. You said you heard it, and it sounded like a diesel."

Had he? In his memory he could only hear her—

No. He had to maintain control. He clenched his jaw. Forced his mind to work like a police officer's should. If Boone had kept quiet because of a payoff, it was possible he had seen a getaway vehicle. He'd been the one best positioned to do so —the floor-to-ceiling window next to the counter he had hidden behind would have given him a clear view when the shooter drove away.

"Some physical evidence was taken of the possible getaway vehicle." Derrick leaned into the screen. "I'll look that up. See if it matches with a van."

A white van.

Torin stared at the photo he held between his fingers. Boone's picture of the possible getaway van was dated fourteen months ago, almost two years after the shooting.

Any similarity to Spring's case had to be a coincidence. There were thousands of white vans in the Chicago area. And the likelihood that the perp would still be driving the same van in the next neighborhood over was slim to none. Any smart thief would've ditched the getaway vehicle immediately, not kept it for three years and then used it to mow down a cyclist.

Then again, every cop knew how incredibly stupid some criminals could be.

"Here we go." Derrick glanced over his shoulder. "Tire prints from the likely getaway vehicle, thanks to an overeager departure."

Torin braced himself. He could handle looking at tire prints without cracking up. He hoped.

He stepped closer and faced the image on the computer. The tread pattern meant as little to him now as it had three years ago. No prints to compare from Spring's collision, thanks to the driver not even trying to stop.

"Analysis says the tire type and size could be used with a van."

Torin backed away with a sigh. "Or about a thousand other vehicles."

Derrick grimaced as he swiveled his chair to face Torin instead of the computer. "Okay. But it could be a van. That van." He directed his gaze at Boone's photo that Torin still held. "I did some digging last night. The Donovan Mackeral we got as the owner when we ran the van's plates does have a drug history."

"User?"

"No. Arrested for dealing a few times, but the charges never stuck. Davis over in narcotics told me Mackeral associated with some low-level dealers and had a lot of users going in and out of his liquor store at odd hours."

"So you think one of his buyers could've used the van to hold up the gas station?"

Derrick folded his arms across his chest. "We think the perp was a user from his symptoms you described, so it would fit. But what doesn't fit is—"

"Why keep the van?"

"Exactly."

Torin stepped to the desk and dropped the photo onto a closed file folder. "So we talk to Mackeral."

"Afraid not."

Torin glanced at Derrick.

"He's dead. Shot at his store six weeks ago."

"You're kidding."

"Wish I was." Derrick spun to the desk and brushed the photo aside to open the folder beneath. "I knew the guy's name was familiar. Monty's been investigating the case, but you know how it is. Drug killing in that neighborhood." He shook his head. "Nobody will talk to a homicide detective."

"Yeah. Story of my life lately. Where'd the shooting happen?"

"Let's see." Derrick flipped the first page of the file over to see the next. "Donovan's Liquor on Jacksonville Lane."

Torin's heartbeat halted. "What'd you say?"

"Jacksonville L—"

"What date?"

"What?"

"The date he was shot."

Derrick looked at the file. "August twenty-eighth, between eight and eleven p.m."

"Pull up Spring Weston's file."

"What?"

Torin glanced down at Derrick, who watched him with his eyebrows lifted. "The collision I'm investigating. Weston, Spring."

"Okay." Derrick's tone said he wasn't following, but he did as Torin asked.

"There." Torin pointed to the file that held the initial report for Spring's case.

Derrick clicked it open. "Line Drive. That's only a street over from Jacksonville."

"They intersect. Look." Torin pointed to the spot in the report where his eyes caught up with his racing mind. "Spring's route took her on Jacksonville, then to Line Drive where she was hit."

"The same night." Derrick stared at the screen.

"The same night. By a white van, we think."

Derrick jerked to face Torin. "You didn't mention that before."

"I didn't think it could be the same one. What are the chances?"

Derrick nodded. "And what are the chances she'd be in the same neighborhood and get run over by our white van, unless she was connected somehow?"

"Spring?"

Derrick met Torin's surprise with a cop's unreadable gaze.

"No, there's no way she's tied to a drug dealer or a

killing." Her cycling team might be doping, but he didn't believe she was part of it. And upper middle-class performance drug athletes didn't run with the same crowd as street crime perps using the hard stuff.

"You sound awfully sure." Suspicion glinted in Derrick's eyes.

"I am." Though doubt niggled somewhere in the back of his mind under his ex-partner's stare. She'd lied to him repeatedly. Someone was threatening her, tried to kill her, and she wouldn't reach out for help. Could he really be sure she wasn't involved in something criminal?

"Well, either way," a smile crept onto Derrick's face, "this might be it, partner. We've got a solid lead on the getaway van."

Torin's heart pounded. Could the two cases really be connected? "Best not get our hopes up. There isn't much evidence in the Weston case either. And if by a long shot the van is the same, the driver probably isn't."

"Maybe. But if you find the driver who hit her, you might get a fresher trail to the shooter. Either way it's a lead. I'm ready to run with it."

"I'm afraid any running you do will have to be on your own." Lieutenant Airaldi's booming voice preceded him to Derrick's desk. His long stride covered the remaining distance to Torin and Derrick as he ignored the alarmed stares of the other detectives he passed along the way.

Airaldi took a wide stance, folding his arms across his thick chest. "You're off this case, Cotter. In fact, you were never supposed to be on it."

Torin's chest tightened. "The Weston case?"

The lieutenant leaned in toward Torin. "Your *wife's* case."

The hope he shouldn't have indulged squeezed the oxygen from Torin's lungs. "Sir, I—"

"He's not really on it in an official capacity." Derrick got to his feet and looked at Airaldi across the desk.

"I see. Then what was he *unofficially* doing with you the night an alleged witness was killed?"

"The witness refused to talk to anyone but Sergeant Cotter, sir." Derrick met the lieutenant's stern gaze.

"I see." Airaldi transferred his attention to Torin. "I understand your desire to be involved in this investigation, Cotter. If I were in your place, I'd want the same." The lieutenant relaxed his broad shoulders. "But the fact that you, an officer with such personal involvement, was present at the scene of the possible homicide of a witness and have been involved in the gathering of evidence puts this department in a tenuous position."

Torin's heart knocked against his rib cage as he waited, hoping for a *but*. An exception the lieutenant would make for him.

"You're hereby ordered to cease participating in the investigation of Ivy Cotter's shooting in any and all capacities."

The breath left Torin's lungs as if the lieutenant had socked him. Not now. Not when there was finally a chance—a hope.

"I'm sorry, Cotter." He turned to leave.

"Lieutenant," Derrick stepped around the desk, "you know Torin."

Airaldi faced the detective.

"You know he isn't going to do anything to interfere, anything dishonest. He wants the truth more than anyone with this case. I'll keep a close watch on him."

Torin held his breath as Airaldi shifted his gaze between them. "I'm afraid it's not my call. The order came from the deputy chief."

"The deputy chief?" Derrick's tone broadcast his surprise.

Torin stepped closer to the desk that separated them from Airaldi. "The deputy chief's ordering me to back off?"

"Apparently, there was a complaint."

"A complaint? But—"

Airaldi held up a hand to stop Derrick's argument. "That's all I'll give you. I'm sorry, Cotter, but you have the order. I expect you to follow it." He didn't wait for acknowledgement before he strode from the room.

Derrick angled to face Torin. "Who would want you off this case?"

"Nobody I know with that much clout." Boone's girlfriend certainly wouldn't have such connections.

Spring Weston's father had talked to the superintendent. But why would he want Torin off the shooting case when he'd purposefully pulled strings to get Torin to investigate his daughter's collision? Wouldn't be a smart move if he were connected to the three-year-old shooting. He'd want to hide the connection between the cases, not draw Torin's attention to it through Spring's crash.

No, even in a short meeting with Henry Weston, Torin knew the man was smart. Too intelligent to make a mistake like that. Someone else must want Torin off the shooting investigation.

"I'm thinking the fish we're trying to catch might be bigger than we thought. With those kind of connections."

Torin nodded at Derrick. There must be someone tied to the shooting who did have lofty contacts. But why would a person like that be involved in an ordinary street crime?

"Were you going to tell the lieutenant that the Weston investigation might connect with Ivy's shooting?"

Torin met his friend's gaze.

"Didn't think so." A slight smile pulled up the corners of Derrick's lips. "I'll keep it to myself as long as I can."

"Thanks." No way was Torin going to risk the lieutenant handing Spring's case back to Jannick, claiming conflict of interest.

"Maybe you can still find what we're looking for by finishing up her case."

"That's the idea." But he had to admit that didn't explain the way his gut twisted at the thought of being taken off Spring's case.

"You going to see her today?"

"Yeah. I'll head over at a more reasonable time." Torin checked his watch, then looked up to see the goofy grin on Derrick's face. "What?"

The detective shook his head, still wearing the same expression. "Nothing."

"I need to talk to her about the white van and the liquor store. Agreed?"

"Oh, sure. Of course. As soon as possible."

Torin couldn't believe a smile fought to reach his face as his friend watched him with twinkling eyes. He held it in check. "Not what you think, Derrick. I'm done with that kind of thing. End of story."

"Maybe it shouldn't be."

Torin blew out a sigh, the urge to smile quickly buried under the pain and guilt filling his heart. "Just solve the case. That's all I need."

He hoped that was true.

CHAPTER
TWENTY-FOUR

October 11. 9:00 a.m.

"VICTORIA!" Spring surprised herself with the bright exclamation when her sister walked into the room. She was okay. Despite making Robert call Victoria twice overnight, Spring couldn't relax until she saw her.

Victoria looked unharmed, even cheerful. She smiled as she approached the bed. "Good morning."

"Quite a welcome she gets." Angie grinned as she went around the bed for the wheelchair as usual. "What about me?"

"I'm always happy to see you, Angie." Not exactly true, but the PT still widened her smile.

"Thank you very much." Angie unfolded the wheelchair and placed the cushion on the seat. "I heard you had an overnight visitor."

Spring's pulse jumped. The dark shadow in the hallway.

"Your brother?"

She breathed again. She hadn't thought about the sinister visitor until after Robert had left in the morning. Then the memory had squeezed her insides in the grip of fear that had become her new normal.

Still no new text messages. Was Robert right? Had she called the texter's bluff? Or was he waiting to—

"Robert said he phoned Sergeant Cotter to ask him to stop by this morning." Victoria grabbed the folded black pants and gray T-shirt that one of the nurses had set on the edge of Spring's bed. "Although the sergeant told Robert he was already planning to come. There's apparently a development in the case he wants to discuss with you."

Victoria reached to lower Spring's blanket and paused, meeting her gaze. "I'm so glad to hear that you plan to tell the sergeant everything."

That tone. The all-knowing, mother's way of saying, *I knew you'd grow up someday.*

"I'm not sure what I'm going to tell him. I've told him most of what I know already."

Victoria arched an eyebrow.

Spring barely held back a frustrated grunt. Why did Victoria always have to make her feel like she was thirteen years old again?

"Maybe we should save all that talk until we get Spring dressed." Angie, ever the peacemaker, gently intervened. "I'd like you to do more of the changing yourself today, okay, Spring?"

She nodded. Anything to stop Victoria's lecturing and pushing. Though as soon as she tried to do the tasks Angie encouraged her to do, humiliation smacked her in the face. She was still weak and unable to do even the simplest things. That would never change. Whether she told Sergeant Cotter everything she knew or not. Even if they found the driver who hit her or the texter sending threats.

She'd never have a life worth living.

Victoria and Angie managed to get Spring's vegetable body dressed and transferred to the wheelchair. Victoria prodded Spring to do more and try harder, but Spring tuned her out.

The brightness the day had seemed to offer before Robert left thirty minutes ago had faded into the gloom of reality.

Nothing had changed. She wasn't free of anything. She'd always be a prisoner as long as she couldn't use her legs.

"Spring, did you hear me?" Victoria's voice forced its way past Spring's thoughts. "That sore isn't healing. Have you been—"

A knock at the door saved Spring from another lecture on the importance of pressure relief.

Her breath caught as the door slowly opened.

"Come in, Sergeant." Victoria acted like they were at their father's mansion, and she was the hostess.

Spring's gaze pulled irresistibly to the sergeant as he entered the room.

He walked closer, looking at her instead of Victoria.

Heat surged to her cheeks, and her pulse decided to play hopscotch. He was even more handsome than she'd remembered in a dark brown sport coat and pale green button-down that made his eyes gleam like emeralds.

Ridiculous. He was only there to do his job. To ask her about things that didn't even matter in the long run. But she couldn't breathe with those electrifying eyes trained on her as he stopped only a few feet away. "Good morning."

She glanced away, trying to hide her rapid breathing. "Hi." Why did he have such a strong effect on her? She was paralyzed. He'd never be interested. She was a glutton for punishment, apparently.

"Your brother called."

More heat infused her face. She must sound like such a child, having her family go over her head and do her talking for her.

"He said you wanted to see me?"

Her gaze jumped to his face.

He looked down and tugged his notepad from the pocket of his sport coat. "I mean, that you'd like to talk to me about the case."

Her pulse picked up speed. Was he embarrassed? Could he actual—

"Yes. There are some things Spring needs to tell you." Victoria would choose that moment to butt in and play the overbearing mother.

He only gave her a brief glance before returning his attention to Spring. "I'd love to hear them." The barest hint of a smile tugged at one side of his mouth.

In spite of everything in her mind that told her there was no point, those green eyes pulled her in and whispered there was hope. That he could help. That if she stepped over the edge and told him everything, he'd catch her.

In that moment, looking into his eyes, she believed the truth might set her free.

"I—" Her chance at freedom died on her lips as a man barged into the room.

Torin instinctively took a couple sideways steps toward Spring as the man in the stained blue polo shirt and torn jeans glanced wildly around the room. Early twenties, pupils dilated, nerves wound like a top—the guy looked like a user. Maybe speed.

His gaze locked on Spring, making Torin's muscles tense. "It's not my fault. It isn't my fault."

Torin inched closer to her as the man muttered the same incoherent sentence repeatedly. Maybe Torin should've brought his weapon with him this time. But he didn't want to think of the results if he had. Safer for everyone this way.

"You can't be in here, sir." Angie walked toward the guy. "You aren't a registered visitor."

He didn't acknowledge her. Just stared at Spring like a cheetah eyeing prey. Did he know her?

Torin took his focus off the guy for a split-second to check Spring's reaction, but her furrowed brow indicated only confusion.

Angie slipped out the door behind the man. Hopefully to get security.

"Can I help you?" Victoria stepped toward him, but Torin stuck out his arm to stop her progress, glancing at her.

His first mistake.

The man reached behind his back and whipped out a Glock, aimed at Spring.

Torin lunged for her wheelchair, shoving her out of the way as the gun went off.

"Hey!" A security guard appeared in the doorway.

The shooter whirled. Fired.

The guard went down.

Torin instinctively reached for his gun that wasn't there as he spotted the butt of the extra weapon the shooter carried behind his back.

The perp stumbled out of the room into the hallway, waving the Glock in his hand as he disappeared from view.

More shots fired.

Screams from the hallway.

"Torin!"

Two shots.

Ivy. Dead in the doorway.

"He's still alive!" Victoria's shout jolted Torin out of the flashes of memory more terrifying than even the present.

He sucked air in ragged gasps as he tried to focus on Victoria, crouching over the guard's body in the doorway. The woman had better crisis response instincts than he did.

Don't lose it, Cotter. Not now.

He checked Spring. Her eyes were huge as she stared at the guard, her face white. But no sign of injury.

She'd nearly been shot. Another woman killed on his watch.

"I'll get a doctor." Victoria got to her feet.

"No." Torin stopped her with the force of the word. Finally coming to his senses, he yanked his phone from his back pocket as he dragged his gaze from the fallen guard. Torin couldn't help him and protect these women. The guard would understand—he had to get the women out alive if he could.

He glanced at Victoria. "Get out of here as fast as you can. Take the exit stairs at the end of the hall, not the elevators." He touched the programmed button on his phone's screen and pressed the cell to his ear. Couldn't hear more shots. "The shooter probably moved on. But if you hear shots anywhere, barricade yourself in a room and hide. SWAT will be on the scene soon."

"911, what is your emergency?" A woman operator.

"This is Sergeant Torin Cotter with Chicago PD. We have an active shooter at the Chicago Rehab Center. Single shooter armed with a semi-auto pistol and another unidentified hand-gun." Torin spewed the information quickly. "Male, hundred and fifty pounds, five-foot eleven, brown on brown, blue polo shirt and torn blue jeans. Shooter started on tenth floor and may have moved to another level. We have at least one victim in need of immediate medical attention."

Victoria started to push Spring's wheelchair.

"Victoria, no." The movement must have jolted Spring out of her shock. "You have to get out of here."

Torin pocketed his phone and went toward the back of the chair.

"I'll just slow you down." Spring twisted her head around to see her sister.

"She's right." Torin reached for the handles, and Victoria backed away. "There's no time to lose. You should've left already." He pushed the chair toward the door, hoping he hadn't delayed too long making the call. "I'll stay with your sister and get her somewhere safe." If he could.

"Why don't we barricade ourselves in here?"

Torin paused and glanced back.

Victoria still lingered in the room.

"The shooter could come back for her."

"For Spring?" Victoria's eyes widened.

"He was aiming at her." Torin pushed the chair again, slowing next to the guard who lay just inside the doorway.

"But he's a random shooter, isn't he?" Victoria's voice held concern but no panic. Amazing response for a civilian.

"I'm not so sure." Torin surveyed the guard's uniform for a holster and gun. None.

The guard appeared unconscious. At least he wasn't in pain.

Torin quickly checked the hallway. No shooter. And no bodies on the floor.

He shoved Spring's wheelchair into the hall and pushed at a fast clip, searching for a better hiding spot. Couldn't carry her down the emergency stairwell and risk getting caught by the shooter.

Victoria jogged to catch up. "Where is everyone?"

"They probably followed their shooter scenario training and ran for the exits. Or they're hiding. You should, too."

Victoria looked in another patient room as they passed. "There are still patients here."

"Keep your voice down." He spotted a man lying in the room.

"He can't get up and run."

"Get in the room with him and barricade it with whatever you can find." The hallway was too empty. No victims. This was not a normal mass shooting scenario. They had to get out of sight. "Hide and stay absolutely quiet until SWAT comes."

"What about Spring?"

"I'll take care of her." Away from other potential victims if she was the target.

"Victoria," Spring hissed. "Will you just listen to him so we can get out of this alive?"

Torin didn't wait for Victoria to answer as he wheeled Spring rapidly down the hallway, glancing at the patient rooms they passed. A storage closet would be better. There'd be shelving units he could push in front of the door, possible items to use as weapons.

"You can leave me." Spring's sudden statement startled him, but he kept moving. "I know I'm slowing you down. You could take the stairs if it wasn't for me."

As if he'd be able to live with himself if he did that. "The shooter was after you, ma'am. I'm not leaving."

Spring's stomach lurched as Sergeant Cotter swung the chair around a corner into another hallway at dizzying speed. This couldn't be happening. She'd almost been shot.

The surge of terror she'd felt when that awful man pointed the gun at her coursed through her veins again.

Why would he want to shoot her? She'd never seen him before. He was clearly insane. Crazy shooters didn't need a reason to kill one person over another. Not from what she'd heard. The sergeant had to be wrong about him singling her out.

The rooms they passed blurred as Sergeant Cotter wheeled her quickly. Some were open. Some closed. Were people behind the doors? Hunkered down in hiding, praying for their lives?

Please, Jesus, protect us all. Her lips moved with the silent prayer—more articulate than the one she'd screamed in her mind when the man shot at her. All she'd been able to cry then was His name…*Jesus*.

But she had prayed the night her bicycle was hit, and she'd flown through the air. And again, when she'd awoken to learn she would never cycle or even walk. There'd been no help from above then.

Sergeant Cotter braked next to a door on the opposite side of the hallway from the patient rooms.

She glimpsed the *Employees Only* plate on the door as he swung it open and pushed her wheelchair into a narrow space between metal shelves that lined both walls.

She heard him shut the door.

He left the switch off, but enough hallway light must have been spilling under and around the door to let her eyes quickly adjust and take in the surroundings.

Towels, linens, and other supplies populated the shelves in neat stacks and rows.

A popping sound cracked outside the room.

Spring jumped, gripping the arms of her chair. She craned her neck to see the sergeant behind her.

His eyes flashed in the dim light, his jaw clenched. He grabbed the metal shelving unit to her right and slid it toward the door. Bottles toppled on a shelf. A couple dropped to the floor.

"Was—" Her voice caught on the whisper. She tried again. "Was that a gunshot?"

Sergeant Cotter got behind the shelves to push them fully in front of the door.

"Is he still here?" Her neck was getting sore from twisting back. She tried to turn farther to see the sergeant better. She lost her balance and careened forward.

Gentle hands were instantly on her shoulders. Strong, warm fingers pressing through her T-shirt as he lifted her upright.

"Sorry. I'll see if I can turn you around." He moved his hands away, leaving her skin tingly.

Definitely still had feeling in that part of her body.

He started to maneuver her chair back and forth in small movements, slowly managing to rotate her to face the door in the small space that didn't allow for an easy turn.

She swallowed. Her mouth was so dry. Whether from the sergeant or the shooter, she wasn't sure. "You didn't answer my question."

He wiped his forehead as if swiping away sweat and met her gaze. "It was a shot." His voice was low, quiet. "He's still here."

Her throat tightened, threatening her ability to breathe. She closed her eyes. *Lord, please help us.*

She opened her eyes at the sound of objects moving.

Torin scrounged through the items on the shelves as if searching for something. He picked up what looked like...

"A hand duster?"

"Any weapon is better than nothing."

She scanned the trim waistband of his khakis. "Don't policemen always wear a gun when they're on duty?"

He turned away, facing the door. "I work in an office a lot. I'd have to display my badge, carry a radio, handcuffs, extra ammo. Don't usually need a gun."

Except today. The tightness of his voice as he explained made her wonder if she'd made him uncomfortable.

"I'm sorry. I didn't mean that I thought you should've—"

"We shouldn't talk." His eyes flickered when he turned to her. "If we don't make any noise, chances are he won't find us."

"What if he does?" She lowered her voice to a whisper, her pulse skittering.

"I'll take care of him." He spoke so confidently, not leaving room for doubt as he angled to the door again.

But the fear pumping through her body didn't listen. "This is so unreal. Stuff like this only happens..."

He looked at her. "To other people?"

The same thing she'd thought about her paralysis in those awful early days. How could another thing be happening to her? Wasn't one freak disaster enough for a lifetime?

"You'll be okay." His voice softened. "I'll get you out of this."

She met his gaze.

Just as a scream pierced the air.

CHAPTER
TWENTY-FIVE

October 11. 9:21 a.m.

A SHOT FOLLOWED THE CRY.

Torin's nerves exploded.

"Torin!" Ivy's scream screeched in his ears as if it were happening now, piercing his heart like the bullet from the gun that pierced hers.

He shook his head. Had to shake off the fear that clawed at him.

His pulse raced as he released the vise grip he'd locked on the shelves without realizing it. Hands shook as he drew them back to his sides.

He should be out there taking down the perp before he injured more people. Maybe Torin had misjudged the situation. Wouldn't be the first time he'd made a deadly mistake.

But everything he'd seen told him the shooter had been looking for Spring. Shooting the guard was unplanned, Torin was ninety percent sure. The guy had panicked, shooting without aim as he ran.

Then why hadn't he left the building? Unless SWAT had responded quickly enough to bottle him up on that floor.

Or he'd stayed to find Spring.

Torin looked at her.

His eyes had adjusted to the dimness enough to see her cheeks were devoid of color, pale lips trembling.

If his gut was right, he was doing what he was supposed to. He had to protect her once he knew she was the target. He didn't have a weapon to take down the shooter anyway.

Idiot move to leave his gun in the trunk of his car. But he'd done it so many times before. It was supposed to keep him out of this kind of situation. As long as he didn't try to play the hero, he shouldn't end up needing to protect someone and paying for his boneheaded mistakes.

His cell phone. He whipped the device out of his pocket to silence it. Another thing he'd have already done if he hadn't been distracted by the flashbacks that wouldn't leave him alone. He was the wrong cop for this job.

He looked up from his phone.

Spring watched him, staring as if she had believed every word he'd said before the latest shot had gone off. He'd promised to protect her. Too bad he knew he was the last person who could.

"Do you believe in Jesus?" Her whispered question couldn't have surprised him more than if she'd pulled a gun on him.

He blinked.

"I just..." Her cheeks darkened, probably flushed that attractive shade of pink he would see in better lighting. "If we're going to die, I want to make sure you know where you're going after..." She looked away, avoiding his gaze as if afraid of his reaction.

Hadn't pegged her as the religious type. But if talking about it kept her calm, he could humor her. "I'm one of the good guys, ma'am. If there is a heaven, I'll get in it. And there sure better be some kind of hell waiting for people like that." He thumbed to the door he stood sideways to. "I've put away my share of criminals even worse than that guy. People do unbelievably horrible things."

She bit her bottom lip, an adorable gesture she didn't seem to know she was doing. "But did you know the Bible says everyone has sinned? We've all done something wrong. Lied, cheated, been selfish. And that sin keeps us away from God and Heaven, because God is perfect."

Torin frowned. Ivy used to say things like that. Any more of the same wouldn't help him forget the memories, hold the flashbacks at bay.

"Jesus lived a perfect life and died for your sins so you *can* be with God when—"

"Shh." He held a finger to his lips.

She shut her mouth, eyes widening.

He turned away from her and the twinge of guilt that tugged at his conscience. He didn't want to scare her. But he couldn't let her go on talking like that either. She may not look anything like Ivy, but she was starting to sound like her twin.

He glanced at Spring one more time. His throat tightened at the sight of the fear tensing her features. Was she shivering? He took off his sport coat and covered her with it from the front since he wasn't sure if she could lean forward for him to slip it around her shoulders. "SWAT will get here soon. You're not going to die."

He only wished he was as sure as he sounded.

CHAPTER
TWENTY-SIX

October 11. 9:44 a.m.

VICTORIA STIFFENED. "I think I heard something." She held the cell phone away from her ear to listen, staring at the curtain she'd pulled to hide them in the corner.

All she could hear was Robert's voice trying to say something to her through the phone. She put it back to her ear, glancing at Stephen in the wheelchair next to her.

"Did you barricade the door?"

Stephen moaned softly as he often seemed to, though she'd only seen him a few other times when he had worked with his PT in the gym.

She gently covered his curved, stiff fingers with her hand. "Yes. I managed to push the bed in front of it." She kept her volume to a near-whisper. "That's the only heavy thing that I could move. I don't know if it will keep him out." Thank the Lord she'd been able to transfer Stephen from the bed to the chair, despite his extremely limited mobility.

She looked at her watch again. "It's been approximately twenty minutes. Sergeant Cotter said the police would be here right away."

"Hang in there, Vicki. I'm almost there. I'll find out what's going on."

How did Robert manage it? He sounded as placid as if he were talking about his favorite pizza flavors instead of a shooting rampage aimed at his sisters.

She closed her eyes and breathed a prayer of thanks for God's providence in prompting Robert to drive back to see Spring again, making him much closer to the rehab center than he otherwise would have been.

Spring. Was she all right? Had the shooter found her again, as Sergeant Cotter said he might?

"The sergeant thinks the shooter intended to kill Spring, specifically."

"What? I thought he was a mass shooter." The normalcy of Robert's car blinker clicking in the background was strangely comforting.

"I don't know. The man seems incoherent. But he came to Spring's room first."

"Did he say anything?"

"'It's not my fault.' He kept repeating that over and over again. He appeared to be on a substance of some kind."

"Then why does Cotter think he's after Spring?"

"He shot at her. The sergeant saved her life."

"I'll have to thank him when—"

"Shh."

Something banged against the door.

"If anybody's in there, you better come out right now!"

The shooter. Only a brief acquaintance, but she'd never forget that voice.

Stephen moaned.

Loud enough to be heard in the hall? She held her breath.

"I heard that. I've got hostages. Come out now or I start shooting!"

Her heart seemed ready to beat through its confines. Did he have Spring? Not that it mattered. She couldn't let him shoot anyone on her account. But if she went to the door, she would put Stephen at risk, too.

"I mean it! Don't make me shoot this cripple in the wheelchair."

She closed her eyes and lifted the cell phone to her ear. "Robert." She kept her voice to a whisper as she stepped out from behind the curtain and closed it behind her. "I have to go out into the hallway."

"What—"

"The shooter says he has hostages."

"That doesn't matter, Vicki. He doesn't need you, too. I'm here now. The police are here. SWAT and police cars like crazy down here. Stay where you are, and we'll get you out."

"You've got five seconds!" The shooter's yell reverberated with frustrated anger.

"I'm coming! I have to unblock the door!" Victoria tried to quell the fear that infused her voice. She set the phone on the bed and pushed with both hands.

Robert's words carried the distance from the mattress. "Don't listen to him, Vicki. Promise you'll stay there."

She shoved the bed away from the door and glanced back to make sure Stephen was still hidden. Pressing the phone to her ear, she steeled her heart against Robert's pleas. "He might have Spring. I have to go."

"Okay." Resignation flattened his tone. "Keep this call going as long as you can, even if you put it in your pocket. Don't end the call. I'll get you out of there, Vicki."

She pursed her lips. "Would you call my pastor? He'll activate the prayer chain."

Silence.

"Please, Robert."

"Sure. Just promise me you'll be careful. Take care of yourself and Spring."

"I'll do my best." But only God could help them now.

The door flung inward.

The shooter stood back, gun aimed at her and other people

clustered in the hallway. She couldn't see how many there were from her position.

Jason, one of the nurses, stood closer—likely the one directed to open the door.

"You were with the chick in the wheelchair." The shooter tilted his head at an odd angle as he watched her. The start of a smile touched his lips in a way that made a shiver spiral up her spine. "You know her?"

"Yes." She pursed her lips. What had he done to Spring?

"Oh, I know. You're her sister, aren't you?"

How did he know that? "Where is she? Did you hurt her?"

"Not yet." His weak smile settled in place beneath eyes full of strife. "Who you talking to?"

She battled the urge to lie and say there was no one on the phone. He'd seen her talking on it, regardless. "The police are here. They'll be coming to find you."

His brown eyes darkened. "Not when I have these people." He waved his gun at the hostages. "Get out here."

She stepped into the hallway, scanning the people gathered.

Spring wasn't among them.

Thank you, Lord. Victoria's ribs expanded as she took in a deep breath.

Dr. Berghuis stood a few feet from the shooter. He caught her gaze with warm comfort in his eyes. "It's all right, Victoria. He promises not to hurt us if we cooperate."

Did that promise extend to Spring?

She glanced at the other hostages. An elderly woman and a man in a wheelchair she'd never seen before made four hostages, including Jason. Five, with her now.

"Anybody else in there?" The shooter glanced behind her to indicate the room.

She hesitated.

"Want me to shoot that curtain and find out?"

She sucked in a breath. He was more cognizant than she

would have guessed. "No. It's only a man in a wheelchair. He's harmless."

Her gaze went to Dr. Berghuis.

He nodded, likely realizing as she did that Stephen would have difficulty on his own if this situation lasted for an extended period.

She looked at the shooter. "I'll bring him out."

"No." He waved the gun at her and tilted his head to Dr. Berghuis. "The doc will get him. Give me your phone."

She looked down at the device in her hand. Her lifeline to the world outside this terrifying scenario. To Robert. But she had Jesus right there with her, the Holy Spirit inside of her. She didn't need the phone for her strength.

She stepped toward the shooter, keeping as much distance as she could from the gun he aimed at her.

He snatched the phone with his free hand. Pushing the device to his ear, he barked into it. "Who is this?"

She held her breath as he paused. What was Robert saying?

"You a cop?"

The shooter laughed—a queer, strangled sound. "You aren't my friend. I don't even know you."

He watched the hostages, his gun aimed at them while he listened to Robert, answering occasionally with a few terse replies. Within a few minutes, his shoulders lowered, and some of the tension drained from his eyes and rigid stance.

Robert was working his magic.

"Okay. You do that. I'll be waiting." The shooter lowered the phone as Dr. Berghuis wheeled Stephen into the hallway next to Victoria.

The shooter pressed her phone's screen to end the call.

Weakness washed through her limbs. Was that the last time she would ever hear Robert's voice?

No. She had to think positively. God would save them. *Please, Lord. Give me courage to face whatever You have in store. And please fortify Spring and keep her safe, wherever she may be.*

CHAPTER
TWENTY-SEVEN

October 11. 12:32 p.m.

SPRING NEVER KNEW fear could last so long. She'd run on adrenaline for the first hour and nerves for the next couple. But no noises had come from outside the closet for a long time, and her nerves were finally beginning to relax out of sheer exhaustion.

Remembering the sore she was supposed to be nursing, Spring pushed herself up to relieve the pressure. Sergeant Cotter's sport coat slipped down as she moved.

"Are you all right?" The sergeant looked up from where he sat on the floor in front of her.

"Yes." She pulled the sport coat back up to cover her arms, its warmth unexpectedly comforting. Something bulky grazed her arm through the material. She felt it from underneath. Bigger and flatter than the notepad in the other pocket. A wallet? Probably held his badge.

The sergeant's legs extended out in front of him in a bent position that appeared relaxed, but he was obviously far from it. He usually kept his gaze on the door, and she could see his

209

shoulder muscles contract under his shirt with every hint of a sound outside.

He hadn't said much since she'd tried to witness to him.

She shouldn't have been so hesitant and embarrassed to talk to him about Jesus, but she hadn't had much practice doing that with total strangers. She usually tried to just live out her faith and build relationships first.

But when it looked like they might be about to die, she knew she had to at least attempt to talk to him about it. She couldn't withhold the lifeboat of eternal life from someone who was sinking with her.

Too bad she hadn't expressed what she was trying to say very well. He had seemed positively turned off. Apparently, she couldn't do evangelism successfully either. Victoria probably would've had him praying the sinner's prayer in two minutes flat.

He pulled out his phone from his back pants' pocket—something he'd been doing frequently.

"What time is it?" Her mouth felt so dry.

"Twelve thirty-four." He pocketed the phone again. "Someone should have been here long before this. I should've gotten a call or text if something was wrong. Unless they didn't want to risk that I hadn't silenced my phone." He stared at the shelves in front of him as if they held the answer to his thoughts. "Which would mean…" He didn't finish.

But she knew what he meant. "The shooter's still here."

He brought his gaze to her face. "Do you know him? The shooter?"

"No." Her surprise at the question lifted her voice. "I've never seen him before."

Those green eyes watched her. Like he didn't believe her.

"Why would I lie about that?"

"I don't know." He spoke slowly, not breaking his stare. "I don't know why you lied about not remembering anything from the collision either."

She swallowed. Looked at the white towels on the shelf next to her.

Wouldn't matter now if she told. Her life was already in danger from someone else. Victoria's, too.

"That man was aiming at you. This wasn't a random shooting." The sergeant's voice cut through her fears. "If you know something, you'd better tell me. It might help me get you out of here alive."

Wonderful. Now the sergeant thought she had lied about some connection to an insane shooter. No wonder he thought the man was trying to kill her. She had created quite a mess when she didn't tell the whole truth.

Maybe telling him everything would make him realize she couldn't be the reason for a shooter's violence. She moistened her lips and pulled her gaze back to his. "Someone threatened my family. My sister." Where was Victoria now?

"In the text messages?

She nodded. What if Victoria was hurt?

"Who sent the threats?"

"I don't know." Her mind wasn't on her answer. It was on Victoria. Could that last scream have been hers? Spring shuddered.

"Miss Weston."

Warm pressure seeped through the sport coat over her arms, awakening her senses enough for her to see that Sergeant Cotter now crouched in front of her, his tanned hands covering her forearms.

"Miss Weston, I need you to stay with me."

The terror started to clear under the warmth of his gaze and his smooth, calming voice. "You can call me Spring." Her words came out in a barely perceptible whisper.

One corner of his mouth seemed to tug slightly upward, then flattened again so quickly she thought she must have imagined the hint of a reaction. "Spring." He gave a curt nod. "I need you to tell me why this shooter is after you."

She shook her head. "He isn't. I don't know him at all. I'm telling the truth."

"But you do know more about the collision than you said?"

"Only a little. But as soon as I was conscious at the hospital, I started getting those texts." She spotted the question coming into his eyes before he asked it. She shook her head again. "I don't know who they were from. The ID was always blocked. But he said he'd kill me. And when I told him I didn't care if I died, he started talking about my sister."

"Did the messages threaten to kill her, too?"

"That's what they meant." She sighed, trying to ease the tension compressing her chest. "I know so little about the crash, it was easy to say nothing."

Sergeant Cotter stood, leaving her arms to adjust to the cooler temperature without the warmth of his hands. "What do you remember?"

She folded her arms under his sport coat. "The rumble of the engine."

"Did it sound like a car or a larger vehicle?"

"I don't know. Well, I know it wasn't like a semi or something. But it could've been anything else."

"What did you mean by 'rumble'?"

She tried to think back to that night, the sound just before her life ended. "I guess it wasn't quite smooth, like it was an old vehicle that didn't run very well."

"Did you see anything before you were hit?"

"Just white. A blur of white."

He nodded. "Like the van the witness saw. It matches the color of paint transfer on your bicycle. We weren't able to trace it because the sample amount was too small."

She knew the little she remembered wouldn't make a difference.

"Did you see anyone?"

"It came up from behind. I couldn't see a windshield at all, much less who was behind the wheel."

"Okay, but what about people not in the vehicle. I mean on the streets, sidewalks—the neighborhood wasn't empty, was it?"

She bit her lip, trying to remember. She never liked riding through that section under the overpass. It was so dark. But it was short, and the rest of the area had less traffic than most. She remembered the sting of raindrops hitting her face with the wind her fast pace created, the fatigue and pain in her legs as she pushed herself to set a personal best time. What she wouldn't give to feel that kind of pain again.

"Spring?"

Torin's voice brought her back to the present. She'd never liked her name much, but she'd never heard anyone say it so gently before. She blinked and tried to recall his question. "I guess there might have been some people, must have been in the neighborhood. But I focus on my ride, not—" The image of the store flashed in her mind. "Wait, I did see something as I rode by."

"Yes?" His emerald eyes widened as he leaned a tiny bit toward her.

"A white van parked next to a store."

"What store?"

"Um..." Her gaze flicked to the ceiling as she searched the foggy memory. "I'm sorry. I was going so fast...I couldn't read it."

"Are you sure?" His eyes narrowed slightly.

Did he think she was lying?

"Yes. I really didn't see it clearly."

"Have you ever been there before?"

"To the store?" Why would he ask that? "No. I told you, I don't even know what it was called."

"Did you see anyone at the store?"

"No."

"Maybe by the van?"

So this is what it felt like to be interrogated. "No."

"I see." Disappointment clouded his features. Or was it anger?

"I'm sorry I can't remember more."

"It's not your fault." His voice softened along with his eyes.

"I'm sorry I didn't tell you before. I didn't know what to do. I wanted to tell someone, but..."

"I understand."

She wanted to believe he did. "All these questions about the store—do you really think someone from a store I've never been to would want to randomly run me down?"

His gaze was unreadable as he looked at her. "More likely it wasn't random at all. I have a feeling you know something else. Something you may not realize you know."

Or something she was hiding from him. Is that what he meant? She wouldn't blame him for thinking she was still lying.

She bit her lip. "Do you—"

A noise outside the door.

Spring held her breath.

Sergeant Cotter put out his hand to signal silence and slowly got to his feet.

There it was again. A soft, high-pitched sound. Like... crying? Maybe from one of the rooms.

The sergeant stepped as close to the door as he could with the shelves blocking it.

"Is that—"

He held up a finger.

The noise grew louder, a whimper. Then crying for sure.

Spring's heart constricted. "It's a child."

CHAPTER
TWENTY-EIGHT

October 11. 12:40 p.m.

"WE CAN'T GO OUT THERE." Torin watched determination and concern replace the fear that had dominated Spring's lovely features for the past three hours.

"The child could be hurt. We have to help."

Torin shook his head. "No way. It's too dangerous, and it could be a trap."

Lines crossed her brow. "We haven't heard anything for hours. The shooter must have left."

He could've smiled at her sudden confidence. The change was charming, bringing color to her cheeks and a glimmer to those dark eyes.

But it was a dangerous change under the circumstances. Nothing good came from playing the hero.

"SWAT would have been here and cleared the whole floor if they'd apprehended the shooter. Something else is going on."

A spark flared in her eyes, and she crossed her arms on top of his sport coat that crunched down into her lap. "So we're supposed to just sit here the rest of the day while a child needs help?"

He did smile this time. Totally inappropriate, but he couldn't help it. He'd thought she was lovely even when hopelessness and fear were the only emotions he'd seen on her face. The new spark made her stunning.

"What are you smiling at?" She frowned, lowering her arms.

"Nothing." He wiped his hand over his mouth, erasing the smile as he turned toward the door. "But we're still not going out there."

Something hard banged against the back of his legs.

He spun in time to see her push her wheelchair at him again. "What are you doing?" He grabbed the arms of the chair to hold her still.

"I'm getting out of here. I'll slam into those shelves until I knock them down and break through the door if I have to."

The woman was crazy.

She glared up at him. "I'm not going to sit here while some child is crying right outside, suffering who knows what." She gripped the wheels of her chair. "I don't care what happens to me."

Something in the statement bothered him. She didn't say it casually, like it was part of a convincing argument anyone might make. "You really mean that, don't you?"

She stared ahead at the level of his belt buckle instead of meeting his gaze. "I care what happens to that child."

Torin watched her. "We could both get killed if we open that door."

She was silent, her hands going limp on the wheels. Then she lifted a watery gaze. "Please. I'd run out there on my own if I could. But we both know I can't." A frustrated sob caught her voice, gripping his heart and twisting.

He shouldn't risk it. He should protect her no matter what she said she wanted.

But he wouldn't do it against her will. Wouldn't take

advantage of the chair that took away her choice to help someone.

He inhaled a deep breath. He'd been beaten as soon as he'd seen the tears in her big brown eyes. "Okay."

Relief filled those melting pools as she looked up at him, and her lips curved into the hint of a smile.

His pulse did an odd skip. He cleared his throat. "I'm going to move this shelving unit as quietly as I can. Then we wait five minutes. If there's no sound outside except for the crying, *I* will go and check it out."

She opened her mouth, clearly to protest.

"That's the deal. Take it or leave it."

"I'll take it." She pressed her lips together, eyes brightening.

He looked away before he couldn't. The woman cast quite a spell.

Watch it, Cotter. That's how trouble started. He'd promised he would never let anything like that happen again. He'd rather face the shooter even with his weapon locked in the trunk of his car.

Torin hefted the shelving unit as quietly as he could, making only a few scraping noises as he shifted it to the side. He let out a breath and lifted the hand duster from the floor, gripped the handle as he stared at the door he never should have unblocked.

Minutes slowly ticked by, the only sounds Spring's gentle breathing and the whimpering outside that wouldn't stop.

If the shooter was nearby, wouldn't he target whoever was crying?

So much of this didn't make sense. There were too many possibilities. If only Torin could get away to investigate, narrow them down. But he couldn't leave Spring. Shouldn't leave her to check out the crying, in fact.

"Sergeant." Her whisper came from close behind him.

He turned to face her where she sat, inches away. "Not going to ram me again, are you?"

She blushed and shook her head, gaze dropping.

That totally inappropriate smile tried to crawl onto his face again as he watched her dipped head, dark waves of thick hair falling forward to cover her cheeks.

She brought her gaze back up. "It's been five minutes. Shouldn't we go?"

"I'm going. You're staying."

She bit her lip, the gesture doing unnerving things to him. "You'll come back?" She was afraid to be alone.

He should've thought of that. "You'll be safer if you aren't seen. In fact, we'd both be safer if we stayed put."

She shook her head.

"Then I'll go. And I'll come back."

She nodded, those brown eyes serious.

He reached for the doorknob. He was going to regret this.

Taking a breath, he slowly turned, opening the door a crack to spy out the hallway.

Clear for the short distance he could see.

He opened the door farther and slipped out, pressing his back against the cool wall as he checked both directions.

Empty. Deathly quiet.

He homed in on the crying. Sounded like it was coming from the room directly across the hall from the closet.

He quickly and silently crossed the hallway, flattening against the wall beside the closed door.

Movement caught his eye.

Spring. She wheeled her chair out of the storage room.

His heart jumped to his throat. "Get back." The harsh whisper sounded like a shout in the silent hall. He looked both directions.

Still empty.

She kept coming, pushing hard.

Exasperating woman. He had to get her out of the hallway now.

He cautiously opened the door of the patient room and checked inside.

A small boy sat propped up in a bed near the far wall.

Torin entered, clearing the room as quickly as he could.

Satisfied the boy was the only occupant, Torin darted back out and grabbed the handles behind Spring's chair, shoving her into the room.

He shut the door behind them, then whirled her chair so it faced him, leveling her with the anger boiling in his stomach. "Are you trying to get yourself killed?"

Spring stared at Torin's flashing gaze. He was furious, and she didn't have an answer. Was that what she was trying to do?

His emerald eyes softened in her silence, tinting with blue. He leaned forward, planting his hands on the arms of her chair. "You may not care what happens to you, but others do."

She couldn't look away as her pulse tripped.

He's a cop, Spring. He was just doing his job.

She moistened her lips. "You're a good policeman, Sergeant."

Something she couldn't read flickered in those eyes. Had she made him angry again?

"It's Torin." He straightened and angled away, looking around the room.

Torin. A name as unusual as the man who was saving her life.

"You'd better see if you can help that kid while I barricade the door."

The boy. How could she have forgotten? Torin seemed to have some sort of spell-casting abilities that made her forget everything around her.

She gripped the rims on the wheels, but there was no way she'd be able to do that turn. Chalk up another point to Victoria. Should have taken her therapy more seriously. "Can you turn me in the right direction?" Heat seeped into her cheeks. Torin would think she was completely helpless.

He stepped back to her chair and swung it around to face the bed.

She started pushing the wheels right away so he wouldn't think she couldn't do anything. She tried to focus on the boy as she wheeled to the bed. Wasn't difficult.

The beautiful tow-headed child looked like he was only about six years old.

Her heart squeezed at the sight of the tears that streaked his flushed face. At least he'd stopped whimpering.

His blue-eyed gaze hopped between Spring and Torin.

She smiled as she stopped next to the bed. "Hi." She kept her volume low, hoping the boy would follow her cue not to speak too loudly. "My name is Spring. What's your name?"

The boy sniffed, and his little fingers trembled on the white sheet that covered him up to the bottom hem of his Chicago Bears sweatshirt.

Poor little kid. Guilt contracted her chest. She hoped Torin wasn't right about the shooter being after her, or this could all be her fault.

She rested her hand on the boy's small, cold fingers. "That man over there," she nodded over her shoulder, "is a policeman. Sergeant Cotter. He's here to protect us."

The boy sniffed again, his gaze going to Torin. "What... what's he doing?"

Spring twisted her head to look, careful not to upset her balance or take her hand off the boy's.

Torin lowered his arms from the large hinge over the door. He'd wrapped something around it. Looked like a belt. His own, judging from the empty belt loops of the waistband his shirt tucked into. The closet didn't have a hinge like that, she now realized. Though she'd never have thought to look for one before.

She turned back to the boy. "He's making sure no one can come in here."

The boy's eyes widened.

"It's to keep us safe. To keep the man with the gun out of

your room." What if he hadn't even known there was someone with a gun in the hospital? She might be scaring him more than he already was. "Did you see the man with the gun?"

He nodded.

Her heart contorted at the fear in his eyes. "Did he come in here?"

He shook his head.

"Good."

"How's Mommy gonna get in?"

The air went out of her lungs. Of course. He must have a parent with him usually. What if she'd been shot? Spring took a breath, trying to think of the best response. She moistened her lips. "Where is your mommy?"

"She said she was gonna get breakfast, and she'd be right back."

Lord, please let his mother be all right. Spring glanced over her shoulder, hoping for some help from Torin.

But he stood with his back to the wall next to the door. He put his finger to his lips.

Her pulse raced. She'd almost forgotten the shooter could still be out there. Could be coming back to the rooms. The idea of the shooter finding this little boy was unimaginable. She breathed a prayer of thanks that God had spared him. *Please help us keep him safe.*

"What's your name?" She lowered her voice almost to a whisper and gently squeezed the little hand beneath hers.

"Bradley."

"Well, Bradley, your mom will be back as soon as she can." She gave him a small smile. "Did you hear the noises in the hallway?"

"People screamed."

"A bad man came into the hospital, but we'll be safe as long as we are very quiet and stay hidden until help comes. Okay?"

The boy's lower lip started to push out, but he nodded.

"Then I'll take you to your mommy."

Moisture started to pool in his eyes.

Time for a subject change. She grabbed the first thought that came to mind. "Do you use a wheelchair yet?"

His expression lightened as his mouth pulled out of the frown. "Uh-huh. Sometimes. Do your legs work?"

She blinked. The bluntness of children. "No, they don't." She glanced at Torin.

He stood in the same spot, watching them. But he didn't signal that she needed to be quieter.

She looked at Bradley. "Do your legs work?"

"No. But I can still use my hands. See?" He pulled out the hand under hers and lifted both extremities with a smile, flexing all ten fingers.

"Yes, I see. That's very good." She had to force out the words. *A little boy, Lord?* He'd have to spend his whole life without the ability to walk. It just wasn't right.

"And when my doctor says I can push myself, I'm going to ride in one of those all the time." He eyed her wheelchair like it was a motorbike. It was exciting to him. A game.

The game would end soon enough. And what would he have to look forward to then?

"Spring."

She started at Torin's whisper.

He made a cut signal across his throat and angled his head toward the door.

He'd heard something.

She put her finger to her lips for Bradley and strained to listen above the pounding of her heart.

Then she heard it. Footsteps.

Someone was coming.

CHAPTER
TWENTY-NINE

October 11. 12:54 p.m.

TORIN CLENCHED the hand duster in his palm and pressed his back against the wall. He shouldn't have let Spring talk to the boy. They'd been heard.

The footsteps stopped outside the door.

Torin held his breath. Every muscle tensed. Eyes locked on the door handle. Watching for it to move.

He would protect her this time.

"Spring?" A male voice. "Are you in there?"

Torin whipped up his hand, palm out toward Spring to signal she shouldn't answer.

He looked at the door. Didn't sound like the shooter. This voice was deeper. Older.

"It's Dr. Berghuis, Spring. The man with the gun sent me to find you and anyone else who's left on this floor."

Torin turned to Spring and mouthed, "Do you know him?"

She nodded, her face pale.

That wasn't enough assurance. The shooter could be right there with the guy, holding a gun on him to make him talk.

But the footsteps had sounded like only one person.

"Spring, are you in there?"

Torin kept his hand up toward her. They couldn't risk this being the shooter's ploy to get Spring in the open.

"I thought I heard you. If you're there, you have to come out."

The doctor wasn't giving up easily.

"He's taken six people hostage, Spring. He's negotiating with the police, but he hasn't let anyone go yet."

That would explain why SWAT hadn't entered by force. They wouldn't if he had hostages and showed signs of negotiating. The doctor's story was believable.

"He says he'll start killing the hostages if everyone who's still in hiding doesn't come out."

Torin glanced at Spring just in time to catch her opening her mouth. He made a slashing motion with his hand.

She pressed her lips together as lines etched her forehead.

"Spring."

The doctor needed to just walk away. Spring couldn't go out there. Their complete silence would make him give up eventually.

"He says he's going to start with your sister."

"Open it." Spring barely got out the words. She couldn't breathe. Victoria was with that maniac. And she was about to get killed.

"Spring!" The doctor's voice lifted. "You *are* in there."

Torin didn't move.

"Torin, it's my sister!" The panic in her voice seemed to make a dent in his stone-cold tactics.

He turned and opened the door a crack, the hand duster raised to the side.

Her pulse jumped when he immediately closed the door again, but he reached up and slipped the belt loop off the hinge. He opened the door just enough for him to pull the doctor inside by his arm.

Torin looped the belt over the hinge again as Dr. Berghuis quickly crossed the room to Spring.

"We can't stay here." He turned sideways to angle his glance at Torin, too. "He's going to start killing people in..." Dr. Berghuis checked his watch, "five minutes."

Spring's throat started to constrict. "Torin—"

"Where is he holding the hostages?" The sergeant's intense gaze locked on the doctor.

"By the east exit."

Torin nodded. "Smart."

"I don't think the boy has all of his faculties."

"Drugs?"

"Yes. Amphetamines. He insisted I bring him more from our supply."

Frustration blended with the panic pumping through Spring's veins as she pushed her chair as fast as she could toward the door. "I'm not going to sit here and let my sister get killed because of me." She faded, realizing she'd get there far too late on her own. "You'll have to push me, Doctor."

"I'll do it." Torin's voice came from right next to her as he bent to set his hand duster between her leg and the arm of her wheelchair. "Hang on to that for me, will you?" His gaze swept to hers, his face close.

A strange warmth filled her chest despite the fear squeezing it. He wasn't frightened at all. Even now. She could face the shooter if Torin was with her.

He went to the back of her chair and wheeled her toward the door.

"Don't go." Bradley's youthful voice caught her from behind.

Spring's heart lurched, and she looked back at Torin.

He paused, turning her chair slightly so she could see the others. "He's safer here."

Dr. Berghuis scanned the boy like he was assessing any

patient on a normal day. "He won't last." The doctor looked at Torin. "We don't know how long this will go on. He'll need food and his catheter bag drained. You two go ahead. I'll transfer him to a chair and follow after you. Tell the man with the gun that I'm bringing the last person hiding on this floor."

"As soon as the boy is ready, check on the security guard in five thirty-one." As he spoke, Torin quickly walked to the door and unloosed his belt from the hinge. "He was shot." Torin slipped the belt around his waist, then stepped behind Spring's chair again.

He'd remembered. She had thought he didn't care about the guard from the way he'd been so quick to leave him behind. But he had been putting others first. *Her* first.

"I already did." The doctor frowned. "I'm afraid there was nothing I could do."

Shock spread through Spring's upper body. The shooter had killed someone. How many others had he killed? Would Victoria be next?

She glanced back at Torin. "Please hurry."

He started to push her again.

"Wait."

Spring twisted around to see the doctor's hand on Torin's forearm.

"The negotiator he's talking to on the phone got him to say his name is Luke. He's very nervous, temperamental. I wouldn't try to get him to talk much."

Torin jerked a nod and took off at high speed, wheeling her out of the room and turning so fast her stomach swirled.

She gripped the armrests without complaint. She only had minutes to get to Victoria. Spring never should have hidden. If Torin was right about the shooter wanting to kill her, then this was her fault. Her sister wouldn't be in danger now if she'd just let the man kill her right away.

She swallowed, her fingers growing numb in their death grip. Would he kill her now? It would be for the best. She needed to remember that. Then she wouldn't have to face living a kind of half-life. She'd never have to see her father again, face his disappointment that she could never be what he wanted.

Maybe if she was gone, he and her siblings would come to think more fondly of her, forgive her failings and remember her as the one who died before she could achieve her potential.

Torin slowed the chair.

They were coming up on the corner that must lead to the east hallway.

He suddenly bent close behind her, his breath warming her ear as he spoke softly. "You don't have to do this."

"Would you let someone else die in your place?"

The chair stopped moving.

Torin's hand covered her shoulder from behind. "You're not going to die." His voice was deep and thick, as if clouded with emotion. "I won't let that happen."

She reached up and touched his strong fingers. "Let's go." She could only whisper, the fear of what she was about to face choking her air. But she had to save Victoria. They were taking too long. "Please."

He removed his hand to push her chair closer to the next hallway, then stopped. He let go and positioned himself with his back against the wall to peer around the corner.

What was he doing? Victoria could get killed in seconds.

Spring couldn't wait another moment. She started to push the chair herself.

Torin's head jerked toward her. His eyes flashed. But he went behind her chair and wheeled it the rest of the way around the corner.

She braced for death.

CHAPTER
THIRTY

"GET YOUR HANDS UP!"

Torin scanned the situation as he stepped in front of Spring's chair, raising his empty hands on either side of his head, muscles primed for action.

The shooter stood just beyond his hostages, aiming his Glock at Torin. Three hostages sat on the floor, Victoria closest to the shooter, and two were in wheelchairs.

"Who are you?" The shooter's shout was high-pitched and tight. Unstable.

"A friend."

"I can't see the girl!"

"I'm concerned you might hurt her." Torin kept his voice calm, level.

"I'm gonna shoot her sister if she doesn't get over here." He knew they were sisters. He had intel.

Torin's jaw clenched. He hadn't been wrong about the shooter's target. He kept the tension from his voice as he spoke. "Can you promise you won't hurt her?" If the negotiators had been talking with the guy all this time, he might be warmed up for conversation and compromise.

"You're afraid of me. Everyone's afraid of me." Despite the

boast, the statement was laced with anxiety, his voice shaky. "Just get over here. I don't want to hurt her."

"I see Victoria," Spring whispered as she craned her neck to peer around him. "Please, I need to make sure she's okay."

"I'll push her over there." Torin kept an eye on the shooter as he slowly brought his hands down and stepped behind Spring's chair. Everything in him screamed not to take her any closer, escort her into danger. He could make a dash back around the corner instead.

"Please, Torin."

How did she know what he was thinking?

His gut in a vise, he put his hand on her shoulder. "You'll both be okay. Don't try to talk to him, and do what he says."

Her soft hair brushed the back of his hand as she nodded.

He wheeled the chair forward. They were arguably too close already to make a run for it. The shooter had a clear line of sight to shoot. It was too late to save her now that way.

Torin forced himself to breathe. Keep his muscles loose, ready to use. He'd promised he wouldn't let her die.

But the promise was about as empty as the perp's not to hurt her. Torin was unarmed and escorting her to an out-of-control drug addict with a gun.

"Ivy, get back!"

Torin tried to blink away the memory of his own scream, of the moment his heart had been torn from his chest. He'd promised to protect Ivy when he married her. He had led her to the slaughter, too.

"Stop there." The shooter's voice jolted Torin from the pain that blocked his awareness of everything.

They were nearly on top of the hostages who sat at the shooter's feet.

Stupid time to zone out. Fear flooded his body. He couldn't do this. He couldn't protect Spring when he couldn't even get ahold of himself.

The shooter's gaze was on her.

Torin itched to jump between her and the Luke character,

but he held himself back. No telling what a sudden move like that would cause the shooter to do.

"Where's Doc?"

"He's bringing the last person on this floor." Torin's quick answer got the perp to switch his attention to him.

"He's just a little boy. Please don't hurt him." Spring's plea drew the shooter's attention back to her.

Along with his gun.

"You can't walk at all, can you?"

The blend of childlike curiosity and cruelty in the shooter's expression frightened Spring and raised her hackles at the same time. She bit her tongue to stop the sarcastic reply that perched there.

From her spot on the floor, Victoria shot Spring a warning look that was completely unnecessary. They were hostages and Victoria was still trying to tell Spring what to do.

"What's the matter? Think you're too high and mighty to answer me?"

Heat fired her cheeks. "No."

"You shouldn't have moved like that. When I tried to… That wasn't nice." His voice pinched, the gun still pointed at her. He really was crazy.

She held her breath. Was he going to shoot her?

"Hey, now." Torin's voice behind her was soft as butter. "You said you don't want to hurt her, remember?"

The shooter's odd-looking gaze lurched to Torin. "I know what I said!" His gaunt cheeks sunk in even more under his spotty facial hair when he inhaled sharply. "But she's going to ruin everything."

Because Sergeant Cotter had pushed her out of the path of a bullet? Spring tensed as the shooter waved the gun barrel at her face. Whatever the guy was on must be making him delusional. She was wheelchair bound and helpless. How could she ruin anything?

"No." The word was sharp, punched out with a gust of energy that made her wince.

Who was he talking to?

His jaw shifted as his free fingers scratched his side through the pale blue polo shirt splotched with what looked like bloodstains.

She shoved the nauseating thought aside. Letting her imagination run away with her would not help.

"You're not going to mess me up again."

A shiver shot up the part of her spine she could feel as he stared down at her with eyes so vacant he could be talking to a ghost in his sickened mind.

He squeezed his hand around the gun.

"Why would you want to hurt her? Do you know her?"

The shooter switched his aim to Torin in response to his interruption. "No...no." A grin twisted the shooter's lips as he moved his head side to side. "I don't know her." His gaze shifted to Spring, and the grin faded.

Footsteps sounded from the other end of the hallway.

The shooter swung the gun toward Dr. Berghuis and Bradley, the boy now sitting in a small wheelchair. "That's not everyone."

The doctor didn't appear rattled by the shooter's shout. He kept pushing Bradley toward them at a steady pace, his mouth in a firm line.

"You said some of them can't get out of their beds." The shooter let the gun loll to the side in his hand.

"That's right, Luke. There are patients like that. They won't be any threat to you." The doctor looked at the shooter as he brought Bradley next to Spring's chair on her right.

She gave the boy an encouraging smile she didn't feel.

He smiled back, far happier and more relaxed than the last time she'd seen him.

The chair. He was probably thrilled to get another ride in a wheelchair. Relief relaxed the pinch in Spring's chest just slightly. If only she could keep Bradley unaware of the danger they were in.

Luke's eyes narrowed at the doctor as he swiped his sweaty forehead with the back of his hand.

An odd sound cut through the tension. Music?

Luke's fingers twitched on the gun's handle as the noise continued.

A classical ringtone? It sounded familiar.

Her gaze dropped to the collection of cell phones, pooled together on the floor in the middle of the hostages who sat in a jagged circle.

But Luke pulled a phone from his back jeans pocket instead. "Nobody move." He waved the gun over the hostages while he tapped the screen of the smartphone that had a pale green protective cover. Was that Victoria's phone?

"Yeah?" He paused with the cell phone pressed to his ear. Who was he talking to? Someone helping him on the outside? "Fine...No, I'm not tired."

Torin came into Spring's peripheral view on her left, slowly moving forward.

Luke's gaze latched onto the movement as he continued speaking into the phone.

Torin kept his eyes on the shooter while he crouched next to Spring's chair, putting his hand over hers where it rested on the arm of the wheelchair. His hand was warm and slightly rough. It felt safe. "You okay?" He kept his voice low.

She bit her lip, fighting against the sudden, inconvenient urge to cry that his gentle question unleashed. She blinked back tears and nodded.

"Are you sure you've never seen him before?"

"Yes, I—."

"Stop that!" Luke's shout made Spring jump. In her upper body anyway.

He glared their way, pointing the gun. "They're talking." He must have been answering some question from the caller.

He paused while Spring froze, waiting to see what he would do with the childlike anger in his voice. "Some guy and a chick in a wheelchair."

She blinked at the sting of the words. That's how everyone saw her now. Even a drugged shooter. If she could move, she'd throw herself at the shooter and let him kill her in the hope everyone else could get away. But she couldn't move. Couldn't do anything. She might as well be dead.

"I said I'll let one go." Luke continued his phone conversation. "But I know the cops are on the stairs. Tell them they have to go away and let me through."

So he wasn't talking to a friend. Maybe a police negotiator?

Torin gently squeezed Spring's hand, bringing her gaze to his face. His mouth curved into a slight smile, his green eyes comforting, confident.

"Okay." Luke's gaze was on them when Spring glanced his way. "No, I haven't hurt anyone. I won't unless they don't listen to me." He licked his chapped lips. "Yeah. Leave the stuff outside the door. If you try to trick me, one of these people dies. I mean it!"

Spring closed her eyes as he shouted the last words.

"Get away from her."

She opened her eyes to see Luke jamming the phone in his pocket and waving the gun at Torin.

Torin calmly stood and raised his hands, palms out. "Just making sure she's okay."

Victoria got to her feet.

Luke swung the gun her way. "I didn't say you could get up."

"Spring can't stay in one position for that long." Victoria lifted her chin, not a glint of fear in her commanding posture. Spring's sister was superhuman. "She has a sore that can't take the pressure."

"That's just too bad." Luke's narrowed gaze contradicted his words. "Sit down and shut up. I need to think."

"There's nothing to be gained by holding these hostages."

Dr. Berghuis took a turn. But would ganging up on Luke wear him down or make him more likely to shoot? "The police will never let you out now."

"Don't you think I know that?" The gun shook in Luke's hand with his yell. "It's all your fault." He took a step toward the doctor but stayed on the other side of the hostages between them. "You doctors. Always think you're so smart. I ought to shoot you right now so the world can have one less."

"But you don't want to do that, do you?" Dr. Berghuis had guts. He stared down the shooter like he was a patient being prepped for operation.

Luke glared. He fingered the trigger of the gun.

"Not smart, Luke." Torin caught the shooter's attention.

He kept doing that. Always drawing Luke's focus whenever he looked mad enough to shoot someone.

Her heart warmed in her chest. Torin would probably say he was only doing his job, but getting paid to be a cop didn't automatically make someone a hero.

"If anyone else gets hurt, you're going to need the doctor here to keep them from dying."

Luke breathed a nervous laugh. "Why would I care?"

Torin's gaze didn't leave the shooter. "Because if you start killing people, the police will take you down."

Luke stared at him. "How do you know?"

"Think, man. You know you're stuck."

Spring's pulse began to race with Torin's challenging tone and the red flush that rose in Luke's face.

"There's only one way this will end well for you."

"Shut up, man! Just shut up!"

Torin briefly lifted his hands at Luke's shout.

The shooter panted as he glared at his nemesis. If Torin was trying to draw Luke's hatred, he was doing a good job. But Spring didn't like it a bit.

"You got a phone?"

Torin didn't blink at Luke's question that sounded more like an accusation. "I left it in my car."

Spring fought to keep the alarm off her face. What if the shooter found out Torin was lying?

"Turn around." Luke tilted his chin.

The line of Torin's jaw tightened as he turned.

Even from the side, Spring could see the outline of the edge of his phone through his back pocket.

The gun went off.

CHAPTER
THIRTY-ONE

Her body lay in the hallway. Blood seeped through her yellow dress, dripping down from her blond hair.

"Torin!"

He shut his eyes, trying to block out the scream, the images that assaulted him.

"Torin? Are you hurt?"

A different female voice reached for him through the crushing memory. Spring.

He opened his eyes.

The rehab center hallway.

Empty.

No body. No Ivy.

What happened? Reality returned in a wave. Luke had shot at him.

Torin took a mental inventory of his limbs to confirm he hadn't been injured. Either the drugs made the perp a terrible shot, or he had intentionally missed.

Torin's fingers trembled as he brought his hands in front of his body, but his shaking and irregular heartbeat had nothing to do with nearly getting killed.

Stupid move. He'd put Spring and the others in jeopardy by testing Luke like that. The shooter's aim was bad enough he could have shot any of them by mistake. And Torin clearly couldn't handle anything to do with gunfire even under these circumstances. Just how many deadly mistakes did he have to make before he'd learn?

He took in a deep breath. Couldn't let the perp think he'd rattled him. It was the memories that had. He turned to face the shooter. "You could have hurt someone."

"That's the point, man." The weapon shook in Luke's hand, his dilated pupils boring holes into Torin. He looked more rattled by the shot than anyone. "Don't try to fool me again."

The perp had a surprisingly elevated vocabulary. Judging from his word choice, accent, and the jeans that looked to be designer denim that had been worn too long, Torin would guess Luke hadn't grown up on the streets. And he still had access to money currently. Or, he knew someone who bought him things. The expensive watch on his wrist and shiny leather shoes had to come from somewhere.

"Give me the phone."

Torin reached for his pocket.

"Slowly."

He slowed his movement as he pulled out the phone and extended it toward Luke.

"Throw it on the floor there."

"Should've sprung for the shatterproof screen, I guess."

The doctor was the only one who chuckled as Torin tossed the device to land next to the other four hostage phones on the floor.

But Spring rewarded him with a slight upturn of her lips.

How could he have put her at risk? He needed to stop playing the big, brave cop routine and play it safe instead. He couldn't see her get hurt.

"Yours, too." He tilted the gun at Spring.

"It's in my room."

Luke's smartphone sounded again—a classical music ring tone. Not what Torin would have guessed for the shooter. Could be a phone lifted from a hostage.

"Don't try anything." He glared at Torin before answering the call.

Torin held up his hands. He'd let the negotiator and SWAT handle this character. All he needed to do was help Spring lay low and stay out of the way. If the situation worsened or he saw an opportunity to end this, he'd take it. But no more unnecessary testing or games.

"Fine." Luke scrunched his chin like a little kid as he spoke into the phone. "There better be nobody waiting." He pressed the screen hard and surveyed the hostages.

What now?

He pointed at Victoria. "You. Go get the food outside the door." He waved the gun to indicate the exit stairwell. "You let anybody in or try to run, and I'll blast your sister." He aimed the gun at Spring to drive home his point as Victoria got to her feet.

Anger stirred in Torin's gut. What a coward. He was holding paralyzed women and children hostage. And Torin couldn't even arrest him, let alone disarm him. At least not yet. But the guy had to get tired at some point, make a mistake, let down his guard. Torin would be ready.

"Hurry up!"

Victoria didn't flinch at Luke's shout. Just looked at him before she walked to the metal door of the stairwell and reached to open it.

"Hold it."

She angled toward Luke.

"Remember what will happen if you try anything. Your sister goes first."

Her gaze flitted to Spring. "I won't try anything." She opened the door partway and leaned out, sliding in two cardboard trays of paper cups with straws. She reached again and swung in two bags labeled with a local fast-food restaurant's name.

So Luke was from Chicago. And apparently liked fast food. The negotiator shouldn't have too much trouble handling this guy. As long as he didn't lose it thanks to the speed the doctor had been forced to give him. Judging from the bulge of Luke's front pocket, too small for a weapon, Torin guessed the shooter was carrying a supply of the drug on him.

At least Torin now knew he could easily get Luke's wrath targeted at him. If he could keep it that way, Spring wouldn't be harmed if Luke blew up and decided to shoot someone.

The perp reached into his bulging pocket and pulled out a plastic bag of powder he must have created by crushing the amphetamine tablets. Torin frowned as Luke held onto his gun while he snorted some of the speed.

If he kept that up, a sudden shooting was entirely too likely. The food or a distraction from taking more speed might help.

"Mind if we pass out the food?" Torin kept his tone casual as he glanced at Victoria.

She still stood near the door, fast-food bags in her hands.

Luke narrowed his eyes. "She can do it. I don't trust you."

The feeling was mutual. Torin forced himself to look away from Luke's stare. He'd made it too clear already that he was a threat.

"But maybe I won't let anybody have any of it." Luke stuffed the bag of speed into his pocket.

Torin casually slid his hand into his back pants pocket, trying for a relaxed position. "You can't be going to eat all that food yourself." Especially since the scrawny guy likely didn't eat much at all thanks to his speed addiction.

"Maybe I'll just let it sit there." Luke's tone was a match for Derrick's nine-year-old son when Torin had watched him one weekend. The kid had to challenge everything, whether it made sense to or not.

"Didn't you promise the negotiator you'd give the hostages

food?" Maybe reminding Luke that there could be consequences would help. These hostages needed nourishment if this was going to last as long as Torin had a feeling it could.

"He's not a negotiator."

Oops. The negotiator must not be playing it straight with Luke. "Okay, I didn't know. I just meant whoever you've been talking to on the phone."

"Are you a cop?" Luke tilted his chin as he glared. "You sound like a cop."

Torin didn't change his casual stance as he chuckled. "Do I look like one?"

"I don't like cops." The perp lifted his gun halfway, as if unsure he wanted to point it at Torin. "I don't want a spy here." He aimed the weapon and took a step toward Torin, his voice growing louder. "Are you a cop spy?"

"He's my boyfriend."

Torin and Luke looked at Spring.

Had she really just said he was her boyfriend? She'd actually shouted it.

Her cheeks flooded with bright red as she dropped her gaze.

Luke broke the silence with a laugh that slithered under Torin's skin. "You're into chicks in wheelchairs?" He lowered the gun and grinned.

Torin ground his teeth together, fingers curling into a fist at his side. *He has a gun, Cotter.* The reminder was the only thing that kept Torin from flying at the jerk.

Spring stared at the floor, looking as if she'd like to melt into it while Luke laughed.

"She's a beautiful lady, man." Torin fought not to let his friendly gaze turn into a glare the perp would interpret as a challenge. "I guess I'm just lucky."

Luke's grin faltered, then faded as he stared at Torin.

"Why don't we eat before the food gets cold?" Victoria sounded like a mom talking to her kids at dinnertime—the perfect tone to keep the peace with this guy.

The shooter swung his gaze to her, then back to Torin. "Fine." He took a step away and angled to watch Victoria. "Chocolate shake's mine."

She set down the bags and lifted one tray of drinks, checking the tops through the lids.

Torin let his gaze leave Luke and drift down at his side to Spring.

She turned her head away, but not before he caught her expression. She'd been watching him with a mixture of surprise and softness in those big brown eyes.

Warmth filtered through his chest. Was she surprised he'd said she was beautiful? Didn't she know that?

He knew she'd only said he was her boyfriend because she wanted to protect him, to stop Luke from following his suspicions that led too close to the truth. But it was interesting that was the first thing she'd thought of in the moment. Could she actually be thinking—

Victoria handed him a cup just in time to bring his thoughts to an abrupt halt. He was not going down that road again. It brought more pain and danger than anything in life.

Victoria's hold lingered on the cup as he tried to take it. She tapped the side with her finger before letting go.

Checking to be sure Luke wasn't watching, Torin examined the paper cup. A label like those used at coffee shops was attached, bearing letters written in black marker.

SC.

Sergeant Cotter.

He took a sip from the straw, cringing when orange soda hit his taste buds. Derrick must not be out there, or he'd at least have sent a Coke. But hydration was important and so was appearing nonchalant, so he drank some more as he started to peel back the label's corner.

It came off easily, and he palmed it in his hand.

Luke stood leaning against the wall, obliviously sucking his shake while dangling the gun from the fingers of his other hand.

Torin lowered the drink and looked at the underside of the label.

Perp drives a white van. Plates match. –D

Boone's photo. Heat traveled through Torin's body as if a fire had been lit in his belly. He glared at the perp. Was he the one who'd killed Ivy?

Luke turned his head in Torin's direction.

Torin dropped his gaze and took a sip of the awful soda. He fought for even breaths as he drank. Had to stay calm, rational.

This shooter might have no connection with the gas station robbery. The van could be the same, but the plates weren't Luke's. No way to ID the driver or what the van had been used for three years ago.

But it did mean that Luke was driving a van belonging to Donovan Mackeral, the victim of a drug shooting. And Spring had cycled past the location of that killing just before she was hit. Had to be a connection.

Spring rested a drink on her leg and stared blankly ahead. Exhaustion and fear strained her lovely features. Whatever the tie was between her and Mackeral's shooting, it clearly didn't include a friendly relationship with Luke.

Had she been buying drugs from Mackeral when Luke showed up and things went south?

"A good cop always suspects everyone."

Derrick's words ground against Torin's raw nerves. Probably right.

But looking at her doe brown eyes, shadowed with fear, her trembling fingers as she clutched the cup in her hand, he couldn't believe she was a user. That she'd be tied to characters like Luke or Mackeral.

He shouldn't be wasting his time trying to pin something on Spring. He should be focusing on getting her out of this alive.

He drank more to hydrate as he forced his mind on assessing, observing, doing whatever he could to apprehend the perp and contribute to saving the hostages as soon as possible. SWAT wouldn't come in anytime soon. Torin had realized that the moment they'd joined the other hostages, and he'd seen the situation they were in.

Whether accidentally or with more intelligence than Torin would've thought Luke had, the shooter had chosen a brilliant location to hold his prisoners. The hallway didn't have any windows. No possibility of snipers taking him out. And the perp could easily see all the entry points.

SWAT agents could force their way in, but not without the collateral damage of Luke shooting at least one hostage before anyone could take him down. So long as he communicated with the negotiator and continued to treat the hostages humanely, the police wouldn't risk an assault that could result in more loss of life.

On top of all that, the response teams knew there was a cop among the hostages. That gave them one more reason to bide their time and hope Torin could protect those inside. And maybe take out the shooter.

Good thing Luke had allowed food in. They could be there for a very long time.

While Victoria handed out the food, Torin surveyed the people he hadn't observed as carefully as he should have before.

Close to Luke, a male of about twenty sat in a wheelchair. He seemed to be able to move his arms, but his fingers curved stiffly inward, and he used the sides of his hands to hold his drink. He made quiet moaning noises off and on. Could be the patient in the room Torin had told Victoria to barricade, but he hadn't gotten a clear enough look then to be sure.

Next to that man sat another wheelchair, which held a heavier male who looked to be in his fifties. His eyes were almost closed, and his head lolled slightly to one side. His lips moved almost constantly, though he wasn't talking. Brain damage as well as paralysis?

Across from them on the floor sat a petite lady who looked

to be in her late seventies or early eighties and a man who caught Torin's interest. Mid to late thirties and one hundred sixty pounds, the man might be able to help with an escape or defending the others if needed. He looked strong, his blue scrubs indicating he might be a nurse. He took a wrapped sandwich from Victoria and glanced at Torin.

Torin nodded.

The man nodded back, then immediately hopped his gaze to Luke as if afraid the gesture might have been noticed.

The guy was nervous and not very tall, probably about five-foot-eight, but in a bind Torin might have to use him. The doctor, though in his fifties, appeared to be the only other able-bodied male who would be able to help if they had to overpower the shooter.

Victoria might be able to assist with a plan, but she seemed too concerned with Spring's safety to risk crossing Luke. And Torin wouldn't want her to change that strategy. The perp was starting to trust Victoria, which could help Spring stay alive and unharmed.

"Do you want a sandwich?" Victoria held up a wrapped package toward Luke across the distance of the hostages.

He snorted. "I don't even like that junk." He sipped his chocolate shake, looking about ten years younger than he was.

Victoria turned to Bradley and handed him the sandwich instead.

Lucky the kid was the quiet type. At least so far. The shooter didn't seem fond of children.

Spring's lips curved into a small smile she aimed at Bradley before the boy started munching his sandwich.

Torin had the feeling she could calm the kid down if he got upset again. The way she'd so quickly and easily brought him from tears to smiles in his room was amazing. And being around the boy had just as quickly transformed Spring into a nurturing, protective mama bear.

That's what she needed. Someone to live for.

Torin couldn't shake the suspicion that she wasn't just unafraid of death. She almost seemed to want it.

He found himself looking into those large brown eyes as she lifted her gaze to his. His pulse picked up speed.

She wouldn't get her wish. Not here. Not now.

He'd make sure of that. Even if it killed him.

CHAPTER
THIRTY-TWO

October 11. 4:36 p.m.
3 hours, 36 minutes hostage.

SPRING FOLLOWED Luke with her gaze as he paced back and forth between the walls of the hallway, muttering to himself. He stopped now and then to snort more of the powdered drug.

Spring sank her teeth into her lip. She'd tried to avoid the inevitable as long as she could, but the last hour had been sheer misery. Couldn't wait any longer.

She took a breath and reached for Torin, who sat on the floor next to her chair. She touched his shoulder with her fingers, surprised at the tautness of the muscles under his shirt.

He turned his emerald eyes up at her, and she thought her heart might stop.

Probably only because she was about to die from embarrassment at what she had to tell him. The humiliations of paralysis never ended.

She bit back what she really needed to say and went for the lesser embarrassment to start. "I'm sorry for what I said."

His eyebrows lifted.

"That you're my..." *Boyfriend*. She couldn't even manage to whisper the word. Heat crept toward her cheeks. "I was just..."

"Trying to save my life." The corners of his mouth tugged upward as his eyes glittered with something exciting and gentle at the same time. "You don't have to apologize for that."

She took a breath as her pulse fluttered. Now this was going to be even more humiliating. But her body's signals reminded her she couldn't wait. She cast Luke a glance.

Still walked back and forth without paying them any mind.

She started to lean toward Torin, then remembered she didn't have much success with that. "I have to go to the bathroom."

He nodded in response to her whisper, his lips straightening into a serious line that didn't betray a hint of amusement or embarrassment. He pulled his legs under him and stood. "Hey, Luke."

The shooter jerked toward them, tensing his grip on the gun he held at his side.

"How about a bathroom break?"

He sneered.

Torin met Luke's derision with a steady gaze. "For the lady. And I'm guessing others might have to go, too."

"Not me. I've got a bag." Bradley proudly held up his quarter-full catheter bag.

Luke's features scrunched like he was about to throw up as he stared at the bag.

Spring could've laughed if not for the gun in his hand... and the fact that she was about to explode if she didn't get to the bathroom. And here she'd been glad to graduate from the catheter.

"I'll take her." Victoria got to her feet and started to approach Spring.

"Hold it."

Victoria stopped, looking at Luke.

"You'll run away if you go together. She can go alone."

Victoria shook her head. "No, she can't. She needs special help."

Spring's cheeks flamed. She couldn't look at anyone. Especially not Torin. She'd almost rather Luke just shoot her. Was this what her life was going to be like if she survived? One humiliation after another?

"There's a bathroom in this hallway." Victoria continued to bargain. "I promise we won't try anything. You'll be able to see us when we go in and when we come out. And I want to be able to take the others who need help, too, so I won't try anything. I promise."

Luke watched her with narrowed eyes.

Victoria would get her way. She always did.

"You can take her. But if you try to run away I'll shoot…" He glanced at the hostages as if trying to guess the favorite. He aimed the gun at Torin. "Her boyfriend. I'll take him out."

"We won't run away." Victoria made her way to Spring's chair, glancing at Torin as she passed next to him.

"Do just what he says." Torin's voice was low and quiet.

Victoria nodded and disappeared out of Spring's vision behind her.

As her sister turned the chair, Spring glanced back at Torin. "Be careful."

He met her gaze for as long as she could see him, until she had to turn her head forward while Victoria took her away.

Spring braced herself to hear a shot.

She wanted to get away from the madman, but for some reason she felt as if she'd left part of herself behind. *Please, Lord. Keep Torin from making Luke angry. Keep him safe.*

She hoped her prayer would be heard this time.

Spring reached under the automatic soap dispenser next to the sink in the women's bathroom. She fell forward, jerking her hands to the counter's edge to catch herself.

Hands clutched her shoulders before she hit the hard granite. Victoria saved the day once again.

Spring gritted her teeth as Victoria pulled her torso back up.

"You should be able to do that without any trouble, Spring. Your trunk control could have been at almost one hundred percent by now if you'd worked at it."

Spring bit her tongue and proceeded to put her somewhat soapy hands under the faucet that started with a motion sensor. This was hardly the time or place for a fight.

"There you go." Victoria kept her hands on Spring's shoulders. "Remember to keep your abs tight."

Frustration bubbled in Spring's chest like the soap suds in the sink. "Good grief, Victoria. This isn't a PT session. We're about to get killed." She turned off the water and pulled her hands from the sink.

"Don't say that." Victoria tore a paper towel from the dispenser and thrust it at Spring. She must be somewhat upset, or she'd have made Spring get the towel herself. "We're going to get out of this."

Spring dried her hands without a word.

"I was so thankful when you showed up in the hallway and you weren't hurt. Though I had hoped you might have escaped."

"How would I do that in this thing?" Spring tossed the wadded paper towel into the garbage slot in the wall.

Victoria's lips pursed in her trying-to-hold-something-back expression. Her brow smoothed as she apparently decided to say something else. "I keep thinking about how worried Dad and everyone must be."

"Yeah. I bet they're worried sick about you."

Victoria managed to look shocked. "They're worried about both of us."

"Sure." Spring's tone signaled her sarcasm.

"Will you stop? You know they love us both."

"Just not equally, right?"

Victoria turned to the sink and started to wash her hands. For the second time. "That's your depression talking. It's normal to become depressed and go through deep emotional downswings after an accident like yours."

"First off, it wasn't an accident, okay?" Spring glared at her sister's back. "Somebody hit me on purpose and left me paralyzed for the rest of my life."

Victoria stepped to the paper towel dispenser. "If you work—"

"Second, this isn't depression. This is me being the only one to voice the honest truth. You know I'm the failure of the family. The odd one out."

Victoria turned to face Spring, wiping her hands with the paper towel. "That's not true. Treese is a personal trainer."

Spring smiled without humor or satisfaction at the remark. "Oh, yeah. I'd forgotten about the *lesser* PT." Victoria obviously knew exactly what Spring was talking about without explanation. Point made.

Victoria closed her mouth, probably realizing what she'd just said.

"Even Treese still got a degree. And in a medically-related field. That's what Dad wants."

"You're being ridiculous." Victoria sighed as she placed her towel in the garbage and pushed it down over the others. "Personal training is not medical, and Dad doesn't put a price tag on his love."

"Just his approval." Moisture stung Spring's eyes, but she blinked it away.

Victoria turned to Spring, crossing her arms over her avocado, long-sleeved polo shirt. "Is that why you refuse to work at becoming more independent? At living?"

Spring looked away, her chest growing uncomfortably

tight. "We should go. People's lives may be depending on us." Especially Torin's. They'd already taken too long.

"Fine. But I want you to know something."

Spring braced herself.

"Whatever happens, I want you to know that I love you. And I'm sorry that I wasn't the sister you needed me to be."

Spring lifted her gaze.

Victoria's hazel eyes glistened with moisture.

A lump formed in Spring's throat. "It's not about you, Victoria. I just can't live like this."

"Promise me you won't do anything stupid."

To end it. The unsaid part of Victoria's statement hung between them in the silence of the bathroom.

Spring dropped her attention to the hand duster Victoria had taken off her chair and propped against the wall. She swallowed. "Sure. Promise."

As Victoria went behind the chair and began to push toward the door, Spring reviewed her promise. She wouldn't take such an action herself, of course. It would be wrong. But if she caught a bullet from the shooter who'd already tried to kill her once, would it be so bad? Maybe it would be God's mercy, sparing her from having to live a life of misery.

"I'm worried about your pressure sore." Victoria spoke from behind as they moved into the hallway. "You can't keep sitting in the same position. And you shouldn't have things like that hand duster on your chair or you could get more sores."

Spring barely heard her sister as she checked for Torin among the hostages.

Where was he? Nerves churned in her stomach.

He wouldn't have done anything to make Luke mad again, would he? The shooter had been glaring at him so much already. And he'd started to suspect Torin was a police officer. Could he have—

Someone stood in front of Bradley's chair.

Torin.

Her heart lurched.

He must've been crouched down to talk to the boy. But now he watched her with a slight smile that made her pulse play hopscotch. Was he happy to see her, too?

She squashed the farfetched thought as soon as it came. It was hardly the time for silly romantic notions, even if she wasn't paralyzed and had a chance with him. He was probably smiling about something Bradley had said.

"You came back." The boy turned his head to beam at Spring as Victoria stopped her chair alongside his.

The welcome warmed Spring's heart. She wished all children would be so willing to overlook her wheelchair. With Bradley, the chair was actually an asset. She smiled. "Did you think I'd get lost?" She thumbed to Victoria behind her. "That's my big sister. She won't let me get lost. She always won when we played hide and go seek."

Bradley's grin widened. "I play with my little brother sometimes. I always find him, too."

"I bet you do." She looked up at Torin. "Everything go okay?"

"I was a good boy." He smiled, his eyes crinkling at the corners.

Her heart skipped a beat.

"I didn't say you could talk."

Torin's mouth flattened as he angled toward Luke.

The shooter aimed his attention at Spring. "Bet you're glad I didn't hurt your boyfriend while you were gone."

Spring glanced at Torin, then dropped her gaze. Why had she ever said he was her boyfriend? She had thought it would help, not make things worse.

"Are you going to let the others go to the restroom now?" The doctor's question mercifully drew Luke's unstable gaze away.

"Only one at a time. And I'll shoot the kid if anybody tries anything."

Spring's breath caught. Now Bradley? What kind of a

lunatic would want to harm a boy in a wheelchair? She moistened her dry lips as she reached across the arm of Bradley's chair to squeeze his hand. *Lord, I don't care what happens to me, but please save this little boy...And Torin.* He didn't know the Lord. That was the reason he was the second person who came to mind. Had to be the only reason that the thought of any harm coming to him wrenched her stomach.

"She can go next." Luke waved the gun to indicate the elderly woman who sat on the floor.

Dr. Berghuis went to the woman's side and helped her to her feet. Once she'd made it past the cluster of hostages and was moving toward the bathroom with a little less stiffness, he turned to Luke. "I should check on the patients confined to their rooms, as well."

Would another request push Luke too far? But the doctor was right to take the risk. If she hadn't been so self-centered, Spring would've already thought about the other patients who hadn't been able to get out of their beds.

Luke stared at Dr. Berghuis.

"You don't want anything happening to those people if you hope to negotiate a release."

"I'll give you ten minutes."

"I'll need more than that."

Luke scrunched up his nose. "How many are there?"

"Three. They're spread out, and I don't know how much attention they'll need. I could use an assistant. Perhaps Miss Wes—"

"No." Luke shook his head. "Everyone else stays here. And I *will* start shooting them if you don't come back."

"I'll come back."

"You can't go until everyone else is here and sitting where I can see them."

"Fair enough." Dr. Berghuis walked to the wall where he resumed his position on the floor, looking as relaxed as if he were sitting down to a picnic. Must be nice to have a surgeon's steel nerves.

"I need to move Spring." Victoria stood behind Spring and spoke quietly over her head to Torin. "She has a pressure sore, and I don't want her sitting on it this long."

"What are you talking about?" Luke stared at them like they were conspiring against him instead of talking about how pathetically needy she was.

"My sister has a pressure sore. I need to move her to the floor for a while."

"She stays where she is." He swung his gaze over the others. "That goes for everyone."

"A pressure sore can be extremely serious." Dr. Berghuis looked up at Luke. "There's no harm in letting her change positions. It could help with the police if you can say you're treating the hostages kindly."

Luke stared at the doctor for a few seconds, his mouth twisting as if he was engaged in a mental battle.

"Go ahead." He spun away from the doctor to pace to the other wall, whipping out his bag of powder to inhale.

"What if *I* don't want to sit on the floor?" Spring let go of Bradley's hand and glared at Victoria as she stepped to the side of her chair.

The famous arched eyebrow. "Seriously? You're going to fight me on this?"

Spring glanced at Torin, Victoria's parental tone making her aware of how immature she probably sounded. "Fine. Just don't make a whole PT lesson out of it."

"I wouldn't dream of it." Victoria pursed her lips as she looked at Torin. "Will you lift her while I get the cushion from her chair and then set her on the floor?"

Torin's startled gaze flicked to Spring, then back to Victoria. "Sure." He couldn't sound or look more reluctant if he tried.

Her heart plummeted. She couldn't blame him. The idea of having to hold her probably repulsed him.

"From here?" He stepped to the side of the chair opposite Victoria.

"Yes. Just put one arm behind her lower back and the other under her knees."

Torin's warm arm slid behind Spring's back, and she quickly turned her head away.

She couldn't bear to see the disgust that would be on his face. But as he lifted her against his solid chest, his arm strong and muscled behind her back, her heart thundered so loudly in her ears, she was afraid he could hear it.

She tried to make herself pay attention to Victoria as she removed the thick cushion from the chair and picked up Torin's sport coat from the floor where it must have dropped when he'd lifted her. Victoria walked away to set the cushion on the floor by the wall.

Spring fought to ignore Torin's masculine scent engulfing her. Like spices and mint.

His chest moved against her arm as he breathed, deep and even. The air passed by her hair and tickled her neck.

She turned her head toward him.

Her gaze collided with his emerald eyes, locked on her with an intensity that sent a shiver skating across her arms. His chiseled jaw was so close. Her fingers itched to discover what his sun-bronzed skin felt like.

His breathing deepened even more, slowing. His gaze lowered. To her lips?

"You can bring her over here now."

Torin pulled his head away at Victoria's ill-timed command.

"Right." He lifted Spring a little higher, not meeting her gaze as he carried her smoothly to where Victoria stood next to the cushion.

Spring's cheeks burned. Had everyone been watching them? She didn't risk checking.

But there was no missing the amusement that played around Victoria's lips and the way she raised her eyebrows at Spring before instructing Torin. "Place her on the cushion, a little on the side of her right hip if you can."

No doubt Victoria would make a big deal out of what had happened, thinking it proved she was correct about Torin being attracted to Spring. For the first time in her life, Spring actually wished her sister was right.

But Torin didn't look at her when he set her down and backed away as quickly as he could.

No, Victoria was wrong. All that little interaction proved was that Spring was painfully attracted to Torin. And that she should have her head examined for even considering the possibility that a man like him would ever think twice about someone like her. Someone chained to a wheelchair for the rest of her life.

She crunched her teeth together as Victoria tried to get her in exactly the right position with her back and shoulder against the wall.

If someone had to crash into her, why couldn't the driver have done a more thorough job and finished her off completely?

Luke paced noisily back and forth across the hallway, watching his hostages like a lion about to pounce on the weakest in the herd.

At least Torin's theory must have been off. Luke hadn't wanted to kill Spring any more than the other hostages. If he had, he would have shot her when she first showed up.

What was she thinking? It would be to everyone's advantage, including hers, if he would rectify the mistake that had been made by the clumsy driver and put an end to her misery. Maybe there was a way she could make sure that happened.

CHAPTER
THIRTY-THREE

October 12. 1:05 a.m.
12 hours, 5 minutes hostage.

THE GUY NEVER SLEPT.

Torin kept his eye on Luke as he finished jotting a second message in the notepad he'd snuck from his sport coat pocket on Spring's lap while she slept.

The shooter pushed off the wall and started to pace again. Those drugs he kept snorting would ensure he didn't have to sleep for some time. The perp wasn't as dumb as he appeared. He likely knew if he fell asleep, this would end. Badly for him.

The shoes bothered Torin the most. They didn't fit. The rest of Luke's garb was made up of ill-kept clothing that was once expensive, but he hadn't replaced any of it. His four day growth of splotchy beard, oily hair, and putrid smell suggested he didn't bother with personal hygiene. The upturned collar of his polo shirt was likely an indicator of sloppiness rather than a fashion statement. Yet he wore fancy black leather lace-ups in mint condition. Why?

Then again, why any of this? Why had Luke dashed into

Spring's room sixteen hours ago and tried to kill her? Or had he only meant to frighten her?

Torin silently tore off the piece of paper, folded it, and stuffed it in his front pants' pocket with the other note.

Too many unanswered questions cluttered his mind. He was used to finding answers. Getting out and investigating until he uncovered every secret and found all the pieces that completed the puzzle. But he couldn't do that here.

He narrowed his eyes at the shooter. He could be the one who had sent Spring those texts. And he could be guilty of the hit-and-run that put her in a wheelchair or knew who was.

Like Cliff? Where did the cycling coach fit into all this? He had motive and intent to harm Spring. He also seemed more capable than Luke of using psychological manipulation like threatening text messages.

Was Cliff the connection between Spring and the shooter? Cliff could've been getting his supply from Mackeral with Luke as the delivery boy. Or Luke might've learned Cliff's secret and squeezed him for blackmail money. That would explain the expensive shoes and watch—payoffs for Luke's silence.

But it still wouldn't explain why he would come to Spring's hospital room during the day and try to kill her. Luke's thinking was clearly clouded by speed, which explained lack of logic and planning. But why try at all?

Even if he was the driver, and Spring could ID him, a drug addict from the neighborhood where Spring had been hit would have no reason to take the risk of publicly shooting her. Chances were, Torin's unit would never have been able to ID Luke from a vague description and couldn't have caught him.

The guy was already hanging by a thread to the underbelly of society. Not exactly the type that had much more to lose. It just didn't add up. Unless Spring had seen more than she was telling. If she'd seen Mackeral—

"Can't sleep?" Spring's soft whisper floated to Torin, cooling the frustration building to a boil inside.

He looked at her face, only about a foot from him as he sat on the floor next to her.

Victoria had rotated Spring's position so that she sat tilted slightly onto her other hip, the side of her forehead leaning against the wall.

"I'm used to it." He couldn't stop a smile at the sight of her beautiful, sleepy eyes that she slowly blinked.

She shifted her head and a thick wave of black hair fell across one eye, tempting him to brush it back.

He captured the rebel hand with his other one and wrapped his arms around his raised knees in front of him.

"Insomnia?" She pushed the distracting wave of hair away from her face.

More like nightmares and regret. "Something like that."

"It's funny. This is the first night I've slept well in days." Her full lips tugged into a small smile. "Ironic, isn't it?" Her eyes pooled with a sadness that belied the smile.

"What keeps you awake?"

She lifted her head away from the wall that her shoulder still leaned against. "Pain, I guess."

His chest tightened, the idea of her being in pain bothering him more than it should. "In your legs?" Like it was any of his business.

"Sometimes." Those mesmerizing eyes watched him, telling him much more than she said. They held the look he recognized. The look of searing loss.

His mouth went dry. "Sometimes in your heart."

Her eyes widened. Then she bit her lip. Nodded. "You, too." It was a statement, an observation as she looked deep inside him, her eyebrows drawing downward.

"Hey!"

She winced at Luke's shout.

"No talking." The shooter glared at them from where he paced on the other side of the hostages.

A few of them shifted or lifted their heads from trying to sleep.

Torin followed Spring's gaze as it went to Victoria, who sat on the floor next to Bradley's wheelchair about five feet away. Spring brought her attention back to Torin and pulled his sport coat higher up over her shoulder. "I'm sorry." She mouthed the words.

He looked past her to make sure Luke wasn't watching before he whispered a reply. "For what?"

"Getting you into this." Her whisper carried the pain in her eyes. "You didn't have to stay for me." She rested her head against the wall, and the wave of hair swept over her eye again.

He couldn't resist a second time. He reached to push her hair aside, but his fingers lingered on the black tresses, softer and thicker than he'd imagined.

Her eyes darkened, locked on his face.

"I'm right where I want to be." His gaze dropped to her parted lips.

Her breathing deepened to match his.

He leaned closer.

"Hey, lover boy."

Torin jolted back at Luke's taunt, reality breaking through the force of awareness that had made him lose his senses.

"You can get your play some other time." Luke grinned, but shook the gun their way. "If I decide to let you go."

Spring's face turned red as a tomato as she ducked her head into the wall.

Torin could've kicked himself. Had he lost his mind completely? It was sheer stupidity dropping his guard like that, allowing Luke the upper hand. Not to mention that he had no business getting…involved with someone he needed to protect as a cop. And he couldn't start a relationship with any woman, period. He shouldn't lead her on. He hadn't meant to, but that's just what he'd done.

Guilt mixed with the self-directed fury that swirled up his throat. He pushed off the floor and stood.

"I didn't say you could get up." Luke swung the Glock toward him.

"You don't mind if I just stretch my legs, do you?" Torin amazed himself with how well he achieved a flippant, casual tone. Not bad, given the emotional war going on inside.

Luke stared at him. "So long as that's all you do."

"Sure." Torin made his way between the two wheelchairs along one wall and the elderly woman and nurse on the other. They were all sleeping, or pretending they were, as he passed. Giving the note to the nurse would have to wait.

Torin tried for an appearance of aimless wandering as he sauntered toward Luke. The shooter watched him closely, so Torin stopped before he got near enough to make the perp nervous.

Torin slid his hands casually into his pockets, fingers rubbing against the folded paper in one. "Man, what I wouldn't give for a smoke, huh?" He rubbed a hand on the back of his neck as he grimaced for effect. Never smoked in his life, but the line usually worked.

Some of the suspicion receded from Luke's gaze, and his jaw relaxed slightly.

"You know…" Torin looked down at his shoe as he rubbed the toe of it on the floor before glancing back up. "I have to admit, you got way more guts than I do, pulling off something like this." He slipped on a partial smile. "How many kilos do you think you'll get?"

Luke's eyebrows dipped. "What are you talking about?"

"I thought you were going for more supply."

"No."

So far so good. The genuine confusion in the perp's voice and expression signaled he was buying the act. "Oh, so it's about the girl."

"What girl?"

"You know." Torin tilted his head in Spring's direction. Thank goodness she was positioned so she looked the other way. "My girl." The words felt more natural than they should.

Luke's eyes narrowed. "Just what are you getting at?"

"I heard the cops were looking for a white van from the crash."

Luke's cheeks sunk to his bones with a quick breath and his gaze darted around Torin, as if looking for witnesses...or an escape.

Bingo. Torin kept his expression as innocent as he could. "Oh man, you didn't drive it here, did you?"

"Shut up." Luke took a step toward Torin, his dilated eyes aiming with his gun. "How do you know all that?"

Torin shrugged. "Spring tells me everything."

Luke's lips stiffened. "Everything? She tell you what she saw?"

A chance to get Luke off of her. He probably wouldn't buy it, but Torin had to try. "She doesn't remember seeing anything."

Luke laughed, a short and shrill, humorless sound. "She's scared. Just like everybody else."

"I think she's telling the truth." Torin kept his gaze steady as the perp's bounced rapidly from him to the hostages. "You don't have to hurt anyone to cover the crash, Luke. She can't finger you."

"You're like everybody else." His voice picked up a hissing edge. "You think you're smarter than me. You don't know anything, man." He lifted his weapon to aim at Torin's head. "And I'm the one with the gun. So you just shut up and go back to your girlfriend."

Torin held up his hands, keeping his expression neutral. "No problem, man. Just trying to help."

"I don't need your help. I don't need anyone's help."

"Okay. Sorry to bother you, man." Torin slowly turned around, his instincts screaming at him not to show his back to an armed perp. He took his hands from his pockets as he walked away, holding them in front of his body to hide the small piece of paper clutched between his fingers.

He glanced behind as he neared the sleeping nurse.

Luke's attention was already divided as he snorted speed from his bag.

Torin walked closer to the nurse's legs, stretched out in front of him as he slept, and dropped the note between them. Continuing at the same pace, Torin moved away and went back to Spring. He stepped to her other side and took his place on the floor next to her.

She opened her eyes as soon as he sat down. "What happened?" She must have heard him talking to the perp, but apparently not what was said.

He wanted to tell her what he'd learned. She had a right to know. But how would she react if she learned Luke was without a doubt the one who'd paralyzed her? Torin couldn't risk finding out in this situation.

He leaned in close to her ear as he pressed the other note he'd written into her hand. He heard her sharp intake of breath and closed his eyes as the scent of her hair flooded his senses. *Focus, Cotter.* "Give this to the doctor." He whispered the words into her ear.

"Back off, lover boy."

Torin pulled back at Luke's predictable reaction, getting to his feet. "She was telling me she's in pain. She needs the doctor to check her out."

"Life is pain."

"Come on, man. I think something's wrong."

"It won't hurt for me to take a look." Dr. Berghuis rose by the opposite wall and crossed the hallway to Spring.

Luke watched the doctor's progress, but didn't voice another objection.

The nurse stirred to the shooter's left.

Torin's gut clenched as the nurse pulled up his legs and paused, probably seeing the note. Torin jumped his gaze back to the doctor in case Luke was watching. Nice timing on the distraction with Berghuis and Spring.

The doctor crouched at Spring's side where Torin had been sitting. "Where do you feel the pain?"

She glanced up at Torin before answering. "Um…my right leg. It comes and goes."

As the doctor leaned toward that leg, Torin shifted to block Luke's view.

Spring slid the note in front of Berghuis. Perfectly timed.

Berghuis didn't miss a beat, taking the note and pressing her leg with his fingers in one fluid motion. As he pulled his hand back, even Torin couldn't tell he was holding a piece of paper.

"I'm afraid they're probably phantom pains." He looked at Spring as if he were performing a normal examination under everyday circumstances. The guy was good. With him as backup, Torin's idea could work. "There usually isn't much that can be done to relieve them. Though you can consult with your neurologist and see if there's something she would advise."

"Okay." Spring's gaze nervously jumped to Torin before returning to the doctor. "Thank you, Doctor."

Berghuis patted her hand. "No trouble at all." He lowered his voice slightly, casting a glance in Luke's direction. "You hang in there."

Spring pinched her lips together and nodded.

Berghuis gave Torin the same paternal smile as he stood and headed back to sit by the opposite wall.

Torin sank to the floor next to Spring and cast a casual glance at the other hostages, slowly bringing his attention to the person he'd wanted to look at immediately.

The nurse met Torin's gaze across the distance. He nodded, then glanced at Luke, who was pacing again. The nurse moistened his lips and wiped his hands on his thighs.

Sweaty palms probably. The guy was more nervous than Torin would like, but there wasn't much choice. The plan needed at least three to work.

He checked on Berghuis.

His gaze already rested on Torin, steady and calm as he gave a slight nod. One person Torin could count on for sure. If the doctor and the nurse played their parts right, this could all be over the next time Luke's phone rang.

Torin just had to stay awake until then. The perp hadn't made a move toward any of the women yet, but Torin wasn't about to risk sleeping in case the shooter decided to turn predator.

Luke paused his pacing to glare in Spring's direction.

Torin steeled his jaw. If the perp wanted to get to Spring, he'd have to go through Torin. Another failure wasn't an option.

———

3:10 a.m.
14 hours and 10 minutes hostage.

Music echoed somewhere in the distance, then grew closer, closer.

Had she set her alarm clock to radio?

"What?"

She knew that voice. Spring's eyes popped open.

Luke was talking. Probably to the police negotiator again. But she couldn't see him thanks to this awkward position Victoria had chosen to put her in.

But she could see Torin very well.

He sat at her side like before. His mouth was set in a grim line when he glanced at her. Fatigue weighed heavily around his eyes. Had he stayed awake all this time? However long it had been.

She focused on the conversation to hear what might have made Torin look so grim.

"No." Frustration cinched Luke's voice. "You can't have any of them until I get some assurances."

"Can you turn me?"

Torin's gaze shifted to Spring in response to her murmured question.

"I can't see anything from here." Nothing but the handsome face she shouldn't be getting so attached to.

He rose to his feet and bent over her. His arms went under hers and he lifted, easily shifting her to a normal sitting position with her back square against the wall.

"Thanks." She couldn't breathe until he pulled back, but he didn't look at her as he straightened, watching Luke instead. Obviously, the attraction was more one-sided than she had started to believe. Maybe she had imagined that he'd almost kissed her hours ago.

"I need to think." Luke barked into the phone. "Ten minutes." He shoved the phone into his back pocket.

Spring shivered and pulled Torin's sport coat up over her chest. Victoria finally had a good idea when she had asked Torin if Spring could keep using his sport coat to stay warm.

She glanced up to thank Torin, but he wasn't there. Where—

He walked up to Luke. "There's something I need to tell you." He held an object in front of Luke, stepping around him in a circle that forced the shooter to turn in order to keep Torin in front of him.

Was Torin holding his wallet? His badge?

A wave of panic smacked into Spring, choking her air as she felt the jacket for the bulky square. He must have taken it out while she slept.

"I'm a cop."

Luke pointed the gun at Torin. "You're what?"

Dr. Berghuis and the nurse snuck up to Luke from behind, where he had another gun tucked in his waistband.

Spring's heart drummed in her ears.

"You're under a—"

The doctor's shoe caught on the polished floor and he tripped, cutting off Torin's words.

Luke spun as Torin lunged for his gun.

A shot pierced the air.

A man screamed.

CHAPTER
THIRTY-FOUR

SPRING TRIED to lift herself higher to see who had cried out. Torin? Was he shot?

Someone slumped to the ground, the doctor grabbing under his arms to slow his fall.

"Stay away from me!" Luke waved the gun at all the hostages as he shrieked. "I'll kill you all!" He aimed the gun at the man still standing.

Torin.

Relief flooded Spring's body as she inhaled a breath. He didn't look hurt.

But why was he just standing there? He stared at the injured nurse as if it were the most horrifying sight he'd ever seen.

Bradley started to cry, growing louder with each frightened sob. His eyes were saucers as he twisted his upper body in the chair. "Mommy. I want mommy!"

Spring looked for Torin to help, but she couldn't see him anymore. Where had he gone? Was he hurt after all?

If only she could get up. She smacked the floor with her hand, frustration exploding inside her. She could only watch the chaos and suffering like a helpless bystander.

Victoria appeared at Bradley's side, her face white. She talked to him quietly as she lifted him from the chair and grabbed the cushion under him. She quickly walked to Spring, glancing down the hallway at the men.

Dropping the cushion on the floor next to Spring, she straightened it with her foot and lowered Bradley to it.

Spring wrapped her arms around the boy, and he melted into her side, clutching her with small fingers.

Musical notes chimed. Luke's phone. He lifted it to his ear with a shaking hand. "What?"

Spring flinched at his shout. She looked at Victoria as she stroked Bradley's smooth hair. "What's happening? Is Torin okay?"

Victoria rose from squatting to check.

Spring could only see Luke standing over the doctor and the fallen nurse. Her heart thumped against her chest as she waited to hear the bad news.

"They attacked me." Luke's voice was a blend of anger and fear stretched tight enough to snap. "Yeah, I shot him. I don't know. Some guy. I had to defend myself!"

Victoria leaned toward Spring. "Torin is sitting by the wall next to the older man's wheelchair."

Oh, no. He must have been shot. "Is he hurt?"

"I don't think so..." Victoria straightened and craned her neck to see him better. "I don't know. He doesn't look right."

"Go and help him."

Victoria looked down at Spring. Probably didn't want to leave her alone with Luke going crazy.

"Please? I'll be fine here."

Victoria nodded and headed toward the aftermath of the fight with more courage than Spring could even dream of having.

"We already have a doctor." Luke continued to argue with the negotiator on the phone. "No." The one word carried defeat. "Fine. I'll let him go. But just him."

Victoria crouched out of sight. She must have reached Torin.

"I want cigarettes and soda." Luke listed the specific brand that he wanted. Like a little boy bargaining with his mother. A horrible, out of control boy with a gun he wasn't afraid to use. "I'm the one in charge here. I could shoot all of them if you make me."

Spring's breath caught as Dr. Berghuis stood and quickly went to Victoria…and Torin. He was hurt. *Lord, please…*

Bradley's whimper grew louder.

She stroked his hair again, trying to keep the movement calm and steady while her pulse raced in irregular sprints.

"I want to get out of here without anyone trying to stop me." The shooter dared to make demands after what he'd done? He'd shot another man. Maybe two if he had hurt Torin. How could everything keep going right for him? "I didn't mean to hurt anyone." The sad note in his voice caught Spring by surprise. He almost sounded like he meant it.

She searched the area to his left. No sign of Torin.

"Okay. I'll give you two. But I'm not doing that again until I get out of here. Bring the stuff and then I'll let them go. You've got five minutes." Luke put the phone in his pocket, looking down in the direction Torin must be.

"I should've shot you, cop." Luke spit the word like a curse as he swept his leg out, connecting with something solid.

Spring gasped. Had he kicked Torin?

"That's enough, Luke." Dr. Berghuis stood, facing the shooter. "I heard you say you're going to let the injured man go and someone else. Who's going with him?"

The injured man. Did that mean Torin wasn't also hurt badly?

"Not him." Luke sneered at Torin. "He's my insurance now. Right, cop?"

Torin got to his feet, allowing Spring to see him at last.

She couldn't spot any blood, but he looked unsteady. His

usual confident stride was missing as he walked away from Luke, his shoulders slumped.

Victoria followed behind him. Was she afraid he needed help for some reason?

"Hey, cop. Get back here."

"He needs to rest, Luke." Dr. Berghuis redirected the madman again.

Luke scowled. "He didn't get hurt. Just couldn't take me, so he went to pieces like a yellow coward."

Went to pieces? Spring studied Torin's face as he drew closer.

His jaw was tight, his skin pale despite his tan. His forehead glistened under the fluorescent lights as if coated with sweat. He didn't look at her.

"There's more to it than that." Dr. Berghuis went to the nurse and helped him sit up.

Blood colored the sleeve of the man's blue scrubs.

"Do you think you can walk out of here?"

The nurse nodded.

Torin walked past Spring's extended legs as if she wasn't there.

"That's far enough, cop."

Torin halted at Luke's command. He sank to the floor a couple feet from Bradley. Still wouldn't meet her gaze.

She tried to swallow back the hurt that swelled in her throat. She should be more concerned about him, not herself.

"One of those can go." Luke gestured to the two men in the wheelchairs closest to him.

Was he really going to let two people go? She moistened her lips. "Please." Her voice shook as she spoke louder than she had since the nightmare had begun. "Let the boy go."

Luke swung his head toward her. Had he forgotten she was there or just didn't expect her to speak?

He took a few steps toward her and stopped under a fluorescent light. His gaunt face had an odd yellowish tinge she hadn't noticed before. He licked his thin, chapped lips. "The cops will do a lot to make sure a kid doesn't get hurt. Won't they, cop?" He threw the barb at Torin, who stared ahead like no one else existed.

"Are you sure you want to keep a child?" Dr. Berghuis stood with the nurse at his side, the man's uninjured arm draped over the doctor's shoulders.

"I know what I'm doing!" Luke's sharp, over-the-edge tone silenced everyone. "You." He waved the gun at Victoria. "Go look outside the door and see if my stuff is here."

She glanced at Spring before she turned and headed for the door.

As she passed Luke, he slid the barrel of the gun across her arm.

Spring sucked in a breath.

"Don't try anything."

Victoria looked at him. "I won't."

He nodded and let her keep going, her safe progress enabling Spring to breathe again.

Victoria stopped when she reached the door and glanced back.

"Go ahead." Luke trained his gun on the exit, throwing a quick glance to his left to check the hostages. At least the men's attempted ambush had made him less confident. Though maybe reminding him to always check his back was a bad thing.

Spring's pulse accelerated as Victoria opened the door a few inches. Would there be shooting if SWAT waited outside?

No. They were probably still keeping their distance. Shooting from outside would just make Luke more trigger-happy on the inside. She hoped she was right, since Victoria would be caught right in the middle.

Victoria opened the door wide enough to lean out. She pulled back inside, holding two boxes of cigarettes in one hand and a twelve-pack of soda cans in the other.

"Bring the stuff here."

"What about the hostages?" Thank the Lord for Dr.

Berghuis. He wasn't afraid to push Luke. Though Torin hadn't been either, and that had backfired.

Spring glanced at Torin.

He still stared at the wall opposite them.

What had happened to make such a change come over him?

"He can push the other one out." Luke nodded to the bleeding nurse.

"Can you do that?" Dr. Berghuis asked his patient.

The nurse nodded. "The chair will hold me up."

At least that's what Spring thought he said. His weak voice was hard to hear, but she'd guess most of the people there would be able to limp out no matter what, if given the chance. Except for her, of course.

Victoria went to turn the wheelchair that held the older man who appeared the most relaxed of anyone, his loose lips and heavy eyelids sagging as his head lolled back and forth. Maybe his mental damage was a mercy in this situation. At least he wasn't experiencing the fear that gripped the rest of them.

Dr. Berghuis helped the nurse to the back of the chair, and the injured man leaned on the handles, pushing the wheelchair toward the door.

"May I open it for them?" Victoria asked the question so politely of Luke. As if he was her boss instead of her captor. Only Victoria could be that professional while being held hostage.

"Knock yourself out, *chica*."

With Victoria's help, the nurse managed to push the man in the wheelchair through the doorway, out to freedom.

Spring's heartbeat slowed to a jog. At least no one else had been shot. And the nurse would get the help he needed.

But what about the rest of them? Were they going to get the same chance to walk out of—

No. She could never walk out of there, even if Luke wasn't holding a gun.

Defeat washed over her in a wave that left her weak. She leaned her cheek against Bradley's silky hair. Maybe she'd be better off if Luke didn't let her go.

"Are you all right?" The voice of Dr. Berghuis to Spring's right startled her. Her thoughts must have absorbed her attention enough so that she'd missed him passing by.

He crouched in front of Torin.

A muscle twitched in Torin's jaw. "I'm fine."

"You have PTSD, don't you?"

Post-traumatic stress disorder? Had Torin had some sort of panic attack?

"I'm not your patient, Doctor." Torin's voice carried an angry edge Spring hadn't heard from him before.

But Dr. Berghuis seemed to take it in stride. "Of course." He stood. "I'm sorry your plan didn't work." He turned away, walking back in Luke's direction.

"Anyone got a lighter?" Luke held one of the packs of cigarettes in his hand.

No one looked at him, much less answered.

He threw the pack against the wall, muttering something she was glad she couldn't hear.

Torin didn't give any reaction. He just glared ahead, his chin shifting like he was grinding his teeth.

Could he really have PTSD? He was so heroic and brave. She'd never met anyone like him.

Spring opened her mouth to ask, then snapped it shut. She had no right to pry into his personal life. They'd been thrown together by a freak situation. He wasn't with her by choice. He was doing his duty.

The way he ignored her now made the facts painfully clear. He would never be interested in her as anything more than someone he had to protect. If they made it out of there, he would leave as fast as he could. She'd never see him again. And she'd have to face life in her prison on wheels, alone.

4:16 a.m.
15 hours and 16 minutes hostage.

Torin rubbed the base of his neck, the tense muscles like rocks under his fingers.

Luke favored leaning against the wall instead of pacing at the moment, snorting the fuel he needed to keep the nightmare going.

"Shouldn't you try to sleep?"

Torin jumped inwardly at Spring's quiet voice, then made himself breathe. His nerves were still taut since the last shooting. Since the epic failure that had left him unable to look at Spring or anyone else. He was just lucky she hadn't been the one to get shot.

He cleared his throat and glanced at the boy tucked against her side, sleeping. "Better if I don't."

She fell silent again.

His gaze yearned to find her face, but he feared what he might see there. Disappointment? Disgust? Anger?

He deserved any and all of those. What a gutless wonder he'd become. A simple plan to outnumber a doped-up shooter, and he'd frozen. Worse than that, he had completely lost it.

When that shot had gone off and the nurse shrieked, all he could hear was Ivy screaming his name, see her blank, dead stare, feel the searing pain as his heart was ripped from his chest. It was real. Happening again.

Luke's kick to his leg had yanked Torin out of the agony only to face the dangerous present reality he had made worse for everyone.

"What you did was incredibly brave."

The surprising words made him look up, meeting Spring's doe-brown eyes. They seemed to reach inside him and wrap around him at the same time. None of the emotions Torin expected were reflected there.

Her gaze hadn't lost a bit of its softness, but it held a hint of caution now. The sight landed like a kick in the stomach.

He swallowed. "Pretty stupid, actually."

She shook her head, the movement brushing that enticing hair across her shoulder. "You were trying to save m—" Her gaze flitted away, then back to his face. "Everyone here. At the risk of your own life. That's bravery."

He didn't know how to answer the sincerity in her eyes.

"I'm very grateful for what you've done."

He glanced away. "There's nothing to be grateful for. I—"

"I know. You were just doing your job." Her full lips formed a gentle curve.

The sight sparked something in his chest. But he ignored it, frowning. "I guess you didn't see what happened."

Her smile faded and her gaze lowered to the boy's head by her shoulder. "The pain in your heart doesn't always come at a convenient time." She paused. "Will you tell me..." She moistened her lips. "I just wondered...what caused yours."

Wondered how he'd become such a coward, she meant. He opened his mouth to say as much, but she lifted her gaze.

Her brown eyes were filled with honest, raw pain. The stuff she usually hid.

He was looking into her soul. And he saw his own sorrow there.

She needed a companion in her pain. He couldn't shut her out.

He glanced at Luke.

The shooter was busy muttering to himself.

Taking a breath, Torin spoke in a low voice. "My wife was killed three years ago."

Lines bunched on Spring's forehead as compassion filled her eyes.

He looked away before he couldn't continue. "It was my day off. We walked into a gas station. Right into a robbery in progress. I should've laid low, played the good witness, but I had my gun with me. And I was a cop, off-duty or not." His mouth twisted in a sardonic smile. "I pulled my weapon, so the shooter started firing." Torin swallowed. "He hit Ivy instead of me."

He'd told the story over and over again during the internal investigation that followed any officer-involved-shooting. But then it was so raw he didn't even hear himself. He had just spoken words, bare facts and technical details—a good cop's reconstruction of an incident. He hadn't thought, hadn't felt. It was the only way he'd gotten through without cracking up.

This time, he felt every word—the depth of his failure, the injustice of a violent thief ending Ivy's life.

"I'm so sorry."

Torin stared ahead. Clenched his jaw to hold back the moisture that stung his eyes.

"It wasn't your fault."

He looked at Spring. The wet track of a tear lined her cheek.

His heart wrenched. He'd never seen her cry for herself, but there she was, crying for him. "Yes, it was." The statement came out as a coarse whisper. "I should have protected her."

"You can't always protect everyone." Spring watched him closely. "You're not God."

God. The ache in Torin's chest hardened. "Ivy believed in your God, too."

Spring's features pinched with confusion, but that didn't soften his anger.

"She used to talk about how good and loving God is." His cynical words hung in the air between them.

"He is." Spring's brow furrowed, and she glanced down. Even she didn't sound convinced.

"Then why didn't He protect Ivy? Couldn't He do that even though I messed up?"

"Yes. He could." She didn't meet his gaze.

"But He didn't."

"No."

Guilt niggled at his conscience when he saw the lines his accusations put on her forehead, the sagging of her mouth. He hadn't meant to attack her beliefs, but maybe she'd be better off facing the truth now rather than continuing to believe in someone who would let her down.

She looked up, bit her lip, then let it go. "He must have had something better planned."

Torin blinked. If she'd punched him in the face, he couldn't have been more surprised. "Better?" He opened his mouth. Closed it. Anger heated his face. He tried to rein in the emotion as he pushed out his words. "Than saving my wife's life?" He shook his head. "Ivy was the kindest, most loving… she didn't deserve that. The perp should've been the one dead on the floor, not her."

"She went home, Torin."

He met Spring's steady gaze. Home?

"Maybe what happened wasn't all about her. Maybe it was about you."

He stared at her.

"Sometimes we won't listen to God until something hard happens. Sometimes that's what it takes to get our attention."

So that's what she was getting at. "I don't much like a God who lets people die just to get my attention."

She didn't bat an eye at the edge to his voice. "Remember when you told Victoria to leave the security guard and run? I thought at first that you were really cold. That you didn't care if people died."

She had thought that?

"I realized later that you told Victoria to run because you thought saving her life was more important." She held his gaze with her own. "Maybe God thinks saving you is that important, too."

Something twinged in his chest, as if a bullet hit its mark there. But Ivy's life was far more important than his own. And so was Spring's. "He's dead wrong." The snap came out louder than he intended.

Luke shot him a narrowed gaze.

Great. Last thing he needed to do was make one more stupid mistake that killed another woman he cared about.

Realization of what he'd just thought hit him like a kick in the ribs. He hadn't meant to care for Spring. To let that happen.

This was where it would stop. He couldn't risk going through that kind of agony again.

"We should get some sleep." He crossed his arms over his chest and leaned his head back against the wall, closing his eyes. But he wouldn't sleep until this scenario ended with Spring getting out of there unharmed. No matter what the cost.

CHAPTER
THIRTY-FIVE

October 12. 6:00 a.m.
17 hours hostage.

SPRING WOKE from her light sleep, not sure why.

The dreadful music played.

"Yeah?" Luke's voice as he answered the phone sounded higher pitched than before, and he jiggled his legs as if he couldn't hold still before breaking into a quick pace again.

Torin was awake, too, sitting silently on the other side of Bradley, watching their captor.

"Doesn't he ever get tired?" She could ask Torin the same question about himself, but her last personal question hadn't ended well.

"It's the speed. If he runs out, he'll crash."

Torin's voice held a guarded tone she hadn't heard before. Maybe it was for the best. If he stopped being so nice, she'd have an easier time keeping her own emotions in check. Maybe she'd stop imagining he liked her or that he ever could.

Bradley shifted at her side.

She half hoped he would wake enough to move a little. Her

279

shoulder had gone numb from the angle of her arm around him.

"Mommy?" He looked up at Spring's face with squinting eyes that widened when he saw her. His mouth scrunched and a sob escaped. Then another.

"Shh, shh, Bradley. It's okay, honey." Spring stroked the boy's head, but he pulled away, unable to move far thanks to his useless legs.

His sobs turned into a wail. "Mommy…"

"Shut him up!" Luke shoved the phone into his pocket as he yelled at them.

"Bradley, sweetie, it's okay." Spring ducked her head, hoping to get Bradley to look at her. "You'll get to see your mommy soon."

Spring threw a helpless glance at Torin.

He finally looked her way. "Bradley, can I tell you something?"

The boy's wail ended with a hiccup, and his gaze darted to Torin. Probably as surprised as Spring that Torin had spoken to him. Bradley sniffed, another sob almost escaping as he nodded.

"I miss my mom sometimes, too."

Bradley's blue eyes widened.

"But then I remember that she'd be awfully sad if she knew I was crying. She'd want me to be happy, even though she isn't here with me." Torin gave Bradley a searching look. "Is your mom happy when you cry?"

Bradley sniffed. "No. She gets sad."

"I thought that might be the case." Torin's mouth held a serious line as he talked to the boy like he would to an adult. "And you don't want to make your mom sad, do you?"

Bradley shook his head.

"Then we'd better find something to cheer you up."

Spring stared at Torin, surprise filtering through her. She had thought he wasn't big on kids since he hadn't talked to Bradley before now. But he'd managed to get the boy to stop crying in a matter of seconds and spoke at Bradley's level as if it were the most natural thing in the world. The man kept surprising her.

"Any ideas?" Torin watched Spring with raised eyebrows.

Heat rushed to her cheeks as she closed her gaping mouth. "Oh. Um, Bradley, what do you do at home when you feel sad?" Hopefully it was something they'd be able to replicate.

"When Daddy comes home, we arm-wrestle."

"Arm-wrestle?" Torin nodded. "I think we can do that." He turned around so that he sat facing the wall instead, his body lined up alongside Bradley's. He held out his arm, elbow crooked.

Bradley's hand looked tiny and pale as his fingers wrapped around Torin's tanned skin.

"You ready?" Torin didn't crack a smile, but Spring thought she detected a glint of amusement in his green eyes.

Bradley nodded, his small mouth downturned with concentration.

"Call it, Miss Weston."

She bit back a smile at Torin's grave tone. "On three. One, two...three."

The battle began, Bradley letting out little grunts as he tried to pull Torin's hand to the side.

Spring could see the muscles in Torin's forearm tighten where he'd rolled up his sleeve, but he didn't look like he had to use an ounce of effort to resist the little guy's pressure.

When Torin's hand started to tilt just an inch as Bradley pushed, Spring knew he was faking to encourage Bradley. Would he let the boy win?

Torin slowly pushed Bradley's hand the other direction, bringing it firmly down.

"Aww." Bradley released Torin's hand with a frown, but his blue eyes danced. "Daddy never lets me win either. He says I gotta earn it."

Torin let a smile break through, and Spring's pulse skittered. "Your dad's a wise man. You'll earn it soon." He stuck his hand out for Bradley to shake. "You're a strong opponent."

Bradley grinned as he proudly shook Torin's hand.

Spring's heart warmed. Torin would make a wonderful father someday.

Pain followed the thought. The experts told her she was still physically capable of having children. But could the doctors supply someone who could run and play with her children, chase after them to keep them from harm? Or find her a man who would marry her in the first place?

"I wish I was as strong as you." Bradley's statement brought Spring out of her thoughts to see a pensive frown on the boy's face as he looked at Torin. "Then I wouldn't be scared."

Torin met Spring's gaze. A battle raged in his eyes, a stormy green. He looked away.

"Everyone gets scared sometimes, Bradley." Spring managed a small smile. "Even grownups."

"Really?"

She nodded. "Do you know what I do when I'm scared?"

He shook his head.

"I ask God for help. He's much stronger than any person."

"Does it work?"

"Yes, it does." She didn't have to look at Torin to know he probably disapproved. But she wouldn't let that stop her from comforting this little boy. "Do you want to pray right now?"

"Sure."

Spring took Bradley's soft hand in hers and closed her eyes. "Dear Jesus, please keep us safe. Protect us and help us to be strong and brave instead of scared. Please get us out of here safely and—"

"Spring." Torin's voice was sharp.

She popped her eyes open. Was he seriously interrupting her prayer?

"What are you doing?" Luke.

The breath whooshed from her lungs as she jerked her gaze to him, standing above her with that gun dangling from his fingers, his cheeks sinking in and puffing out beneath his thin facial hair.

She tightened her hand around Bradley's. "Praying." She braced herself. She'd heard of shooters killing people for saying they believed in Jesus. Would Luke do that?

A snicker. Then a high-pitched laugh.

She watched him finish his cackling as her heart formed a desperate plea. *Protect Bradley, Lord. Please.*

"*You* pray?"

Irritation surged with the adrenaline shooting through her veins. "Yes."

He let out another short laugh. "What a con game. It's always people like you who believe in religion. Sick people, old, cripples..." He waved his hand over her like she was the definition of the word. "You people think it'll help you to believe in God, but it doesn't."

"How would you know?" The rebuttal shot from her mouth before she thought, but she didn't regret it. Even when Luke narrowed his eyes.

"Didn't stop me from hitting you."

Her heart lurched to a halt. She was falling, plunging as if someone had pulled the floor out from under her and she was dropping the ten floors to the ground.

She grasped at something to break her fall. He was a random shooter. A crazy drug addict. He couldn't be the driver.

But the plummeting sensation in her soul called her a liar and a fool.

She was looking at the person who had taken her legs, her life...everything.

"Spring." A touch on her hand, Torin's face in front of her. "Spring." His green eyes stared intently at her as her vision began to clear.

Air returned to her lungs, and she heaved a breath, then

another rapidly as she tried to get ahold of her swirling emotions.

"I'm sorry I didn't tell you." Torin crouched in front of her, gently cradling her hand in his.

She tried to speak, but no sound came out. She swallowed, her mouth like sandpaper. "You knew?"

"Not for very long."

She searched his face. "That talk you had with him."

He nodded.

"You could have told me."

"I wasn't sure how you'd take it."

Not very well, apparently. She pulled her hand from Torin's.

"I didn't want to make this any harder for you than it already is."

Was she being that pathetic? So weak that Torin thought of her the way Luke did—as a handicapped, delusional nobody destined to be a victim to some and an object of pity for others? Anger fired her chest, flowing into her arms. But Torin didn't deserve her wrath.

Their captor did.

His phone sounded just as he reached his normal spot at the other end of the group of hostages, mercifully far from Spring. "Are they going to do it?" He must have asked the negotiator for something during the last call, when she had focused on Bradley instead of listening. "Just get them to back off, and I'll leave."

Torin stood and turned to watch Luke.

The shooter waited, apparently listening. "No, you have to promise they'll be out of the building." Another pause.

"You're lying." Luke's voice pinched as he lifted the gun like there was someone to shoot standing before him. He moved the phone in front of his mouth. "I know you're lying!" He threw the device to the floor and kicked the wall.

All the hostages stared at him.

Spring put her arm around Bradley and pulled him closer, her heart pounding.

"This wasn't supposed to happen!" Luke's scream echoed through the hallway. "I was smart." A sob choked his voice. "I was. My scholarship..." He turned around, scanning the hostages. "*You* know, Doc." He pointed at Dr. Berghuis, who watched him from a sitting position on the floor.

"Your people did this to me. Throwing drugs at me. ADD, ADHD, ADDDD whatever!"

Bradley shook against Spring's side.

She looked down at him.

His fingers trembled on his lap. He was terrified.

Because of her.

The truth hit her like a shot from Luke's gun. She was the reason all of this had happened. Luke had come to kill her. To keep her from telling anyone he was the driver in the crash. He only took all these innocent people hostage because Torin had protected her.

He killed the guard. A human being was dead because of her. And he might not be the only one before this ended.

Guilt compressed her chest until she thought she would suffocate. It was all her fault. None of these people were ever supposed to be harmed. She should be dead, and they should be free.

"I didn't ask for this! Do you hear me?"

Bradley buried his face in Spring's side, trying to hide from Luke's rant.

This had to stop. And she knew how to do it.

"Luke."

He angled toward her.

Out the corner of her eye, she saw Torin's head swing her way. "I understand."

"What?" Luke stalked past the other hostages, pointing the gun at them. He huffed as he neared her.

"I said I understand."

"Spring." Torin stepped in front of her, facing Luke.

"Back off, cop." Luke looked like he was aiming the gun at Torin, but Spring couldn't see.

Her throat turned dry. Torin wasn't supposed to get hurt. "Torin, please." She sounded like she was begging, but she didn't care. She had to do this. "I know what I'm doing."

He reluctantly stepped to the side, his intense gaze locked on Luke.

"It's not your fault." She forced herself to forget about Torin and watch only the shooter. Those odd-looking eyes that gave her the shivers. "I know you only wanted to get me when you came here."

He stared, his mouth pinched in a thin line.

"I know you didn't mean to involve any of these other people." She moistened her lips. Now or never. "I promise I'll stay if you let everyone else go. There's no reason to keep them."

"Spring—"

"Shut up!" Luke barked at Torin, keeping his gun aimed while he darted a quick glance at her. "You're trying to trick me."

"No, I'm not."

"You think I'm stupid?" He threw her another look before focusing again on Torin. "I know I won't get out of here without hostages. I'm not going to let everyone go just like that." He shifted his jaw. "Not until I get what I want."

He pulled away and started back where he'd come from.

Desperation clawed up her throat. She couldn't lose this chance. "What do you want?"

He whirled around. "I want you and everyone else to shut up!" He pointed the gun at her.

She closed her eyes.

The gun went off.

CHAPTER
THIRTY-SIX

"Torin!"

Torin blinked to banish the sight of his wife's body, lying in front of the door to the gas station.

"Are you okay?"

He couldn't answer as the memories assaulted him from all sides.

Something warm touched his arm. A warmth that slowly seeped through him, calming his firing nerves and the fear spiraling from his gut into every part of his body. He worked to calm his breathing. Slow, quiet breaths.

"Torin?" Spring. Her arm stretched across Bradley to rest her fingers on his forearm.

Torin must have ended up sitting, probably cowering while the flashback engulfed him. The gunshot had set it off again. The shot that could have killed Spring if not for Luke's rotten aim.

Torin swung his gaze to check on the perp.

He was busy on the phone again, probably trying to explain the gunshot. Maybe the negotiator could get another hostage released out of this.

"Are you okay?"

He brought his gaze back toward Spring, stopping on a bullet hole that punctured the wall only six inches from her head.

He scowled. No, he was not okay with that. "What were you trying to do?"

She pulled her hand back, blinking at him.

"You really are trying to get yourself killed, aren't you?"

She turned away, jaw tensing.

He shouldn't have been so sharp. But the thought of seeing her get shot and being helpless to stop it still made his hands shake. "Spring."

She wouldn't look at him.

Fine. Then he'd just say it. "If you're so okay with dying, then why are you so afraid of living?"

Her gaze lurched to his, hurt registering in her eyes.

He almost regretted the words. He was hardly in a position to call someone else out for being a coward. Luke could've finished what he had started while Torin was out of it, battling the memories that wouldn't let him go.

Torin swallowed. "I'm sorry."

She pulled Bradley closer, the boy's face already buried in her side.

"I had no right to say that." Torin wouldn't blame her if she called him a hypocrite or never spoke to him again.

"You know what my dad said when I won the first cycling race I entered?" She brought her gaze to Torin. "Looks like Spring's brain is in her legs."

He only glimpsed the pain reflected in her eyes before she looked away.

"I was sixteen years old. I couldn't get higher than C's in science. That meant I was the only Weston who wouldn't go into medicine." She stared at the wall opposite them. "Five kids and they're all following in Daddy's footsteps. Except for one." She pointed to herself. Took a deep breath. "But when coaches started to tell him I was good at cycling, Dad allowed me to do that instead of medicine, so long as I excelled at it. I was supposed to go pro and win. Be at the top."

"Why?"

"To make up for failing at medicine or getting an equally impressive degree, I suppose." She raised her eyebrows. "Didn't your parents ever pressure you to meet their expectations? Or maybe they wanted you to be a cop?"

Torin transferred his gaze to Luke as weariness settled on his shoulders like a heavy weight.

The shooter paced while he tried to bargain for something on the phone.

"I don't know." Torin lowered his stare to a spot on the floor. "They didn't live long enough to tell me."

"I'm so sorry. I didn't know." Her voice held compassion that seemed to reach inside his heart, exploring the dark, hidden crevices he didn't share with anyone.

"They both died when I was young, Dad in a car accident and Mom from cancer a year later." He gave a half shrug. "You get used to it."

Heavy silence hung between them.

"My mother died when I was twelve." Spring's voice was nearly a whisper, but he could still hear the pain.

He lifted his gaze to hers, the feeling of connection stretching like a lifeline between them.

The loss in her eyes said more than words. She understood. "Who raised you?"

"My grandmother." His chest warmed as he pictured her wrinkled and affectionate face. She had been happy so long as her grandson didn't end up on the street.

"She did a great job." A small smile undercut the sympathetic sadness in Spring's gaze.

"She was a great lady."

A glint of understanding lit Spring's eyes, and the corners of her mouth turned down. "You lost her, too."

Torin pulled in a long breath. Let it out. "Family's a special thing to have."

She met his gaze. "Yes. It can be."

"But I have to say your dad must not be too bright."

Her eyebrows lifted. "He's one of the best neurosurgeons in the country."

"Then why can't he see there's so much more to you than cycling or medicine?"

Her eyes widened as she watched him.

Then her expression changed, lips pressing together as a shadow darkened her features and her gaze dropped. "Now all I am is a wheelchair."

"That's not what I see."

Her startled gaze landed on his face, and he looked deeply into her eyes, wanting her to know he meant it. He wished he could say more. Wished he was half the man he used to be so he could promise her things…promise to love and protect. But he couldn't.

"I guess none of that matters right now." He directed his attention to Luke as if he was referring to the shooter.

When he glanced back, disappointment sagged her features. Stabbed his heart. He'd failed again. Failed to protect her from himself this time.

He'd been an idiot to let his feelings for her grow so much, and even more of a fool to let them show. She deserved much more than a shell of a cop who couldn't risk loving anyone the way he had loved Ivy.

But what he'd said to Spring was true. The feelings he was trying to fight didn't matter while they were there, under Luke's thumb.

The shooter's nerves frayed more with each hour that passed. He was edgier, more unpredictable, more irrational. And he still had enough speed left in his bag to only get worse.

Torin had to end this before Luke started blaming Spring for the spot he was in again. Torin couldn't be what Spring deserved, but he could get her out of there safely. Or could he?

He frowned, resting his elbows on his knees and gripping his wrist with the other hand. So far his attempts had only ended in disaster and risking Spring's life. He needed to develop a plan that wouldn't jeopardize her safety. And one that didn't allow Luke to get off a shot. If he could avoid that trigger for his flashbacks, he could keep his head and take down the perp.

"Bathroom break?" Victoria stood in front of Spring, the empty wheelchair at an angle by her side.

Spring nodded, glancing down at Bradley under her arm.

The boy watched Victoria with a frown, fear still shadowing his blue eyes.

Victoria smiled at him. "I know. *You* have a bag."

A hint of a smile replaced the boy's frown.

"Dr. Berghuis is going to come over and help you with your bag in a little bit. Mind if I take Spring away for a few minutes?"

Bradley looked up at Spring, who gave him a sweet, reassuring smile Torin wouldn't mind having aimed at him. "Okay."

Torin glanced at Luke, but Victoria seemed to guess his thinking.

"It's fine. I already got his permission. Would you mind sliding Bradley on his cushion to the side so we can stand next to Spring?"

Torin nodded and got to his feet. He slid Bradley as carefully as he could, but was completely unprepared for the boy's, "Weee!"

A grin popped onto Torin's face despite himself.

He glanced at Spring in time to catch her amused smile and the tiniest sparkle in her eyes.

His heart thudded against his ribcage.

"Will you lift from that side, please?"

Torin snapped to attention at Victoria's instruction and stepped to Spring's side where Bradley had been sitting. He didn't know whether he was more disappointed or relieved that Victoria only wanted him to help this time instead of lifting Spring alone. It had been impossible to keep his growing feelings in check when he'd had to hold her so close.

"One, two, three." Victoria nodded to Torin, and they lifted Spring between them.

Spring's hair brushed against his cheek as he lifted with one hand under her arm, the berry scent of the dark wave intoxicating his senses.

He backed up as soon as they set her in the chair, letting Victoria adjust Spring's position on her own. He couldn't think when he was so close to her. Couldn't keep the feelings at bay.

He watched Victoria push the chair up the hallway toward the bathroom, his ribs squeezing inward. He was losing the battle with his emotions. One more reason to get out of there as soon as possible.

Dr. Berghuis finished doing something with the young man in the wheelchair closer to Luke and headed in Torin's direction.

Torin braced himself for some objection from Luke, but he stayed leaning against the wall and snorted powder.

Hair on the back of Torin's neck stood up as an idea started to form. While Luke seemed to watch Torin anytime he moved an inch, the shooter let Victoria and Dr. Berghuis move freely among the hostages. They'd been doing so off and on, checking on the patients in wheelchairs since Luke had released the injured nurse. Luke had even let the doctor leave again to care for the bedridden people in patient rooms.

Luke thought Berghuis and Victoria were harmless. Which meant they could have a chance to surprise the shooter.

Torin smiled at Berghuis as he approached.

"You look chipper considering this is..." the doctor stopped in front of Torin and checked his wristwatch, "hour seventeen and counting. Everything all right?"

"Having the time of my life."

Berghuis gave a sideways grin at the sarcasm, dropping his gaze to Bradley. "I'm here to check this lad's bag."

"It's not very full." Bradley held up the bag in question.

"You're right." Berghuis glanced at Torin. "I'm afraid everyone's dehydrated. I'll have to speak with Luke about procuring more beverages."

"He's letting you talk to him?" Torin kept his voice low.

"Yes and no." Berghuis crossed his arms over his open white lab coat and striped shirt. "It seems since I brought him the amphetamines, he feels confident he can control me. I've continued to be friendly in the hope of gaining his trust. Perhaps some influence, too."

"Do you think you could get close to him and keep his focus on you while I come in from behind?"

Berghuis frowned. "Didn't we already try that?"

"With me as the bait. But I make him too nervous and edgy. He seems relaxed with you. He might not suspect anything."

"Might."

"How badly do you want to get out of here?"

Berghuis shifted his jaw. "When do we do it?"

"Now." While Spring was still gone. If any shots were fired, he didn't want them aimed at her.

CHAPTER
THIRTY-SEVEN

October 12. 6:28 a.m.
17 hours and 28 minutes hostage.

SPRING FINISHED DRYING her hands with the paper towel and chucked it into the garbage slot.

This trip to the women's restroom had been mostly silent, Victoria's face a study in the quiet thoughtfulness she so often favored. Judging from the frown that shaped her lips and the lines across her normally smooth brow, Spring was glad her sister was choosing to keep the thoughts to herself.

But she also wasn't grabbing the handles of the chair to push Spring from the bathroom.

Spring lifted her gaze to meet her sister's in the mirror.

"You like Sergeant Cotter, don't you?"

Spring pretended to pull a spot of lint off her black pants as she fought the heat that tried to reach her face.

"That's not what I see," he'd said, with a look that had sent shivers shooting to her fingertips.

"Are you asking if I mind if *you* like him?" Spring raised her eyebrows in what she hoped looked like an innocent, detached expression.

"Don't do that, Spring." Victoria folded her arms across her shirt. "You can be honest with me."

"Can I? You never want to hear the truth when I say it."

"If you mean the lies you believe so you don't have to—" Victoria pursed her lips.

The heat of anger rose in Spring's chest. "Don't have to what?"

"So you don't have to face life."

"Why are you so afraid of living?"

Spring pushed the memory of Torin's question away. Why was everyone suddenly a bunch of psychiatrists bent on analyzing her?

"Blaming others for your circumstances is only a way of avoiding the need to face scary, hard things. Your own choices and act—"

"How dare you?"

Victoria's eyes widened slightly.

"How dare you accuse me of blaming others because I'm scared? You have no idea what my life is like. You have no idea what it's like to wake up and not be able to feel your legs." Spring fought to hold back the tears that blurred her vision, but one slipped out. "And you have no idea," a sob tried to strangle her voice, "what it's like to disappoint Dad...from day one." She wiped at the falling tears with her thumb and fingers.

"I'm..." Victoria cleared her throat. "I'm sorry, Spring."

Spring peered at her sister through the blur. "You're so much like him, he couldn't help but love you."

"It's not..." Victoria turned away, but Spring could see her furrowed brow in the mirror. "I never knew you felt this way."

No surprise there. Before the crash, they hadn't talked often, and when they did the conversation was filled with Victoria's unsolicited advice and Spring throwing it back. Maybe if Spring had managed to actually take some of that advice through the years, she wouldn't have had to taste so much of her dad's disappointment.

She sighed. "We should get back. I'm afraid Luke is just waiting for an excuse to hurt Torin."

Victoria raised an eyebrow, probably because Spring hadn't called him Sergeant Cotter. She went to the back of the chair, gripped the handles, and wheeled Spring toward the door. "He seems like a special man."

Spring warmed at the praise from her hard-to-please sister. "He is."

Victoria paused before opening the door. "You don't have to push him away. I hope you know that."

With the way he'd pulled back from her as soon as she started to think he felt what she did, she wouldn't need to push him away. He wasn't interested. Or maybe he couldn't get past the wheelchair even though he was nice enough to say he didn't notice it. Of course the chair was a problem. Would be for any man.

"Can we just go? Or are you afraid to?" Spring picked a different fight to get Victoria off the topic.

"I guess I am." Victoria's voice was small, quiet.

Spring had never heard her sound like that. As if she was actually scared. But she couldn't be. Victoria was always strong, always confident, and knew exactly what to do.

"I'm starting to wonder…" she took a breath, "if we'll get out of here."

Hearing her stalwart sister voice the fear growing in her own mind twisted Spring's stomach into a knot. It was Spring's fault Victoria was even here. Luke had come for her, not Victoria or any of the others.

Spring gripped the arms of the chair. "You'll get out." She'd do whatever she had to in order to keep that promise.

Victoria put her hand on Spring's shoulder and gently squeezed. "We'll both get out. God will protect us and show a way. I've been praying every minute."

Maybe God would listen to Victoria's prayers. He probably liked her better, just like their dad.

"God even kept Robert on my phone with Luke. I think He has a plan in using Robert's gifts."

Spring craned to see her sister's face. "Luke's been talking to Robert this whole time?"

"Yes. I was speaking with him when Luke found me. The police must have decided to let him function as negotiator. Robert is experienced with people like Luke. He might be able to persuade him to surrender."

If only it were true. Before someone else got hurt because of her. Someone like Torin.

The knot in her belly cinched tighter. They needed to get back. Victoria had said Luke threatened to shoot Torin if they tried to escape or hide. Hopefully they hadn't been gone too long already.

As Victoria pushed her from the bathroom into the hallway, Spring voiced the weak hope growing in her mind. "Torin will protect us." Even if she didn't want him to.

"I think you're probably right."

Spring could hear the smile in her sister's voice, but she didn't care. Torin may not be as attracted to her as she was to him, but she knew she could trust him to protect her no matter the cost to himself.

The trouble was, she didn't see him as just a police officer or bodyguard anymore. He was another person she'd entangled in the troubles of her ruined life. She couldn't let him keep risking his life to help her. Especially when the thought of him getting hurt scared her more than the thought of waking up paralyzed tomorrow.

She looked for him as they approached the group of hostages. Just like the last time, she couldn't see him at first.

Bradley sat in his wheelchair with his back to them. Torin or Dr. Berghuis must have put him there.

But where was Torin?

"Oh, dear."

Spring's heart paused at Victoria's words. "What is it?"

"On the floor by Luke."

She strained to see as Victoria pushed the chair past Bradley's and kept going toward the shooter.

A vise seized Spring's chest, squeezing painfully.

Torin lay on his side a few feet from Luke.

"Is he—"

Victoria's hand pressed Spring's shoulder. "He's alive."

Torin shifted then, rising up from his shoulder to a sitting position. He winced like the movement hurt. His hands were bound in front of him with something brown. His belt?

His gaze came up, locking on Spring. "Keep her back." His voice was rough and hard.

Victoria halted the chair.

Luke cast a wide-eyed, hysterical glance at them. "No, bring the girlfriend here. Maybe I'll shoot her to teach the cop a lesson he'll never forget."

"Don't take it out on her, man."

Luke launched a kick into Torin's thigh.

"Stop it!"

"Aw." Luke stuck out his lower lip with a glance at Spring. "Your crippled girlfriend cares."

"Spring, stay out of it." Torin's eyes were darker as he glared her way, his teeth clenched.

How many times had Luke hurt Torin while they were in the restroom? Pain and nausea flooded her stomach like she'd been kicked herself.

Dr. Berghuis walked between the two men. "You don't want to do anything to jeopardize your plan. You have the negotiator right where you want him. He's given you everything you've asked for, hasn't he?"

Spring held her breath, waiting for Luke to lose it and shoot the doctor in the chest.

He nodded instead, his cheeks sinking in and puffing out with heavy breaths.

"You don't want to abuse the hostages or the police might not cooperate. I'll just move the sergeant over to the wall, where you can keep an eye on him better." The doctor helped Torin to his feet.

Torin limped badly, every step jabbing Spring's heart. This was all her fault.

If Luke had only finished the job when he'd first crashed into her, or she'd died on the operating table, then Torin and everyone else wouldn't have to go through this. And she wouldn't have to face the prospect of life without her legs.

At least that future was becoming less of a possibility with every minute they were held captive. Luke's tension was palpable as Victoria pushed the chair past him, giving him as wide a berth as she could.

She stopped the chair by Torin and angled toward him as Dr. Berghuis helped him sink to a sitting position on the floor.

Spring willed Torin to look at her, but he kept his gaze away, the muscles in his jaw flexing. Frustration surged in her belly. She wanted to reach out to him, to lean close to find out what had happened, if he was okay. But she couldn't move from the prison of the wheelchair.

The notes of Victoria's ringtone pierced the air, making Spring jump.

Luke lifted the phone to his ear. "Are they going to give me what I want?"

"What happened?" Victoria whispered before Spring had a chance.

Dr. Berghuis glanced at Luke, who kept his eyes on them while he talked on the phone. "We tried to disarm him." The doctor lowered his voice to a whisper. "I was supposed to distract him, but I couldn't hold his attention. He turned at the wrong moment and saw the sergeant coming." Dr. Berghuis looked down at Torin, who didn't even glance up. "I'm sorry."

"Did he hurt you badly, Sergeant?"

Victoria was asking the questions Spring should, showing the concern she wanted to. But she couldn't get words past her tightening throat. She had been right. Torin would do anything to protect her, to get her out of there. Even what she would never want him to do.

"He was kicked several times." Dr. Berghuis glanced at Torin, still silently sitting by the wall. "I'm afraid Luke forced me to bind his hands with the belt. He got that gun on us before we had a chance."

"Listen." Torin's sharp command froze them all. His gaze locked on Luke, drawing the others' attention to what the shooter was saying.

"Get me food and the drinks, and I'll give them two more. Five minutes."

Two more hostages were getting out?

Spring's heart leapt. Victoria could go. And Bradley. And Tor—

No, only two could go. Torin might not be looking at her, yet she still knew beyond a doubt he wouldn't leave her. But could he protect her with his hands tied?

"Please let Mrs. Stewart go." Victoria stepped toward Luke with the suggestion before Spring could think about voicing hers.

"Who?"

"That lady there." Victoria nodded to the elderly woman who sat with her back to the wall opposite them. She was so quiet that Spring had barely noticed the woman for hours. Her skin was pale, and she looked weak even to Spring's non-medical eye.

But if Luke released her, Victoria and Bradley couldn't both go free.

"Sure. She looks too much like my grandma anyway."

Victoria quickly walked to the woman and helped her to her feet.

Spring took a breath and went for it. "And my sister."

Luke slanted his gaze at Spring.

She swallowed. "Please let her go."

Victoria's eyebrows nearly touched her hairline. "No."

Luke glanced at Victoria.

"I don't want to leave. Not without my sister."

"It's what Dad would want."

Victoria shook her head. "Nonsense. He wants us both."

"Shut up." Luke pointed at Victoria. "She knows how to do as she's told. I like that. She stays."

Spring's hopes sank as their captor cast his gaze over the others as if looking for the lucky winner of his life or death lottery.

"That one can go." He nodded to the young man in the wheelchair with braces on his wrists, fingers curled under.

Spring couldn't help but feel glad for him. But she didn't know how much longer she could take watching Bradley, Victoria, and Torin suffer because of her...worrying that worse might happen to them.

Maybe she could talk to Luke, tell him she wouldn't press charges for the crash if he let everyone go.

Wishful thinking again. Luke had gone too far for the police to allow him to go free now. Did he know that? He seemed to be stalling, just biding his time and asking for small favors instead of a getaway vehicle and clear passage. Maybe the drug he kept inhaling left him incapable of forming a plan.

Which would mean there was no predicting how much longer he would hold them. And whether or not he would start shooting in a fit of emotion.

Lord, if someone must die, please...let it be me. She'd do everything she could to guarantee it.

CHAPTER
THIRTY-EIGHT

October 12. 8:34 a.m.
19 hours and 34 minutes hostage.

TORIN'S WRISTS burned where the belt dug into his skin. He gritted his teeth and continued to work at sliding his hands out of the leather binding. Wasn't as tight as it could've been, thanks to the doctor having bound Torin instead of Luke. And Torin had the presence of mind to angle his wrists at the time, taking up more space than necessary.

About the only thing he had done right. He leaned his head back against the wall. The embarrassment of this failure was almost worse than the first. No flashbacks had disoriented him this time, and a doped-up shooter had still bested him.

The plan should have worked perfectly if Berghuis had been able to hold Luke's attention just two seconds longer. But Torin couldn't blame the doctor. The idea was riddled with risk and assumptions, and Torin had known it. He went ahead with the plan out of sheer, foolhardy desperation.

The foreboding sense of the fate that might await Spring was growing, gnawing at him from the inside. Luke was highly unstable and wasn't forgetting that she had been his original target.

But once again Torin had only made things worse. And taken a beating this time. His body ached all over thanks to Luke's repeated kicks.

Torin had wanted nothing more than to grab the perp's foot and deck him, but his hands were tied at that point and Spring was in the hallway. Safer to play possum and hope to gain an advantage by leading Luke to underestimate him.

He just wished the subterfuge didn't come at the cost of Spring's respect. He'd seen it in her eyes when she'd looked at him.

Shock. Disappointment. Pity.

Now she knew what he really was. Weak. Unable to protect her or anyone. A pretend cop giving the force a bad name.

His gaze went to her now, where she sat in her wheelchair a couple feet away. Victoria had positioned Bradley's chair next to Spring's after the two hostages had been released. Spring had stopped looking Torin's way after a while, focusing on entertaining the boy instead.

Maybe now that she saw his weakness confirmed again, she would understand why he had pulled away earlier. She'd probably push him away herself. He would never be able to offer her what she deserved. He hadn't been enough for Ivy. He wouldn't be enough for Spring or anyone else.

A soft, lilting sound came from Spring, interrupting his gloomy thoughts. Was she singing?

"Jesus loves me, this I know, for the Bible tells me so..." The familiar children's song Torin had heard at his grandma's church decades ago echoed in the cavernous hallway.

Bradley's high-pitched, boyish tone joined Spring's.

The tightness in Torin's chest eased. She had a lovely singing voice, but it was her expression that caused him to stop manipulating the belt and listen.

"They are weak but He is strong..." Peace rested on her

face as she sang, creating a glow that perfected her features to a level of beauty that sucked the air from his lungs.

"Next person who sings gets their head blown off." Luke spoke the threat loudly to be heard over their voices.

Torin tightened his jaw, barely stopping himself from another stupid move—trying to throttle the shooter.

Spring's face reflected Torin's anger, the look of peace replaced by flashing eyes and red-tinged cheeks. "Why won't you let us sing?" She glared with the fire he'd only seen one other time, when he'd tried to prevent her from rescuing the boy. "It's comforting to Bradley. You shouldn't be keeping him here, away from his parents."

She was pushing it.

Victoria shot Torin an alarmed glance. She was right. Spring shouldn't call attention to herself.

Luke shrugged, calmer than Torin would have expected. "I haven't seen my parents in years." He lifted his hand with the gun out to the side. "I'm fine."

The gross inaccuracy of the statement would've made Torin laugh if his gut wasn't twisting into a painful knot. Spring had Luke's full attention now. Not good.

"No, you're not fine."

Torin's contorted stomach flipped. What was she thinking?

"You're addicted to drugs and have shot two people, not to mention holding us hostage."

"So?" A smile played around Luke's lips, but his eyes weren't amused.

Something changed in Spring's expression, as if she'd had an idea. One Torin was sure he wouldn't like.

"You said you didn't mean to hurt anyone."

Luke frowned, watching her.

"I believe you. And I don't think you want to hurt anyone now."

Torin had to remind himself to breathe as his gaze jumped from Spring to Luke. Was she asking for it on purpose? The suspicion that she might want Luke to kill her returned to Torin's mind, making his pulse pick up speed.

He flexed his wrists in the belt. He could slip out of the binding whenever he needed to now.

"This little boy needs his mom and dad."

Luke's gaze shifted to Bradley for a moment.

"Just like you do." Her voice softened. Was she seriously feeling bad for their captor? Or maybe she was just trying the sympathetic approach to gain Luke's understanding. "I can't stop your hurt, Luke, but maybe you can make things different for Bradley. Don't let him go through the kind of pain you have."

She was mesmerizing, her voice steady and calm, gaze full of comfort. Maybe Torin had been right about her spell-casting powers.

Even Luke listened, the hostile mask of his power trip falling away for a moment, revealing the raw misery of a broken life.

"Too late." Luke's voice was weak and dry. His gaze appeared to see something miles away.

"It isn't too late. Not for Bradley or you. Jesus can help you, Luke. He can save you."

The mask slammed onto Luke's face, and he strode toward her. "You're trying to trick me!" He lifted the gun. Aimed at Spring. "There's no such thing as Jesus."

"Leave her alone." Torin pushed up from the floor, drawing the shooter's attention and making him brake.

"Torin, it's okay."

He didn't look at Spring to acknowledge her protest. "She's just trying to help you."

Luke snorted. "Why would she want to do that?"

"I have no clue."

"Sit down."

"She's right about one thing."

"Sit down!"

Torin lowered to his knees. "It isn't too late. You should

ask the cops for a car and a clear path out. If you don't hurt anyone else, they might do it."

Luke's gaze switched to the other hostages, then back to Torin.

"I'm a cop, remember? I know how these things work. They'd rather let you go than have a bloodbath on their hands." He hoped Luke was out of it enough to believe the story. At the least he was stealing the shooter's attention from Spring.

Luke narrowed his eyes. "You're lying."

"I could be. Or I could be telling the truth. Your only way out is to try."

"I'm not going to get shot by a bunch of cops." Luke shook his head. "It's safe here." His gaze danced around the white walls of the hallway. "No windows. No way in I can't see. We can stay here as long as I want." He nodded as if he'd convinced himself.

He turned a glare on Torin. "Now everybody shut up and leave me alone."

Luke opened his bag of powder to snort more, and Torin finally let his gaze drift to Spring.

The look she gave him wasn't what he'd expected. Instead of gratitude or even fear, her eyes glinted with what looked like anger. She was mad at him?

Understanding dawned with another twist to his mangled gut. She had realized he was weak, and she hated him for it.

He had expected such a reaction. But that hadn't prepared his heart for the blow.

10:17 a.m.

21 hours and 17 minutes hostage.

Spring's pulse pounded as Luke argued with Robert on the phone. The conversation was the most heated they'd had.

Luke was losing his grip, or Robert was getting more threatening.

Would SWAT officers blast their way in? Would Bradley and Victoria get hurt if they did?

Torin would. He would shield her from everything, putting himself in harm's way.

Spring's frown deepened. She would rather die herself than have him get hurt. But he stood in the way of every attempt she made to draw Luke's attention. And if Luke ever decided to finish the job he had started on the street six weeks ago, she knew he'd have to go through Torin.

She couldn't bear that. Her gaze dropped to the dark brown sport coat Victoria had returned to her lap after she'd used the bathroom.

Lifting the sport coat off her legs, Spring looked at Torin where he sat on the floor, watching their captor.

"Thanks for the loan."

Torin turned his head to face her, his emerald eyes jolting her pulse. His brow furrowed when he saw the sport coat she held out to him. "I don't need it back if you're cold."

"I'm not." Though her legs did seem cold without the secure warmth. But considering she couldn't even feel her legs anymore, she knew the sense of something missing was emotional, not physical.

"Okay."

His hands were tied. The realization caused heat to crawl up her neck. He'd think she was an idiot. She leaned forward to drop the sport coat onto his bent knees in front of him.

She nearly lost her balance but caught the arms of her chair just in time, exerting muscles she didn't know she had to push herself upright.

Fueled by that success, Spring blurted out what she needed to say before she lost her nerve. "I don't want you to protect me anymore." She almost wished she could take back the words when she saw the expression in his eyes.

His eyes flashed with pain as if she'd struck him.

She looked down, swallowing the sudden lump of guilt that made her wish she could take back the words. She stared at her black pants, smoothing her dead thighs with her hands. He didn't care because of any personal attachment. She had to remember that. She'd probably just injured his pride. She dragged her gaze back up.

His eyes had darkened to the color of pine trees. "If you didn't want to get killed so badly, I wouldn't have to keep protecting you."

Her mouth dropped open. "I don't want to get killed." Heat rushed to her face.

"You sure have a funny way of showing it. You don't have to try to make him shoot you at every opportunity."

"Isn't that what you're doing?"

A muscle in his jaw flexed as his eyes glinted. "I am *trying* to take the heat off you."

"I never asked you to."

"You didn't have to. Anyone can see you need help."

Hot tears sprang to her eyes. "And anyone can see that you are in no condition to protect anyone."

"Spring." Victoria's snap held a warning.

Spring gladly yanked her gaze from Torin's face. She didn't want to look at him again. How could she let herself become so vulnerable to more pain? Wasn't it enough that her life had been stolen from her?

"Did you hear what Luke said?" Victoria's worried tone broke through the hurt.

"What?"

Victoria put her hand on the back of Bradley's chair.

Only then did Spring see the look of terror on the little boy's face.

Because of her argument with Torin? More guilt gathered in her throat.

"I think Robert may have threatened to send SWAT." Victoria moistened her lips. "Luke said he'd kill Bradley if they try to enter."

"Robert? Your brother's negotiating?"

Victoria nodded to Torin. "Yes."

"They won't risk the boy's life." Torin sounded as strong and confident as ever. Clearly their argument hadn't hurt him the way it had stabbed her.

When had she let herself believe he actually cared for her? She knew it wasn't possible. He only wanted to protect her because it was his job. Because he clearly thought she needed help. The worst part was that he was right. She did need help. With everything.

But she wouldn't let others get killed trying to help her. She would die first.

CHAPTER
THIRTY-NINE

October 12. Noon.
23 hours hostage.

THE TENSION in the air nearly crackled.

Luke paced with quicker strides across the width of the hallway, cheeks sucking in and out as he worked his jaw, crumpling the shrinking supply of speed in his hand. He was starting to come apart.

On Torin's right, the air hung even thicker. Spring hadn't spoken to him since their argument, and he'd only caught her looking at him once with an expression he'd seen on plenty of perps' faces.

It was clear she'd lost any respect she might have had for him, and that she was furious. She had good reason to be. He'd never meant to suggest she was helpless or weak. But that was no doubt exactly what she thought he had intended by what he said.

Never had been great with words. Another reason to spend his time behind a desk or poring over evidence instead of dealing with people.

For some reason, she brought out a different part of him. A part that cared about people. Too much, as it turned out.

At least her angry silence worked to help him regain perspective. To step back and grab hold of the objectivity that was necessary for all his investigations, and usually so easy for him to maintain. He'd let emotion cloud his judgment for too long. He might have made progress in figuring out a way to manipulate Luke by now if he hadn't been so caught up in thinking about Spring and his roller coaster emotions.

He'd even forgotten about the unease that had bothered him at first—the incongruous elements of Luke's actions and motivations. Focusing on the pacing shooter instead of Spring's whispers to Bradley, Torin mentally reviewed the facts.

Luke was clearly the one who had hit Spring, but his motivation for coming after her at the rehab center wasn't so clear.

Or it was perfectly clear, and Torin was just refusing to see it. The revelation hit him like a truck doing sixty.

His pulse picked up speed. *Idiot.* He'd have made sense of it before if he hadn't let his emotions run out of control.

The hit and run had been intentional. Luke had wanted to kill her. So he wasn't after Spring now out of fear she would finger him for the collision. He had a different motive. Probably the same reason he'd wanted her dead when he had hit her that night.

Donovan Mackeral's killing.

Was she a witness? Or an accomplice?

Torin's gut twisted at the possibility.

He carefully glanced at Spring without moving his head.

She held Bradley on her lap in the chair, murmuring to him as she stroked his hair. She had insisted on holding the boy when he'd asked, ignoring her sister's protests that the weight would aggravate her pressure sore.

He didn't think he'd ever met anyone so filled with compassion for the most vulnerable. Someone so kind, strong only for others, and so willing to sacrifice herself for them.

Unless those moments of riling Luke had been carefully scripted scenes. Or the drugged puppet dancing with the master's pull of the strings?

Torin could be risking his life to protect a criminal, an accessory or perpetrator of two killings now that the security guard was dead.

And if she was involved in Mackeral's murder, was she somehow tied to Ivy—

No. It was unfathomable. His heart knew the truth better than his desperate mind.

Spring had to have been in the wrong place at the wrong time. Luke had likely killed Mackeral and then thought he should eliminate the chance witness. Stupid to try to finish the job in broad daylight in front of witnesses at a hospital, but his drugged mind left little room for rational plans.

If Torin's theory was right, the hostage scenario was as serious as Torin had originally suspected. Luke had risked everything to come there and do what he'd failed to when the collision hadn't killed Spring.

In his mind, he would still need to.

There was no chance Luke would ever let Spring go. No chance he'd try to escape himself and leave the hostages, unless he first…

The unfinished thought pinched Torin's chest. He shifted his wrists in the loose binding under cover of his sport coat.

He could be wrong. He didn't have irrefutable evidence that his theory was correct. So he probably shouldn't act on it. Yet.

A hiss came from Spring.

Torin made himself stay on the floor, not wanting to draw Luke's attention. "Spring?"

She didn't answer. Her chair was angled enough that he couldn't see her face head-on, but her profile revealed a rigid jaw and closed eyes, sweat popping out in beads on her forehead. Was she hurt?

"Spring, talk to me. What's wrong?"

"You okay?" Bradley peered into her face from his close proximity a few inches away.

She opened her eyes. "Fine."

Hardly assuring when she had to force the word through gritted teeth.

Victoria got up from the floor and stepped around her sister's chair. One look at Spring's face was apparently enough. "Phantom pains?"

Spring managed an abbreviated nod.

"Try to breathe. Deep, long breaths."

She took in air, and something twisted behind Torin's ribs as if her pain was his.

"Now let it out, slow and long."

She followed Victoria's instructions, not arguing like she usually did. Probably meant she was in a great deal of pain.

Torin leaned forward. "Can't you do something about it?"

Victoria shook her head. "I'm afraid not. They should go away soon."

Spring continued to grimace as Torin clenched and unclenched his fingers under the sport coat. There should be something he could do. If he could take the pain for her, he would in a heartbeat.

Bradley patted her shoulder as if that would help until Victoria told him to stop.

Spring finally let out a slow breath and opened her eyes again, her jaw relaxing. "You don't have to hover."

Victoria straightened, crossing her arms over her shirt. "You don't have to be such a bad patient."

"Is that what I am? A lifelong patient now?"

Victoria sighed. "Hardly the time to pick a fight. I didn't know you were having phantom pains. How long ago did they start?"

"Hardly the time for an exam either."

Victoria unfolded her arms and lifted them out from her sides. "Fine. I give up." She spun on her heel and marched back to the wall where she gracefully lowered herself to the floor.

She was just a convenient target at the right time. Torin didn't doubt he was the real reason for the heat in Spring's rejection of her sister.

"Is your owie all better?"

Spring smiled at Bradley, sliding her hand over his hair. "Yes, it is. I'm sorry if I scared you."

"It's okay. I'm not scared."

Would Spring accept an apology from Torin so easily? He took a breath, checked to be sure Luke was still busy pacing, and tried in a low voice. "I'm sorry, too."

Spring turned her head, finally looking at him. The confusion and hurt in her eyes knocked the wind from his lungs.

He'd expected anger, not pain. He swallowed. "I didn't mean to hurt you."

She met his gaze. "I didn't mean to hurt you either."

"Don't worry about it. You didn't."

Something flashed just briefly in her eyes, and her lips tugged into a deeper frown.

He'd apparently said the wrong thing, but he wasn't sure why it was wrong.

"I still don't want you to risk yourself for me anymore. I don't need people to protect me. I can handle this on my own."

"On your own?"

Her chin tilted. "Yes."

"You don't actually believe what you said to him, do you?"

She glanced at Luke, the action stripping away some of the defiance that thinly masked her fear.

"He does want to hurt you, Spring."

She briefly met Torin's gaze. "How do you know that?"

"The evidence. He didn't try to brake when he hit you. Didn't try to swerve. He had a reason to want you dead before he came here, remember?"

"He said he wouldn't hurt me if I kept quiet."

The text messages. He'd forgotten. "I can't explain that other than he must have been trying to trick you into thinking you were safe." Or Cliff had written them? Still hadn't figured out what role the cycling coach played in all of this. Had he sent Luke to eliminate Spring because she learned of the team's doping? That could mean the crash had nothing to do with Mackeral's killing.

The answers to those questions didn't really matter at the moment. All that mattered was making sure Spring knew she was in danger and getting her out of it.

She didn't look at him, smoothing Bradley's hair as the boy leaned his head back against her shoulder.

Her silence, the resignation on her face, spoke as loudly as a yell. She didn't care if Luke still wanted to kill her. She didn't want Torin's protection either way.

Even as his heart sank, he reminded himself it didn't matter. Cops were used to not being wanted—sometimes hated. Wouldn't stop him from doing his job.

If his theory about the shooter's intentions was correct, then whether Spring liked it or not, Torin was her only chance of getting out of there alive.

1:15 p.m.
24 hours and 15 minutes hostage.

The sound of the phone made Spring start, prompting Bradley to look up at her from where he sat on her lap. She wrapped her arms around the boy, hoping that might help to calm the nerves that had kept her chest tight and pulse irregular for the past hour. She'd never think of Victoria's classical ringtone as calming again.

Luke frowned as he listened to Robert, she assumed, on the phone. His features scrunched. "You think it's been long? Try it from this side." He called Robert a dirty name.

Spring winced and covered Bradley's ears as quickly as she could, lowering her hands when the boy pushed them down. Maybe she was being silly. He had already seen a man get shot.

"Yeah, I want to get out of here. But they won't let me go." A tone very like Bradley's crept into Luke's voice as he morphed into a little boy. "I don't need you. I've got my own plan."

Spring didn't have to look at Torin to feel him tense.

"You'll see." Luke nodded as if Robert were standing in front of him. Then his cheeks pinched inward. "They can't do that. I'll kill them." His voice rose to a high-pitched squeak.

He listened another moment. Then ended the call. His face paled more than his normal yellow-tinged pallor.

A shiver rolled across Spring's arms.

Torin watched Luke with a relaxed, careless expression from his sitting position on the floor, but Spring could see his shoulders were tight, arm muscles wound like taut rope under the thin sleeves of his shirt. The sport coat covered his hands as he sat on the floor, making her suspect he might be trying to get out of the belt that bound his wrists. What would he do if he got free?

Her pulse sped up.

"Perhaps you should give them more hostages." Dr. Berghuis's voice seemed to startle the shooter as much as Spring. The doctor stood on the opposite side of the hallway from her and the other remaining hostages. His hands casually rested in his pockets, his white lab coat pushed behind them as he watched Luke with his unflappably peaceful expression.

Luke met the doctor's look with a tormented twisting of his features, as if he were desperate for someone friendly to just tell him what to do. "He said they're going to close in soon. They can't risk the lives any longer." Luke sucked in a sort of hiccupped gasp. He rubbed the gun against his pant leg, lowering his gaze. "They won't let me go."

"Why don't you ask them to?"

He pulled up his chin to give the doctor the shocked stare Spring felt like sending him herself.

"Ask them for a car and a safe way out."

"That's what he said." Luke swung the gun toward Torin, making Spring hold her breath.

Dr. Berghuis glanced at Torin. "It was a good suggestion." He met the shooter's stare without a smidgen of fear that Spring could detect. "Just ask them and offer to give them a couple of hostages in return. You might be surprised."

The ringtone sounded. Luke's hand went to his back pocket, but he paused, glancing at the doctor.

"Go ahead."

Luke lifted the phone. "Hello?"

Spring strained to hear him above the blood rushing in her ears. She was glad Bradley had gone still and silent in her lap, likely sensing the tension and maybe her fear.

"I want a car parked at the back of the building." Luke's voice quivered. "Nobody can be near it or watching it. And I want nobody in the staircase when I leave." He paused to listen.

Would the police let Robert agree?

"Tell them they can have more hostages." His gaze traveled over the remaining captives. "Two."

Her heart constricted. Not three. Just one more would have been enough. Then everyone she cared about would be safe.

"Fifteen minutes." Luke slid the phone into his back pocket as he surveyed the hostages.

Please, Lord. Make him let Bradley go. And Victoria.

Even as she inwardly breathed the prayer, she wondered why she left out Torin. She wanted him to be safe. Couldn't bear the thought of him getting hurt.

She swallowed as she realized the difference. The thought of not having him with her scared her even more.

She closed her eyes. How incredibly selfish. He didn't even return her growing, confused feelings. He never would.

"Please let Spring and Bradley go." Victoria's weak voice popped Spring's eyes open.

No. He couldn't listen to her. Not this time.

Luke transferred his gaze to Spring.

She tried to return his look without fear. "I don't want to go."

His cheeks sunk in farther, but she couldn't read his expression. Then he glanced at Victoria. "You'll go. Somebody has to push the kid."

Spring couldn't breathe from sheer disbelief. Then air came with joy. Bradley and Victoria would be saved. *Thank you, Lord.*

But Victoria looked at Spring with agony in her eyes, her skin as white as the night she'd awoken Spring to tell her their mother was gone.

Spring reached out her hand, and Victoria took a couple steps to close the gap between them.

She grasped Spring's fingers tightly in hers. Victoria hadn't held her hand since that night and the following days of devastating grief. Since the funeral, when she had kept Spring's hand in a comforting grip the whole time.

A lump clogged Spring's throat. She would not cry.

Looking at Bradley, she directed her relief into a smile for him. "You're going to get to see your mommy now."

His blue eyes brightened like a summer sky. "Really?"

Her smile broadened naturally, powered by the joy on his sweet face. "Yes. Really."

"When?"

"In just a few minutes. Victoria will put you in your chair, and then she'll push you out of here to people who will help you find your mom."

"Cool!" Bradley eagerly reached for Victoria.

She let go of Spring's hand to transfer the boy to his own wheelchair.

Spring's arms felt empty as she watched Bradley sit in his chair with a huge grin. It was a good thing. He'd be safe. He'd be with his mother. True words, but they didn't soothe the wound she felt tearing her heart. She'd become attached to more than one person there.

"Can we go now?"

Victoria looked at Spring instead of Bradley as she answered. "In a few minutes. I have to say...goodbye to my sister."

"Isn't she coming?" Bradley's eyebrows scrunched together as he directed his gaze to Spring.

She tried to smile, hoping Bradley wouldn't notice it was watery with tears springing to her eyes. "No."

"Why not?"

"I can't. But I want you to tell your mom 'hi' for me. Will you do that?"

Bradley's mouth tucked into a thoughtful frown. "I want you to come with us."

"I want to go with you, too."

"But you said you didn't want to go."

Leave it to a child to hear and understand more than she wanted him to. Spring glanced at Luke, who watched them as if he was listening, for some reason allowing them to speak. "I wanted my sister to be able to go instead."

"Oh. Can't you both come?"

"I'm afraid not."

"Not yet." Victoria looked at Luke, but his watchful, impassive expression didn't change.

"It's okay." Spring met her sister's gaze, trying to convey through her expression that she didn't object. "It's better this way."

Victoria's lips pinched together as moisture glimmered in her hazel eyes. But Victoria never cried. Not even on that darkest night of their lives.

Spring turned her head away, emotion squeezing her

throat as her gaze fell on Bradley's frown. She took hold of the wheels of her chair and pushed toward him.

Standing beside Bradley, Victoria watched, her slim eyebrows reaching up to her hairline.

Spring stopped in front of Bradley and gave her sister a smile.

Victoria let out a sound that was a half-cry, half-laugh. She reached to take Spring's hand with a smile as a single tear dropped onto her cheek.

"I just wanted to show you I'll be fine without you." Spring infused her voice with a teasing sass she didn't feel.

Victoria sniffed, her smile shaky. "I never doubted it for a moment."

"Time's up."

Spring jumped at the sound of Luke's voice. She locked her gaze on Victoria and squeezed her sister's fingers. Victoria's face was pale, tired, beautiful. Spring suddenly wanted to memorize every detail, but she didn't have to. She already knew her sister by heart.

Victoria bent over and clasped Spring's shoulders in a desperate hug.

Spring closed her eyes as Victoria's lilac scent, just like their mother's, engulfed her like a warm blanket from home.

"Remember what you promised." The whisper flowed into her ear as her sister squeezed once more, then straightened, looking into Spring's eyes.

"Nothing stupid."

Victoria nodded, another tear tracking down her cheek. "I love you. The whole family does."

"Hey, get going before I change my mind." Luke took a step toward them.

"Back off, Luke." Torin's hard tone sent a shot of warmth through Spring. He still cared enough to take a risk so she could say goodbye to her sister.

"Shut up or I'll put a gag on you!"

A tremor coursed to Spring's fingers at the unhinged anger

in Luke's yell. "You better go." She released Victoria's hand and transferred her gaze to Bradley. "Goodbye, young man. You're a very special boy. Don't ever forget that God loves you."

Conflicting emotions tugged at his small features. "Okay. See you later?"

Luke suddenly grabbed Victoria's arm.

She gasped.

"Push the kid over to the door." He gave her a shove, and she hurried to grab the handles of Bradley's wheelchair.

She met Spring's gaze as she pushed the chair forward, passing by faster than Spring expected.

Spring gripped the rims on the wheels of her chair and tried to turn so she could watch them leave.

It suddenly rotated for her. She jerked her head around to see Torin standing behind her, moving the chair with one hand, his wrists still bound together in the belt.

She angled forward just as Victoria looked back from the exit.

Bradley raised his small hand to wave.

Spring gulped back a sob and lifted her hand in return, her gaze locking on Victoria's tearful face.

"I'm here. I love you." The words Victoria had whispered to Spring over and over again that night sixteen years ago echoed in her ears. She'd forgotten. Forgotten the warmth in Victoria's voice, the comforting stroke on her forehead as she had clung to her big sister, sobbing into her nightshirt until it was soaked.

Spring had never thanked her.

Victoria opened the door with the automatic button on the wall and wheeled Bradley through.

Spring should be happy to see her go. Their family needed her. They didn't need Spring.

The door slowly closed behind them, just as a grim certainty closed part of her heart forever. She would never see her sister again.

CHAPTER
FORTY

October 12. 1:35 p.m.

"Thank you."

Victoria tried to smile at Bradley's mother and father as they bent over their son, weeping and laughing while they smothered him with their joy.

She couldn't say, *You're welcome*. The credit for Bradley's freedom belonged to Spring. She had gotten Luke to look on the boy with pity and compassion, leading to his release.

If only Victoria could tell her sister how proud she was of the woman she'd become. Her chest constricted.

"Victoria!" A female voice called her name.

Treese and Robert hurried toward her, also inside the perimeter the police had established to keep bystanders and reporters at bay.

Victoria's anxious heart warmed at the sight of her siblings.

Even Treese wore a sparkling smile as they came close, and she flung her arms around Victoria. The first time for that in at least twelve years.

When Treese pulled back, her brown eyes glistened. "Thank God you're okay."

God? Victoria stopped herself from commenting on the uncharacteristic remark.

"Vicki." Robert pulled her into a hug.

When they ended the embrace, she met his gaze. "Thank you for helping us in there. It was a comfort to know you were on the other end of the line."

"For me, too." Robert lifted the phone he held in his hand. Their only connection to Spring now.

Treese lightly touched Victoria's arm. "Hank is taking care of Max."

Tears pricked Victoria's eyes, but she held them back. She had tried not to worry about her fearful dog. To trust God. And He'd provided the one person other than her whom Max didn't fear.

"How's Spring?" Treese's features clustered with worry.

"She's…" Victoria paused to stop the waver in her voice. "I'm concerned for her. I'm worried Luke isn't going to let her go."

"You mean he'd take her with him?" Treese's eyes widened.

"He might do worse than that." She glanced between her siblings. "Did you know he's the one who hit her in the collision?"

Robert's eyes blackened. "How do you know?"

"He confessed it. He told Spring point-blank he had hit her."

Robert pushed a hiss through his teeth. "Nice."

"I'm afraid he might not let her go."

"He'll let her go." Robert's bearded jaw firmed in a confident line. "I've told him the police are going to back off and give him a car. The drug he's taking is dulling his reasoning faculties, and he has a desperate need to follow a leader, for approval from a father figure who will tell him what to do. I'm fulfilling that need for him right now."

Robert was always convincing, but the anxiety fluttering in Victoria's stomach didn't cease. "What if Sergeant Cotter is correct that Luke crashed into Spring intentionally, not accidentally?"

"Oh, you're right." Treese glanced from Victoria to Robert. "He could still want her dead for the same reason, whatever that was. Maybe we should tell the police."

"No, he has no reason to kill her at this point." Robert shook his head. "Whatever his original plans were or his mission before, he abandoned that long ago when he took hostages in a panic. He clearly didn't plan to do that, and with every hour his focus has become more on himself and his fear that he won't get out of this situation. Trust me, all he's thinking about right now is how to get out of the center alive and free."

Victoria looked up at the rehab center, lifting her gaze to the tenth floor.

"She knows how to do as she's told." Luke's words clung to her as if Cillian had returned as a ghost to haunt her. What if Cillian's accusation when he had walked out of her life was accurate in this instance? What if her adherence to rules and authority would lead to Spring's death?

The memory of Spring's expression when Victoria had looked back at the door clouded her view of the sunlight that bounced off the building's tinted windows.

The farewell in Spring's eyes wasn't an *au revoir*. It was *adieu*. Goodbye forever.

She didn't want to leave the center alive.

CHAPTER
FORTY-ONE

October 12. 1:40 p.m.
24 hours, 40 minutes hostage.

TORIN'S worst fear was confirmed. Luke had no intention of letting Spring go.

The release of Victoria and Bradley in exchange for a car and a free path out didn't smell right. Luke hadn't asked for anything of the kind before...when he had more hostages.

Had this been the goal all along? To get rid of the other hostages so that he didn't have to kill them when he eliminated Spring? They were down to the bare minimum now. Aside from the few patients confined to their rooms, which Luke seemed to have long forgotten, it was only Torin, Spring, and Berghuis.

Torin complicated things by being a cop and protective of Spring. Luke would have to take him out, too. And the doctor? The perp was probably keeping him around to access one last dose of speed before he either killed himself or made a suicidal run for it.

Doped-up as he was, Luke didn't act like someone who believed he was about to gain his freedom. Usually, a perp would be either elated or nervous while waiting to hear that the police had his car in place.

But Luke was more relaxed than Torin had seen him since the chaos began. The shooter leaned back against the wall, drug bag tucked away in his pocket, looking down at the Glock he held in two hands in front of him. He lifted his head now and then to check on his remaining hostages, his cheeks sunken in and a look of decision in his eyes.

Torin couldn't be more relieved that he'd listened to his instincts and taken advantage of the distraction during the last hostage release to pass another note to Berghuis. A simple plan, similar to what had failed before, but this time he wouldn't be going for the perp's gun. He would get Spring away from him.

It was a risk, but one they had to take. If they didn't, Spring would be dead within the hour.

Torin looked down at her dark hair from his stance behind her wheelchair.

She hadn't said a word since her sister left. Hadn't looked at him or stirred, so he'd held his position, too. Waiting for Luke to make the first move.

She sniffed. Was she crying?

He put his hand on her shoulder, and she looked back halfway. Enough for him to see the red rim around one eye and moisture on her cheek.

His stomach knotted. He should've been comforting her. Even as an observer, he'd seen that Victoria's departure had been like a surgical separation. The sisters' emotion had caught him by surprise, since they didn't exactly behave as best friends. But he couldn't have missed the pain in Spring's voice when she had tried to pretend she was teasing her sister at the last.

Torin would give anything to drop the subterfuge that his hands were bound and wrap Spring in his arms until all her tears dried and her pain melted away.

But right now saving her life was more important, and he

couldn't let his emotions make him fail again. This time, there would be no mistakes, and he wouldn't let his flashbacks get in the way.

If he could control them. Doubt cut at his confidence. He shook it off and focused on his plan.

The perp could have anywhere from one to five more rounds left in his first Glock. Torin wished he knew for sure, but Luke could have fired more rounds in other hallways during his early rampage when Torin couldn't hear him. Or he may have only shot what Torin had heard.

If they got lucky, Torin might only have to dodge one bullet before Luke would need to switch to his other gun. That moment would give them time to get out of range.

But no matter how many rounds were left, he would have to make sure Luke missed. Spring's life depended on it.

What was the perp waiting for?

Whatever it was, Torin wasn't going to wait, too.

He looked at Berghuis, standing by the wall opposite them. Torin nodded.

The doctor nodded back.

Now or never.

Berghuis started walking toward Luke, who casually lifted his head.

Torin slowly turned Spring's chair as the doctor moved closer to Luke, partially blocking the perp's view of them.

"What are you doing?" At least Spring kept her voice quiet, her tone softened by sadness.

He pulled his hand free of the belt and rested his fingers lightly on her shoulder. "Trust me."

She tensed under his touch.

He let go, gripping both handles of the chair, belt dangling from the one wrist it still wrapped around. He kept the chair at an angle that allowed him to see the doctor and be ready.

Berghuis stood in front of Luke. The shooter straightened away from the wall, and Berghuis slowly walked around him as he talked.

Torin blew out a breath, muscles prepping.

Luke rotated to watch the doctor, turning his back to his other hostages.

Torin took off.

Spring let out a small squeak as he pushed the chair as hard and fast as he could up the hallway, headed for the corner that had brought them there.

"Hey!" Luke had seen them. "Stop!"

Torin launched into a zig zag pattern, running behind the chair. Luke's bad aim better hold.

A shot whizzed too close to Torin's ear. He ducked as a scream echoed.

"Torin!"

No. Not now. He tried to fight the flashback while dodging.

"Ivy!" His own scream seared his soul.

He shook his head. Pushed. Blinked like mad.

The corner.

He veered the chair around it.

Ivy's body lay on the floor.

"Torin? Where are we going?" The panic in Spring's voice yanked him from the memory's grip.

His hands shook. He clenched them around the handles of the chair.

Had he stopped? The chair was still, the different hallway empty. Silent.

Luke yelled somewhere behind them, around the corner.

The fog cleared and Torin surged forward, adrenaline rushing in his ears. Had to get Spring somewhere safe.

He'd known he couldn't outrun Luke pushing or carrying her all the way. Only chance was to hide and barricade themselves.

Torin wheeled the chair a few doors down, then dashed into an open room on the left. Shut the door.

No lock.

No hinge above the door he could secure with his belt.

He cursed himself under his breath. He would pick that room.

He quickly scanned for their options.

Looked like an exam room. One chair, equipment bolted to the wall.

The desk and low table were the only options to barricade the door. But the desk was small and...He lifted the low table. Not as heavy as he'd hoped. Even the two together wouldn't block the shooter from entering.

Maybe the table could serve as protection? Torin eyed Spring in her chair. No. The table wasn't tall enough to protect her from a shot if he tipped it on its side.

Brilliant, Cotter. Way to lead a woman into another trap.

No time to beat himself up. He had to come up with a plan.

He went to the desk and yanked out the drawers, searching for anything that could be used as a weapon. He pulled out a small pair of scissors and turned to Spring. "Okay, here's the deal."

She met his gaze with trusting eyes.

His chest tightened. Did she believe he could protect her? Despite his obvious weakness? "We can't barricade this room enough to hold. Best option is to let Luke come in, and I'll ambush him from behind the door."

Her eyes widened. "No."

"It's the best way."

"No. Please, Torin." No anger or fight in her voice this time, just fear and an emotion he must be imagining. "Please go. I know you can get away without me." Tears glittered like stars in those beautiful eyes. "I want you to go."

The air slowly compressed out of his lungs as his gut twisted. Did she care? About him? He closed the gap between them and crouched in front of her so he could meet her gaze at the same level.

But she looked away. "Please, just go. Go before it's too late."

"Because you can handle it on your own?"

The gentle jab did the trick. She brought her gaze to his. "You know that's not true."

"Not really." The clear drop that trailed down her cheek made him ache. He could bear anything but her tears. "With your spunk, I don't think you've really needed me at all."

Her eyes stayed serious, lips pressed together. "Thank you."

"For what?"

"For protecting me and everyone else."

Did she really think he'd done that? In reality he'd only failed her time and again. Was it possible she didn't hold that against him?

"But I need you to go now." Her voice dropped to a whisper. "I can't watch you get hurt because of me."

The tear touched her full lip.

He brought his gaze back to her eyes. "I can't imagine anyone more worth it." He leaned forward and covered her lips with his. She returned the kiss, her mouth tasting of berry, salty tears, warmth, and passion.

A noise in the hallway startled them apart.

He straightened, keeping his gaze locked with hers. "We could try to be quiet and hope he doesn't find us. But it's only a matter of time, probably not much, before he does."

There was something different in her eyes when she looked up at him, making his pulse beat faster than adrenaline could.

"What do we do?"

"We're going to be found. We need to be ready to take the offensive." Doubt kicked up in his mind again. Taking the offensive hadn't worked out well the last several times in his life. One ending in Ivy's—

He braked the thought. He'd forced them into this situation now. The only chance they had of getting out alive was to attack first.

"Here." He extended the scissors toward Spring. "I want

you to take these. If he gets close enough, you need to use them. Jab his face if you can or anything else if you can't reach his head."

She just stared at the weapon, the pallor of her face suggesting she might be sick.

He tucked the scissors between her leg and the arm of the chair. "Humor me, okay?" He kept his tone even and calm. "If things go like they should, he won't get anywhere near you. It's a last resort, but if I go down, you need to defend yourself."

She moistened her lips, gave the tiniest of nods.

"We need him to walk all the way into the room." Torin went to the back of Spring's chair, gripping the handles and turning her toward the corner.

"You can't hide forever!" Luke's shout pumped anger through Torin's veins. If the perp wanted a fight, he was going to get one.

This time, Torin had the advantage. At least of surprise.

Positioning Spring in the far corner, facing toward the door, he stepped away from her. "I won't let him hurt you."

She looked at Torin, her skin still white. "Just don't let him hurt you."

His heart squeezed as if it was being crushed in a vise. Why now? If he was going to fall in love again, why did it have to be Spring, the target of a lunatic with a gun? Either his life was a study in irony or God just enjoyed playing cruel jokes.

Torin took his position to the left of the door, the direction it would swing when opened.

"I'm going to shoot the cripple first and then you, cop!" Luke's shout was close.

And just what Torin needed. The threat lit a fierce wrath that curdled in his gut and burned upward.

Luke would not hurt Spring. Never again.

CHAPTER
FORTY-TWO

Spring's pulse pounded so loudly, Luke could probably hear it from the hall.

"I mean it, cop!"

She cringed at Luke's yell. It sounded like he was moving closer.

Torin stood next to the door with his back to the wall. His eyes filled with what she used to think was anger at her. Now she understood it wasn't. It was for the person trying to hurt her.

He was going to protect her once again...whatever happened.

An ache filled the crevices under her ribs.

He turned his head and met her gaze. "You'll be fine."

She must have looked as terrified as she felt or he wouldn't have whispered the attempt at reassurance. What if he got hurt or...worse? She feared that much more than her own fate. She had meant what she'd told him. She couldn't see him get hurt. Not when he was protecting her. Not ever.

He didn't even know the Lord. She should have used these last moments to talk to him more about Jesus. How Torin could have eternal life. If something happened to him now and he didn't know Jesus...

She bit her lip. *Please, Lord. Protect Torin. Get his attention and open his eyes before it's too late.*

"You ready, cop?"

She froze.

Luke was right outside the door.

It opened. Slowly.

The shooter stood in the doorway, gun raised as he scanned the room.

His gaze locked on her.

She didn't breathe.

"Knew you were in here. You shouldn't have run away." Luke stepped into the room, aiming his gun at her. "I never wanted to hurt you. I had to. It's not my fault."

Another step.

"I still have to do it."

Please, Lord. Help Torin.

"It's the only way I—"

Torin launched from behind the door and slammed into Luke, whipping the belt over his gun hand.

Luke let out a scream as he tried to spin, but Torin held him tightly, yanking the belt to shake the gun from Luke's grip.

Luke threw his free elbow at Torin.

He dodged.

Luke tried again, writhing as he jabbed, catching Torin with the hit and breaking free.

The belt fell, but in a split second Torin was on Luke again. He launched a kick at the gun.

Luke swung it away.

Torin tackled him, grunting as he dodged a punch, grabbed Luke around the waist.

Something clattered to the floor. A gun.

Torin got it from him?

No. Luke still held one. The other must have dropped from his waistband behind his back.

"Sergeant!" Dr. Berghuis appeared in the doorway. He moved toward the battling men.

"Stay back!" Torin's shout stopped the doctor in his tracks.

Torin gripped Luke's arm as he threw his body weight into the lighter man. They fell to the floor.

A shot went off.

Spring's heart stopped.

But Torin landed a hard punch to Luke's jaw. The shooter's head whacked against the floor. His eyes closed.

Was he knocked out?

Torin reached for the belt on the floor and turned Luke's limp body onto his stomach. Torin belted the shooter's wrists, then picked up the gun Luke had finally released.

Could it be over? Spring looked from Luke to Torin and back again, shock delaying her response.

Torin had the gun. Luke was down.

It was over.

Oxygen surged into her lungs as if she'd been deprived of it for weeks.

Torin wasn't killed. He wasn't hurt.

She could hardly believe it.

"Well done, Sergeant." Dr. Berghuis was the first to speak as Torin leaned on one hand pressed to the floor. The doctor pulled a cell phone from his pocket. "I managed to grab a phone from the hostage collection. I'll call the police."

Torin nodded, his face paling to a grayish hue.

Alarm jumpstarted Spring's pulse. "Torin?" What was wrong?

He shifted, dropping back onto his elbows on the floor.

Then she saw it.

Dark red liquid seeped through the side of his pale green shirt.

"Doctor!" Spring pushed her chair forward. "He's hurt."

Dr. Berghuis crouched next to Torin as Spring reached them.

Torin winced. "Never mind me. Call the police first."

Spring's heart strangled at the pain in his voice.

Dr. Berghuis got to his feet and took two strides to the paper towel dispenser on the wall. Yanking out some towels, he came back and shoved them into Torin's hand. "Press these against the wound." He stepped away to call the police as Torin pushed himself up with a grunt and held the paper towels to the wound in his side.

Spring wanted to help, wanted to do something. But she couldn't do a thing. She could only sit there like some lifeless doll on a shelf, watching Torin's blood color the brown towels a blackish hue.

"Hey." Torin's soft tone brought her gaze to his face. "Don't look so sad. We won." The tense lines around his mouth relaxed a bit, despite the pain in his eyes. "It's over." His lips curved into a small smile. "You're free to get away from the irritating cop now."

"Don't say that." She frowned and stared at the blood that tinged his fingers where they pressed the towels.

"The police are on their way." Dr. Berghuis came back to Torin and crouched beside the wound, pulling Torin's hands away briefly.

Luke made a moaning sound.

Spring jerked to look at the shooter's face.

Eyes still closed. But was he waking up?

"It might take them some time to clear every floor." Torin watched Luke, too. "I'd feel better getting Spring away from him just in case." He shifted his attention to her. "I'll take you down instead of waiting."

Dr. Berghuis shook his head as he replaced the bloodied towels over the wound. "You need to stay put. Press that there, hard." Straightening, the doctor grabbed more towels from the dispenser and handed them to Torin. "Any excessive movement could lead to too much loss of blood."

"It's fine. I don't have to go." Spring tried to clear her features of the fear that must still be showing enough to concern Torin. "We can wait here."

"You don't have to wait, Spring."

"Exactly right." Dr. Berghuis stepped behind her chair. "I'll take her down and come back with the medics myself."

"No." She placed her hands on the rims of the wheels, though she wouldn't really be able to stop the chair from moving if the doctor pushed. "I won't leave you."

Torin touched her knee with a blood-smeared hand, looking at her with those intense emerald eyes. "The doctor is right. Until Luke is in cuffs with more cops around, I don't want you anywhere near him."

"I don't—"

"I'll be fine, Spring." His voice was weaker, but carried an edge that sounded like irritation as he dropped his hand and looked away. "I'll be much better if I don't have to worry about you."

So that was it. Mission accomplished for the sergeant. Spring's heart plummeted in a downward spiral as Dr. Berghuis pushed her chair forward.

"See you in a few minutes."

She couldn't respond or look at Torin as they passed him. Couldn't let him see the surprise that was no doubt written all over her face. She'd been humiliated enough without making it obvious that she'd been so stupid as to believe she had become more than a job to him.

Dr. Berghuis patted her shoulder as he turned the chair into the hallway. "You'll be safe in just a little bit now."

But her heart wouldn't be. It was still back in the exam room, held by the cop who couldn't have been more eager to get rid of her as soon as he could. Why had she let herself believe he cared for her? He clearly didn't or he wouldn't be in such a hurry to rush their parting.

Once they were rescued, he'd have no reason to see her again. He knew who had hit her in the collision now, and that investigation was the only reason he'd shown up in her life in the first place.

Dr. Berghuis turned the chair around another corner, then again into a passageway that widened as it intersected with other hallway openings.

A row of six elevators stood toward the end of the passage, waiting to take her out, away from Torin forever.

She should be thrilled the terrifying ordeal had ended and she was getting out alive. But survival didn't mean what it used to.

The life stretching before her seemed all the bleaker now that she'd let herself hope there might be a bright spot in her future—a man who would overlook what she couldn't. The only man who might actually be able to love her, despite—

Her heart choked at the far worse terror she now faced. *Why are you sparing my life again?* The inward cry to God burst from the despair that swallowed her from the inside out. *Thank you for saving Torin so he'll have another chance with you, but I don't want to live like this. I can't.*

"Feels good to be free, doesn't it?" The doctor's question interrupted Spring's wrestling match with God.

Free? She squeezed the armrests as they approached the elevators. "I'll never be free. Not chained to this thing."

"I'm sorry about that." Dr. Berghuis pushed the chair past the first elevator, the second, the next.

Everyone was sorry. No one more than Spring.

They passed the last elevator. Why weren't they stopping at one to take it down?

"I never meant for you to be paralyzed."

Spring's breath caught. What did he mean? Her pulse accelerated as he took her around the corner past the elevators.

He stopped.

He moved in front of her. Pulled something from behind his back under his white coat.

A gun.

"You were supposed to die."

CHAPTER
FORTY-THREE

STAY AWAKE. Torin grunted as he pushed himself higher, hands braced on the floor behind him to support his upper body. At least the pain from the movement made him more alert. Temporarily.

He could feel the strength draining out of him along with the blood that dripped from his side, pooling on the floor. He should press towels against the wound again, but he'd started fading when he had lain still on the floor to do that.

He didn't dare give in to the darkness that was closing in until SWAT arrived. He couldn't risk Luke waking and slipping free from the makeshift binding.

At least Spring should be out of the rehab center by now. Unharmed.

Relief softened his pain as he pictured her soft eyes. Remembered how she hadn't wanted to leave him.

He could hardly believe she hadn't been hurt. He'd done it. No regrets this time. Although he could've done without the close shave with Luke's weapon.

The gun. Luke had two of them. Torin had one tucked in the front of his waistband. He'd better secure the other one.

He scanned the floor around the perp, then a wider circumference.

Nothing.

That wasn't right. The perp had it when they fought. It had fallen to the floor. Torin had seen it.

Where was it now? Under Luke?

The perp moaned, shifted his hands lower on his back.

Torin pushed onto his knees, causing a surge of pain in his side. He gritted his teeth. "Where's the other gun?"

"Where am I?" Luke tugged his wrists, but the belt held them together.

Torin shoved himself to his feet and looked down at the perp. "Where's your other weapon?"

"Is my car here yet?" The muffled question barely made sense. Maybe he hadn't fully woken up yet.

"There's no way the police were going to get you a car."

"No, Doc's car. He said we'd take his car." Luke craned his neck to look the other direction. "Where is he?"

Torin narrowed his eyes at the back of the perp's head. Berghuis could have said that to get Luke to trust him and not hurt anyone.

"He's gone. To the police."

"No, he's going to get me out of here without getting hurt. He said I wouldn't have to go to jail." Luke twisted like he was going to get up.

Torin pressed his hand against Luke's neck. "Stay down."

Luke stilled.

As Torin drew his hand back, his eye caught a mark on the perp's neck above the collar that had crumpled under Torin's hold.

A tattoo. Two swords, crossed over a blue shield.

Rage broiled in Torin's stomach, flaming out to every muscle, every nerve.

The man who'd murdered Ivy lay on the floor beneath him.

Fury blazed hot through Torin, fogging his vision, searing his eyes. He blinked hard. Stared down at his wife's killer.

They were alone. The murderer had tried to kill others. Torin couldn't ask for a better set up for justice.

His hand pulled the gun from his waistband as if by instinct. He pushed his knee against the killer's back and pressed the gun barrel to his head.

"What—"

"Remember me?"

The killer tried to twist his head to see. "Huh?"

"Three years ago, you robbed a gas station."

The perp froze.

"But I came in, remember? A woman came in, too. And you killed her." Torin leaned his head down close to the murderer's. "She was my wife."

"It wasn't me, man, I swear." Panic strangled the perp's voice.

"You have the same tattoo, and you drive the same van."

"No!" He tried to sit up, but Torin held him down. "I was there, but I didn't go inside. It was Jason. He shot her."

Was he lying? "Who's Jason?"

"My best friend."

"Where is he now?"

"I don't know."

"I've got a gun on you, man."

"Seriously, I don't know! He ran off to Mexico or somewhere." The perp was scared enough to be telling the truth.

Torin released his hold and stood. He glanced at the gun in his hand, his breathing shallow and fast. Would he have shot Luke if he hadn't denied killing Ivy? He didn't believe in that brand of justice. Would that conviction have been enough to stop his anger from pulling the trigger?

He pushed the gun into his waistband before he had to answer that question.

"Where's the doc?"

"Gone."

Luke was silent for several long seconds. "For real?" His

tone pinched, whether with fear or some other emotion, Torin couldn't tell.

"Yes."

A whimper floated up from the floor. He was crying?

"Why'd that chick have to see us? I had it made. I could get all the speed I wanted." The words escaped between small sobs.

Torin's heart thudded against his ribs. Luke had to be talking about the collision. "What do you mean?"

"He said he wasn't going to give me any more after I messed up and didn't kill her. He said it was too risky because she saw him. He didn't even care anymore about me and Jason. He was gonna cut me off anyway."

The hair on the back of Torin's neck stood on end. He hoped the instinctive response was way off base. But his eyes drifted to Luke's shoes. He'd just seen the same style on someone else. "Who was going to cut you off?"

The perp twisted his head to aim one eye up and spoke the answer Torin was terrified to hear. "Doc."

CHAPTER
FORTY-FOUR

THE DOCTOR JUST STOOD THERE, watching Spring and his expensive wristwatch. They were only a couple of halls away from where Torin was. Bleeding.

"You didn't call the police, did you?" She could barely breathe through her constricting throat.

"Of course I did. But I gave them only enough information to postpone their arrival." His thin lips curled into a smile.

She used to appreciate that he was an unusually friendly surgeon. Now his smile made her skin crawl.

Torin was hurt. And they were just waiting there. For what?

She moistened her dry lips. "Torin needs help. He could bleed to death."

"Could he?" Berghuis didn't lose the reptilian smile.

Spring's heart slammed to a halt. "That's what you're waiting for."

"Smart girl."

Her pulse started again at a double-time rate. This couldn't be happening. They'd escaped. It was supposed to be over. How had they leaped from the frying pan into the fire?

None of this made any sense. Why was a prominent

Chicago surgeon standing there, holding a gun on her? Luke was the one who had run her down on the street, who'd tried to shoot her and taken hostages. Dr. Berghuis had nothing to do with that. Did he?

It didn't matter. Torin was bleeding, and he wouldn't have any help unless she could get away from the doctor. He could—

"This isn't the first time I've appreciated your intelligence. You're the rare sort that's smart enough to keep quiet when you're told." The doctor's gaze carried the extra meaning in his words.

"*You* sent the texts?"

"Well, I should hope they were more coherent than anything Luke could manage."

She hadn't thought to dissect the wording of the threats. "But why would you—"

"Isn't it obvious?"

She stared at him.

"I couldn't let you tell the police you saw me."

"Saw you?" It still didn't make sense.

"Of course. When you heard of the shooting on the news, you would've put two and two together."

"Shooting?" The popping sound she'd thought she heard that night. It had been a gun. "You shot someone?"

"It was a drug killing. One of his customers shot him. The police will never think otherwise as long as you can't tell them I was there."

"But I didn't see anything."

He laughed. "I do believe you've convinced yourself. You repressed all your memories of that night along with the collision, apparently. Convenient for me, but I knew it was only a matter of time before your memories would return. You cycled right past us, too quickly for me to see you coming."

"Us?" Luke must have been there, too. A drug killing. "Were you giving Luke drugs? From the hospital?"

"Your shock is very convincing."

She thought back to that night. Had she seen them and repressed the memory? No, the store had been a blur. There could've been people in the shadows by the van, but she hadn't seen them. Frustration mixed with the fear pumping through her veins. "At the speed I was riding, do you really think I could identify faces in the dark? In the rain?"

"I couldn't take the chance regardless, though I never should have trusted Luke to eliminate you. Clumsy idiot couldn't even drive straight enough to kill you."

She could barely grasp what the doctor was saying. She'd been paralyzed because of something she hadn't even seen?

"As I said, it was never my intention for you to have to live like this."

Anger trumped her horror. "Then why didn't you just kill me when you operated?"

"And ruin my reputation as a surgeon?"

"Your reputation? You're a drug dealer. A murderer."

The doctor looked as offended as if she'd accused him of malpractice. "Certainly not. I had a duty to Luke as my son's friend." Berghuis glanced away. "Jason is unfortunately addicted to cocaine. His addiction led him to make a rather costly mistake once, and Luke couldn't be trusted to keep that information to himself."

"So you got him addicted to drugs?"

"Of course not. The boy was already on drugs. I merely did my best to keep him happy."

And quiet. "Why couldn't you simply help your son face up to his mistake?"

"You must be joking. The medical community wouldn't distinguish between father and son in a case like this."

"So?"

"I'm going to be named chief surgeon in another six months. I can't allow anything to stop that. I've worked too hard."

Disgust swirled in Spring's stomach. "So you'd rather kill people than have your reputation ruined?"

"Some kinds of lives aren't worth living." His gaze skimmed over her wheelchair. "But you know that."

The words pierced her anger, deflating it faster than a flat tire. Hadn't she thought the same thing herself, hundreds of times since the crash?

"It's nice to know I'll actually be doing you a favor."

"A favor?"

"Putting you out of your misery when I kill you. You said it in your text. You'd rather be dead."

"I was trying to stop your threats."

He shook his head. "It wasn't a bluff. I've seen the look in your eyes. You don't want to live like this, paralyzed for the rest of your days. I was going to end things for you then, before Luke showed up with his gun. I would have made your passing more peaceful. No violence. Only a happy ending for you."

How could a man so sick in his mind echo so exactly her agonized thoughts? Her gaze met his. And for a terrifying second, she knew he saw her tortured heart.

This was it. The moment she'd hoped for. She was actually going to die.

There was no one left to save her. No Victoria, no Torin. She was alone.

She wouldn't have to live a life of failure in her dad's eyes. Wouldn't have to be chained to a wheelchair, unable to walk or do anything for herself. Wouldn't have to be rejected ever again by a man she cared for. She'd go home to be with Jesus.

The list of positives weren't as comforting as they should be.

A new question bothered her too much. What would God say about how she had used her life? Would He tell her, "Well done"?

"Why are you so afraid of living?"

Conviction gripped her with the memory of Torin's question. He was right. She was afraid of living. And that fear had kept her from doing anything significant with her life.

Her botched attempt with Torin was the first time she'd ever told someone about the Gospel. She hadn't tried to witness to the other hostages. She hadn't done as much as she could to comfort Bradley either because she was so caught up in her own problems.

Had she done anything with her life even before the crash? Or had she been afraid of living then, too? She'd committed to being the best cyclist she could, whatever it took, because then she might actually be able to gain her dad's approval.

But what about God's approval? She had never once considered what God wanted her to do with her life. She'd been so focused on trying to please her earthly father that she had forgotten to figure out what would please her Father in heaven.

She looked at the gun in the doctor's hand.

Now it was too late.

Father, forgive me.

Torin dragged himself up the hallway. His left side felt like a blob of hurt that kept lagging behind the rest of his body.

He fought to keep his mind off the pain and on his destination—the elevators. He only hoped Berghuis had taken Spring there.

The doctor wasn't stupid enough to take her down to any other floors. The police would be waiting.

Berghuis would keep her on that level, probably until Torin bled out. Just long enough to ensure Torin wouldn't be a threat with the weapon he had.

The doctor clearly didn't like head-on conflict and didn't play odds. He'd go with the surest solution to his problem. He couldn't let Luke or Spring walk out of there alive. Which meant Torin had to go, too. He would die if he didn't get medical attention, so he was easy to eliminate with a little patience.

If Berghuis was as smart as Torin thought, he'd wait until Torin was done for or too weak to handle the gun, then bring Spring back and shoot her in the same room. He'd kill Luke, too, and make it look like the shooter had committed suicide after executing the last hostages.

The doctor would have a clever story to explain how he had just barely escaped the carnage. Maybe he'd even be gracious enough to make Torin out to be a hero who'd helped Berghuis escape.

Pain ripped through Torin's side. He slowed his pace, tried to keep breathing. He couldn't stop. Couldn't let Berghuis get away with this.

The mantra of a cop. But the truth was Torin didn't care about Berghuis. He cared about Spring. The second woman he had failed to protect.

How could he have been so stupid as to let Berghuis take her? Torin had handed her over on a platter to the real killer. He should've seen Berghuis's true colors sooner. How had he missed the evidence?

He'd known something seemed off about Luke's behavior. And his instincts had been right. Luke wouldn't have gone after Spring in the hospital if not for the doctor's threat to cut off his drug supply. Torin had known there had to be another explanation.

But he had missed connecting the evidence of the shoes that had bothered him all along. They were a duplicate of the doctor's. Luke had probably demanded Berghuis give him a pair and that fancy watch while he had the doctor on hooks for silence about his son.

Torin had lingered with Luke in the exam room just long enough to make sense of who Jason was and why Berghuis would have given the perp anything in the first place.

Now he knew what he should have figured out a long time ago. If he'd only done his job. Investigated the evidence instead of trying to play the hero.

Now Spring would pay for his mistake. Just like Ivy.

The gravity of his error seemed to fuel the bullet wound, and his side burned as if flames devoured his skin. Weakness weighted his limbs.

He slowed. Stopped. Sank to the hard floor.

He might not even be going the right way. Berghuis could have taken Spring anywhere. She could already be…

The end of the hallway blurred. He was losing consciousness. He had failed again.

CHAPTER
FORTY-FIVE

"SHOULDN'T BE MUCH LONGER NOW."

Spring emerged from her dark thoughts to see the doctor's disturbingly pleasant smile, as if he were informing her that her surgery had been successful.

She tried to swallow, but there was nothing to go down. Her mouth was so pasty and dry. How long had it been since she'd had anything to drink? Not that it mattered anymore.

Time seemed to crawl as she awaited the death she had longed for. But now she saw it for what it was—an escape from what she feared most.

Was Torin facing death, too? *Let him come to you before it's too late, Father. Please.*

"I don't mean to make things difficult by drawing this out for you. There's really no need to be afraid. I will make it as quick and painless as possible, I promise you." He gestured to her legs. "And then you won't have to worry about living like this for who knows how many years."

How did he know she feared that more than dying?

The answer shamed her even more. He knew because he thought that way himself, thought that people and life only had value if they were perfect. No disabilities, no flaws, no oddities. It was the thinking of the world that didn't know God, that hadn't a clue where real worth came from and why life mattered.

When had her thinking become so warped? She knew the truth, but she had fallen right into thinking that her life no longer had any point or value because she'd lost the use of her legs. Mainly because she was too scared to live that way.

But her value wasn't in her legs. Her life wasn't in her legs. Her strength wasn't in her legs.

Jesus loves me, this I know. For the Bible tells me so...

The song she'd sung on autopilot to comfort Bradley echoed in her ears. She was loved. She had forgotten how much. That was why she mattered, why her life was still important whether she had a disability or not—because Jesus loved her.

We are weak but He is strong...

Warmth spread through her arms and fingers, making goosebumps pop out on her skin. She didn't have to fear life in the wheelchair or the doctor threatening to shoot her, because God was stronger than anything she would face.

Torin was right. It didn't make sense that she trusted God to take care of her life after death—for her salvation and for all eternity—and yet she didn't trust Him to take care of the much smaller affairs of her earthly life. Maybe she was the one who needed something drastic for God to get her attention.

The humor of that irony brought a laugh to her lips. She actually laughed. Out loud.

The doctor took a step toward her, gun raised as he checked the empty, short hall behind him and then scanned all directions.

A powerful, blissful sense of freedom filled Spring's soul, flooding her with a joy she'd never known. It welled up inside, bubbling over in another laugh.

"What are you laughing at?" The doctor's assured smile was nowhere in sight.

"I don't need to be afraid."

"That's what I told you."

She barely registered his response, still marveling at the freedom opened up before her. "I don't need to fear living with my paralysis. I don't have to fear Dad's disappointment. God is in control."

Dr. Berghuis released a sarcastic chuckle. "If that's the case, He doesn't seem to be doing a very good job with your affairs."

"Oh, but He is." All of this was part of His plan for her. And she knew His plan was always good because Jesus loved her.

It wasn't too late to embrace His will for her, to embrace this life He'd given her. She wasn't going to waste another minute of it, even if there wasn't much left.

For however long she had to live, she would live for God not men. And she would do it without fear. Because God was stronger than any evil or tragedies she would face. Strong enough even to show her how to live without her legs.

Or to die without anything but Him.

Torin blinked several times, shook his head to clear his vision as he crawled to the end of the wall behind the elevators.

Spring's voice carried to him around the corner. She sounded so…happy. Like he'd never heard her sound before. It didn't make sense.

Judging from the direction of the voices, Berghuis had apparently taken Spring to the elevators after all. But not to save her, not to escort her out of the building to safety.

Torin adjusted his grip on the gun that kept slipping thanks to the blood that coated his fingers.

His worst nightmare—the one he had lived once and promised would never happen again—was unfolding right there and now.

Berghuis was about to kill Spring.

And Torin didn't even have the strength to stand.

"If you don't stop talking, I'm going to have to shoot you here instead." Berghuis's threat held an edge that said it was real. "I hate to risk blood getting in the wrong place, but I could do it."

Why did Spring have to keep talking to him? And about Jesus, no less.

"I know you're doing this because you're afraid, Doctor. Afraid of losing your career, your reputation. But believe me, Jesus can set you free from your fears. All of them. Just like He did for me."

"Not likely. I'm an atheist."

"God doesn't stop existing because you don't believe in Him. He can forgive you. Even if you get away with what you're doing now, you'll have to pay the price with eternity in hell. It's not worth the—"

"Shut up. No one's going to find you by the sound of your voice if that's what you're up to. There's no one to save you."

She'd hit a nerve. Berghuis was losing it.

"Who will save you, Doctor? When you're alone and about to die, who—"

"Stop it! I'll kill you right now."

"I'll kill you!" The robber's shout screeched in Torin's ears as if he were standing in the gas station again.

He waved the gun at Torin and Ivy. "I'll kill you!"

"It's okay." Ivy held out calming hands with a peaceful smile. "You don't have to do this. Jesus can save you."

Shots rent the air.

A scream.

Ivy, dead on the floor.

"You say one more word and you are finished right now. I'll risk the blood." Berghuis's threat yanked Torin from the nightmare that had already happened, dragging him into the one in progress.

He had to get up. Had to at least try to save Spring.

But he spotted his hand holding the gun. It shook wildly. He tried to steady it. Couldn't.

Fear pumped through his body instead of adrenaline, churned his stomach as his remaining strength seeped out along with the blood.

Even if he could stand, he couldn't shoot without risking Spring the way he was shaking. And the Glock only held one more round.

He would fail again. He knew it.

And she'd be the one to pay the price.

He shut his eyes.

The trembling coursed through his whole body as flashes of memory pelted him in debilitating bursts.

Gunshots.

Ivy's scream.

But somewhere in the midst of relived horror, Spring's voice found him.

"He must have had something better planned."

Hard to believe. Especially now, when Torin was Spring's only hope of rescue, and he was going to pieces.

But Spring believed it. So much that she would talk about it to the man who was about to kill her.

God, I know we're not exactly friendly. Torin kept his eyes closed, grimacing as he took in a painful breath. *And I know I don't deserve help, but I'm asking for it anyway. Spring says you can save us from our fears. Can you free me from mine, from these memories, so I can save her?*

Salty moisture touched Torin's lip. He didn't know when the tear had fallen, when his heart had started to ache.

Why would God want to help him? He was guilty of all those things Spring had called sins. He'd lied, been selfish, and a hundred other things. God had no reason to help him now.

But Spring had just told a killer with a gun that God could forgive him. Maybe there was hope for Torin.

Please, God. Forgive me.

He waited, half-expecting some audible answer from above. Some different feeling inside.

He opened his eyes, and then he saw it.

His hand holding the weapon was perfectly still.

His erratic pulse beat steadily, breathing was calm. No dark memories flashed before his eyes.

Peace.

He'd forgotten what it felt like.

"That should be long enough." Berghuis's statement carried around the corner, recapturing Torin's attention. "Let's check in on your friend." His voice was traveling. He must be starting to push Spring back past the elevators, moving on a course parallel to the hall where Torin waited.

Now or never.

Just give me the chance to tell her I finally paid attention. Adrenaline surged through Torin's body with the prayer, and he tried to push himself up.

He managed to gain his feet but pain seared his side. He doubled over, teeth gritted. *Give me strength.*

If he could get behind Berghuis as he came out by the elevators or in the next hallway, Torin would have a chance. One shot to take him down.

He squeezed the grip in his hand as he straightened and pitched his weight forward, forcing himself to move as fast as he could up the hallway behind the elevators.

As he reached the end of the passage, he caught sight of something emerging from the other hall.

Spring in her wheelchair.

His heart lurched.

Berghuis came into view behind her, pushing the chair.

Torin's pulse pounded in his ears. He waited for the fear to kick in. The flashbacks.

But neither came.

The peace held strong under the adrenaline.

God had something good planned. And Torin was pretty sure God could save Spring even if Torin failed.

Torin's vision started to blur as he watched Berghuis push her. *Hang on.* He had to move now.

He stepped out from the hallway. Aimed his weapon steadily at the back of Berghuis's white coat. "Freeze, Berghuis!"

The doctor whirled, gun pointed.

He screamed. Dropped to the floor.

What had happened? Torin held his finger over the trigger. Stared at Berghuis as the man squirmed on the floor, clutching his leg.

Torin darted a glance at Spring.

Her chair was angled slightly toward him, her trembling hand extended over the armrest, clutching something.

The scissors, blades coated in dark red. She had stabbed Berghuis?

Torin pushed aside his astonishment to focus on securing the perp. Keeping his weapon trained on the doctor, Torin moved forward as quickly as his wounded body would allow.

He bent to pick up the gun Berghuis had dropped on the floor. The movement tore pain through him, but he squeezed his teeth together and forced a breath through his nose. He stuffed the Glock with only one round in his waistband and reached for the handles of Spring's chair.

He leaned into them, pushing her chair farther away from the perp before turning it around. Growing weaker by the second, Torin managed to pull his weight off the handles and walk around the chair to check on Spring.

She stared at him with the big, brown eyes he'd feared he would never see again. "You're alive." Her full lips pulled into a joyous smile so beautiful he wondered if he'd died and gone to heaven.

When his breath returned, he managed a weak smile in return. "So far." He gripped the edge of her armrests to keep from collapsing. "Are you okay?"

Her smile didn't budge. "You're alive. I couldn't possibly be any better."

If he wasn't about to pass out, he'd plant a kiss on those curved lips. Weakness was quickly replacing the adrenaline that had powered him briefly. He didn't know how much longer he could stay conscious.

The phone. Had to get to the phone.

He forced himself to turn away from her and locate the cell phone that had fallen a few feet from the doctor.

Torin aimed his weapon at the perp as he grabbed the device from the floor.

Berghuis still grimaced in pain, his blood flowing to the floor as he clutched his leg like he'd never been hurt before.

Torin returned to Spring and handed her the phone. Pulling the emptier weapon from his waistband, he switched on the safety and tucked the gun next to her in the chair. He held the other Glock out to her.

Her eyebrows lowered, and she lifted her gaze from the gun to his face.

"I'm about to pass out." He set the weapon in her lap. "Call 911 and explain the situation. Keep this gun aimed at Berghuis. Help will get here in three minutes or less."

The corners of her mouth pulled downward as lines of concern crossed her forehead. "Torin?" She reached toward him, her hand grasping his as he sank to the floor in front of her and leaned his head back against her legs.

He smiled as rest welcomed him. His Spring was safe.

EPILOGUE

November 13. 10:00 a.m.
4 weeks and 1 day free.

"YOU'RE STILL GOING to stay with me the first night, right?" From the back of the van, Spring watched her sister's reflection in the rearview mirror.

Victoria glanced back before turning the van onto another road. "Yes. But the way you've been handling your own transfers, bathroom, changing clothes...you know you don't need me."

Spring smiled, her courage buoyed by the reassurance, though her pulse still kept a nervous pace. "I'll always need you, sis."

Victoria's lips curved in a small smile, but she didn't answer. She'd been so much quieter lately. Less forceful since the hostage experience.

It had changed them both. The other Weston siblings had noticed the difference. But Spring wasn't convinced the change in Victoria was a good one. Though Treese and Hank weren't complaining that their big sister wasn't as pushy and controlling as usual.

"Still nervous?"

Spring stopped drumming her fingers on the armrests of her wheelchair and smiled. "Yes." She blew out a breath, wishing her chair was parked a little closer to the windows of the van so she could be distracted by the sights. "I haven't been this nervous since I had to give my testimony at the preliminary hearing." At least that had gone well.

If the trial proceeded as it should, Luke and Dr. Berghuis would be going away for a long time. The doctor especially, since he would have to face two murder charges plus the attempts to kill her and Torin.

The details of how the doctor had committed so much evil still confused her. It had apparently all begun with his son killing Torin's wife. Donovan Mackeral learned of the killing because Luke and Jason regularly did drug runs for him, using his white van. Mackeral agreed to keep quiet about Jason in exchange for free drugs from Dr. Berghuis. The doctor tired of the blackmail and thought he could get rid of the problem by making Mackeral's death look like a drug shooting.

He thought he could get away with killing Wiley Boone, too, so long as he made the death look like a heart attack. The drug the doctor had used for Boone was discovered in the autopsy, and Torin's detective friend Derrick had pulled together more evidence for a conviction.

Spring shuddered. The thought that the police had found a tiny camera hidden in her room at the rehab center still made her skin crawl. Berghuis had apparently linked the camera to his cell phone, which made the job of tying him to the camera and the texted threats easier for the police.

She blew out a long breath. It was over now, and Berghuis would pay for his wrongs.

Except, perhaps, for his involvement in the case she knew Torin most wanted resolved—his wife's killing. Torin now knew who had shot Ivy, but may never find him. If Berghuis knew where his son was, if he was still alive, the doctor wasn't sharing.

The fate of Cliff and the cycling team wouldn't be known for a while either. They were under investigation, but Spring thankfully wouldn't have to be involved beyond giving her statement about what she had seen.

"There's no reason to be nervous." Victoria's encouragement broke through Spring's rambling thoughts. "Angie said she's never had a patient make so much progress in such a short amount of time." Victoria smiled, though it didn't brighten her eyes like it used to. "You're ready to live on your own."

To live. Nervous as she was, she did feel ready, even excited to begin the next phase of her life. To see what God would do.

"Too bad Torin had to work today."

"It's okay." Spring shrugged, though she had been disappointed when he'd said he was scheduled to work. She was thankful he'd healed from his wound enough to be back at his job and that he was seeking help with the PTSD so he could enjoy his work again.

"Did you get any news from admissions yet?"

Spring nodded, not able to hold back her smile. "Just today. I'm accepted into the education program."

"Spring, that's wonderful. You're going to be an excellent Pre-K teacher."

"Thanks. I haven't told Dad yet."

"Want me to?"

"No, that's okay. I can do it." She was determined to at least try to communicate with her dad better. Their division and the pain that came from it had gone on long enough. Even if he wouldn't accept who she was and what God called her to do, Spring could still accept her dad as he was, loving him better than she had most of her life.

"Here we are." Victoria pulled the van into a parking lot by the apartment building Spring would soon learn to call home.

Since her dad's house still wasn't wheelchair-accessible, Spring had gladly accepted his offer to pay for a new apartment until she earned enough to cover the rent herself. A little personal space might make the effort to love her dad easier.

She smiled at the thought. She still had a long way to go and a lot to learn. But the Lord was patient and would complete the work He'd started in her heart.

"Is that—" She leaned forward to peer through the windshield.

Looked like a small cluster of people waited on the sidewalk that led to the apartments, though Spring couldn't see very clearly from her position.

A smile played on Victoria's lips as she pulled into a stall. Something was up.

The side door of the van electronically slid open. And there stood Treese, Hank, and...Torin.

Her heart flipped in the cartwheel it could only do for one man.

Torin's broad smile signaled he was enjoying the surprise that was probably on her face.

She pushed her chair down the ramp out of the van and stopped in front of her little welcoming committee. "I didn't expect to see any of you here." She directed a perturbed look Torin's way but could only hold it for a second before her happiness broke through. "I thought you were scheduled to work."

"I was." He shrugged a shoulder under the blue sweater that infused his emerald eyes with a blast of sea green. "I traded shifts."

"And we," Treese stepped forward with a bouquet of flowers, "couldn't miss seeing your apartment before you get it as messy as your room always was at home."

Spring wrinkled her nose as she took the bouquet in her lap. "I was just a kid then, you know."

Hank rolled his eyes as he stepped to Spring and bent his tall frame to give her a hug, his wavy, chin-length blond hair falling forward. "You should see *her* room now."

"It's in perfect order." Treese held her chin up like a queen.

"Seriously, Spring." Hank touched her shoulder. "Congratulations. It sounds corny, but you are such an inspiration to me." Moisture glistened in his blue eyes, shooting the words to Spring's heart.

"Me, too." Treese nodded.

A lump formed in Spring's throat. "Thank you." She lifted the bouquet. "And the flowers are lovely."

"Rob wanted me to tell you he's planning on Chinese takeout at your place soon." Hank smiled as he gently squeezed her shoulder. "He had to work today, but I know he wanted to be here."

Spring sniffed and nodded.

Treese took in a big breath. "Enough weepiness, guys. This is supposed to be a party. Do you have stuff to be brought in?"

"A suitcase and some other things." Victoria directed Treese and Hank to help her at the van.

Torin moved closer to Spring, making her heart race. "Walk you to your door?"

Her pulse fluttered at the simple romantic request. She was seriously a goner where this man was concerned. She nodded, afraid her voice would sound too swoony if she spoke.

She wheeled her chair along the sidewalk that curved toward the entrance of her apartment building.

Torin walked at her side, his silence making her nervous. It shouldn't. She knew he was often quiet.

But she felt that she was at a turning point now—the start of her new life outside of rehab. Would Torin want to be part of it?

He had visited her nearly every day at the rehab center once he had healed from his gunshot wound. They'd talked about so much, never running out of things to say, thoughts to share. They had studied the Bible together, and her love for him had deepened even more as she watched him grow closer to the Lord and challenge her to do the same.

She thought…*hoped* Torin might love her, too. But the doubtful, cynical part of her still said Torin Cotter loving her would be far too good to be true.

Now that she was out of the hospital, safe and independent, he might feel his duty toward her had been fulfilled and walk out of her life forever.

Spring's heart contorted with the possibility as he held the outer door open for her. She wheeled past him and continued to her apartment, the second door in the ground-floor hallway. She bit her lip, bracing for the goodbye that could be coming. *Father, please give me strength to handle whatever you have in store.*

She inserted her key in the lock and pushed the door open.

"Spring."

She spun her chair around to face Torin, trying not to let the pain in her heart show on her face.

"I need to tell you something." The gaze he rested on her looked serious and nervous at the same time.

He was going to tell her this was the end. He was leaving now that she was fine.

It hurt even worse than she'd expected.

But after all he had done for her, the least she could do was make it easy for him. She opened her mouth to tell him it was okay, even though it wasn't.

"I love you."

Her heart stopped. She stared at him.

"You know I'm not good at saying things, so I can't say it the way you deserve." His mouth lifted in a half-smile that stole her heart completely. "But I've fallen in love with you more every day that I've had the privilege to know you."

He stepped closer to her chair and lowered himself to one knee. Taking her hand in his, he looked deep into her eyes. "I know it's too soon to ask you what I'd like to."

Her pulse restarted at a sprint. Did he mean what she thought he did?

"I still have a lot of healing to do with the Lord's help. And I know you have a lot of plans for your life, a lot of things you're going to be doing and…" He looked at her hand in his, running his thumb over her fingers. "I guess what I'm trying to say is that I know you don't need me, but I'm hoping you'll let me continue to be part of your life." He brought his gaze to hers, his emerald eyes shimmering with intensity and love. "Because I need you more than I can say."

Tears blurred her vision as she leaned toward him and cradled the chiseled line of his jaw in her hand. "I need you, too. And I love you." She smiled through her tears. "I don't want to even imagine life without you."

A slow smile crinkled the corners of his eyes and spread across his handsome face, filling her heart with joy.

He started to stand and, before she knew what was happening, he swept her out of her chair, into his arms.

Laughter burst from the happiness overflowing her soul as she wrapped her arms around his neck and welcomed his sweet kiss.

Thank you, Father. This life God had given her was so good.

Turn the Page for a Special Sneak Peek of
WINDY CITY WESTONS, BOOK 2

WASTED

EXCERPT OF WASTED

"WHAT DO YOU WANT?"

Victoria Weston's smile slipped away at Jamica Trent's unfriendly greeting.

So much for the hope that this home health visit would entail less drama than Victoria's initial evaluation visit. She hadn't even made it inside the house yet. And might not anytime soon with the way Jamica held the door open halfway and blocked it with her body.

But as Victoria took in the weariness around Jamica's angry eyes and the tears on her one-year-old baby's dark cheeks, the boy sliding from Jamica's hip, compassion replaced any irritation. "I'm here to see your mother for physical therapy."

"You ain't the therapist." Jamica surveyed Victoria as if she was a solicitor or con artist. "She's a short, chubby chick."

Not the kindest way to describe Ginny Lenton.

Lord, please give me patience and compassion. After repeating the same request she'd prayed when she'd approached the Trents' house, Victoria forced a smile. "I believe you're thinking of Ginny, my PTA."

Jamica's eyes narrowed. "PTA?"

"My assistant."

"Jamica!"

Victoria nearly closed her eyes in relief, although she could have done without the sharpness in Delilah Trent's tone.

"Let the woman inside for Pete's sake! You want me to be laid up forever? Don't think so with the way you been carrying on."

Victoria held back a smile. Deliliah evidently still had as much lively spirit as when they'd first met.

Jamica rolled her eyes and left the door to hang open on its own, apparently an invitation for Victoria to enter.

She stepped inside, switching her therapy equipment bag to her left hand so she could close the door behind her with her right.

Her gaze jumped ahead to find Delilah, sitting up with both legs stretched out on the brown sofa in the living room. A television blared across from Delilah against the far wall.

The path to reach the sixty-two-year-old patient was littered with clothing, toys, empty soda cans, and boxes. All potential fall hazards. It looked like Victoria would have to discuss fall prevention again, though Ginny had said she'd already been emphasizing the problem at each of her visits.

"Hello, Mrs. Trent."

The woman waved a dismissive hand as Victoria picked her way across the living room.

"Told you to call me Deliliah last time."

"Of course." Victoria hadn't forgotten, but since she'd only met Delilah one other time at her initial evaluation appointment, she didn't want to presume the invitation to be informal still held. "It's good to see you, Delilah." Victoria smiled as she reached the sofa. "How are you feeling?"

Delilah harrumphed. "Depends on how much Jamica's been getting' on my nerves."

Victoria laid a disposable pad under her bag before setting it on the nearby wooden chair that looked like it had once been part of a dining set. "Family dynamics can be tricky sometimes." She retrieved a pair of nitrile gloves from the outer pocket of her bag and pulled them on. "Did Ginny tell you what we'd be doing at my visit today?"

"Seein' if I pass the test, I guess." Delilah chuckled.

Victoria smiled. "No test, I promise. We're only going to assess how you're doing and determine if we need to make any adjustments to your exercise and treatment program. I'll go over your meds with you, too, and make sure everything is good there."

Delilah shrugged one shoulder under her pink cable-knit sweater. "It's all the same."

"Good. Then there shouldn't be any surprises." Victoria gently drew up Delilah's loose cotton pant leg until she could see the dressing covering the incision. Thankfully, Dr. Tennison had agreed with Victoria's recommendation that Deliliah keep the wound covered longer than normal due to the questionable sanitation of her living conditions. "How do you feel about your progress since your knee replacement?"

A snort from behind Victoria made her look over her shoulder.

Jamica stood about eight feet away, glaring at Delilah, no baby in sight. "I can tell you. She just lays there and says she can't do nothin'. And she moanin' and groanin' all the time."

"Don't you tell them lies, girl." Delilah's dark eyes flash as she craned her neck to see Jamica past Victoria. "And you be polite now. We got company."

"She ain't company. She's a therapist. And why you need her anyway? I thought the surgery was supposed to fix you. Ain't you supposed to *go* to therapy like everybody else? You don't gotta bring all these strangers in here."

Victoria straightened and stepped to the side so Delilah could see her daughter. Better not to try to check the incision in the middle of a fight.

"Why you so edgy?" Delilah's eyes narrowed at Jamica.

Jamica tried for a shrug, but the obvious tension in her

shoulders wouldn't cooperate enough to convince anyone of nonchalance.

The notes of Chopin's *Nocturne No. 9* broke through the tension. Victoria's ringtone. "Excuse me." She peeled her glove off and grabbed her phone from another pocket in her bag. She'd have to thank whoever had such perfect timing.

Relief slid through her as she stepped out of the line of fire and glanced at the caller ID.

CareFull Home Health.

She put the phone to her ear. "Victoria Weston."

Delilah and Jamica restarted their verbal sparring before Victoria could clearly hear the person on the other end of the line.

She covered her ear with her fingers. "Ginny?"

"Hey, yeah. What's with all the noise in the background?"

"I'm at the Trents'."

"Oh, gotcha. At it again. At least you know I wasn't making it up."

"I knew that from my first visit, unfortunately." Victoria chose her words carefully, though with the shouting match going on, it was doubtful Jamica or Delilah would hear anything she said.

"Yeah. They sound pretty heated this time. You good alone there?"

"I think so." Though Victoria wouldn't mind wrapping up the visit as soon as possible. "What did you need?"

"Oh, Dr. Tennison's office called with a question about—"

A slam cracked through the house.

Victoria jerked to see the front door bounce back from where it must have been smacked into the wall.

A tall man in a dark jacket stood in the doorway, a red bandana layered under a black winter hat on his head, and fury twisting his features.

Light glinted off something in his hand.

Was that—

The long, silver blade left no doubt. He was holding a knife.

She always follows the rules. But what are the rules for murder?

Victoria Weston encounters tough things as a home health physical therapist, but this is a first—a dead body. The police call the patient's death accidental. Victoria knows that can't be true. Her efforts to convince the police they're dealing with a murder get her labeled a troublemaker by all but one man— the troubler of her youth.

When Cillian Doherty returns to right the wrongs of the past, he finds his high school flame in a different kind of danger than he expected. As a social worker, he's in the perfect position to corroborate her cry of murder or give her what she wanted—to handle her problems without his help.

But someone wants to silence Victoria. When lies escalate to violence and threaten more lives, the Weston siblings join the battle to save their sister. But it will take a God more powerful than all of them for Cillian and Victoria to make peace with their past and catch the killer. Before the killer catches them.

Shop *Wasted* at
JerushaAgen.com

She never invites visitors. But visitors sometimes invite themselves.

When a winter storm brings more than snow, May Denver is forced to flee from her home and fight for her life. Can she trust an unwanted neighbor and risk her greatest fear in order to survive?

GRAB THIS ROMANTIC SUSPENSE STORY FOR FREE
WHEN YOU SIGN UP FOR JERUSHA'S NEWSLETTER
www.FearWarriorSuspense.com

GUARDIANS UNLEASHED

"Fast-paced suspense at its best."
- DiAnn Mills,
bestselling author of Concrete Evidence

JERUSHA AGEN
RISING DANGER

JERUSHA AGEN
HIDDEN DANGER

JERUSHA AGEN
COVERT DANGER

JERUSHA AGEN
UNSEEN DANGER

JERUSHA AGEN
LETHAL DANGER

JERUSHA AGEN
TERMINAL DANGER

GuardiansUnleashed.com

ABOUT JERUSHA

Jerusha Agen imagines danger around every corner but knows God is there, too. So naturally, she writes romantic suspense infused with the hope of salvation in Jesus Christ.

Jerusha loves to hang out with her big furry dogs and little furry cats, often while reading or watching movies.

Find more of Jerusha's thrilling, fear-fighting stories at www.JerushaAgen.com.

The Sisters Redeemed Series

JerushaStore.com